LadySmith

BY

RHAVENSFYRE

Ladysmith

DEDICATION

To the Goddess in all her forms.

ACKNOWLEDGEMENTS

To all of our wonderful readers, of course, and to our hard-working Beta Readers; Marion, Dava, Gail and Tammy. Thank you for all you do.

When day and night meet
at the forge of souls,
the midnight sun will
bring mixed blessings.
The one who is two,
shall lose and gain
a crown.
One will be given
their hearts desire,
while another
shall be torn asunder.

PROLOGUE

"Bellaria, you have betrayed Faerie for the last time. Your greed and jealousy have led to unforgivable acts."

Cringing before the powerful voice, only one of the many who circled about her, the cowled woman hid her face deep within the dark shadows cast by the heavy brocade covering her head. While her posture outwardly spoke only of subservience and regret, inside she seethed with anger. She wanted to face her accusers openly, with all the hatred and defiance she held within her but now was not the time to be bold.

To throw back her cowl and bare her teeth at the ones seeking to judge her would be certain death, so she wisely kept her face hidden, averting her eyes from the ones who towered above her. To stare at the ground when she deserved to stare down the stars chewed at her gut like a venomous serpent spewing its poison, but she took the pain and used it to focus on tonight's goal—survival. Bellaria knew her fate was being decided in this moment, and she could only hope for leniency.

A quick glimpse at the stony faces standing around her did not bode well, but with every avenue of escape blocked by cloaked figures and the circle of stones they sought to emulate rising up behind them, there was nothing she could do. The sacrifice stone beneath her feet grew cold with frost. Bellaria shivered and her eyes widened in fear when she realized she could see her breath gathering like a cold mist around her. She inhaled, preparing to try one last time to argue her case, and her lungs froze along with the power of speech. Her heart pounding in true fear now, Bellaria realized the extent of the danger she was in too late. She had underestimated her enemy, and she would now suffer the consequences.

"What say you?" a disembodied voice intoned the question with all the power of rite and ritual behind it. Another voice spoke. "Oblivion." Then another. That one word was a death sentence, and it echoed in the dark chambers of Bellaria's heart. She was not to be given leniency then.

There was no reason to hide anymore. She threw off her cowl and turned to face each of her accusers; defiance stretched her mouth into a feral grin. She watched as her jury faded into the mist. The bright light of the full moon gathered itself among the shadows of stone before even its solid light distorted and faded into the night. There was nothing left but the stones around and beneath her, their shapes quickly lost to the blackest of black as she fell into nothingness. She screamed but could not hear her own voice—it was swallowed as quickly as her body by the velvet darkness. She could think but could not feel, and without her senses she knew madness—true madness—would not be far behind.

It was a cruel sentence, and for one silent moment she was truly impressed that her "betters" had been willing to do something so vile as to leave her in this timeless cell. It was something she would have done without thought or mercy.

Still, her drive and desire kept her searching, her eyes open and seeking in the void around her until her muscles strained from the effort. She blinked; confusion lacing her thoughts even as her mind screamed for her to take note of the small light shining within the blackness. Desperately, she clawed at nothing to reach out towards the wavering glow. Touching it, she tasted it with her magic and spoke in wonder.

"I thought they were all gone. Dead and gone with the war, and certainly since the veil closed," she spoke aloud, then blinked in surprise. She was able to hear her words and sound did not carry within the void. Joy as black as her surroundings shot through her body, igniting nerves and inviting sensation back to lifeless fingers. The light was her salvation and a means to her revenge. Scrabbling and scraping her way into the light, she followed its siren call until she escaped from her prison...and emerged in a blizzard of pure white snow.

"No!" Bellaria cried out, howling out her distress so realistically a wolf returned her call. Turning wildly, she took in the deep drifts of snow and the barren trees surrounding her, whipping the cold winter air into a dusted frenzy. She stood within a smaller version of the stone circle, and like the other, it held no warmth. Only here, there was no power to be felt in the dark grey forms. Scooping up a fistful of snow into her hand, she focused on her clenched fist. Fear welled up inside her at the prospect of failure. Before it could overwhelm her, she forced the unacceptable weakness deep down into the blackest parts of her soul, to be consumed by her ravenous anger. It never snowed in Faerie—ever. What she held within her hand now was proof that, even though she had escaped her prison, she was still far from home.

She was back in the land of mortals, a land stripped of its magic when the veil closed eons ago, no longer able to feel the ebb and flow of currents that was the lifeblood and pulse of Faerie. Or had it? A taste of something sweet and powerful lingered on her tongue, past the cold taste of iron that everything here carried, living or dead.

In defiance of the bitter cold, Bellaria pushed her hood back, revealing long red hair as bright as blood. Fury ignited within her like a hot coal. The desire for revenge burned so strong that she shook with the need to destroy. Looking down, she found steam rising from between her clenched fingers. She uncurled her fingers, then watched as a thin stream of water run hotly from the palm of her hand. Each drop of water landed with a distinct hiss onto the cold snow beneath her feet.

So, she thought wickedly, *they have not managed to take everything from me.* She smiled, though it was more a baring of teeth than anything resembling joy, her eyes lit up with a different sort of fire. She plucked her long cloak out of the falling snow and left the stone circle with long, determined strides. She intended to do quite a bit of mischief here, but first, she would concentrate on finding herself somewhere a bit more comfortable and worthy of her status. A deposed queen was still a queen, and she had no intentions of living like a beggar in a world of lesser beings.

***

Mrs. Lillian Gertrude Carr wasn't sure what she was hearing at first, then she realized that the rhythmic thumping she thought was a loose board on the barn was actually someone knocking on her door. It was an easy mistake. Since her husband died, the barns were starting to look more than a little ragged, and with each winter were closer to falling down completely. She pulled back a faded yellow curtain and peered out the window, then shivered. Frantic flakes of snow beat wildly against the windowpanes, some managing to stick for a few brief seconds before the powerful wind regained control of them, blowing the fine powder back into the storm.

"Who would be out in this weather?" she mumbled to herself as she shuffled to the front door. Not that it really mattered to her. In her opinion, no one should be out in this kind of storm. *Not fit for man or beast,* she thought, relishing the memories the old saying brought to her, a lifetime of winter storms kept at bay within the warmth of her family home. Nowadays, her memories had to serve her well, since she was the last Carr left alive who even remembered the old family homestead. She was sure there were nieces and nephews out there somewhere, spread across the country and with modern lives too busy to be interested in such a pastoral life as farming. *Too busy by far to come visit me,* she thought. Becoming a widow at the ripe old age of 54 had made her feel old before her time. Now, in her late seventies, her creaking bones had given up arguing with her widow status. Alone in the great house for almost twenty years with only her cat for company, it was no wonder she didn't recognize a knock on the door, considering how few and far between those knocks had become.

At least she hadn't succumbed yet to the temptation of inviting one of those neat young men that went door to door passing out free pamphlets into her house during a lonely spell. Of course, she could talk the ins and outs of the Holy Bible around them just as well as the good Reverend Peavey at Holy Trinity. It might even be fun to do it once, just to see how long it would take before they tried escaping. Tonight she was sure it wasn't them at the door, mostly because they had never bothered travelling down her long gravel driveway on their bicycles just to talk to one little old lady, not even on a nice summer day. An image came unbidden then, of the two young men she had passed on one of her rare trips into town, bouncing and sliding down the poorly tended drive, their ties flapping madly as they made their way painfully down her small country lane. Shaking her head in amusement, she was unable to keep a youthful sounding giggle from escaping her. Her eyes crinkled merrily within a face as worn and weathered as the bark on the ancient oak tree that grew in the back yard.

"Foolish old woman, babbling to yourself while someone knocks on the door, begging to be let out of this weather?" She wondered if losing her manners was a sign of forgetfulness, of old age finally taking its toll on her mind.

Grinning at her irrational happiness from having a visitor, even one blown in by a winter storm, she hurried to open the front door, her scuffed slippers whispering softly against the worn wooden floor.

***

Bracing her frail body against the wind, Lillian squinted at the grey figure standing on her porch but was unable to make out any particular features. The snow swirled around them violently and she shivered in the frigid air; her favorite housecoat wasn't designed to keep that kind of cold out.

In her kindhearted way, she ushered the stranger inside without bothering to worry who it was first. Unfortunately for Lillian, her act of kindness would not be rewarded. As the tall stranger entered the foyer, she was sure her visitor was male due to the height, which was close to six feet. Her eyes widened in shock when the stranger turned and pulled back her hood, proving her assumption so very wrong.

The woman before her was impossibly beautiful, regal looking and poised. Her studied gaze as she silently took in her surroundings was commanding, a queen surveying her realm.

Lillian stood gaping at what the wind had literally blown in. Poetic descriptions from childhood books flowered within her mind. Freshly remembered and begging to be spoken aloud, they were held at bay by a fear colder than any storm she had weathered, and then were lost for all time. Hot tears flowed down her face. She was caught in the direct gaze of the tall woman before her—in steel grey eyes so pale they seemed carved from midwinter ice, while a small voice inside her screamed to look away, to save herself. She was dimly aware of her tears freezing painfully against her cheeks, caught in the wrinkles that time had carved into her face.

Her body refused to obey her commands. Unable to move, she could still feel everything around her. She felt the storm outside gather its strength, howling in delight when it found its way into her home, then sighing almost blissfully while it stole the heat from inside her along with her frail life. The storm held no remorse for its victim. Its frigid winds gathered her tears and played with them, tossing the salty drops into the air and making them dance. Taken as souvenirs, they quickly became indistinguishable from the million other drops of snow and ice that whirled madly around the two women. Against a blinding sheet of white, it was the stranger's unearthly eyes that followed her down into the darkness, her body crumpled to the wooden floor almost as an afterthought.

CHAPTER ONE

Maeve MacLeod joined her granddaughter on the small rocking bench tucked away on her back porch just in time for them to watch the sunset together. Over the last year, her visits had become more sporadic until they were so rare she worried that each visit would be the last time. Her son's new wife didn't appreciate her or her stories so she wasn't keen on letting Rohanna visit, no matter how much the child begged to see her. Maeve was sure that if Belinda could have it her way, she wouldn't be allowed to see the little girl at all.

Rohanna was watching the horses with a rapt expression on her face that reflected the late afternoon glow. They moved about restlessly, crowding the worn and muddy area right outside the pasture gate. Muted noises, meant to reassure each other, sounded like a gaggle of old women grumbling about having to wait for dinner. Pricked ears flicked back and forth like antenna, nervously splitting their attention between the large bale of hay sitting on the other side of the gate and the wooded edge of the meadow behind them.

The sun had given up the brightest of its light, deepening to a striking vermilion glow that cast reddish-purple shadows across the valley and darkened sorrel hides to a rich burgundy. Maeve laughed at their foolishness. It never did any good telling them that the shadows weren't going to eat them. If it moved and they couldn't identify it, then it was a horse eater and they expected their humans to protect them from the shadow monsters. The bravest of the bunch broke away from the herd and trotted a few feet towards the darkness, tossing its head and snorting before ambling back to the gate. *Such a brave soul that one has,* Maeve thought, smiling at the horses' nightly antics.

She cast an eye up at the cloudless sky. Soon she would have to open the gate and let them in for the night. They would run for the hay as if they'd been starved all day, despite the fact they had been eating rich grass the entire time, and she would chuckle and tease them about how plump they were becoming from all the clover. Until then, she was content to sit and tell stories to her granddaughter.

"You will always have a special bond with horses, Rohanna, just like your mother," Maeve said. The affection she held for her granddaughter filled her heart to the point it was almost painful, a sensation she would gladly feel her whole life...a fierce love that promised to protect and care for another without reserve or hesitation. Maeve pulled her granddaughter into a hug and smoothed the fine gold-blonde hair with her palm then placed a reverent kiss on her brow.

Unable to stop herself, she ran her fingertips through her own hair. As thick and coarse as one of the horse's manes, her own ruddy-blonde hair had paled with time and had lost the silken quality past suitors couldn't resist caressing. It was now streaked with more white than she cared for, though not so heavily that it made her look truly old. She was blessed with her bloodline's tendency to age gracefully and for that she would be eternally grateful. Her face was still unlined, pale as fresh cream despite hours spent out of doors and just as smooth, with cinnamon brows that made her emerald-green eyes all the more striking in contrast. She could still turn a few heads when she went into town. Maeve smiled, amused at the direction of her thoughts. The forgetfulness of busy people was a blessing. No one had bothered to count just how many years she had been making her monthly drives down the mountain for supplies.

"I don't remember Momma."

Anger rose in Maeve's chest at the sadness in her granddaughter's voice. Memories of warmth, love, blonde hair, and sheltering arms were all the poor girl had left of her real mother. Her stepmother, Belinda, had removed everything that belonged to her mother from their home. Rohanna didn't even have a picture to keep in her room.

That was another reason her new daughter-in-law didn't want Rohanna to come visit. In Maeve's house, Rohanna was free to remember her mother; her photographs were not kept hidden and Rohanna could gaze on her mother's face whenever she wished. Maeve had made sure of that. *Erin MacLeod would not be forgotten by her own daughter.*

Maeve felt a deep sadness inside her, but the ache she felt in her heart was just a pale shadow of Ro's tragic loss. Maeve had loved her son's first wife as a daughter. Erin's death two years ago was but the first blow—her son's decision to marry Belinda Carr was the second. John's decision to replace Ro's mother so soon after Erin's death filled Maeve's heart with dread. It was so unlike him. Maeve couldn't shake the feeling that he had somehow dishonored the memory of his first love by taking a second wife so quickly. She confronted him and he had given his mother what he thought was a good excuse. Ro needed a mother, and he felt inadequate to take care of a small girl by himself. This would have been believable if it had been any other woman than the one he had chosen to marry.

Ro's new stepmother was cold and imperious, and as unlikely a woman as she'd ever seen to be considered mothering. So unlike Ro's mother as to set Maeve's teeth on edge the minute she met her, the woman's only gods were money and prestige. There was no warmth in her smile or compassion for an orphaned child in her heart and no matter how hard she tried, Maeve could not read Belinda. She kept her thoughts and feelings closed off from everyone, hidden from both the seen and unseen world, and it troubled Maeve to no end.

No. Belinda Carr was not the woman Maeve would have chosen for her son.

Maeve gazed over the porch railing at the evening fog and tried to dispel her troubling thoughts. The damp, grey mass hung heavy along the rolling hills edging the back pasture, roiling like a living thing seeking an equally wraithlike meal. She reached out and made a passing motion with her hand as if she was wiping a chalkboard clean. *Dark thoughts as night was falling was a sure way to bring disaster on them all. It was better to keep such things locked away until they were needed.*

The sun had set now, making the tree line soften and fade like an old pastel. Edged in crimson and gold, the night waited to transform the brilliant colors into the cobalt and amethyst of dusk. A few impatient frogs already called out to each other hesitantly, looking for assurance that their time to sing was coming soon. Without having to look, she knew that the full moon was rising farther into the eastern sky. She had waited for the sun to vanish below the horizon before taking her ascendance in the darkening sky.

"You look just like your mother when she was a little girl, Ro. It is like looking into the past and seeing her again." Maeve smiled down at her granddaughter. It was true, down to the unruly blonde hair and the light sprinkling of freckles across her nose, she was her mother's daughter. Rohanna was the spitting image of her mother, with very little of her father in her except for the eyes. Her eyes carried the coloring of the MacLeod line, reflecting the fertile glens and golden sunlight of the old country. They were the same eyes that stared back at her in the mirror every morning.

Erin had grown up on a farm just down the road. A regular tomboy in her early years, she was always coming by and sneaking carrots to Maeve's horses. When she first met John, they were in immediate competition with each other. It wasn't until later that fierce competition turned into studied indifference as they grew into adolescence, then transformed again into something else altogether. It was no surprise to her when John came home one day, asking her husband how to approach Erin's father so that they could get married.

Maeve stood up and stretched, noting every creak and groan as her muscles and bones woke up. She enjoyed shuffling through the pleasant memories of her past but it was time to bring the horses in for the night.

"Come on, little one. Let's get the horses to bed and then I'll tell you a story."

That was all it took for Rohanna to launch into a full run towards the barn. Maeve shook her head and followed at a more sedate pace. Even though her soul begged to join the young child in skipping and dancing through the grass, she was past the time in her life when it was seemly to do so.

Maeve knew that her time of teaching would soon be coming to an end. Before long, John and Belinda would be back from their honeymoon, and she doubted if his new wife would allow an old woman to continue filling Rohanna's head with "nonsense" once she settled in to her newly minted status. A wife could demand what a fiancé could not.

***

"Your mother is alive through you, little one, with all her gifts passed to you as well, as is your father's."

"What gifts, Grandma?"

"Ah. To explain that, I need to tell you a story about our family, the MacLeod's." Maeve cleared her throat before beginning. "Your story starts a long time ago, back in the old country, and involves such things as faerie folk and magic."

Dropping into story-telling mode, Maeve's voice took on a singsong cadence, her faint Irish accent becoming thicker with the telling. "There are many shapes and forms to the magical folk, Ro. Some look like people—just like you or me. There are others that look like animals, but who speak and have thoughts much like our own. Then there are those who are not held to any one form and can change at will from human to animal. One such creature is the Mere. A Mere can take the form of either a fair woman or a horse, a mare to be exact. The Merefolk are mysterious creatures, who can choose to lead a man to his doom, or become their saving grace. Some legends say they were the royal mounts of the Great Hunt, chasing down their quarry with all the bloodlust of a hellhound. Others knew them as Nightmares, black mares with flaming eyes who brought

14

evildoers to justice when no others could or would by driving them mad—visiting their dreams and making their nightmares real."

Wrapping a thick woolen blanket around the two of them against the evening chill, Maeve settled deeper into the porch swing cushions. Rohanna was a small spark of warmth pressing against her side. Swinging gently, Maeve thought carefully about her next words, then began again.

"Many, many years ago, back in Ireland, your great-great-great-grandfather Connor became lost in a bog—a swamp." Maeve paused to make sure Ro had understood what she meant.

"Go on, Grandma." Rohanna's voice wavered a bit, but her eyes shone with excitement. A small hand gripped two of Maeve's fingers in a punishing grip, and she gasped. Rohanna was strong for one still so young.

"Okay, child," Maeve chuckled, retrieving her clutched fingers and surreptitiously rubbing them back awake. The child was so eager to hear the rest of the story she practically vibrated with energy.

"His cart and horse had become stuck in a deep patch of sucking mud that had lay hidden beneath the fallen leaves. Now, many men would have given up, and left the horse to its fate to save their belongings. But, he loved that gelding like an old friend and sat the night with him, holding his head above the murky water so that he might continue to breathe. He called out with all his might until his voice went hoarse, even though he knew that there was only a slim chance that another human being would hear him so far from the main road. Cold and wet, Connor lay there shivering for hours, ignoring his own discomfort to give some to his trusted companion. He sat there crooning to the old horse so that it knew he was there, knowing full well that the gelding's soul was close to fleeing his tired and mud-trapped body.

"Just when he was about to give up all hope, he heard the sharp snap of deadwood breaking, and movement coming from deep within the darkened woods. He called out one last time before his voice cracked, spent from hours of crying out. What stepped out of those woods was another horse, but one unlike any he had ever seen. This horse had never been tamed by bridle or harness, and its coat was so black it seemed to gather the night about it like a velvet cloak. Its eyes glowed like the brightest moonlight, and silver sparks flew from obsidian hooves whenever they hit bare stone. Now Connor, being a bright man usually, became very afraid. He knew the creature before him was nothing mundane, but one of the faerie folk. And this was not just any Fae, but one of the Meres of the Great Hunt. Connor dropped to his knees and began to pray, he was that sure he would never see his family or friends again, let alone the next sunrise.

"Instead, with great gentleness, the Mere approached him and nudged the discarded harness lying on the ground, stomping her hooves at him in irritation when he looked up at her blankly, all hope having been poured from him like a cracked pitcher. When that did not move him, the Mere plucked the very cap off of his head and tossed it into the mire. Now, if you've ever had a horse laugh at you, you'll know how that fortified the man to find his backbone. He gained the courage to scramble to his feet, and with great trepidation, he placed the leather straps upon the Mere so that she might pull his old gelding out of the water and mud. When the gelding was safely pulled to dry ground he turned to thank the Mere. He bowed and stuttered, and wished he knew what else to do, but she simply shook herself free of the leather harness as if it was never cinched around her. Slack jawed and in shock he watched her gallop back into the bog, all the while managing not to make a single bit of noise to mark her passage."

Mindful of her granddaughter's young age, Maeve crafted the last bit of her tale carefully.

"Only after drying the old gelding off and giving him grain did Connor take care of his own needs. He built a peat fire to warm them both before dropping from exhaustion. Despite his best effort to stay alert in the strange bog, he drifted off into a deep dreamless sleep. Later into the night, before the dawn came and offered the safety of daylight, a visitor entered his camp. It was a woman, with flowing hair colored black as night, and skin so pale that it shone under the moonlight with an ethereal glow. She stoked the fire and tended to his gelding and when he woke, she did not run away from him or show any fear at being alone with a strange man in the wilds. When Connor caught sight of her, he could barely breathe, she was so beautiful. The fire had died down while he slept, and damp had crept into his bones, while the woman was warm and bright and offered to share his blanket with him.

"Now," Maeve clucked and patted her granddaughter's knee. "You are still too young to understand what goes on between a man and a woman. All I can say is that the two lay together that night and kept each other warm. When Connor woke the next morning to the heat of the sun beating down on him hot enough for steam to rise from his clothing. His gelding was busy nuzzling his pockets for a treat and the woman was gone. He was alone, with nothing to prove his tale, and a serious desire to get home.

"With the early morning sun to guide him, Connor was able to find his way out of the bog. He found his tongue remained wrapped around the strange happenings of that night, even though the telling and retelling of the fantastic tale would have earned him more than one free ale at the pub. Many months passed. He often found his thoughts returning to that night and the strange woman he had met, but in all his travels he never saw or heard of anyone matching her description again.

"Almost three years to the day went by from his adventure in the bog when he came home to find a small boy sitting on the hearthstone in his small cottage. There was no note to explain who the boy was or how he came to be inside his home, which was just as well since Connor couldn't read very well. The only clue he had was a simple rune pendant tied to a leather thong around the small boy's neck. The knowledge of that rune was forbidden but Connor still recognized the bold design. Ehwaz, the symbol for the horse and friendship. The child carried within him and upon his face a shadow of the dark haired woman from the bog as well as the marks of his own fair features. He ran his thumb across the carved rune and looked into emerald green eyes and knew without a doubt that this child was his. He took him into his arms and cried in joy because he had no children of his own. You see, Connor had lost his wife at a young age and had never found another to love."

Maeve smiled as she looked down at her granddaughter, the small wrinkles in the corner of her eyes creasing merrily when Rohanna smiled back. *So innocent,* Maeve thought, *would she even remember this old woman's tale after tonight?*

"Do you know who that little boy was, Rohanna? That boy was your great-great-grandfather. Connor named him Owen after his own father, and as he grew up people noticed that he was special. He had a way with horses like no one else, and word spread far and wide of his abilities."

"Just like Da?"

"Yes, little one," Maeve nodded, "Just like your father."

"And Momma, she was good with the horses, too!" Rohanna spoke fiercely, ever ready to defend her mother.

Maeve chuckled at the little girl in her arms. Having John and Erin as her parents had doubly marked her with a fiery temperament. Maeve hoped that was enough to see her through all the trials of her life.

"Yes, Rohanna, your mother was very good with the horses, almost as good as your father is. I have no doubt that their gifts will pass on to you, as well," she added quietly, not wanting to push the child's young mind too far today. *But, eventually when she is old enough, she will learn the whole story. Eventually she will be ready to embrace her destiny.*

"Now, where was I?" Maeve asked herself. She paused for a moment to gather her thoughts back in like wool to a skein and continued to weave her story.

"Oh, yes, I remember now."

"People who were at their wits end sent their unmanageable horses to Owen, and they soon gentled under his care. It wasn't long before he was the most sought out trainer in the region, so much so that others became jealous of him. Where once Owen's talents were spoken about with pride, rumors flew faster than the wind that his ability with horses was an unnatural thing. The least of the rumors said he had made a deal with the faerie folk, the worst of the rumors held that he made a deal with the devil himself. People started to talk about strange happenings around his farm. They said he spoke to the horses, and that they spoke back to him. That on the full moon, the Merefolk would come and dance within his fields, their eyes glowing a fiery blue within the silvery mists.

"Now Connor, he didn't fear a soul when it came to his own self, but now he had a family, a son to worry about. He chose to leave his home and his land and journey across the ocean to America, where he had learned there was plenty of open land and he wouldn't have to deal with superstitious neighbors. He ended up here, in West Virginia, and purchased several large parcels of land to raise and train horses. This cabin here is the first place our family settled and has been in our family since then."

"Are there faerie folk here too, Grandma?" Rohanna asked, peering out into the darkening forest from behind the blankets safety.

"The faerie folk are anywhere the deepest woods and wilds still exist, child, but you don't need to fear them, Rohanna. They won't harm you."

"But how can that be, Grandma?" Ro asked. "Miss Belinda says they are just stories. She says that they are just faerie tales you made up and aren't real at all."

Ro's grandmother frowned at the child's statement. She didn't want to interfere with her son's family, but she refused to lie to her granddaughter. "These are not just made up stories to keep you entertained. These stories are a part of your family history. No matter what your new stepmother says, you can always believe in me, child."

Smoothing down the soft, blonde hair that so reminded her of Erin, Maeve lovingly kissed her forehead to sooth away the sharpness of her tone. "No matter what,

Ro...if you are ever in need of me, I will always find a way to be there. Do you understand?"

"Yes, Grandma, I think so."

Maeve chuckled in amusement, a soft noise that echoed the sound of the bubbling stream below them as it continued its merry trip down the hillside. Rohanna was too young to completely understand what she was telling her. For now, she would remember these nights filled with pleasant but innocent seeming childhood stories. When the proper time came, Rohanna would realize the truth behind them.

***

Ro was tired, but like the man in her grandmother's story, she was trying desperately to stay awake.

"Grandma, can you tell me another story?"

"Not tonight, little one. It's time for you to go to bed."

Rohanna yawned. She wanted to hear more about the faerie folk and the wild horses that were as smart as people. She started to doze off in the safety of her grandmother's arms with the stories of the old country still buzzing in her ears. Visions of black horses with blazing eyes galloped across her dreamscape. She wasn't afraid of them, not as she thought she should be. Instead, her dream-self grinned wildly, giddy and free as she followed the thundering hooves into the darkness of night, past the pale moon hanging low over the quiet earth...until only she and the beautiful mares shared the starlit sky.

CHAPTER TWO

Rohanna treasured the illusion of freedom that riding Perseus offered her as they trotted past the hills and forests surrounding her family's farm. The gelding was her favorite, a solid bay pony just shy of a full horse size, with a big horse attitude and an even bigger heart. It was a beautiful day, a day meant to enjoy rather than simply endure. She turned her face toward the sun, her pale skin warming immediately. She would have to be careful not to burn.

Taking a deep breath, she caught the scent of clover and wild roses mixed with the smell of meadow grasses almost tall enough to cut for hay. The gelding smelled it too, his nostrils flaring greedily as they trotted past the tempting fields. An inquiring flick of an ear back at her made her laugh—he was already too fat as it was.

"Sorry, buddy. You know the rules. No snacking until we get you home," she apologized, laughing again when Perseus' ears drooped in disappointment. She patted the reddish brown hide affectionately before she clicked and nudged him to move out faster. There was no need to tease the poor beast, and she wanted to get deeper into the forest before she had to go back.

It would have been a perfect day, if only she could forget that her stepmother was waiting for her back at the house—along with a dozen or more guests invited to celebrate Rohanna's birthday. Or, Ro sneered, *more like Belinda's version of a birthday party for her "beloved stepdaughter."*

Rohanna's sarcasm was well placed. Anyone even remotely considered a friend, let alone in her own age group was rarely invited. It was more of an annual event that benefited her stepmother. An excuse to invite every important person in the county to their home so she could showcase how well off they were.

Ro believed it was also an excuse for her stepmother, who delighted in filling her birthday with boring trivialities, to torment her. Her duties included kissing the wrinkled cheeks of powdered old women who clucked and cooed at her, then commented with age-endowed assurances that she would eventually grow into a "proper young woman" if she would just pay more attention to her selfless and obviously well-bred stepmother. If Ro heard one more veiled comment this year about "appropriate behavior" for a young woman, she swore she would scream in frustration at one of the old biddies until her voice gave out.

It was her thirteenth birthday and Rohanna had been dreading the day since she'd been informed she was to be fitted for a formal dress to honor the occasion. A dress! She had stopped voluntarily wearing dresses years ago. That is, except for the horrid affairs Belinda subjected her to. Boring afternoon teas filled with speculative old ladies looking her up and down as if she was a prized brood mare, trying to decide if she would be a good match for their grandson in a few years.

She was expected to act respectful and suffer through the most god-awful and uncomfortable outfits she had ever had the displeasure of wearing. They would appear on her bed in the morning along with an admonishment not to disappear before breakfast. In turn, she had developed a knack for finding ways to avoid the painful social affairs by saddling up her horse and heading for the hills—literally. It was well worth the occasional missed meal, but she thought she had figured a way past that problem, too.

It turned out that she was wrong. She made the mistake of sneaking into the kitchen early this morning, foolish enough to think she could avoid Belinda and still manage to fill her belly. Rohanna hadn't expected to find her stepmother in the kitchen, since Belinda usually avoided any place in the house she considered beneath her. Evidently, today's event was important enough for her to personally supervise the extra staff she had hired.

All Rohanna had wanted to do was snag some fruit and bread to take with her on her ride. The telltale riding breeches and tired flannel shirt she wore gave her plans away, which didn't include playing nice with the local blue bloods, and that had set Belinda off.

Rohanna closed her eyes, trusting Perseus to follow the trail while she replayed this morning's argument with Belinda.

"Rohanna, you act like it is going to kill you to be nice to our guests today!" Belinda reproached her, managing to sound like the aggrieved party. *"I can't tell you what an embarrassment it is for your father and me when you show up covered in dirt and grime from running around those hills...instead of doing what you should and behaving like a proper young lady."*

"I am not an embarrassment and my da' would never say so," Rohanna fired back.

"And that accent..." Belinda continued, speaking over Rohanna and completely ignoring her argument. Every syllable Belinda spoke in her overly cultured voice dripped with disdain for the faint Irish brogue Rohanna carried. *"How many tutors is it going to take to get rid of it? It is very unbecoming for a young lady of your station."*

Furious and unable to contain herself any longer, Rohanna spat back at her overbearing stepmother. "Oh, and would you be telling my father that you don't like his accent either, eh?" She emphasized the soft burr just to irritate Belinda further.

Ro had let her temper get the best of her. Irritating Belinda was like poking a wasp's nest—it was never wise and it was always painful, but she couldn't help herself. Luckily, Belinda was always careful to maintain a pleasant attitude whenever an audience was present. Curious eyes were watching their altercation, and for once, Ro was actually happy that Belinda had a habit of overdoing everything. Before the embarrassed chef and his assistants could find an excuse to leave the room, Rohanna made sure she beat them to it. Casting a grateful eye at the maid who surreptitiously held out a small package to her, she ran out the kitchen door before her stepmother could call her back.

Belinda's voice had followed her out the door. "Make sure you are back in time for the party, Rohanna...and that means enough time to clean up and change."

Rohanna groaned. She knew how far she could go and what she could usually get away with. She knew she couldn't avoid the party, not completely, but at least she could enjoy her morning until then. Thinking about the pink atrocity she found hanging from her closet door this morning made her groan even louder. *I swear that woman has extra lace added to make the stupid dresses even itchier, as if she designs them specifically to torture me.*

Rohanna's troubled thoughts kept landing solidly back onto the one person whom she could honestly say she hated with all her heart. Cold and calculating, Belinda seemed to see her as a commodity to be paraded about for the best social and financial connections, and her birthday was just another opportunity to promote her personal agenda.

Rohanna was young, but she wasn't blind or stupid. She had seen too much over the years to believe her stepmother was as nice as she pretended to be in front of other people. She still remembered the first time she met Belinda. She was only five years old and her mother had died less than a year before that. Rohanna instantly hated the haughty woman who talked down to her and pretended to fuss over "the poor motherless child." Rohanna had looked up into the perfect oval face of her father's soon-to-be new wife and proclaimed to the whole world that she would never call Belinda "mother". While her father laughed at his daughter's precociousness, Belinda fumed, unable to hide her anger and embarrassment. She laughed, pretending to shrug it off, and told Rohanna that she could call her by her first name instead. Even then, Rohanna instinctively knew that it was all a ruse, and did her best to avoid being in a room alone with the woman.

Over the years, Rohanna watched Belinda carefully, resenting the woman for taking her father away from her. Each year he seemed to work harder and harder until she barely saw him anymore. He seemed like a man possessed. He was driven to make the farm grander, to bringing in the best stock and ensuring that their horses were always in the ribbons at every show.

Rohanna missed spending her days with her father, especially their trips to the racetrack where he had started his career in horses. She enjoyed running around the barns and talking to the stable hands and jockeys. They were always happy to keep an eye on her while her father worked. Some of Rohanna's happiest memories had been at the track, watching the horses being trained and prepared for the upcoming races. There were no other children on the farm, and it was a great treat for her to have other people to talk to. The jockeys always had a kind word and a smile for her, and for the most part, they were about the same height as she was. She knew they would hate it, but she often pretended they were playmates her own age.

***

Rohanna had been so lost in her thoughts that she hadn't realized how far they had gone. She had reached the halfway point on the trail, a high point on a ridge overlooking the valley below. Her stomach growled, reminding her that she hadn't eaten yet and she took that as a sign that she should stop and rest there. She ground-tied her gelding and pulled out the wrapped paper package the maid had given her. It wasn't the fruit and bread she had hoped for, mostly some cheese and meats from the cold cut platter. Still, she would have to thank her later. The maid always made sure to have something hidden about her as a snack or treat and that made Rohanna feel ashamed. She didn't even know the woman's name, but for a good reason. Any servants she became too fond of seemed to disappear, dismissed by Belinda for some unknown grievance.

The rock outcropping was the perfect place for a picnic. She could look out across the valley from there, dotted with small figures she knew were her dad's breeding stock grazing in their pastures.

The morning fog had burned off so she could also see her house, shining like a white beacon in a sea of green. The barns sat farther off, their red tin roofs also clearly visible against the cloudless sky. Even from here, you could tell that the house was almost as large as one of the barns, but whereas the barns were a new addition, the house had stood there for years. When it was built, she was sure it would have been considered a mansion, something only the richest could have afforded. Belinda seemed intent on bringing the grand house back to its former glory, servants and all, with a mindset closer to the late 1800s than modern times. Rohanna watched enough old westerns to recognize the similarities.

Rohanna had explored the huge house from top to bottom when she was younger, especially when the weather was too bad to go outside. It was one of the few things she could do to break the incredible boredom of being stuck indoors for hours on end. By constantly being on the move, she learned she could avoid Belinda. Her stepmother always found some unpleasant chore for her to do if she thought Rohanna was just "lazing around the house," as she put it.

It was during a heavy snowstorm that Ro's explorations found something unusual. The house was riddled with old passages and hidden cubbyholes that led to several different rooms, and one that led to a secret cellar where someone had dug a small tunnel all the way out to the old barn. Ro had been thrilled. She had found a way to hide from Belinda and still know what was going on around her. She was like a mouse hiding in the walls, unseen and unobserved. It was a thrilling game for quite a while until...*Until what?* Rohanna's mind drew a blank. She squeezed her eyes shut, visualizing the details of the small panel inside her closet until it felt real enough to reach out her hand and open it. Ro would crawl inside the slim passageway, following the smell of her father's cigar smoke.

Rohanna blinked. The memory was gone. She tried to bring it back by closing her eyes again and concentrating on the feel of her wrist twisting just so until she felt the latch give. The feeling of walls closing in on her almost overwhelmed her. She couldn't swallow, couldn't breathe. Her heart started pounding in her chest as fear rose in her throat, a wave of nausea following close behind. Rohanna scrambled away from the edge of the rock outcropping, her meal forgotten as her mind rebelled. Perseus whinnied and scuttled away, forgetting his manners for a moment as he danced behind her, responding to her distress.

"Whoa...whoa, boy!" Rohanna grabbed at reins that whipped through the air in time with the swing of the gelding's head. Occupied with making sure her horse was safe, Rohanna was able to push her own fear aside and clear her head.

It suddenly became clear to Rohanna what she really wanted to do. She was already halfway there. Why couldn't she go see her grandmother? It was her birthday after all. Rohanna counted back the months and realized that she hadn't seen her grandmother in almost a year. How she could have let that much time pass by? Something always seemed to come up that kept her away, even though she could count over a dozen times she had made plans to saddle up and visit her.

"Well, Perseus...there's nothing keeping us from visiting grandma today, is there? How would you like to go for a long run, huh?"

Her grandmother's cabin sat at the very edge of the main property, a good hour's ride from where she stood now. Perseus tossed his head and nickered at her, making it look like he was agreeing with her. She grinned at the silly horse then mounted swiftly before turning his head towards the track that would lead her to a secondary trail at the bottom of the hill. They would have to hurry if she wanted to make it there and back again without Belinda finding out.

CHAPTER THREE

Rohanna rode wildly along the trail without paying much attention to her surroundings. She was familiar with every trail, every rock, and every tree on her father's farm. It was beautiful property, and she never tired of exploring it, but that wasn't her goal for today.

The trees to the left and right of her were nothing but a blur in her periphery; the only thing that mattered was the ground in front of them. There wasn't time for sightseeing and even though she trusted her gelding, Perseus, it was her job to keep them both safe.

Even her father would object to her galloping through the densely wooded forest like she was, but she had no problem navigating the occasional overgrown root or deadfall they encountered. Despite the danger, the ride was both soothing and exhilarating. The motion of her horse beneath her, the sounds of ironclad hooves hammering a muffled drumbeat against the cushioning leaf fall—that was the sum of Rohanna's universe and it made her happy.

Lost in the scent of leather, horse, and freshly turned earth, Rohanna barely noticed a subtle change in the air. Moisture gently kissed her face where before there was only heat and dappled shadows. Swirling tendrils of fog gathered across the trail in front of her, creeping low and heavy along the ground. Rohanna pulled back on the reins and Perseus slid to a stop, then tossed his head at the sudden command. His bit jingled, then quieted down when he did.

She squinted up through the canopy of trees around her and saw nothing but blue sky and the sun shining between the leaves and branches directly above her. It was close to noon, the time for fog and mist was over for the day—yet there it was. It was unusual enough that Rohanna hesitated before clucking Perseus forward. "I've seen weirder weather than this," she said, reassuring herself as much as the horse beneath her. The mountain region was known for strange and unexpected weather changes, she was sure there was some simple reason for this as well.

He high stepped a bit as if unsure about walking through the unexpected fog. "Whoa there, buddy, you're okay," Rohanna whispered, patting the nervous gelding on the neck.

Another twenty feet down the trail and the fog completely surrounded them. Rohanna twisted in her saddle, the well-oiled leather creaking loudly in the near silence, and peered back in the direction she had just come. The swirling grey mass of fog was now just as solid behind her as it was beneath them. The thin trail beneath his hooves now resembled something closer to a deer track than the wide, flat trail she had been galloping along just a few minutes ago.

More curious than afraid, Rohanna clucked at her gelding, urging him to continue.

It was deathly silent around them, except for the occasional snort from Perseus. He wasn't a nervous horse normally, but Ro could feel his hide twitch and shiver beneath her. The jingle and creak of her tack sounded abnormally loud within the quiet of the forest, echoing hollowly against the trees that crowded close to the trail. If there were other creatures in the forest with them, they weren't announcing their presence. Not a single bird chirped or squirrel chattered at them as horse and rider walked carefully forward. The bay was taking his cues from her, so Rohanna deliberately relaxed her posture, conveying a sense of calm confidence through her saddle that she wasn't quite feeling.

Patting the gelding's neck again in reassurance, she spoke softly, more to break the odd silence than anything else.

"It's okay boy, you're doing great." The sound of her voice was strangely hollow. Perseus's ears pricked up, flicking back at her, and then twitching nervously forward again. Perseus finally settled on a compromise, one ear pricked back at his rider, ready for any command, while the other ear pricked attentively towards the trail in front of him...the equine version of early warning radar.

After several minutes of scanning the forest around her, Rohanna realized the grey mist was developing a golden halo. The pale yellow globe of the sun re-emerged high above them, its muted rays steadily gathering the fog into a crystalline rainbow of swirling color. Rohanna took a deep breath. The air was heavy and humid and carried with it the sweet scent of wild roses and clover. She squinted against the sudden brightness and urged Perseus forward, following the sunlight along another thin trail cut out of the woods. The forest suddenly gave way to bright sunshine and thick grass dotted with brightly colored wild flowers.

Try as she might, she couldn't remember ever passing this way before. Rohanna thought she knew every square inch of her father's land, yet the small clearing ahead was unfamiliar. The grassy meadow was bowl shaped, cupped between two low hills and framed by tall hardwoods that swayed gently in breezes that didn't seem to touch the still air along the edges of the clearing. Looking around her, Rohanna couldn't help but be amazed at the beauty of the place. Despite being absolutely wild and natural, it held a cultivated air of perfection. After crossing a small bubbling brook tucked along the edge of the meadow, Rohanna guided Perseus farther into the grassy clearing.

Without warning, Perseus just stopped, then refused her command to continue on. Rohanna was too shocked to be upset over his bad behavior. Her eyes were glued on what stood in the middle of the meadow. Her heart sped up and she would have clapped her hands together in excitement if she wasn't holding a set of reins.

She had heard of faerie circles from her grandma's stories, but Rohanna had never expected to see one—especially not on her father's farm. Rather than fight with Perseus, she slid out of her saddle and walked towards the center of the small meadow. Even being led, Perseus balked at getting any closer to the stone circle so she let him go. He wouldn't wander far from her, and he was too busy happily munching the abundant green grass to care what she was doing. She knew she shouldn't let him eat like that after such a hard ride, but she couldn't keep her eyes or her feet away from the odd sight in front of her.

A dozen grey stones pushed out of the ground, jagged obelisks that stood in a perfect circle and surrounding a center stone set slightly off center. Despite the abundant grass everywhere else, the area within the circle was immaculately clean. Only the finest spongy covering of moss grew between the stones. Two of the stones were slightly larger than the rest and were capped with a horizontal stone that could never pass as a chance occurrence.

Perfectly square angles made it a doorway, and the familiar shape beckoned her. She stopped at the entranceway and pressed her palm against the rough surface. Rohanna was surprised at how warm it felt. Her palm tingled, and she swore she could feel the stone vibrate subtly beneath her fingers like a living being. Mindful of her grandmother's stories, Rohanna retreated, backing away from the strange circle to retrieve Perseus before he ate himself silly. A sandy hill topped by a wide oak tree stood a few yards away and looked comfortable enough so she headed for that.

Rohanna led Perseus to a grassless patch and tied him to a low-lying branch. She was still hungry, and from where the sun was sitting, Rohanna knew it wasn't that far past noon. She had enough time to enjoy her discovery and eat before attempting to find her way back. Digging into her saddlebags, she brought out the rest of the food she had stuffed in there earlier. A familiar looking tree caught her eye, and she was thrilled to find a few ripe apples the birds hadn't found already. A wild raspberry bush added to her meal and gave her the fruit she had been craving all morning. Ignoring the woeful eye of her companion as she bit into the crisp apple, she chuckled at him sympathetically.

"You've had plenty to eat already today, my friend." She laughed, well aware of how much of the lush grass he had stuffed himself with while she was otherwise occupied. Unable to help herself, she found her eye drawn to the stones again.

She couldn't explain it, but she felt an intense connection to them after having listened to so many of her grandmother's stories about the faerie hills and great stone circles dotting the countryside back in Ireland and

England. She hurriedly divided her food in half and ran back to the circle, but then pulled up short before walking through the stone entranceway. She stood there and wondered again if it was truly a good idea to enter, then admonished herself for her superstitious fears.

"Get yourself together, Ro. I can't believe you're afraid of a little superstitious nonsense." She snorted, then laughed at her own words. "If I didn't believe in that nonsense, why am I leaving food for the faeries?" she asked, nervously rubbing one damp palm on her breeches. "At least try to be consistent, Ro."

Her pulse quickened in anticipation, expecting something to happen when she entered the circle. She was halfway disappointed when it didn't.

Once inside, she walked briskly to the center stone and gingerly set the fruit and cheese down. Long and low and shaped like a church alter, it seemed like the right place to leave an offering to the fairies. As an afterthought, she added Perseus's forfeited apple, then lost her nerve and turned to leave. Stumbling in her haste, she flailed her arms out, reaching for anything to keep from falling. Her hand landed solidly on the surface of the flat stone. This time there was no mistaking the hum and sensation of movement beneath her palm.

Ro snatched her hand away and retreated, running back to the safety of Perseus. A prickling sensation, similar to a static charge, clung to her right hand. She rubbed at it briskly, trying to get feeling back into numb digits that somehow also felt icy hot. What she had sensed when she touched the stone was too much like a heartbeat, slow and heavy like the stone it emanated from, but a heartbeat nonetheless.

Perseus crowded beneath the shade of the large oak tree she had tied him to, calmly waiting for her return. Rohanna smiled at the intelligent gelding. The heat of the day beat down upon her shoulders, hot and sticky feeling. Between the shade and the bubbling creek running along its edge, the small hill was cool and inviting and she eagerly rejoined her pony.

She slid down the rough bark and crossed her legs beneath her. The creek chattered across smooth-worn rocks as it flowed past her. Wildflowers welcomed a small army of bees that moved heavily in the air covered its banks. Their faint hum was a welcome noise, simply because it was so mundane. As long as her back was to the circle, Ro could identify the smells and sounds around her without wondering if they were real. She closed her eyes, breathing in the fragrant air, letting it calm her as it relaxed her muscles and settled in her bones. Without intending to, she fell asleep and tumbled into a dream while Perseus stood guard above her.

***

Rohanna peered into the darkness and shook with excitement. The hidden latch she found in the back of her closet opened a small door, revealing a space between her closet and the wall behind her room. It was dim and dusty, but she couldn't resist the urge to explore. She was small and easily fit through the door, and once inside, the small space was high enough for her to stand up in.

She took a few tentative steps before looking behind her. The open door was the only light illuminating the area, which seemed to continue much farther than she could see. If she kept going, she would walk into darkness. She was brave for an eight-year-old, but not that brave. Besides, if she left the door open, she risked Belinda finding it. This was her discovery, and she wasn't about to lose it to her stepmother. She would need to find a flashlight if she wanted to explore further.

Rohanna whimpered and shifted beneath the oak tree. Perseus snuffled her hair and nickered softly. She quieted down and fell back down the rabbit hole of her dream.

It took her three weeks to find a flashlight and another week before she had the chance to explore again. It was hard, knowing the place was there and not having anyone to share her secret with—but the waiting—that was the worst thing of all. Ro's barely contained patience was well rewarded when she finally absconded with a flashlight. That very night she went exploring, waiting until everyone thought she was asleep before sneaking out of her bed and carefully closing the small door behind her to hide the light.

The passageway led down a flight of stairs and past her father's study. Once she knew that, there was nothing that could keep her visiting, night after night, whenever it was safe for her to do so. An ornate wood and brass vent along the back wall of the room let her sit, unobserved, while her father took an evening brandy or read in the quiet, book-lined room. Hiding there, breathing in the familiar scent of her father's cigars, Rohanna would lay her head against the cool brass grate and wish that things were different.

Finding the hidden passageway was a Godsend. She rarely saw her dad during the day anymore. Dinners were awkward and mostly silent, with Belinda listening to everything they said with a critical ear, and Ro expected to go to her room soon after that. These late night adventures were a forbidden necessity. They let her feel like she had some control over her life. It was something that Belinda didn't know about and couldn't forbid her from doing. She had to be careful to not fall asleep. It wouldn't do to have Belinda check in on her and find her missing from her room.

Then, in that strange way you can dream about a dream inside a dream, Rohanna tumbled into a nightmare and cried out in her sleep.

Rohanna crept out of her bed and into the passageway. It had been a couple of weeks since the last time she felt safe making the trip. The comforting smell of cigar smoke greeted her in the dark passageway, the sweet smoky scent of good tobacco gaining strength as Rohanna approached her vantage point.

She hadn't expected to find Belinda there, standing in her father's sanctuary. She faced the fireplace, her profile lit by the bright flames of a healthy fire. She wore a thick robe wrapped around her as if she was cold despite the heat of the flames. Rohanna touched her cheek. Even behind the grate, she could feel the heat.

Her father sat in a chair near the fire, but she couldn't see his face; only the back of his head was visible over the high backed chair. His still lit cigar lay forgotten in its tray. Rohanna could see the long tail of ash sagging beneath a smoky trail that circled lazily towards the ceiling.

Belinda was talking. Her voice was low but urgent, and despite Rohanna's best efforts, she couldn't make out the woman's words. Belinda spoke for a while, her father listening but not speaking. The longer she spoke, the more upset Rohanna became. She didn't know why Belinda was in her father's study and she didn't like it. The study had always been the one place that was solely his, off-limits to the rest of the family. Sanctuary. She was only eight years old, but she knew the word had special meaning. Belinda shouldn't be there.

Anger boiled up inside her, bringing the hot taste of bile into her throat. It burned her, even as her budding hatred burned inside her. It was Belinda's fault she barely saw her father anymore, and now she intruded even here.

Belinda turned from the fire and faced her father. Rohanna fell back and hid behind the wall, sure the woman would see her eyes peering out from behind the ornate grate, then freaked out when her heart pounded so loudly in her ears, she was sure the woman would pick up on that drum like noise as well. Her jaw dropped when she heard Belinda dismiss her father in the same tone she used with the servants. Anger flamed across her cheeks at the woman's audacity.

"You may go now," Belinda said, her imperious voice dripping with malice. How could he not hear it?

Rohanna had a temper, but she held it along with her breath and waited for him to respond. He would never tolerate anyone talking to him like that! Rohanna anticipated a showdown as she watched her father slowly stand up. As his full height rose from the deep chair to tower over his wife, Rohanna's shock turned to horror at the sight of her father's face. Craggy lines, usually quick to form themselves into an easy smile or stern frown, lay slack and grey against normally sun-reddened skin. He appeared pale, almost ashen, and Rohanna's heart quickened in fear at the thought that her father might be sick. His warm brown eyes were flat and dull and did not seem to see the room around him. He moved slowly, his body jerking awkwardly as if it didn't belong to him.

Rohanna's heart thumped painfully against her chest. Every instinct told her to yell—to scream out to her father in warning. There was no doubt that Belinda was a threat to her father's life. Rohanna strained her field of vision to follow his passage to the door, willing him to speak. But to her dismay, the only sound in the room was the creak of the door hinges as he left the room and the pops and crackles from the logs in the fire.

Rohanna turned her attention back to Belinda. She watched grey eyes grow cold and hard, as dangerous and deceptive as black ice on pavement. Belinda's pupils dilated swiftly, the darkness eating away the grey like a black hole eating a star. Her face seemed to come alight then with some secret thought, obsidian eyes glinting harshly against the firelight. Her stepmother smiled then, a smile that chilled Rohanna to the bone and sent another wave of metallic fear through her.

It wasn't that the smile didn't reach Belinda's eyes—it did—but her smile wasn't one of joy or happiness. It was a baring of teeth more suited to a feral creature, a smile that made Rohanna shiver. Belinda was a creature out of a nightmare, a demon clothed in human form. The shadows cast behind Belinda danced madly in time with the flames like a host of tortured souls. Clasping her hand over her mouth to muffle her ragged breathing, Rohanna slid carefully out of her secret hiding place, praying that the slight sounds her bare feet made against the cold wood would be unheard.

Rohanna slipped back into her bed and lay as still as possible, willing her body to relax into a semblance of sleep. She strained to hear past the nightly creaks and groans of the house, her heart pounding at the thought of footstep in the hall, of Belinda opening the door to her room.

Despite her best efforts to remain vigilant, exhaustion took her small body where her mind could not. Sleep

*overtook her—the nightmares found within that darkness a
pale comparison to her waking world.*

***

Ro woke with a start, her heart pounding until the
memory of the day came back to her. Perseus stood close
by, practically hovering above her, his eyes and ears
remaining alert to their surroundings. Nickering happily, he
seemed relieved that Ro was awake and able to protect both
of them.

"Poor thing, it must have been hard work, standing
guard for so long," she crooned, patting him on the nose
and scratching his favorite itchy spot. His usual comic
response didn't appear; instead of making a face, he swung
his head around to stare at the stones behind them.
Following his gaze, Ro noted the shadows starting to gather
beneath the stones.

"I know, Pers'. They make me nervous as well, but
don't worry, I won't let them hurt you."

Ro sighed. She hadn't meant to fall asleep and now it
was well into the afternoon. Visiting her grandmother
wasn't going to happen now.

Rethinking her earlier generosity, she figured the
faeries wouldn't mind if she gave Perseus back his apple.
He deserved it for being such a good boy. Walking back to
the circle, however, only revealed that her shared lunch
was no longer on the flat stone. Every crumb was gone.
Must have been squirrels, she thought, squinting against
the afternoon sun. Except there was something there; she
just couldn't quite see what it was. She placed a cautious
hand on the upright stone beside her, remembering the odd

sensation from earlier. Nothing. The stone felt rough and warm from the sun, but it was just plain stone.

Relieved, Rohanna strode back inside the stone circle and kneeled down in front of the flat stone sitting in the center. There was something there. She picked it up and cradled the small item in the palm of her hand. Running her finger along the smooth edges, she traced what looked like a crude stone cross. It had a slight green-black tint, as if it had taken some of the color of the moss carpeting the ground beneath her. Ro grinned and closed her hand around the small stone cross.

The food being gone could have been accounted for by squirrels or other animals, but this? Wait till my dad sees this. A real life Faerie stone! Animals couldn't have left this behind. It was proof that there really were faeries, just as her grandma had told her.

CHAPTER FOUR

Rohanna kept Perseus to a trot on the way back, giving him his head and trusting his nose to find the way home. The ground-eating trot, while easy on the gelding, was not as easy on Ro. The bouncing gait required a lot of work from her already tired muscles, but she didn't dare show up at the stables with him blowing hard and covered in sweat.

Oddly enough, it was just a simple matter of turning down one trail to another and suddenly they were back on familiar territory.

"We're back on track, Perseus. Now let's get home before someone notices how late we are," Rohanna said as they passed by an old wooden gate she knew by sight but had no other purpose. It was rusted shut and didn't connect to any fence on the property, but because of the sharp, thorn-like nest of barbed wire wrapped around it, Rohanna always marked it in passing. She might ride like the devil on a moonlit night, but barbed wire and horses were a bad mix she was careful to avoid.

Rohanna didn't question why she was lost one moment and on a familiar track the next, she was too happy to worry about it and already focused on the next obstacle. Perseus would need to be untacked and washed down before she could even get to the house—and she was still running late. She threw caution to the wind and clucked Perseus into a cantor. It was easier to hide a sweaty horse than her absence.

Her plan worked, at least the part where she made it back unnoticed and had Perseus safely tucked into his stall. Unfortunately, Belinda found her before she could ditch her riding clothes.

"And just where have you been?" Belinda drawled. Her crossed arms and tapping fingernails didn't make Ro step back, but the cold gleam in her eye did.

"I, uh..." she stuttered, then caught sight of her saving grace driving a beat up old pickup truck towards them and ran for it. "Hey, Dad!"

Belinda narrowed her eyes and glared at her. Ro tried not to grin, but it was hard not to. It was almost worth being yelled at to see Belinda painfully swallow whatever it was she was going to say next. She looked like she swallowed a bug, pursing her lips together into a razor thin line as she tried to rein in her considerable temper. Ro watched as the mask fell back into place with a silent click. Like closing the lid on a box, Belinda's face remade itself into something pleasant and practically motherly.

By the time her dad turned off the noisy engine and joined them, Belinda had regained her composure. She smiled at her husband sweetly, one hand clasped lightly to her neck and the other wrapped tightly against her elbow. She no longer seemed angry, but conveyed the perfect "worried parent" posture any child would recognize.

She wished her father would see the other side of Belinda, the one she kept hidden away when he was around. *He has*, a small voice whispered inside Rohanna's head. *He has?* Confused now, Rohanna's eyebrows knitted together. He couldn't have, or he would have done something. Ro believed that with all her heart. Her dad would not let Belinda bully her so, not if he knew about it. *What am I not remembering?*

Belinda tilted her head the slightest bit and her father dutifully kissed her cheek before absently reaching down and ruffling Ro's hair.

"How's my two favorite people?" he boomed. Always larger than life...even his voice got carried away with his enthusiasm for life.

Ro felt foggy headed, like the time she had the flu and couldn't hardly hear from being so stuffed up. The more she tried to focus on the memory that nagged at the corners of her mind the further it ran from her, as elusive as the owls she could always hear calling to each other at dusk but never saw. Her smile slid from her face. The sun suddenly seemed too bright, sending a sharp pain across her forehead and making her shield her eyes against the painful light.

"Well, to be perfectly honest..."

Grandmother always said the first story heard was the first story believed. Ro shook her head free of the cobwebs clouding her mind and butted in before Belinda could finish what she was saying.

"Everything's great, Dad. Belinda let me go riding today since it was my birthday. I was just thanking her for all my gifts." Ro beamed up at her dad, avoiding Belinda's glare. *There, see if she'll call me a liar to his face!*

"Well, that's great. I'm proud of you, girl. I saw you riding when you came in. I don't think any of our trainers are even close to you in skill." John tousled Rohanna's long blonde hair affectionately.

Belinda's frown deepened.

"You don't look happy, dear. Is there something I need to know?" John asked.

"I was worried, John. She was out so long, and all by herself. She could have gotten hurt or...?" She left the sentence hanging, as if she was unwilling to say aloud what kind of trouble Ro could have gotten in. Her hands were clasped tightly to the front of her dress, practically wringing themselves in worry.

Ro watched her stepmother's act in fascination. She knew it was an act; there was no real concern for her there. Belinda might convince her father that it was concern creating such a white-knuckled response, but Ro knew it was barely contained anger.

"I'm sorry, Belinda. I am sure that Ro will be more careful next time so as not to upset you."

"I was fine!" Ro started in heatedly, forgetting herself for a moment and too angry to care. Ro stepped between her father and his wife, ready to start a fight. Her grin widened until she was practically baring her teeth at Belinda, daring her to do something in front of her father.

Rohanna wasn't sure why she was willing to start a war today, especially since she spent most of her time avoiding one. Belinda's face darkened like a thundercloud and leaned towards her. Her father wrapped his arm around her, pulling her away from her stepmother and against him. *Please, please, Dad, stand up to her*, Ro wished, *Just for once—stand up to her for me.*

"You worry too much, dear. Ro's been out on these trails since she was the tiniest thing. She knows them like the back of her hand."

"You spoil the child too much, John," Belinda replied petulantly.

"I am not a child," Ro started in again, but her father hushed her.

"Well, that may be so." He nodded his head in agreement, then continued before Rohanna could protest again. "But it's her birthday today, and I have another treat for her." He turned to face Ro and winked at her. "How'd you like to go get an ice cream?" he asked. Ro squealed and threw herself into her father's arms, hugging him fiercely.

"Yes! Oh, yes. That sounds great, Dad!" she shouted. "With sprinkles and everything?"

"Of course, Sunshine."

Rohanna beamed up at her dad. It had been a long time since her father had called her Sunshine. For a moment, she relished the feeling of victory. Its sweetness was something she had never tasted before. Then her father turned around so he was facing away from his wife and Ro had a clear view of Belinda. The woman was glaring at her with as much venom as a snake could muster. Ro shuddered. She may have escaped for now, but she knew that Belinda would find a way to make her pay for her joy later.

"Are you cold, Ro?" her dad asked. "We can stop and get a sweater from the house."

"No Dad, I'm good. Let's go," she said. No one else cared if she was wearing riding breeches and tall boots into town, her dad surely didn't. Her flannel shirt was loose and clean and if she looked like a horse person, then so be it...that's who she was.

She grabbed her dad's hand and pulled him towards the pickup truck. As she buckled her seatbelt, Ro felt an odd sadness at how excited she was to leave. She spent way too much time trying to escape the farm. It wasn't fair. She loved the farm and all the horses and she loved her Dad. She felt guilty about wanting to leave, and she resented

Belinda for making leaving sound more appealing than staying.

***

Belinda glared at the rapidly shrinking image of the beaten up old truck as it bounced down the road. She waited until the dust cloud kicking up behind it obscured their view of her before dropping her façade. Her eyes narrowed in frustration, leaving only the slightest sliver of slate grey iris showing. Even in the bright afternoon sunlight, her eyes held all the warmth and color of a cold winter storm.

Crossing her arms in front of her, she tapped her fingertips lightly across one pale forearm while she considered the events of the last few minutes. Her plans for the day were completely and utterly derailed. Her guests, all thirteen of them, slunk out of whatever hidden place they had found and gathered around her.

"Something is wrong," she muttered beneath her breath. *They shouldn't have been able to leave like that, not when I wanted them to stay.*

A tremulous voice piped up behind her, the mocking tone instantly grating on her nerves and fueling her already sparked temper.

"Belinda! I thought you had those two under control. What are we going to do about tonight?" the woman asked, blithely ignoring the waves of anger coming from the taller woman. The admonishment held an inexcusable note of disrespect that sent Belinda's rage burning out of control.

She spun on her heels, turning so violently the other woman had no time to react. Long fingers wrapped around the older woman's skinny throat and squeezed. Ignoring the

52

choking noises coming from the woman as she clawed at her arm, Belinda brought the wrinkled face up to hers, making her balance on the tip of her toes like some ridiculously aged ballet dancer. Belinda's red hair flamed around her, a nonexistent wind whipping through and around her. The huge oak tree dominating the front yard danced behind her, its limbs whispering against each other in a dire warning. Her eyes glowed with displeasure as she spoke.

"First of all—you will never address me again in that way, Siandra. Secondly, you will never again presume to know everything I have planned."

The old woman gasped in her grip, her face turning beet red as she tried to breathe past Belinda's vice-like grip. A gloss of fear floated opaquely across the old woman's rheumy eyes like a lump of spoiled lard. Belinda grimaced in disgust, then tossed her away as easily as waving her hand. Siandra landed in a crumpled heap on the manicured lawn. Belinda wasn't worried that she had seriously hurt the human witch. Siandra wasn't as frail as she made herself look. Not that it mattered—Belinda was in the mood to hurt someone and Siandra was a convenient target.

"My apologies if I offended, Bellaria," Siandra rasped, rubbing at her tender throat with one hand while awkwardly trying to get up with the other.

"Do not use that name again, Siandra," Belinda bellowed, turning on the woman who had made not one, but two mistakes in less than a minute. "I will not stomach such idiocy."

Belinda turned in a circle, glaring at each and every one of them, making sure they understood her warning. Carelessness put her plans at risk, and she would not be thwarted in her quest for revenge. Each one of the women cast her eyes down to the ground and backed away, affording her the courtesy her position required and she demanded, but they gave themselves away. One moved a bit too slowly, another held her shoulders too proudly to perfect her obeisance.

Belinda growled, and the sound was nothing that should ever come from a human throat. The situation required action to satisfy her need for violence as well as reinforce her dominance over this little group of hers. She had twelve witnesses waiting to see what would happen, circling the two of them with all the intense hunger of a kettle of vultures.

Belinda drank the fear in Siandra's eyes and found the taste sweet. She ignored the outstretched hand, begging for mercy even as Belinda took from the woman the only thing she had left to offer—the power carried within her fragile shell of a life. The old witch wasn't going to need it anymore, and Belinda did. Even if it was a meager meal, the woman's power added to her growing strength.

"Clean this mess up and find a replacement. Preferably someone with a stronger heart and a quicker mind than this old fool," Belinda spoke into the silence that followed her little demonstration.

Twelve pairs of eyes followed her as she stepped over the crumpled body lying on the ground, but none repeated their cohort's mistake. The breeze changed direction and brought the scent of fear with it. Belinda's nostrils flared. The twelve woman left reeked of delicious terror. *So tempting*, she thought, closing her eyes and taking a deep breath in. She had to walk away before she succumbed to the temptation and simply destroyed them all. She could start over, there were always women looking for power and willing to do anything to get it.

"Too much time and effort," Belinda grumbled, generating a flurry of movement behind her. *If I didn't need them, they would be gone tonight,* she thought. The old woman had been right about one thing—she would have no need for them tonight.

CHAPTER FIVE

Ro hung on tight while the old pickup truck bounced along the dirt road that ran along the back of the farm. If her Dad's wink hadn't given their destination away, his choice of route surely did. It was a shortcut they had used often in the past, one that avoided the highway and lead directly to the racetrack. The old gravel road was a lot more fun than plain pavement but it also had a habit of tossing rocks about, which is why her Dad took the old pickup— another scratch or dent wouldn't be noticed or cared about.

The ancient Ford was worn and abused and from the way the truck bottomed out in one of the deeper ruts, probably needed new shocks 50,000 miles ago. While she slid around on the faded and cracked bench seat, she wondered if the teeth-rattling ride compared to the wild bronco rides she loved to watch at the rodeo.

The poor thing had seen better days. The paint job was peeling off in places, but under the heavy layer of dust, dirt, and rust you could tell that it used to be a glorious green and gold color. There were no embellishments on the old truck, no proud lettering that told anyone that the truck belonged to the MacLeod's or their farm. Ro suspected that her stepmother would have a fit to see the MacLeod's farm name anywhere near the racetrack, it being beneath her stature. The old truck was beneath notice too, she guessed. It sat far in the back of their lowliest barn most of the time, hidden beneath a paint encrusted utility tarp. *Out of sight and out of mind,* she thought. Sighing heavily, she wished she could do the same sometimes.

Back out on the main road, Ro and her father rode together in comfortable silence. The racetrack sat just outside of town, easily accessible from the main highway. Choosing the back road allowed them to take the more scenic route. The single lane road that snaked through the valleys and hills of the surrounding countryside took longer, but it was worth it to avoid all the traffic.

Now that the risk of a stone bruise was past, Ro rolled down the window to enjoy the breeze. The sweet smell of freshly cut alfalfa took over the truck cab, along with the wind that playfully blew through the truck's interior. Her long blonde hair danced around her head, threatening to blind her whenever it whipped across her face. Her father noticed one of her repeated attempts to pull long strands of flyaway hair out of her mouth and grinned down at her. "Having trouble there, Ro?"

"A little bit." Ro grimaced. She hated tying her hair back, but this was getting a little ridiculous. Not for the first time she considered how much easier it would be if she had short hair.

Reaching into the back, he grabbed a worn straw cowboy hat and plopped it on Ro's head. The hat had been there for years and Rohanna had never paid it any mind.

"Here you go, sweetie," he said, "try that on for size." His eyes were glued to the road so when he tried to put the hat on her, it landed lopsided, plastering her hair against her face in an overgrown mess.

"Dad! I can't see." Laughing, she removed the tired hat so she could pull her hair back. As she gathered her hair in one hand, she saw something written inside the brow band. A name, the black ink faded from years of use and barely legible anymore.

The letters were written boldly, the backward slant told her that the writer was most likely left-handed. Her own scrawl held a similar slant, no matter how hard Belinda tried to correct it. Rohanna ran her fingers along the worn and sweat stained leather.

ERIN

My mother was left handed. This is my mother's hat.

Hot tears gathered at the corner of Ro's eyes, misting her vision before she could blink them away. "Dad?"

"Hmmm?" her father answered absently, keeping his eyes on the winding road ahead of them.

"Can I get my hair cut?" Her hands cradled the hat gently, its presence a welcome reminder of her real mother. She had worn this hat, and from its appearance it was obviously a favorite. Now it was Ro's. *A piece of her mother that Belinda hadn't found and destroyed.* Rohanna vowed that it wouldn't "disappear" as other bits of her past had.

John risked a quick look over at his daughter. Rohanna's eyes were bright with unshed tears, and she held the hat in her hands like it was the Holy Grail.

Repressed grief and guilt assaulted him simultaneously, sending a sharp pang deep through his chest and making it hard to breathe. John's throat worked furiously, trying to swallow past the pain. Hot tears gathered and threatened to fall. He had to blink rapidly to clear his vision.

A red light gave him a moment to recover. He squeezed his eyes shut tightly, willing the grief away. Rohanna had so little to remember her mother by.

With her gold-blonde hair and pixie face, Rohanna was a miniature version of his dead wife and a constant reminder of his loss. He had given Erin that hat the first year they were married. It had cost a lot of money back when they didn't have much to spare. She wore it every day, traveling in the same seat that Rohanna now sat during their travels.

Erin rode in the western circuit. It didn't make a lot of money, but was well worth the gas and time in how much happiness it gave her. She would come in from the arena after running her pattern, covered in dust from head to toe and smiling from ear to ear. He didn't think she could be much happier. Then she would look at him, and her smile would become something more. Her whole face would glow, just for him.

His heart ached as he watched his daughter slowly place the old cowboy hat squarely on her head, brushing a few loose strands of hair behind her ear. His breath caught at the casual motion, it was so like her mother he shivered at the similarity.

Rohanna stared out the truck window. For a child of thirteen, she was entirely too serious. John had never seen such a somber child. His mother would have called her an old soul, and he would have been happy to believe that her quiet ways were due to that, but he had to face reality. She had been a happy little girl once. Now she didn't even have playmates her own age to socialize with. Marrying Belinda had seemed like a good idea at the time, when he was dealing with his loneliness—or, he should say, not dealing with it very well. Together, they had made the farm profitable beyond his wildest expectations, but at what cost? Why had he not seen how lonely and isolated his daughter had become until now? Things needed to change, and change usually started with admitting you made a mistake.

"Dad? A haircut?"

John cleared his throat. He had gotten lost in thought and hadn't answered his daughter's question. "Sure, Sweetheart. Anything you want."

Turning left, he headed away from the track and towards the center of town. A quick time check told him he could run this one extra errand and still make it to the track on time for his appointment—and Ro's Ice-cream.

The small downtown area looked a lot like any other small town in America. Main Street was mostly a long row of brick buildings that had probably been built a hundred years ago, interspersed with a few fast food joints easily identified by their cookie-cutter appearance.

John parked in front of the salon and left the truck running. "I'm just going to run to the feed store real quick and pick up some supplies since we're in town. Are you okay here by yourself?"

"Sure, Dad." Ro took the money her dad held out and stuffed it in her pocket.

Rohanna watched her father drive away, then pulled open the door and looked around. A bell tinkled above her, and she scooted in to make it stop ringing. Once inside, the acrid scent of hair products and chemicals assailed her. Her nostrils flared. Rohanna felt out of place in the clean white interior of the salon. Peering down at her boots, she worried that she had dragged some part of the farm in with her, dreading the looks that an errant piece of horse dung would cause.

The sound of someone softly clearing their throat made her look up. A well-dressed young man stood in front of her, watching her expectantly. Looking past him, she stared at her image in the mirror behind him. Her eyes were large and frightened looking, her face overly pale despite the light tan she managed to hold each summer, making her freckles stand out darkly against the faded gold of her skin.

She didn't know what she was supposed to do. She felt her stomach clench uncomfortably, the icy cold fear competing with the hot flush that colored her cheeks. She stood there dumbly, embarrassed and unsure what she should do.

The stylist smiled at her, his straight white teeth gleaming in the bright light. He introduced himself as Geoffrey and his kind voice put her at ease immediately. She returned the infectious smile with one of her own.

"Come on back, Sweetie. No one will hurt you here," Geoffrey said, glancing out the window. "First time all alone?"

"Yes," Ro admitted.

"You'll be fine, sweetie." He guided her to a chair in the back where she received her first salon shampoo. It was pure bliss. The young man's fingers worked magic on her tangled hair, massaging her scalp firmly with a minty smelling shampoo until it tingled. Rohanna relaxed into the salon chair, comforted by the friendly but subdued voices around her. The idle chatter contained nothing of importance, but held some humor. Rohanna found herself giggling at some of the young man's stories.

Rohanna stared into the mirror, a black cape wrapped tightly around her neck and draped across her lap. Geoffrey held limp wet strands of her blonde hair out from her head while he talked to her about her options.

"What do you want done today?"

Rohanna felt a delicious sort of terror take over. It was her decision, no one else's.

She licked her lips, almost afraid to say it. Then she looked up at Geoffrey and smiled. "I want it gone. I want to look like her," she said, pointing at the poster on the wall.

"You're the boss lady today." Geoffrey picked up his scissors. He looked pleased at her choice and quickly dived into his job.

Ro watched in fascinated horror as long strands of gold hair dropped ignobly to the floor, while a girl not much older than herself idly swept them up from around her chair. The discarded hair joined other sprigs of hair cut from customers in nearby chairs. What the girl swept up into her pan looked a lot like what would happen if a calico cat sneezed too hard and lost its coat all at once. That thought made her giggle.

"Don't move, sweetie," Geoffrey reminded her.

"I'm sorry." Rohanna bit her lip. She was afraid that if she started laughing again she wouldn't be able to stop. Closing her eyes, she took a deep breath to calm herself and focused on the rhythmic snip-snip sound of the scissors above her.

Rohanna fell into a pleasant daydream as Geoffrey did his work. She didn't notice when the subtle noise of the scissors stopped until he touched her face.

"All done."

She stared at the image in front of her. Short blonde hair framed an oval face, her high cheekbones stood out dramatically beneath large green eyes that widened even further in amazement. Geoffrey had put some kind of gel in her hair that had given her natural wave some body. The short strands lay like subtle flames licking the air around her head. She felt transformed. The new hairstyle made her look older, more mature "You're beautiful, honey," Geoffrey said. He looked proud, like an artist unveiling his newest creation. "Do you like it?"

"I do." She gave him a quick hug, an action completely out of character for her, then turned back to look at the familiar yet different face again. "I love it."

She more than loved it; she loved how it made her feel.

Her mother's cowboy hat lay on the table next to the mirror. She picked it up and covered her beautiful hair beneath the wide brim, then turned her head from side to side. With the hat on, she looked much like herself. She smiled an apology at Geoffrey's look of horror, then pulled the hat down tighter above her ears, regretting having to hide all of Geoffrey's wonderful work.

Thanks, Mom, she whispered to herself—strangely anticipating the dreaded confrontation with Belinda once she saw how short her hair was. *Oh well.* She shrugged. *The woman is already mad at me, what more can she do?* Somehow, the thought of Belinda being angry with her wasn't as scary as it had been this morning. Before she could think further on this odd development, her father appeared at the window, beckoning her to the waiting truck.

Something fell out of her jeans pocket and clattered onto the floor when Rohanna pulled out her money to pay the cashier. Geoffrey bent down and retrieved it from under the counter, then held it in the palm of his hand for a moment before handing it back to her. "Here, sweetie, you don't want to lose this."

"Thanks, Geoffrey." Ro plucked the cross-shaped stone from the hairstylist's hand and stuffed it back into her pocket. She had just found the fairy stone, she didn't want to lose it.

"It's very pretty, Ro. You should find someone to mount it on a chain for you. It would make a nice necklace," he suggested. "Then you won't risk losing it again. Maybe your grandmother will do it for you?"

"Really? You think it's that pretty?" Ro asked, concentrating on the cashier as she counted out her change. She didn't want to keep her father waiting any longer.

"Yes. A unique pendant for a unique girl."

Geoffrey's parting words were lost in the sound of tinkling bells. He waited until Ro and her father drove away before clapping his hands together and readying himself for the next customer. There was nothing else for him to do. The stone had found her, it was up to Rohanna to keep it close.

CHAPTER SIX

"Hey Ro, I was going to buy you ice cream at the track, but since we're already in town, do you want to hit The Creamery instead?"

Ro gaped at her Dad; of course she wanted ice cream from the best place in town. "Really? You have to ask?"

Then she turned a sly eye towards him. "Do we still get to go to the track?"

"Of course. I have to meet a man about a horse, and I know everyone will be thrilled to see you."

Rohanna whooped loud enough to be heard in the next county.

Ro's dad laughed, truly laughed as if he was happy again, and when he did that she didn't even care about the ice cream. It was her birthday, and she had somehow gotten her wish for the day. That didn't keep her from buying a double scoop of rocky road on a waffle cone with whipped cream. It took both hands to keep it balanced, and even if her eyes proved to be bigger than her stomach, she was willing to give it a try.

She was in heaven when her father told everyone there that it was her birthday because the lady behind the counter added extra cherries and sprinkles for free. Once back in the truck, Ro found another reason to love her new haircut; she didn't have to pick hair out of her ice cream as they drove down the road.

They followed the winding road back to the racetrack barns, pulling into the back lot reserved for trainers and owners. A familiar body popped out of the small guard shack and waved them through the gate without checking their passes. Rohanna waved back, excited to see that her old friend was still there.

Ray had grown some since the last she was here—not taller, but certainly wider. Ro had a sneaking suspicion it had something to do with his fondness for the hot sausage sandwiches that Dora, the food vendor, gave him for free every time she passed by. The guard shack looked smaller than she remembered it, small enough to not look very comfortable for a man that large to squeeze into. Rohanna grinned. Maybe that was why Ray sat down on the stool outside the shack door, his clipboard perched precariously on the window ledge, rather than going back inside where it was cool.

Her father parked the old pickup near the stables. A long line of trucks, most of them connected to horse trailers of various sizes and shapes, hid the long building from her, but she could smell the horses and taste the excitement that always seemed to flavor the air there. Most of the trailers were plain white, with a few bronze and black ones mixed in for color. The more expensive trailers matched their trucks. Covered in chrome and fancy paint jobs, they put some of the older, rust-trimmed trailers to shame.

Small clouds of tan dust billowed up behind each horse that trotted by. Ro's faded blue jeans were rapidly turning an even lighter color from the dust settling on them as she followed her father through the wide rows of stalls. Every fourteen feet or so a dark square broke up the solid wooden wall of the building where a line of elegant heads peered curiously out from most of the split stall doors.

The racetrack was always a busy place, filled with people walking across the dirt and grass, full of purpose and self-importance. The horses pranced by as impatiently as the people holding their lead lines, eager to get to their race on time, while jockeys dotted the landscape in their brightly colored outfits. Human butterflies gracing a field of otherwise bland humanity. Ro was shocked to find out that the jockeys were shorter than her now. The last time she was here, she had to strain her neck to look up at everyone.

Her father marched towards one particularly tall bay mare just ahead of them. She stood proudly, her intelligent dark brown eyes surveying the steady stream of horses and humans passing her by. She ignored the small group of men surrounding her, much as a queen would ignore her retainers unless needed. In contrast to her calm demeanor, the men were arguing in that animated way only old friends could manage to pull off—arms waving and fingers stabbing the air above them.

A thin, dark man stood slightly off to one side, his grey pinstripe suit and posture marking him as someone out of place in the stable area. He oozed superiority with every look and gesture, and Ro instantly disliked him. Neither he nor his suit seemed to be holding up very well in the hot dusty aisle. He didn't seem very happy to be there, and Ro could tell that despite his apparent disdain for the men surrounding him, he was paying keen attention to their conversation. Sweat ran freely off his forehead in small streams, as if the warmth of the day was slowly melting him away in dusty rivulets. If it wasn't for the continual dabbing with a limp handkerchief, a motion that was bordering on becoming a nervous tick, his shirt collar would certainly be closer to the reddish tan of the dust that swirled around them all.

Rohanna grinned when another familiar face looked up from examining the mare's front leg. Relief flashed briefly across his otherwise grim features when he saw her father standing there, then lit up when he saw Ro. Frown lines disappeared like magic and a wide welcoming smile transformed his face. There was no mistaking her father's best friend. Buddy looked a little more worn and weather-beaten than she remembered, but otherwise he hadn't changed a bit.

"Ro!" he bellowed. Buddy stepped out of the ring of men, his arms open wide.

"Buddy!" Ro launched herself away from her father. She sprinted across the dry, dusty distance between them, kicking up her own small dust cloud behind her. Buddy enveloped her in a crushing hug, spinning her around once before letting her down. Thrilled at seeing Buddy again, Ro forgot that she was supposed to be thirteen going on thirty, not the silly child she used to be.

"Whoa there, Little Bit," he said with a laugh. He stepped back to look her up and down, one eye squinting against the light. Ro felt a bit self-conscious when he paused momentarily on the old straw hat sitting low on her forehead, sure that Buddy would note her shorn hair and comment on it. Ro giggled at the semi-serious inspection, clapping her hands over her mouth to smother the threatening laughter. Buddy's face looked exactly how it did when he was looking over a horse, and Ro couldn't help but feel like one of Buddy's prize racehorses.

"Not so little, anymore, are ya? I swear you've grown a foot since I last saw you. Guess I'll have to find you a new nickname now." Buddy nodded at her father. His voice, though still friendly, became all business. His country drawl tumbled roughly across a gravelly voice that seemed perpetually hoarse.

"It's been a long time, John," Buddy said. He thrust his large, square hand out to shake her father's. "But, I'm glad you decided to come by on such short notice. I need a second opinion on this filly, and the rich idiot who owns her won't listen to me."

Buddy nodded his head in the direction of the bay mare behind him, then spit his annoyance into the dry earth.

"I don't see what I can do that you can't, Buddy. You're just as good as me when it comes to picking winners." He peered over Buddy's shoulder at the mare standing placidly in the midst of the swarm of men.

Momentarily forgotten, Ro listened to the men talk. The clear tones and slight lilt in her father's voice sounded so different from the soft country drawl of Buddy's voice. Ro followed her dad and Buddy while they continued to talk quietly. Introductions were made, then her father took a closer look at the mare. He checked each leg, running his hands across her hide with a practiced touch. The filly snorted and dropped her head, relaxing under her father's calming hands. Ro found herself staring directly into a pair of liquid brown eyes that reflected only gentleness and calm beneath long brown lashes and half-closed lids.

Ro's father was discussing the mare with the rest of the group. Her lineage was impeccable, and her practice runs had been impressive. One of the men asked a question.

"Is she sound to race?"

"Yes, technically she is."

Ro could hear the reluctance in her father's voice to say so. The more they talked, the harder it was for Ro to separate the heated voices as they discussed the fate of the mare. It was all quite silly to her. Petting the mare's satiny muzzle, Ro spoke before she could think.

"But she doesn't want to race," she stated calmly. Seven pairs of eyes turned and looked at her. Under such scrutiny, Ro felt over matched. She wanted to run but her feet wouldn't move. Ro didn't care what the other men thought, but her father's frown worried her.

"I'm sorry," she stuttered. Her apology was lost when the filly's owner started yelling.

"What do you mean, she doesn't want to race? It's what she's bred for—what she's trained for!" The man's voice rose to a high screech, his arms flailing wildly around him. The filly's head swung up and towards the loud noise, dancing lightly away from the irate man.

What did I say to set him off? Confused, Ro backed away from the scared filly and the angry man.

"You." The man spoke venomously, stabbing a sharp finger at her father's chest. "You're supposed to be a professional. According to him, you're the best." The offending finger gestured angrily at Buddy, then swung around until it pointed directly at Rohanna. "The track is no place for a girl, especially one with an opinion!"

A creeping flush travelled slowly along her father's neck and along his cheeks, his lips pursing so tightly they were nothing but a thin white line beneath his nose. He was angry, very angry, but so far had said nothing to the man before him.

It was a supreme act of self-control, especially when Ro knew he could darn well toss the smaller man around like a bale of hay if he had a mind to. The longer her father stayed silent, the more worried Ro became. She was sure her dad would burst if he didn't breathe soon.

Ro felt her own anger rise in defense of her father. How dare this ratty little man speak to him like that? Ro stepped out from behind the safety of her father's back. Jaw thrust forward, every line in her small body spoke defiance and anger. Ro was discovering that it was easier to swallow your fear if you were angry enough, and her anger now gave her the courage to shout back at the man.

"You heard me. She doesn't want to race, and if you do race her she *will* lose. Her heart's not in it, and it's just plain cruel to force a horse to race if they don't have the will to do it!"

That did it. The man stopped yelling and just stood there, sputtering. His face turned an unhealthy shade of red, like a ripe cherry. Ro wondered if he was going to keel over right then and there. Before he could catch his breath for a second run, Ro's father stepped up and placed his hand on Ro's shoulder. He spoke softly, his voice barely loud enough to hear even a few feet away. Every metered word was uttered in a careful voice that would have been a warning to a smarter man.

"I agree with my daughter, sir. The mare is sound in every way, but like my daughter said, she hasn't the heart to run. I'm sorry that I—we haven't been of more use to you." Tipping his hat at Buddy, he guided Ro away from the men.

"Let's go, Ro."

"Yes, Dad. I'm sorry."

"There's nothing to be sorry about. Don't fret over it."

"You aren't angry with me?"

"No, I'm not angry with you." A muscle twitched along his jaw as he spoke, telling her that he was still angry, just not at Ro. He looked down at her and smiled. "Come on, let's get something to eat a little more substantial than ice cream."

Ro's stomach growled, making them both laugh.

They walked in silence after that, heading towards the track restaurant that served the private boxes reserved for special guests. Ro took advantage and ordered an old favorite she rarely got at home, hot dogs and French fries. As her father chatted with the waitress, Ro turned her attention to the horses as they posted for the first race.

"Ro." Her father brought her attention back from the field beneath them. "I'm not mad at you—okay? Sometimes people just don't like to hear the truth, and it upsets them. That man back there, he's put a lot of money on that filly just to place her in a stakes race. If she doesn't win, he's going to lose his investment. Losing that kind of money can make someone a little crazy."

"She's going to lose," Ro said without a single ounce of doubt. "I feel bad for her."

The waitress arrived with her food just in time. It all smelled wonderful, and she tucked into the treat like she was starving. Her dad just shook his head at her before reaching over and stealing a handful of fries.

"Now, let's have a look at that haircut you've been hiding. I need to know how much trouble we're in when we get home," he said. Rohanna held her breath while he made a show of wiping his hands off on a napkin. She blew it out a relieved sigh when he looked up at her with a playful gleam in his eye. Ro took off her hat and placed it on the table, then waited.

"Ah, yes." Rohanna's father cleared his throat and leaned back in the chair. "That's different. I like it, Ro. You know, you look more and more like your mother every day."

"Wow, you think so? Thanks, Dad," Rohanna said around a lump in her throat. Before the moment became awkward, her father pushed away from the table and stood up.

"Hey, I've got to take care of something real quick, then we'll head out, okay?"

"Sure, I'll be fine," Ro answered. She was perfectly safe where she was, and he wouldn't leave her for long. Tearing into the messy hot dog covered in sauerkraut and mustard, Ro turned her attention back to the track just as a field of brown streaks thundered past. The jockeys perched precariously atop their mounts were urging them to go faster—to win. Ro could feel the excitement of the crowd. The roar of a few thousand voices extorting their favorite to pull ahead was almost deafening—even from where she was. She shared in the cheers, urging the horses on without caring who won, simply reveling in the joy of the race itself. Sometimes she would pick a horse on a whim as they trotted past, noting the color of the rider's jersey. Most of the time, they won.

In the next race, the bay filly her father had inspected trotted by on the way to the gate. Ro already knew the outcome before the horn sounded, but she had to watch anyway. The filly finished a dismal last, despite the desperate urgings of the jockey liberally and shamefully applying the whip to her unwilling frame.

When her father returned, Ro found the courage to ask him what would happen to the filly since she lost.

"Well, if she's lucky, someone who needs a good broodmare will bid on her in the stakes race. Otherwise, she'll go home with her owner. She's a fine mare," he said. "She'd make an excellent broodmare in the right hands."

"I hope someone buys her," Ro said. "He's an awful little man and doesn't deserve to own her."

"I hope so, too, Ro," he said. "Now, let's get home before it gets dark out."

Rohanna made a face. They had been having such a grand day she had almost forgotten about Belinda. Her good mood started to dry up long before the old truck turned into their driveway, and for good reason.

Belinda was waiting for the two of them when they got home, every inch of her height exuding displeasure and anger as she looked down at Ro. Her father patted her back and sent her to her room, not as punishment, but as an escape from the escalating pressure building between the two adults, forecasting an impending explosion she could sense like a coming storm. Ro had no desire to be anywhere near the thunder rumbling between them. From the stern set of her father's jaw, she knew tonight would be different from other nights. Tonight her father wasn't going to back down.

CHAPTER SEVEN

"She's thirteen, Belinda, let her be. There isn't much else for her to do on the farm during the summer. Let her ride. Her grandmother is enjoying having her around and school is going to start in a couple of months."

"I don't like it. Her gallivanting about the countryside day after day. How is she supposed to learn responsibility?"

"She's fine, and I can't think of any better way for her to learn how much there is to do on the farm than by riding through it. She found that old section of fence down just last week, remember? We could have lost a couple of colts through that fence, not to mention the neighbor would have been mighty upset to find our horses munching on his fields."

Rohanna plastered herself against the hallway wall, a small backpack and her boots clutched against her chest, and waited. She guessed she should be grateful. This wasn't the first conversation they've had about her summer...but it was one of the more civil ones.

Hidden from sight but not sound, she continued eavesdropping until the subject changed, then she tiptoed back through the kitchen and out the door.

The back porch was relatively safe. She plopped down on the bottom step and stomped her feet into her riding boots. Belinda had removed most of the thick runner carpets in the house and had the floors redone. The exposed hardwood was newly glossed and dangerously slick to run about in her socks, but wearing her boots in the house was the same as rapping out her location with a stick.

The path to the barn, on the other hand, was soft and grassy and easy to bolt across as silently as a deer. She checked the straps on her backpack one more time and she was gone. Perseus would be waiting for her, and as soon as she tacked up, she would be back where she belonged...riding the trails in the woods.

"Hey, Boy'o...how are you doing today, huh?" she whispered, then clipped the lead line on his halter and led him out of his stall. "You ready to ride, huh?"

Perseus nickered at her then pushed his head against her thigh, almost knocking her over. Rohanna chuckled. "Ah, you smell that, huh? I've got a treat for you today."

She dug around in her pocket for a couple of sugar cubes, but before she could pull them out, Perseus nudged her again. "Impatient?" she asked, cocking an eyebrow at him.

Something tumbled free from her pocket on the second try and Perseus lipped at her palm eagerly. Distracted by the noise, she let him steal both cubes, her eyes were on the ground beneath them.

"Crap." Rohanna bent down and snatched up the small stone cross she'd been religiously carrying around with her for the last month before Perseus could stomp it into nothingness beneath his feat. Perseus stretched his neck to snuffle at her hand. Ro clamped her fist around the small stone and elbowed him away before he could taste test it. "This isn't for you, Pers'. You'd crack your teeth on this one."

This wasn't the first time she had almost lost the Fairie stone. If she didn't do something, she would lose it and that would be a shame. Rohanna tightened Perseus's cinch and patted his shoulder. "You know what, it's early enough for a long ride. How do you feel about visiting Grandma?"

Perseus tossed his head and pawed at the ground. Ro swore if he could've smiled at her he would have. She grinned at the silly horse, then mounted up quickly. "I'll take that as a yes."

Her other foot found the stirrup, and they were off. She had been hoping to use the second hole she had cut into the heavy leather a few months ago, but it seemed that after that initial growth spurt this spring, Mother Nature had given up on her. She hadn't sprouted much past five feet, and from the look of things, it didn't look like she was going to get much taller. *It's just as well*, she thought. Perseus was basically an oversized pony and it would look funny if her feet were hanging down near his knees.

Before she clicked Perseus into a gallop, she checked her pocket again. The small lump was right where it belonged, but she still stood up in her stirrups so she could stuff it as far down as it would go. *What was the hairstylist's name? Geoffrey? He said something about getting it mounted.* That made a lot of sense to Ro. She ran her fingers along her neckline where a slim silver chain hung—her father's official birthday present to her. It would work perfectly for the small stone pendant.

Pleased about coming up with a good solution, Ro let the rest of her concerns temporarily slip away. The next hour was spent concentrating on the ground, the trees and the wind whipping past her head. Perseus's hoof beats marked both time and distance, but she really didn't feel either until she pulled up outside her grandmother's cabin.

The sun was bright out in the open, but she swore she saw a shadow where one shouldn't be. She twisted her head to look closer, but something flashed in her eye, blinding her for a moment and leaving small motes of color dancing across her field of vision.

"Ro! I didn't expect you today!"

Ro peeked out of one eye to find her grandmother standing on the porch, a dishtowel in her hands and a smile on her face.

"Hey, Grandma," Ro said, sliding down off of Perseus's back and leaving him ground tied. Like always, she felt filled with happiness whenever she came here, and a big part of it was the hug she couldn't say no to and never wanted to. "Do you have company?"

"No, child. Why do you say that?" Rohanna's grandmother, asked.

"I just thought I saw someone, something moving near the back porch when I rode in." Rohanna blushed, feeling silly about bringing it up all of a sudden. "It was probably nothing, the sun in my eyes is all."

"Don't be embarrassed. Why don't we put Perseus away in the barn and we'll check it out. There are critters about...who knows? Maybe I've got a family of raccoons casing the place for a midnight heist, hmm?" Maeve took Rohanna's free arm and headed for the barn with Perseus in tow. "Now, why don't you tell me how you're doing?"

Rohanna balked. She didn't want to talk about Belinda and her father today, and she couldn't talk about her mother. One always led to the other, because in her mind, they were part of the same horrible story. Sometimes, in her deepest, darkest thoughts...her anger would turn on her mother and she wanted to yell and scream at her and demand to know why she had to leave them. Belinda wouldn't be here if her mother hadn't died, if she hadn't left her and her father all alone in the world. It wasn't right, to be punished twice for her loss.

Ever since her birthday, her mother was in her thoughts...more so than normal. She had hidden Erin's cowboy hat in the space behind her closet, as safe a spot as she could think of from Belinda's prying eyes, but took it out as often as possible just to run her fingers along the lettering. She often wondered where the crawlspace led past the closet light, but any time she thought about slinking past the cobwebs and entering the darkness her heart would skip a beat or two then fall into a wild gallop that made it hard for her to breathe. Rohanna squeezed her eyes shut against the intense emotions the past churned up, pummeling her like a maelstrom. As it always did, thinking about her mother made her misty eyed, her throat tightening into a tight band of pain.

"I'm fine," she rasped, roughly scrubbing her eyes with her shirt sleeves. She didn't want to break down and cry in front of her grandmother again, sobbing like a little girl while she rocked her to sleep.

Maeve stopped and touched Rohanna's arm. Her smile was sad and the look she gave her almost made Rohanna break down anyway. It was as if the older woman knew everything she had been thinking and understood how miserable she felt.

"Caring isn't a weakness, Ro," Maeve spoke sagely. "Feeling things intensely is one of the things that makes you human. Don't ever close yourself off from your emotions, Sweetheart. You might think it's easier, being hard all the time, but all it does is make you cold inside." She knew from experience. It hurt to feel. The temptation was so great at times to pull away from life and embrace revenge, but she couldn't do it. She would lose something in the process, something so precious to her she would never risk it. *And if you lost her, would you risk it then?* Maeve shuddered at the thought. "Pray that never happens."

"What was that, Grandma?"

"Nothing, little one. Just an old woman talking to herself." Maeve gathered her shawl tighter around her shoulders despite the summer heat. "Would you like something to eat? I was just making a bit of lunch."

Rohanna grinned and Maeve rolled her eyes, chuckling at herself because the answer was so obvious. Ro was as skinny as a rail and had grown six inches since last year. "Of course. That was a stupid question. Come on, little one, let's feed you. Growing bones and all that, right?"

***

"Is that the Fairie stone Geoffrey told you about?"

Maeve looked up from the kitchen table at the woman standing in the doorway.

"Come out of the shadows, Shyann. It's uncanny how quiet you can be," Maeve grumbled, "and yes, it is."

Such a small, modest looking thing to hold so much power, Maeve thought, returning her attention back to the small stone cross.

Rohanna had ridden off on Perseus barely five minutes ago. "Did you make sure she didn't see you?"

"I always do. I still don't understand why I have to hide from her." Shyann joined her at the table. Bright red hair the color of autumn leaves rustled around a smallish face and wide, almond shaped eyes that looked a lot more innocent than they were.

"Because you are you, and one day I might need her "cousin" to show up," Maeve said, tired of repeating herself. "And no, you don't always 'do' because she saw you leaving when she rode up."

"What? How did she manage that?" Shyann's eyes widened in surprise. Very few could spot her if she didn't want to be seen.

"Calm down. She only saw a shadow."

Shyann leaned back in her chair and pulled at her lower lip. Pale green eyes looked up at Maeve, serious beneath ginger eyebrows not used to sharing a frown. "I'll be more careful."

"See to it that you do." Maeve stood up and rapped the heavy wood table with her knuckles. "Come now, we have a lot to do between now and moonrise. Rohanna wants the stone set for a necklace, and I must find my silver. We weave tonight."

"So soon?"

"Yes. I understand why Geoffrey made his suggestion. The girl's almost lost the thing a dozen times over already. The necklace will keep her from losing it again, but that doesn't mean I like it gone from her any longer than necessary."

"Yes, my lady." Shyann pressed her fingers to her forehead and bowed. Her eyes danced with humor and her old grin was back, resetting her smooth face into more familiar lines. Maeve pulled at her braid, a sure sign of irritation that only made Shyann's grin widen even more.

"None of that, now. Not here, and not now." Maeve grimaced at Shyann's antics, then shooed her from the kitchen. "Go, you know what I need you to do."

Once alone, Maeve looked down at the stone again, then plucked it up between her thumb and forefinger. When Rohanna had put the Fairie stone in her palm and asked if she could make it into a necklace, Maeve was surprised by how light the thing was. It barely carried any weight to it at all, as if part of its substance resided elsewhere. Dull green and black, there was no outward sign of how much light was hidden inside of it, or how much power resonated within its rough lines.

She closed her fist around it and listened to the rhythm of the earth. Held inside her hand, it should have been the merest echo, yet it thumped against her hand like a war drum, warming her blood and inviting her heart to join the bass rhythm.

"After tonight, you'll be even stronger," Maeve crooned. "You'll protect her and keep her safe until it's time."

CHAPTER EIGHT

John patted his breast pocket and smiled. Rohanna was going to be so thrilled. Not as thrilled as she was going to be when she met her new filly but thrilled, nonetheless. Ro loved her Perseus, but she needed something a bit more elegant and a little taller...if she was going to really shine at the horse shows this year, and the three year old filly he'd been training for the last thirty days was showing a lot of promise. It was going to be difficult, keeping the new filly a surprise until winter break, but hiding her out at his mother's homestead helped a lot—not that Maeve didn't have to keep reminding him to control his exuberance. If she didn't, he'd have given in and told Ro about her Christmas present a dozen times already. Half the problem was finding time to sneak off and train her in secret, what with Ro riding about the farm every day.

He had to make sure she wasn't on her way to visit her grandmother before heading that way himself. A quick trip into town for supplies usually hid the missing time, then it was back home to work on the farm. Today took longer because he had to speak to their hay guy about placing a winter order for square and round bales. The old guy, replete with overalls and a toothpick at the corner of his mouth, was a chatter. After two glasses of lemonade and an enthusiastic tour of his cow barn, John finally escaped with a handshake and a decent price for an additional 200 bales of high quality hay for the winter. He also got an invite to go deer hunting if he wanted...and a white waxed paper packet of sausage from last season that the wife had ground up. *Friendly folk*, he mused. *Too bad they don't have any kid's Ro's age.*

He stopped at the only four way stoplight outside of town and peered up at the sky through the windshield. There were some heavy clouds coming in over the mountains that were starting to worry him. So far, they seemed content to stay put but there was a feeling in the air that worried him. Heavy and humid, he could practically taste the potential for one doozy of a thunderstorm.

John yawned behind his hand, then jumped when a horn blasted behind him. A young woman in an SUV waved at him, obviously irritated that he missed the light change.

"Sorry," he muttered under his breath, shaking his head at the impatience of youth.

The rest of the drive was uneventful, up to the moment he pulled into his driveway and drove past the barn. Ro was outside, leading Perseus behind her. He was tacked up and saddled and she was headed for the trailhead.

He slammed the truck into park and jumped out of the truck. "Ro! Rohanna!" he bellowed.

Rohanna whipped her head around. Even as far away as she was, John could tell she saw him. He raised his hand to wave her in, but she ignored him and mounted up. The wind was starting to pick up, and it grabbed her voice and sent it whooshing past his ears. Rohanna kicked Perseus' flanks and urged him forward with a western inspired whoop. Unused to Ro being so aggressive with him, Perseus jumped and took off like a streak, great chunks of sod flying up behind him.

"What's gotten into that girl?" John muttered, casting a worried eye up at the sky. She knew better than to go riding when the weather was turning, but from the look on her face, he would say she was angrier than the dark, ominous clouds gathering to the west.

"Belinda?!" John raised his voice inside his house for the first time in many years. He walked into the living room to find a mess. He bent over and picked up a lamp, then tossed a pillow back onto the couch. It looked like a small tornado had whipped through the house and left a path of destruction leading straight towards Rohanna's bedroom.

"What the hell is going on in here?"

"John?" Belinda's tremulous voice greeted him a second before the woman entered the room. "Oh, thank God you are here. Ro...she just went crazy. Yelling at me and tearing the place apart, just because I told her she couldn't go out riding today."

John stared at her in disbelief. He walked around the room, slowly, taking in all of the damage. He doubted one small girl could do so much...especially one that didn't break ninety pounds soaking wet. He ran his fingers across the coffee table and came back with something wet...and red. It spread, thick and sticky, between his thumb and forefinger. "This is blood, Belinda! Why is there blood here?"

"I have no idea! The child must have harmed herself." Belinda managed to sound affronted at the tone of his voice. She didn't expect John to grab her arm and hold it up in the air. Her wedding ring, the one he had spent so much money on...was marred with a streak of red...turning the large diamond into a ruby.

"This doesn't look like she harmed herself, Belinda." Johns face turned as hard and cold as stone, but that was nothing compared to his voice when he spoke again. The way he ground out every word reminded her of an ancient grist mill.

John started pacing the room, mainly because if he took a step towards Belinda he didn't know if he could contain himself. His arms shook from the effort of not fisting his hands and taking his rage out on anything solid.

Through a haze of red hot anger, he glared at the woman he thought he loved and forced his jaw to unlock. His tongue felt strange against his teeth but he managed to make himself understood. "It took me a long time to see it, but I see everything so very clearly now. How miserable Rohanna is, how much she hates you...and now I see it has been for good reason. I made a terrible mistake after Erin's death. I thought Rohanna needed a mother, but what she really needs is to be happy and to have the childhood she deserves. We will talk when I return, and after that the next time I see you will be at the lawyer's discussing the terms of our divorce. That is, if I don't call the police first since you saw fit to strike my daughter."

The threat hung there for a moment, heavy between the two of them. Belinda stared at him, for the first time since he met her, she actually looked out of sorts. Speechless in that way someone looks at a beloved pet that suddenly decided to bite the hand that fed them.

"I am going to leave now, Belinda. I need to find my daughter and make sure she's okay."

He turned on his heels and headed back out the door.

"Stop! John. Come back and have dinner with me. Rohanna is fine. She's just out on one of her rides and will be back soon." Belinda's voice had taken on an odd quality. Oily and falsely sweet at the same time, it poured over his skin and made the hairs on the back of his neck rise. He turned slowly, the urge to listen to Belinda, to believe what she was saying, was almost overwhelming. A bright light flashed across the front window, followed by a deafening crash that broke the spell. He shook himself like a dog, then grabbed for the wall. He felt dizzy for a moment, but it passed and his head cleared.

Rohanna, she's out there, possibly hurt...and a storm is coming in.

The thought was sufficient to keep him on point. He glared at his wife. "What kind of game are you playing, Belinda?"

"No game, John." Belinda dropped any pretext of being nice. "I never play games...not unless I plan to win." She smiled and poured herself a drink from the carafe at the liquor bar. "Go, find your precious daughter. You better hurry though, I have a feeling this storm is going to be hellish."

John shook his head, looking back at Belinda not once but twice in his confusion. "I don't really know who you are, do I?"

He didn't wait for an answer.

The storm was coming in fast and he had to make sure Rohanna was safe first...then he would deal with Belinda.

***

Belinda whirled around the minute the front door slammed shut and headed for the basement.

"Get out here, now."

Twelve cowled figures crawled out of the shadows, their backs hunched over as if the verbal lashing caused them actual pain.

"You were supposed to be watching for him!" she hissed, pointing at one in particular. Tallish and thin, the middle aged woman shook beneath Belinda's stern glare.

"I'm sorry, Belinda. The girl ran from me and I was trying to find her. She found another way to the barn and I could not retrieve her before he saw her. By the time I made it back here, he was already inside."

Another woman stepped forward. "As to that. How is it that he broke through all the wards in the first place? I thought this problem had been taken care of. You had control of the girl, why not the man?"

Belinda narrowed her eyes until they were mere slits of hot anger and thought about that. "A good question, Thia. He should not have been able to speak to me so. What are we missing?"

Thia cleared her throat before speaking again, casting her eyes down diffidently just in case Belinda took umbrage at her suggestion. "Perhaps he has something in his possession that prevents you from dominating him?"

"A token of some sort?" Belinda turned away from the others. Her wedding ring caught the light from the stairwell and sparked an idea. She huffed, irritated that she hadn't thought of it before. "Maeve. The woman hasn't said a thing or made any indication that she knows who I am...but what if she does and has been content with watching from afar—ensuring that we fail with Rohanna?"

"Because she knows the stories from the old country? That doesn't make her a threat. Sure, she has Fae blood...but who doesn't this far out in the backwoods?" Thia spoke more boldly this time.

Belinda turned on her. "And you would guarantee this with your life, Thia? Hmm?"

The witch blanched and backed away. Belinda ignored her and closed her eyes so she could think in the pure darkness of her mind. Of course, the woman was right. Maeve was a tired old woman, and if she was an enemy...she wasn't one Belinda would ever worry about. John, now. He was becoming a problem.

Belinda sighed and pinched her nose between her fingers at the headache all of this was causing...all for one fool girl who may or may not hold the key to finding her way home.

"I'm done with this. We have a problem that needs to be taken care of, the sooner the better."

"What do you need us to do?" Several eager voices sounded delighted in the coming carnage.

"He's protected, what can we do?" The dissenting question overlapped and ran through the first.

"He may be protected from me, but there are other things in this world that can be quite dangerous. Humans are fragile creatures and a storm is coming." Belinda smiled. Lightning flashed through her eyes, followed by a rumbling crash outside the house that made the walls around them shudder. "I do so love a good storm."

CHAPTER NINE

A few miles down the road the heavy cloud cover sent the evening racing into night. The sky opened up soon after that, eating up the light from John's headlamps and reducing his world to the rhythmic squeal of the windshield wipers. The rain ran like a river along the blacktop until it was hard to tell where the road ended and the dirt shoulder began. There was no other light to guide his way and the dummy buttons popping in and out of focus between the overworked windshield wiper blades reminded him of shy rabbits blinking at him before running away into the dark.

John checked his cellphone, hoping to see a message from Ro, but there was nothing. Disgusted, he tossed the thing down in the passenger seat. The road was familiar, one he drove every day, which was why he felt safe pushing the envelope, driving just below the speed it took for his wheels to start hydroplaning on the slick surface.

The entire valley was a dead zone, it was stupid for him to try the damn thing, but sometimes a message would make it through. He hadn't bothered calling Maeve, she refused to keep a cell phone or much of anything else electrical at the old cabin. He should have called from the house phone, but he hadn't been thinking straight at the time. He had initially thought to take the gravel road that followed some of the horse trails winding through the farm, but with the rain coming in, it had become too risky. Ro was smart. She would have gone to safety in something like this, and the safest place she would run to was her grandmother's. He headed for his mother's cabin, crossing his fingers that he had guessed right and would find them sitting in front of the old wood stove, trying to dry out and Maeve forcing a cup of something hot in Ro's hand for her troubles.

Going home meant travelling back to a simpler time. Maeve seemed to prefer working within the natural rhythms of the farm around her, waking up with the dawn and retiring at sundown. The breezes were all she used to cool the cabin in the summer and a solid wood stove heated the place and cooked her meals in the winter. He was surprised she didn't use one of the horses to ride into town for supplies, instead of her familiar old pickup truck. Father had bought the darn thing a year before he died, and she had kept it since then...never trading it in for a newer model. Knowing how often she drove, it probably still had less than 100,000 miles on the engine.

John's jaw tightened against the old memories. The year his father died was the same year his mother sat him down and told him he was a grown man now...that he should call her Maeve and not Mother. It felt strange at the time, but he got used to it. Then after Ro arrived, she had simply become Grandma and everyone left it at that.

He didn't realize he had sped up until he felt the tires slipping. Tapping the breaks as carefully as he could, he managed to slow down a bit before hitting one of the nastier curves on the way down to Maeve's cabin. Lightning flashed, whiting out the windshield and blinding him temporarily. Blinking the afterimage away, he didn't even have to count to one before the thunder struck so close it rattled the truck doors.

"Damn, Ro. This was a hell of a night to take off," John muttered, wishing that she had trusted him enough to tell him what happened rather than run away. Now she was out in this crap with only Perseus to keep her safe.

The next curve came up sooner than he expected. The lightning struck again, even closer...only this time it illuminated the entire road ahead of him. A figure stood in the middle of the road, arms raised, palms forward and thrust out in front of them. "What the..?" John cried out, cranking hard on the steering wheel. The truck skidded out, then hit the mud embankment and tumbled down the hillside. Something huge and dark reached out and grabbed the truck and all of a sudden it wasn't moving. The windshield cracked against his forehead and he was thrown back into the seat. Something hot and wet ran down his face and all he could think of was that it couldn't be raining inside the truck.

"Belinda?" he gasped, not out of love but out of fear. *Oh, God. What have I done?* In the clarity that persists in the moment between life and death, John remembered a dozen, a hundred times silver grey eyes stared at him with barely concealed contempt...the words she had spoken and his inability to stand against them. Those eyes had passed through him on the way down the embankment, much like his truck had somehow passed through an image of a person who was there yet not there. *I've left my daughter in the hands of a monster and I can do nothing to protect her.*

He managed to force his fingers to do as he bid, pushing past the pain to fumble around in his chest pocket for the small packet Maeve had given him. The truck door was twisted partially open. It only took a nudge to force it farther. The pain was excruciating, but that wasn't what frightened him most. A creeping numbness was taking over his body stealing what little warmth was left in him. A second before he passed out, giving into the inevitable, he managed to push the envelope out of the cab. He felt the rain then, joining the red blood running down his hand to pour into the carved ground beneath him. He didn't question why he could see the envelope, or why it shined like a beacon when everything else dimmed and faded away. He felt, rather than watched, it slip away as the rain fell and made small rivers of mud and blood that joined a dozen other rivulets.

It's safe now, he thought, and smiled. *She won't find it.*

But Ro will.

"Who's there?" He coughed, then laughed weakly. There was nobody there with him. He looked up just as another bolt of lightning struck close, illuminating the gnarled limbs of a giant oak looming above his head. A great crack followed, followed by the smell of burning wood.

He felt the warmth and smiled past eyes too tired to open. "That's nice. I was getting cold. A good fire fixes everything."

"John? John, can you hear me?" The voice came from far away, jolting him out of his nice cozy nest. He shivered against the sudden cold.

"Maeve? Mother?"

"Yes. Stay still, the fire department's on its way."

"No, wait. You have to find Ro," John whispered, grasping at Maeve's shawl and pulling her close to him.

"She's in danger, Mother. Find her."

"Where, what happened?"

John waved his hand weakly. Speaking was becoming difficult. "Perseus. Out there. She took off. In the storm."

Maeve watched the spark die in John's eyes.

"Nooo." She raised her chin and screamed her rage into the storm. *The stone, where's the fairie stone?*

"Maeve?"

A gentle hand pulled her away from the wreckage, from her frantic search for the Fairie stone.

"What do we do now?" Shyann asked. Maeve's eyes were wild, her loose silver hair plastered flat against her face.

"The stone, the stone is gone." Maeve plucked at her shawl.

"And Ro might have it..." Shyann reminded her.

"Ro! Oh, Goddess, Shyann!" Maeve turned and clutched at Shyann's collar. "Go! Find her, make sure she's safe. Bring her back here."

Shyann hesitated. She'd never seen Maeve so distraught. She had to make sure Maeve knew what the consequences were. Ro didn't know her on sight...had not met her on Maeve's insistence. "Are you sure?"

"Yes, yes," Maeve muttered, turning her attention back to the wrecked truck. "How am I going to tell her that her father is dead?"

The woop-woop of an emergency vehicle brought Shyann's head up. Flashing red lights and the sounds of men yelling was her warning to leave.

"I'll be back as soon as I find her," she said, leaving Maeve to the noise and controlled chaos. The cabin was barely a quarter mile away from where they stood now. She would start there and backtrack. Shyann cast one last worried look back at Maeve before she took off running. *I hope they don't notice that she's standing in her bare feet, or ask how she got there so fast.*

She ran until the storm stopped and then she ran faster, following trails into the dead of night that were barely visible beneath the dark canopy of trees...and nothing more than a muddy creek where the land lay open to the thin moonlight that showed up late for the search.

She returned to Maeve's cabin just before the sun came up. A lone rooster crowed, announcing the coming dawn a minute before the first rays slipped above the horizon. This time Maeve didn't hear her slip inside the door, nor did she seem to notice her sit down at the table across from her. Red rimmed eyes stared blankly at a cold cup of tea, and for once, Maeve looked as tired and worn as the body she had lived in for so many years.

"You didn't find her."

"I did not," Shyann said. "But I know where she is."

"Tell me."

Maeve's gaze hardened as Shyann told her story, then she bowed her head and hid her face in her hands. "I have failed her."

"You haven't, and she is safe...for now," Shyann argued. "Perseus...now. He had a great soul. He fought to protect her, all the signs were there. I couldn't just leave him like that."

She held out her hands and bid Maeve to look. Cupped within her palms was a small light, a firefly like thing that pulsed with life. "I could have left him. Let him go to the Summerland, but I don't think his story is finished yet. I can do for him what I did for you. All I need is a vessel."

Maeve wiped her face and sniffled. It was such a very human thing to do, but it warmed Shyann's heart that she had managed to do something to ease her pain.

"We can do that. As soon as the sun rises fully, introduce John's filly to the stallion. I can't risk giving her

John's gift now, but that filly will help bring Perseus back to her."

"Yes, M'Lady. We can do that."

***

Rohanna woke from a terrible nightmare and tried to sit up. Her head exploded the minute it left the pillow, and she cried out against the sudden pain. She grabbed at her head, then moaned when her fingers accidentally dug into the bandages wound across her forehead. A more tentative exploration discovered another bandage taped to her cheek. That one itched.

"Shush, child, you'll hurt yourself moving like that." Gentle hands helped her back down, then tucked the blankets around her. Ro watched in silence, trying to gather her thoughts around her. She was having trouble remembering anything past breakfast with her father this morning.

"I don't understand."

"I'll go get your mother. She'll be glad to hear that you're awake." The woman clucked at her, then smoothed down the front of her plain white uniform before turning to leave.

"Awake? What do you mean? What happened?" Rohanna undid the nurse's neat work by throwing the blankets aside again and trying to stand up. She gave up, huffing and puffing from the exertion, after only a few seconds of trying. She was as weak as a kitten.

"You should talk to your mother, but from what I was told...you were thrown from your horse a few days ago...took quite a tumble. Hit your head." The woman shook her head, obviously not happy with Rohanna's irresponsible ways. "Your mother's been beside herself and I don't blame her. Riding off like that? You're lucky you didn't break your neck. I can't say as much for that poor horse. I hear they had to put him down."

"Perseus!" Rohanna roared. The woman's eyes crinkled around a terrible smile. She had enjoyed telling her that, of that Rohanna had no doubt. *Leave it to Belinda to find a nurse as callous and cruel as she was,* she thought.

"I don't believe you! Let me see my horse, now!" Rohanna did manage to get up this time, the room swayed dangerously beneath her feet, then she felt the cool wood floor beneath her cheek and then the pain in her head blossomed and sent her back into darkness.

CHAPTER TEN

The long grey ribbon of driveway wound its way through a thick veil of militant trees, thick trunks capped by heavy green and gold canopies. A line of straight-backed sentinels that marked their passing as if they were marching past the slow moving vehicle. Their even spacing mirrored their counterparts, left and right...an honor guard of soldiers armored in rough bark, as unnatural in their placement as Rohanna felt. An immense stone building that looked more like an ancient castle rather than a boarding school slipped into view between each passing tree in a marked cadence, only to disappear behind verdant leaves again.

The stress of the last few weeks had left Rohanna's finely chiseled face gaunt, her high cheekbones standing out sharply against pale, almost translucent skin. Dark circles beneath her eyes made them appear bright in contrast to her eyelids, which remained swollen and red. They were evidence of how many tears she had shed in private, as well as the ones she had publicly and unashamedly shed at her father's funeral.

Ro gazed blindly out the window at the raindrops sliding across the glass, lost in her own thoughts. The overcast sky and dreary landscape suited Rohanna's mood just fine. Fair weather on this day would have felt like the world was mocking her.

Too much had happened, and she felt lost and alone. Her head throbbed painfully, even with her forehead pressed against the cool hard glass of the car window. The view of her future home became unfocused in time with her breath, the window fogging against her hot breath, revealing two overlapping handprints pressed along its surface. *Was someone trying to get in or get out?* The odd thought intruded on Rohanna's grief, sadness welling up yet again to flood out the numbness she preferred. Numb didn't hurt, it was just...numb. Much more comfortable than thinking or feeling. Thinking and feeling led to anger, and she was too tired to be angry right now.

Unfortunately for Ro, her mind rebelled against her enforced lethargy, and she found herself thrown back into memories so fresh and painful, she felt like she was bleeding from them. Maybe inside she was.

Rohanna couldn't believe what was happening. Even the death of her beloved father became a social event lorded over by her stepmother Belinda. Somehow, she managed to create an aura of loss so convincing that most of the guests spent their time fawning over the "grieving widow" instead of honoring the man who had died. Rohanna sat quietly in a corner, suffering the long afternoon while she silently observed the milling crowd. She couldn't differentiate the buzzing in her head from the low murmur of the guests as they walked about the great hall. Their grief didn't seem to affect their hunger. Most of them spent a good deal of time sampling the expensive catered food that Belinda had brought in.

If Rohanna hadn't just watched her father's casket being lowered into the ground a few hours earlier, there wouldn't be any difference between this atrocity and any of Belinda's other parties. All the right people were here and Belinda was soaking it up, the center of attention as always. The handkerchief in her hand was purely for show, as neither her tears nor her makeup stained it. Rohanna thought that was quite a feat, since Belinda routinely brought it up to her face to wipe away a grieving widow's tears.

When they finally ushered the last guest out the front door with a polite "thank you for coming" Rohanna sighed in relief. Now she could finally seek out the silence and solace of her own room. She stood up, slowly and painfully, and started to shuffle towards the staircase that led to her room. A cool voice intruded upon her exhausted state, just as she lay her hand on the smooth wood of the banister.

Rohanna turned and faced her stepmother wearily. The grieving widow was gone. That persona had disappeared along with her last guest only to be replaced with the cold, haughty woman Rohanna knew so very well. Belinda stared at her, then turned and disappeared back into her father's study. The staccato rhythm of her heels sounded angry, taking their owner's self-importance out on the shiny wooden floors. Belinda obviously expected Rohanna to follow.

What more can she do to me?

Rohanna felt a small seed of fear forming deep within her stomach; she didn't want to follow Belinda. She didn't want to know what Belinda had to say. She wanted to run away from this woman who now held her future in her hands. A woman who hates me as much as I hate her, she thought.

"Rohanna, I know you are still grieving for your father," Belinda started to say as soon as Rohanna entered the room. "But, it is time we talk about your future."

Walking into her father's study to find her stepmother seated comfortably behind his desk let alone occupying his favorite chair, was too much for Rohanna. Her temper flared, threatening to loosen her tongue. She was barely able to contain herself but managed to remain silent, despite her desire to physically rip the woman out of her father's chair and away from his desk.

Schooling her voice to a calm tone that she didn't feel inside, Rohanna reluctantly responded to her stepmother, "My future?"

Smiling viciously, her stepmother spoke in a crisp voice more suited to a boardroom than her late husband's den. "Yes. As you know, with your father's passing, I am in charge of running this estate. I see no reason for you to mope around here wasting your time on frivolity, when you should be finishing your education and learning to become a proper young lady."

Confused, Rohanna tried to gather her thoughts. Her father had always told her that the farm would go to her when he passed away. What was going on?

"My father left the farm to me, Belinda, not you. And if not me, at least it should be returned to my Grandmother!" she argued, but was interrupted by harsh laughter.

"You are mistaken, child. I am the executor of your father's estate. As a minor in my care, I have every right to do as I please with you." Belinda's voice cut harshly through the silence, carrying a malice so palpable that it almost struck Rohanna like a physical blow.

"I have arranged for you to start at The Academy this session. It's unusual to get in on such short notice, but the headmaster has graciously allowed you to start right away, considering the circumstances."

The Academy? The Academy was over 200 miles away, far from her home and family. Once there, Rohanna was sure she wouldn't see her home except for summer break and holidays.

Protesting, Rohanna sputtered, "You can't, I won't go, I refuse."

Belinda stood up and leaned over the desk. "I can, and I will. I suggest you start packing. You will be leaving on Monday. Oh, and just in case you have any bright ideas, I will guarantee you that if you give me any trouble whatsoever, you will never see this farm again. I own you and this farm until you are twenty-five. I suggest you take my advice if you ever want to inherit your father's farm."

"So, I did inherit the farm?" Rohanna asked, confused at her stepmother's admission.

Belinda waived her hand dismissively, then responded casually, as if it was nothing more than an unimportant afterthought. "Yes, yes you did. But like I said, not until you are twenty-five. Until then, I have the reins, so to speak. I am telling you this now as an act of faith. You can check with the attorneys in the morning, if you like."

So, Rohanna thought, Belinda finally has what she has always wanted. She's in control of everything, including me, and I can't do anything until I turn twenty-five. Rohanna wanted to howl in frustration. Why did her father do that to her?

Her grandmother hadn't been at the funeral, and despite begging for leniency, Belinda refused to let her go visit. "The woman is dealing with her own grief, Rohanna...let her be."

Rohanna rubbed the scar on her cheek. It had needed stitches, and the skin was still red and angry where they pulled out the sutures. The doctor insisted it would fade in time and be barely noticeable, but right now it was an ugly reminder of her guilt. She had no doubt that her grandmother didn't want to see her, but how else could she apologize for what she'd done?

She didn't remember saddling up Perseus...or riding out when a bad storm was coming in. That seemed so unlike her. She might be a little headstrong, but risking Perseus? She closed her eyes and tried to remember that day, but like always...a vague discomfort grew inside the darkness behind her eyelids and she was forced to give up.

Tears of shame slipped down her cheeks. She was told that amnesia after a head injury was normal...but that didn't excuse her actions. Actions that sent her father out into the storm after her with balding tires and no concern for his own safety. Now, she had to live with that guilt.

Perhaps being sent away is a Godsend, she thought. Belinda had no qualms about reminding her that Perseus and her father had paid the price for her foolishness. At least among strangers she could lick her wounds in private.

The car pulled up to the front of the school. She looked up at the stone walls and tall, thin windows and grimaced. The place looked like an ancient church...*or a prison.* Either way, it looked sturdy enough to contain her guilt. She took a deep breath and opened the car door. For the first time in her life she was going to be surrounded by strangers, and for all her past wishes to be around people her own age, she would take back the isolation of her farm to have her father back.

CHAPTER ELEVEN

Rohanna woke up before the sun rose and glared at the now familiar dorm room ceiling. She hated being at the boarding school. She hated being so far away from her farm and she hated being away from her horses. *The only good thing about being here is that it is far away from Belinda,* Ro thought.

She had already made several enemies at the school, mostly other rich girls who were used to lording it over the campus. They didn't want to give up their social standing to a new girl, and Ro simply hadn't been up to the necessary meanness needed to earn their respect. It wasn't her fault. She simply didn't see herself that way. People who saw themselves as better than everyone else due to chance and circumstance of what family they were born into or how much money they had reminded her too much of Belinda. There were only two types of people in their world, the ones that fit in and the outcasts. She preferred the isolation of the latter.

Rohanna was now in her junior year. She had easily qualified for the school equestrian team despite her lack of a personal mount. Belinda had refused to allow Ro to have one of their own horses to show on, and after losing Perseus, she didn't have the energy to argue past the woman's insistence that she didn't deserve one. Still, she wasn't completely immune to the taunts and whispers from those who had somehow heard of her misfortune. Having to use the school horses would have embarrassed a lesser person, but for Rohanna it was simply a reminder of what she had lost, so was the thin white scar across her right cheek. It still itched at times, and when it was cold outside, it burned like fire.

Rohanna realized she was rubbing at her cheek again and pulled her hand away. She could have given up and stopped riding altogether, but the farm was always the first thing on her mind when she woke up and the last thing she thought of when she went to bed.

I will get the farm back from Belinda, Ro vowed, turning on her side just to stare at something new while she thought about her life. It wasn't just getting the farm back either...it was keeping it alive and well while Belinda did her best to ruin everything her father had tried to do. That meant she had to ride, and not just ride, but ride well enough for people to take notice. The MacLeod name had a reputation, and no matter how much it hurt, she would do whatever it took to keep that reputation fresh in everyone's minds.

Luckily for her, there were always students who abandoned their interest in showing upon graduation. Their rich parents would shrug off the cost and make a donation of the poor horse rather than deal with a four legged creature that needed care and grooming. It was a much better fate than going back home to be ignored or abused, and it left a few well-bred souls available to those less fortunate students who dared the gauntlet of sneers and uppity attitudes. Most of her competition had their own mounts and relished teasing her mercilessly when she first arrived—then they started competing against her and the mocking turned into something else. Rohanna didn't know if consistently taking the blue ribbons away from her tormentors made things better or worse—but she didn't ride for them. She rode for her father and her grandmother, but in the process, she discovered something else about herself. She loved the thrill of competing and winning. It made her heart race and her soul fly, much like it had whenever she watched the thoroughbreds thundering past her at the track.

The window panes lightened from unrelieved black to a dull grey. It was enough to see by, and that was all she was waiting for. Rohanna threw off her blanket and stood up, eager to be the first one in the barn. People thought she was strange, being up this early in the morning on an off day, but she enjoyed the quiet solitude early morning offered her. The horses were fresh and eager for attention with very few people around to intrude on her private time. It was Saturday. There weren't any classes today and most of her homework was already done for the weekend. After stamping her feet into her tall black leather boots, Ro gathered up her helmet and riding crop. She tucked her crop into the top of her right boot then inspected herself in the mirror. The tall boots were paired with tight tan breeches and her usual untucked red flannel shirt. Her schooling helmet hid her normally wild hair, now properly braided and hidden beneath the protective plastic and felt hat. Ro grimaced, still dissatisfied with her appearance. She looked too much like a cookie cutter version of every other rider in the school, even with her favorite flannel. She slid a pair of heavily tinted sunglasses on, their reflective surface flashing silver against her pale skin. The sunglasses allowed her to observe everything around her while maintaining her distance, unapproachable and untouchable. Rohanna grinned at her reflection in the mirror. She was ready to go now. The barn should be quiet for a few hours unless another rider decided to motivate and get in some last minute training for tomorrow's show.

Her saddle, a birthday gift from her father, lay atop several layers of horse blankets beneath an oak saddle stand. She didn't dare leave the saddle in the barn where it would inevitably be used or lost. It was the last present her dad had given her and she couldn't bear the thought of losing it. She ran her fingertips over the saddle, focusing on the slightly oily feel of the fine leather and relishing the quality of the workmanship. Sadness welled up in Rohanna's chest, scraping open a wound that hadn't quite healed. A single tear slid down her cheek, it dripped onto the black leather, staining the otherwise pristine surface with salt.

The saddle had been custom ordered and made—a handcrafted process that took several months and God only knew how many hours to complete. The saddle maker delivered it the morning of her fourteenth birthday, per her father's instructions. She was forever grateful to the artist for taking the time to drive so far just to hand deliver a single saddle, even if he never told her how he knew where she was. Burly and short, almost as wide as he was tall, he had just smiled at her and tugged at his beat up old ball cap before turning his van about and leaving. He had family in the area, he insisted, and therefore the trip hadn't put him out. Besides, he liked her father, and wanted her to know that many of the local businesses were there for her if and when she needed anything from them.

Rohanna picked up her saddle and headed for the door, enjoying the cadenced staccato of her boot heels as they snapped sharply against the hardwood floors. A muffled curse through one of the dorm room doors was followed by the sound of something soft smacking into the door. *Probably a pillow,* Ro thought, mildly amused at the girls choice of words, which included one or two she hadn't heard before and filed away for future use. She picked up her pace just in case they decided to stumble out of bed and ruin her pleasant morning.

She entered the main barn through the back aisle. Like the rest of the school, it was a huge monstrosity of a building, stacked stone to the height of the stalls, topped by huge timber framing. Copulas sat along the roof at spaced intervals, letting in light and ventilation. It was a beautiful old barn, and it smelled like home, making it her favorite place to be. Familiar faces greeted her. Long noses poked out of their stalls for a passing rub or nickering gently for a treat as she walked past each stall. At the end of the aisle, she noticed a set of tack boxes that looked straight out of a catalog stacked outside the last two stalls. Shiny and clean usually meant one thing—a new horse had arrived.

Rohanna's curiosity was piqued. She wanted to know who the barn's newest resident was. Ignoring the woeful looks of the other horses as she strode past them, she made her way to the last stall and peeked in.

The new horse was gorgeous—an elegant and bold looking blood bay gelding standing almost seventeen hands. Rohanna marked his conformation, desperately looking for any flaws. She couldn't find a single one, and didn't know if she should be thrilled or disappointed. If he was as talented as he looked, Rohanna would actually have some competition this year. *Scratch that,* she thought as she petted the inquisitive muzzle, "If your rider is as talented as you look, I might have some competition," she murmured.

"You must think highly of yourself, then?" The unexpected voice behind her made her jump, causing the horse to snort and dance away.

"I'm sorry, I shouldn't have said that." Embarrassed to her core, Rohanna felt heat on her cheeks. A young red-haired woman Rohanna had never seen before grinned gaily at her.

"Don't worry. As far as I'm concerned, you never did." She winked, laying her tack on a convenient bale of hay. The newcomer leaned against the stall door and affectionately stroked the bay's aristocratic nose.

"Do you like him? His name is Galileo, mine's Shyann," she said, extending her hand out to Rohanna. Grasping her new friend's hand firmly, Rohanna responded to the infectious grin in kind. Her mood lightened instantly until laughter seemed to bubble up out of her of its own accord.

"He's gorgeous," Ro admitted, reaching out to stroke the velvet nose enviously. Galileo's nostrils widened as he snuffled Ro's hand, taking in her scent before blowing softly against her palm.

"Whoa, now, don't embarrass the man," Shyann scolded. "He is a handsome boy, I'll give him that. But don't fawn over him too often or he'll get a swelled head."

Galileo lifted his head from Ro's subtle scratching and looked at her so innocently, shaking his head at her as if to say, "No, I wouldn't!" Both girls laughed at him. It was too much for the aristocratic horse. Galileo wandered off in a huff, tail swishing in irritation at both of them, and proceeded to examine the far corner of his stall carefully. He pretended not to take notice of them and almost succeeded until he turned a baleful eye to them from over his shoulder. That set the girls off again, falling against the bale of hay as they laughed even harder.

"Wow, you would think he understood you, acting like that." Ro giggled. "Oh, that was too funny," she gasped, clutching her sides. It had been a long time since she had laughed so hard. Her jaw ached from lack of practice.

"Well, I'm never surprised by that one. He's smart, and he knows it. Woe to the poor rider who tries to tell him what to do, and I mean it. If you don't know what you're doing, he'll take full advantage of you. Now, if you treat him with the respect he deserves he'll be your best friend forever."

Ro chatted with the newcomer, who insisted on being called Shy, "now that they had met and were practically friends already," as she said.

"Which is the biggest joke ever," Shy continued non-stop, "since I am definitely NOT shy in the least!"

Ro had to agree with her on that one.

"Will you help me bring in the rest of my stuff?" Shy asked.

"Sure, but let me give you some friendly advice...don't leave your gear lying about, it won't stick around for long."

Rohanna was more than happy to let Shyann monopolize the conversation as they walked back through the barn, adding in a few words here and there whenever Shy came up for air. Normally reserved, Ro usually had little tolerance for the perpetually happy people who populated the school. They usually weren't very bright, and their continual babbling was generally about things Ro had very little interest in, like makeup, clothes, and boys. Shyann, on the other hand, was as excited about horses as Ro was, and the lilt in her voice held a familiar cadence that reminded Ro of home.

A wave of homesickness crashed through Rohanna, riding in on the sound of Shyann's accent. She missed the hills around her home. She thought of her grandmother, whom she had not seen since her father's funeral.

Just thinking of her seemed to conjure up the beloved woman's voice.

"Rohanna? Quit your daydreaming, girl!"

The admonishment rang in her ears loud enough to believe it was real. She cast a quick look at Shyann, surprised that her new companion didn't hear the distinctive voice. Of course, Shyann's mouth was travelling a mile a minute, and Ro wasn't sure if the girl's ears could hear past her own words once she got going.

"Did you hear that?"

"Well, sure I did. 'Tis my great-aunt. She brought me here." Shyann stopped her monologue long enough to answer her.

Rohanna emerged from the dim shadows of the barn and was instantly blinded by the sun. Squinting against the light, she didn't immediately recognize the nimble older woman scrambling out of the horse trailer parked outside the barn.

"Shy, grab this won't you? It's a bit heavy for an old woman."

Rohanna stopped dead in her tracks. Various emotions raced through her, starting with surprise and ending with sheer joy at seeing her grandmother after so long a time. The poor woman barely had time to step down from the trailer door before Rohanna was there, wrapping her arms around her.

"Grandma! Oh, my God, you're really here. It's so good to see you." Rohanna's words spilled over each other as she hugged her grandmother.

"Careful Ro, you'll break me. I'm not as young as I used to be."

Remembering her manners, Ro turned to introduce Shyann to her grandmother then realized that Shyann and her grandmother obviously knew each other, only Ro had no idea who Shyann was.

"Great Aunt?" That was what Shyann had said. Stepping back in confusion, she took a closer look at the young woman. Rohanna noted the reddish hair framing a somewhat oval face, a slight jaw giving her an elf like appearance that would have looked innocent, if it weren't for mischievous green eyes. Shyann was practically dancing from one foot to the other, her lips pressed together tightly as if trying not to speak. Somehow, Ro knew this was something that was very, very difficult for her to do.

"What's going on?" Rohanna asked, her gaze passing from the familiar lines of her grandmother's face to the much younger and unfamiliar face of Shyann. There was an unmistakable family resemblance in their features, although her grandmother's hair had faded to that magnificent shade of silver that red heads often did, compared to Shyann's copper-penny red. Despite their obvious age differences, two similarly mischievous smiles peered out from beneath equally untamable hair, mirroring each other in a way that gave away their common heritage.

Her grandmother beckoned Shyann forward. She wrapped a thin, denim-covered arm around the taller girl and squeezed her tightly. The younger woman flushed red in embarrassment at the public display of affection, but managed to widen her grin at the even more confused expression on Rohanna's face.

"This is your cousin, Ro. I meant to do the introductions, but it seems like you two have found each other on your own." Looking past the two girls, she focused on the large wooden barn they had just emerged from a few minutes ago. "Although, I should have known you would be in the barn with the horses," she added.

So, Shy was her cousin, Rohanna thought, but the information didn't lessen her confusion. She cocked her head sideways, begging the question on her mind.

"Aye, my mother's, mother's sister, she is," Shyann explained, pretending to add up the generations by ticking them off with her fingers.

"Behave, Shyann." The wrinkles around Maeve's eyes deepened when she smiled. "Shyann is going to be attending here this year, Ro, so make sure you keep her out of trouble."

Casting an inquisitive glance towards her cousin, Ro caught the other girl's quick wink at her and smiled ruefully. Somehow, Ro got the impression that keeping Shy out of trouble would be a full time job.

"Um, Grandma?" Ro asked, suddenly serious. For all her joy at seeing her grandmother again, there was still something she needed to get off her chest. The guilt over her father's death remained a heavy burden on her heart, and she needed to tell her how sorry she was. Ro had lost a father, but Maeve had lost her son. She needed to know why, after all these years, she finally searched her out.

"What, child? You look troubled," Maeve asked, noting the sudden change in Ro's demeanor. Shyann slunk off, remaining close by yet managing to give them some privacy.

"I am so happy to see you again, but...but, I thought you were angry with me. Belinda told me you didn't want to see me, and then, nothing. I sent so many letters, telling you how sorry I was...how much I regretted what I did." Rohanna choked up, her apology caught in her throat.

"Oh, Ro...I don't blame you at all. What happened to your father wasn't your fault, and don't let me catch you thinking that way again! The storm was to blame, and bad luck. And as for Belinda?" Maeve's eyes narrowed when the name passed her lips. "I'll not speak badly about your step-mother here, but I never told her to keep you from me. Your letter's never reached me, of that you can be sure, or I would have written you back."

"But, how did you find me now?" Rohanna was trying to wrap her head around everything Maeve was telling her.

Maeve winked at her. "A certain saddle maker showed up at the farm looking for you. It's a long story, but suffice it to say...we turned over a lot of stones to find you here."

Maeve shook herself, and with her old shawl wrapped loosely around her shoulders, the action reminded her of a crow trying to settle ruffled feathers. "Now, you two girls hurry up and get Calypso unloaded. She's been stuck in the trailer all morning."

Rohanna followed Shyann around to the back of the horse trailer then stood back as her cousin emerged with another horse. Almost the twin of Galileo, Calypso also stood a solid seventeen hands, with the same intelligent eye and elegant head that the other horse possessed. But where Galileo was a brilliant blood bay, Calypso was a dark black bay. The gleaming black coat was trimmed elegantly with red gold highlights gracing her delicate muzzle and accented her legs and underbelly. A patch of white on her forehead shaped like a new moon glowed against the dark coat. A true horsewoman, Ro had to look her over from head to toe. She whistled softly; the mare appeared flawless in conformation.

"What do you think?" Shyann asked, obviously proud of the tall mare she led into the box stall across from Galileo.

"I think you're very lucky to have these two." Ro couldn't suppress the small stab of jealousy admitting that gave her. Her cousin had not one, but two beautiful horses to choose from. "There's not a single mount in the barn that can hold water to them."

"Are you worrying about how you're going to fare at the shows this year?" Shyann asked, raising one ginger eyebrow.

"Ah-ha! I see your evil plan. But remember, you have to be approved for the team first, then we'll see how you do against me."

Galileo was doing his best to get their attention. Laughing at his "love me" expression, she almost expected him to bat his soft brown eyes at her. He was actually pouting, sucking his bottom lip in at the other horses who were receiving *his* attention. Rohanna felt drawn to the bay gelding gently nuzzling her for treats. He seemed more solid, more trusting than the darker mare.

I wish you were mine, Boy'o, Ro thought, then patted Galileo one last time before regretfully turning away from the gelding.

"I guess we should head back to the truck before Grandma comes looking for me," Rohanna said. There was no way she was going to miss spending time with her grandmother before she had to go back home.

Shyann agreed, but before they went too far...she pulled her aside.

"Listen. Maeve will kill me if she finds out I told you before she did, so act surprised, okay?"

"Okay?" Rohanna half agreed but only because Shy was making her incredibly curious.

"I'm not so lucky as you think I am." Shyann looked behind her as if expecting Maeve to suddenly appear behind them. "She's going to ask you to choose one or the other."

Rohanna almost jumped out of her boots, her excitement was so great. Shyann practically clamped her hand over Ro's mouth to keep her from making too much noise.

"Well, I guess you've got excited down pat. Do you think you can do that again in, say, five minutes?" Shyann asked, a droll expression on her face.

"My choice? Galileo or Calypso?" Rohanna whispered loudly, peering back towards the stalls. She thought about the two of them, so alike and yet so different in temperament and attitude.

"Yes." Shyann laughed at Rohanna's indecision, then waggled her eyebrows at her. She shouldn't be enjoying this so much, but she really wanted to know if Rohanna would recognize the familiar soul and be drawn to it. "Is it so hard to choose? They're twins you know, I can see why it would be hard. Like two peas in a pod, they are."

"No, they aren't. Calypso is definitely the flashier of the two, but there's something about Galileo that I can't put my finger on."

"I know what you mean. Maeve said he has an old warrior's soul. Fierce to protect, but old enough to know better than to start useless wars."

"Hah! So, you've gotten your fill of her stories as well, I see." Rohanna chuckled, then frowned slightly. "I find it strange then, that we've never met before. Grandmother must have kept you hidden in the pantry when I came to visit."

She was joking, but Shyann seemed distracted and was a second late responding to it. Then her eyes focused back on Rohanna and she broke out into a hearty chuckle.

"To be sure, I could see her doing something. But truth be told, I travelled a lot when I was younger. I'm sure if we were supposed to meet before now, the fates would have ensured it." Shyann grinned at her. "But now that we have met, I'm sure we are to be the fastest of friends. This school won't be the same, you can be sure of that!"

"Why do I feel like you are going to be trouble for me?"

"Ah, perhaps because my mother named me that as a wee child, eh. A wonderful middle name that would be, hmm?"

She didn't even mind helping Shyann haul all her luggage up to the dorm—at least until the next morning when she woke up stiff and almost too sore to move.

She barely made it to the show on time, and if her face was more grim than normal, none of the judges noticed. She still collected the blue ribbon, even if she did have to use a hay bale to dismount at the end of the day.

CHAPTER TWELVE

Rohanna woke screaming, flailing her arms wildly. Something was holding her down. Red flashed behind her eyelids, blurred images of a figure draped in black, a voice whispering in her ear, urgent, demanding—wanting something from her. Other voices joined in, sibilant, whispering in the dark around her. It was terrifying.

"Ro, wake up Ro!"

Rohanna struggled to open her eyes but the nightmare still claimed her, holding her hostage with gossamer strands of fear that bound her arms and legs until she managed to break free from the imaginary shackles. Groaning, she tossed off the thick blankets and swung her legs over the side of the bed. She dug her palms into her eyelids, trying to push the jumbled images out of her head.

Raking her fingers through sweat dampened hair, Ro shivered in the cool night air. She could feel her heart beating rapidly within her chest, as if she had been running a marathon in her sleep. Taking in deep gulping breaths that burned with the sulfurous stench of fear, she attempted to calm her racing heart.

"Dammit, that hurts. You hit me!" Shyann yelled, fingering her left cheek tenderly. She winced when she found the bruise left by Rohanna's elbow or fist. Rohanna wasn't sure which one.

"Shit, Ro—you could have warned me!"

"I'm sorry, Shy," Ro apologized.

"Ask me again and call me a fool if I ever try to wake you up from a nightmare," Shyann muttered, her quick temper already losing its flame. Ro was incredibly glad her cousin was more of a match than a wildfire; she rarely stayed mad, and she never brought up past grievances. She was the epitome of someone who lived fully in the moment, and Rohanna loved her for it.

"Are you okay, I didn't hurt you, did I?" Rohanna asked. The nightmare was quickly fading into a memory of terror and rapidly losing the power it held over her.

"No worries, Ro. A little bent, but not broken," Shyann joked, breaking the serious moment with a crooked smile. "But remind me to poke you with a long stick the next time, instead of trying to shake you awake, okay?"

"Sure, Shyann," Rohanna agreed, "but I still feel horrible about the whole thing."

Shyann sat down on the bed next to her. Despite the humor in her voice, Shyann held a measure of concern.

"It must have been a bad one. You were screaming at the top of your lungs. I thought you were going to wake the entire dorm up. Thank goodness we have thick walls," Shyann said, then added with a wink, "You need to do something about that, Ro. I can't afford those kinds of noises coming out of the room, now, can I?"

Rohanna laughed. Shyann didn't make much of an effort to hide her preference in company. In her short time at the Academy, she was already the subject of gleefully whispered rumors. As far as Rohanna knew, though, Shyann had never brought anyone back to their shared room. Rohanna had a sneaking suspicion that Shyann was all tease and no action, but the rumor mill was brutal and cared little for actual facts.

"You know you're going to get into trouble someday, don't you?" Rohanna asked. Shyann was handsome, aggressive, and in competition with all the boys at school for the heart of every available senior girl who batted their eyes at her. Ro worried that Shyann's behavior would get her kicked out of school and that would deprive her of the only close friend and serious competitor she had. Her concern was purely selfish, life would be incredibly boring without her cousin around.

"I won't get into trouble. There's nothing for them to catch, I promise. Besides," Shyann added in her uncanny way of reading Ro's thoughts, "that would deprive you, my dear cousin, of me." Laughing heartily, Shyann was almost knocked off the bed by the carefully aimed pillow that landed squarely in her face.

"Oh, you! You are so full of yourself." Rohanna jumped out of bed to wrestle her pillow back from Shy. Shy, on the other hand, was intent on keeping it, at least long enough to return a pummeling rain of blows across Ro's shoulders and back before retreating to her side of the room. Their short burst of energy didn't last long, their giggles wound down until only tired smiles remained. It was almost morning, and they both needed more sleep.

"I have a test in the morning, Ro," Shyann spoke around a yawn. They didn't so much crawl back into their respective beds as fall into them, exhausted. Rohanna curled up in her blankets with her back to the center of the room. She was so tired but her brain was running in high gear. She stared at the wall and willed her body to relax, feigning the sleep her mind wouldn't allow.

"Ro?" Shyann's voice floated between them in the dark. Rohanna weighed the idea of not responding, then sighed. It was so hard to lie to her cousin.

"What, Shy?" she asked, hoping she at least sounded sleepy.

"These nightmares of yours, do they happen a lot? I mean, obviously not as bad as tonight...but, often?"

"No, they don't happen a lot, Shy. I can barely remember already, there's no reason to worry about them." It was hard to lie to her cousin, but not impossible.

The room fell silent for a couple of minutes. Rohanna was starting to believe she was off the hook, then Shy spoke up again.

"You know, if you need to talk about them, I'm right here. Maybe I could help you with them."

"Go to sleep, Shy. We both have a busy day tomorrow." Rohanna punched at her pillow then burrowed in deep, pulling her blankets all the way up past her shoulders. She lay awake for a long time, listening to the deep even breaths of her sleeping cousin while the images from the familiar nightmare played behind her eyelids. With each necessary blink, blurred snapshots of movement passed across her vision, frustrating and incomplete. She had lied to Shyann, but what could she do? Tell her that the nightmares came almost every night?

Rohanna had learned a long time ago to recognize the strange voices heralding the beginning of the nightmare. Their metered cadence was more frightening than the out of focus images flashing along the sleep dimmed edge of awareness, almost recognizable but just beyond her ability to put a face and name to them. If she could drag herself awake before the nightmare had her in its grasp, she had a chance to escape it. Tonight, she had been too tired to wake up in time and it had caught her in its terrifying web.

She doubted she would get back to sleep tonight. As much as she enjoyed Shyann's company, her presence proved to be a double-edged sword. Rohanna couldn't slip out of bed and go to the barn, where the comforting smell of hay and horses often allowed her to catch some much needed sleep. Dreamless sleep. For some reason, the nightmares never seemed to find her there. There were many mornings she had run back to her room, picking straw out of her hair before heading to her first class. Those mornings were few and far between now, and the sleepless nights were starting to wear on her. Shyann was a heavy sleeper, but Rohanna didn't feel like explaining a late night excursion if she woke up to find her gone. *Although if this keeps up, I might have to change my mind. If I don't get a good night's sleep soon I'll be useless in class and dangerous in the saddle.*

Rohanna closed her eyes. They burned like fire from staring too hard at a blank wall in the dark. She knew that when she said good morning to the mirror in a few hours, they would look as bloodshot and puffy as they felt. *Tomorrow night, if it's bad again, I'll go to the barn.*

Rohanna wasn't the only one staring at a blank wall and thinking about serious things in the dark.

Shyann was awake, listening to Rohanna pretending to sleep. She knew Rohanna was still wide awake, unable or unwilling to go back to sleep and risk another terrifying nightmare. Since coming to the school, Shyann had painfully watched Rohanna suffer from terrors that visited her almost nightly. Once in a while, Rohanna would get up in the middle of the night and sneak out of the room, only to return rumpled and cold just before Shy's alarm went off.

There was no doubt in her mind. The unrelieved nightmares were taking their toll on Rohanna. She had always been slim, but now her clothes were starting to hang off her small frame like a scarecrow in a cornfield.

Perhaps no one else had noticed how pale and withdrawn she was starting to look, but Shyann did. Closing her eyes, Shyann made a painful decision. Maeve had sent her to keep Rohanna company and to keep her safe. That she could do without much effort, but night terrors? Those were outside the realm of her experience. She had no idea how to protect Rohanna from nightmares. Nightmares didn't feel pain or fear and they didn't bleed, but then she had another thought. In a way she had already done as Maeve had bidden her. She had brought Galileo with her.

If I go, I won't be leaving her alone. Galileo will protect her...and this time, he has the body and strength to match the heart and soul. Perseus had been a brave and loyal pony, an old soul in his own right...and he loved Rohanna with all his heart. As Galileo, he will do no less.

Turning on her back, Shyann threw her arm over her eyes. Tomorrow she would call Maeve and see what she recommended. She had sworn to serve, but her presence here seemed to be doing more harm than good. Perhaps if she was gone, Rohanna would feel free to roam the halls at night again, and find what solace she could in the barn with the horses. *If not solace, then at least some uninterrupted sleep*, she thought.

CHAPTER THIRTEEN

Four long years. Now, in a couple of days, I'll be home again.

Rohanna glanced at the stack of luggage sitting next to her bed. The neat pile was a lot smaller than she expected, considering how much of her life it contained. A few things remained on the dresser. The dark gown and cap for graduation, a few changes of clothes. That was it.

Rohanna's mind drifted into that time consuming state where you weren't quite asleep but weren't fully awake either.

"What the hell?" Rohanna jumped and almost fell off the bed when someone opened her door. She hadn't even heard the latch click, and they sure as hell hadn't knocked. That, she would have registered.

"Shy! I wasn't expecting you until tomorrow at the earliest," Ro practically squealed. Her cousin lounged against the doorframe with the same insolent grin plastered on her face she remembered. Ro pulled Shyann the rest of the way into the room and gave her a big hug before holding her at arm's length. "Damn, Shy, you haven't changed a bit since the last time I saw you."

"I missed you too, Ro." Shyann returned the favor, giving Ro a quick once over that made her blush. "I can't say the same about you. You definitely grew up."

"You're horrible, you know that?" Rohanna laughed, playfully punching her cousin in the arm. "But honestly.

You don't look a day older than...what? The day we graduated from the Academy."

"Hey, it's not my fault the family genes are so awesome, now, is it?" Shyann waggled pale eyebrows at her then plopped down onto the mattress and leaned back on her elbows. "Speaking of graduations, tell me all about the last four years. I am sure you've been plenty busy."

Ro blushed again, knowing exactly what her cousin meant. Rohanna was twenty-two years old now and had four years of college between her and the last time she saw her cousin. She could only imagine what Shyann had been up to, and wasn't sure she wanted any details.

Despite what the mirror showed her, Rohanna didn't consider herself particularly attractive. She envied others their dark hair and golden skin, which didn't painfully burn each summer. Rohanna's Irish heritage made her prone to freckles and sunburns unless she slathered on huge amounts of suntan lotion, which meant that despite her many hours out in the sun, her skin refused to deepen to anything you could even remotely call a tan.

"Not really, Shyann. Sorry to disappoint you."

"Oh, man. Don't tell me you became one of those girls who never went out. You know, the ones who cried if they didn't get an A in every class." Shyann groaned and grasped at her stomach as if the idea was physically painful.

"No, not really. I went on a few dates, but it really didn't seem worth it. After seeing some of the other girls cry themselves silly over one guy after another, it just seemed stupid."

"Guys? Or gals?" Shyann sat up from where she had flung herself down on the old mattress. "Or should I say women...now that you're a college graduate?"

Rohanna rolled her eyes. "That again?"

"Well, you never seemed interested in any of the boys back at the boarding school, so?" Shyann left the question open.

Rohanna shook her head. Shyann was going to be disappointed because Rohanna had no intention of answering that question. She had seen what relationships did to people. Her father had been miserable because of his need to be with someone. Why would she ever risk that?

"So, what?" Rohanna asked, narrowing her eyes at her cousin before giving in and laughing at their old, but familiar argument. Shyann had the right of it. She never led any of her dalliances on. There wasn't any preconceived notions of love or a relationship to follow; it was all about having fun and new experiences not promises and expectations.

"So. If the boys didn't interest you, something else had to." Shyann leered at her, trying to get her to tell all her deepest darkest secrets.

"Yeah, my textbooks," Rohanna drawled, abandoning her serious act when Shyann lifted one shrewd eyebrow at her. Shyann made her feel seventeen again, or perhaps seven. It was hard to tell somedays. It wasn't that her cousin was immature, per say, it was more that she refused to grow up. Ro giggled and tossed herself down on the bed next to her cousin. "I really did miss you, Shy. I wish you could have come to college with me. Who knows? Maybe with your influence I might have had more fun."

"You're probably right, Ro. I bet college would have been a lot more fun for me. Everyone looks so deliciously grown up here."

"I hadn't noticed," Rohanna admitted. For all their teasing that was the most honest answer she'd ever give

Shyann. There were plenty of handsome men…and women, for that matter, at the university, and not a single one ever moved her past admiring their looks.

Ro's silence sobered Shyann's mood. She cocked her head, staring at Ro so hard she shifted uncomfortably beneath the intense observation. "You know, somehow I don't think you're kidding."

"I'm not." Rohanna had been so glad to see her cousin that she hadn't bothered asking why she was there. Rohanna had been disappointed when Shy told her she was needed back on the farm and wouldn't be following Rohanna to the University. Rohanna's only consolation had been Galileo. He was hers to keep, but it was time to give him up. Graduating college meant going home. Never again would she keep an animal at the MacLeod farm, not while Belinda remained in charge. Galileo would go home, but not her home…he would return to Maeve's place, where he'd be safe. Rohanna's thoughts put a damper on their comfortable banter. "You're here to take Galileo."

"To be sure. But, Ro, you're the one who asked that we take him back."

"I know." Ro felt small, miserable in a way she didn't think Shyann would understand. "Somehow…and this sounds terrible, it just didn't seem real until you showed up. A part of me wanted to be gone before you came to take him, even though I knew you were coming, isn't that horrible?"

"Meh." Shyann brushed off the comment with a wave of her hand. "You're going to be home now. You'll see us often enough."

"I'm not so sure about that. I'll visit at often as I can, but there's so much to do, and you know Belinda will give me a fit whenever I want to come over."

"If you want to, we can take him home to your farm?" Shyann worried her lip with her teeth before asking.

"No! I don't want anything happening to him. I won't be home for a few more days." Rohanna paced across the small room. She caught herself chewing her nails and forced her hands to her sides.

She looked around the small room. Despite it being her home for the last four years, she didn't hold a single ounce of nostalgia for the cookie-cutter dorm room. The University had been such an improvement from the boarding school. No pseudo-military uniforms, dreary rules and regulations, or bullshit politics.

The four years had passed quickly, earning her a degree in business with a minor in equine studies. Everything she needed to run a horse farm efficiently, except she didn't have a farm to run, did she? Not yet. She was going home, but Belinda was still in charge for another three years. It was frustrating as hell, but her father's will tied her hands and she had to abide by his wishes.

"Ro?"

The quiet voice interrupted her pacing. "Geez, I'm sorry, Shyann. I guess I got lost in my head."

"It's okay. Say, you're done with all your finals aren't you?" Shyann asked, her words moving fast as they always did when she got excited.

"Yes. I'm just waiting for final grades." Rohanna stopped and waited. When her cousin got this excited it usually meant she had had an epiphany that was either completely brilliant or was leading the two of them into complete disaster. Ro couldn't sense which one it was this time, but had a feeling it was both.

"So why hang out here? You know you passed everything." Shyann gave her a sly look.

"What about graduation?"

"What about it?" Shyann shrugged. "Is crossing the stage that important to you?"

"No, not really. I mean, if you all were going to be here for it, maybe. But otherwise, why bother?"

"Good question. Is there any reason you have to stay here?" Shyann asked.

"Hmmm. Belinda has a driver coming out to pick me up after graduation. I guess he could pick up my things even if I'm not here. What do you have in mind?"

"I'm thinking of a little belated hooky, that's what." Shyann grinned. "It's been a while since you've been at the old homestead and you won't have to say goodbye to Galileo just yet."

Rohanna started pacing again, her mind going a mile a minute.

"If I just show up at home, she can't say anything because it will already be a done-deal." Rohanna was shocked at her own words. She was actually contemplating this. A nervous thrill passed through her at the thought of defying her stepmother. *But it isn't really defying if she doesn't know and didn't say I couldn't,* Rohanna thought. She stopped pacing and grinned back at Shyann.

"Let's do it. I'll get what I need for a couple of days and then we'll load up Galileo. It's time to blow this popsicle stand."

***

When they turned off the main road and headed deeper into the countryside, Rohanna turned and beamed at Shyann.

It always felt like coming home whenever she visited her grandmother. As they rounded the last curve in the crush and run driveway, they passed through a thick grove of oak trees invaded by the occasional pine and then across a large rolling meadow.

It had been ages since she had visited her grandmother's house. The house and property sat on the northern edge of the MacLeod farm. It had been the original MacLeod homestead, but when Ro's dad got married to her mom, Ro's grandmother had divided the property and gifted the newlyweds with the majority of the acreage as a wedding gift, along with the great house.

Rohanna secretly found the old log cabin more to her taste. It was simple and beautiful and held so much character with its hand-chiseled logs. Dark with age, the ancient beams contrasted with the bright white chinked in mortar. The river that wound through most of the property passed nearby, then widened into a small lake thanks to a stacked stone wall a past ancestor had built to dam up the swift moving water. There was even a small waterwheel at the dam, attached to an antique grist mill. With no obvious signs of modern conveniences, the whole effect was like stepping back in time, or out of time. Rohanna loved it.

Once they were at the cabin, it didn't take long to unload the complacent gelding from the horse trailer. "I'll miss you boy," Ro murmured quietly, rubbing Galileo's muzzle. "You behave for Shyann now, you hear?" Shyann took the lead line from Rohanna and walked Galileo towards the barn.

"I still don't know why we can't just swing around and drop him and you off at the farm," Shyann muttered as she opened the gate.

The gate squealed and protested as she pushed it open, sending a couple of the younger, more skittish horses running. They stopped and turned towards the offending noise, snorting loudly and tossing their heads in a belated show of bravery. Normally, Rohanna would have found it amusing, but she was to upset about leaving Galileo to appreciate the colts' comedic antics.

"Because, if Belinda knows he's special to me, he'll disappear somehow," Rohanna explained, sighing in frustration. She already felt horrible about it, and the woeful look Galileo was giving her wasn't helping at all. "I wish there was a way I could sneak him onto the farm without her seeing him."

"Well, he's here at least. You can come anytime you want to see him." Shyann squeezed Rohanna's shoulder sympathetically. For once Shy didn't bring up Rohanna's problems with Belinda. It was odd that she didn't since she was usually the type to suggest a direct plan of attack when challenged. The compassionate expression on Shyann's face was more disturbing than reassuring. It meant that Shyann agreed with her, which also meant she believed that Belinda was capable of doing exactly what Rohanna said she would do.

The thundering noise of horses running towards them broke the mood as the two women refocused on the herd. There was little risk of any of the better trained horses running them over, but an overenthusiastic colt or two was another thing. Shyann pulled off Galileo's halter and gave him a quick pat on the shoulder.

"Off you go, my friend. It looks like you were missed." Galileo bounded off, racing towards two bay horses running towards him from the edge of the pasture. They met and spun around, whinnying and tossing their heads at each other in greeting.

Ro squinted her eyes at the trio. "Is that Calypso?" she asked.

"Yes, it seems Galileo missed his sister."

"Who's the other horse?"

"Ah, that's his mother. Your dad dropped her off here years ago. I think he got her from the racetrack. She's a good mare, and she crossed really well with your grandmother's stallion, don't you think?"

Galileo and family circled around and came back to the large round hay bale sitting in its holder near them. Rohanna laughed. It never failed; you could have an entire pasture of good grass, and a horse will sit and eat the hay bale. Rohanna ran a practiced eye over the mare, noting her confirmation and markings. She was older and Ro could tell that she was pregnant, making her look ungainly, but still...she looked awfully familiar.

"Um, Shy? When did my dad drop this mare off?"

"About nine years ago."

The two girls jumped and turned around. Ro's grandmother, Maeve, stood right behind them. Maeve still stood straight and tall, her slim frame defying time and gravity to either shrink her presence or bow her back. She held a carved walking stick that looked more like a decoration than a necessity. Her pale hair was loosely tied back, the long tresses free from her usual braid. It looked like a cascade of snow flowing across her back almost down to her knees. Rohanna fingered her own hair and wondered if it would turn as white and elegant as her grandmother's when she got older.

"Is this...?" Rohanna swallowed against the sudden surge of emotion tightening her throat. She didn't realize that happiness and grief could simultaneously occupy the same space in her heart, but they did in that moment.

"Yes, it is. Your father told me all about this mare, and what you did that day. He couldn't bear to see you upset and he agreed with you, wholeheartedly. She wasn't meant to race. He bought the mare and brought her here, thinking to train her for you. She was supposed to come with the saddle on your next birthday."

Maeve's explanation left out a lot, but it didn't take much to figure out how the elegant mare ended up becoming a broodmare instead of showing up on Ro's 14th birthday.

"But, come in now, lass. You've been driving all day, and we at least have you for the night. There is food and a warm fire tonight, and of course, me." Maeve pulled Rohanna in for a hug, gathering her in whipcord strong arms that belied her age. The smell of something good cooking mixed with the scent of burning wood met them on the way towards the cabin.

"I won't argue, not with dinner waiting for me," Rohanna said, raising her nose to sniff the air. She was all too happy to stay, she just wished it could be longer than just a night or two.

CHAPTER FOURTEEN

"What the..?" Rohanna woke up with that odd disoriented feeling you get from sleeping in a strange bed, when it takes a few moments to remember where you are. She felt dizzy, as if her internal compass needed to reset her physical location in the universe. The bed she was sleeping in faced north rather than south, which just felt innately wrong after so many years of sleeping in the opposite direction.

It was almost a full moon, and the cold blue light shining through the window seemed doubly bright so near the lake, illuminating everything inside the room enough to see shapes and forms instead of just shadows. She glanced at the clock. It was three in the morning.

She threw back the blanket and stood to look out the window. Twin moons, one riding the sky low on the horizon while the other walked upon the smooth surface of the lake, managed to captivate her despite the cold.

Rohanna shivered. Rubbing her arms against the damp chill in the room, she seriously contemplated moving her pillows to the foot of the bed and crawling back under the blankets. *Three o'clock.* The witching hour wasn't a friend of hers. This was the time she usually awakened from her frequent nightmares. Tonight was blessedly different. She felt calm and well rested. Her head was clear, and she didn't feel that sense of unease that wouldn't leave her until daybreak.

On the flip side of that welcome coin, she was wide awake now. For once, she had the silence and solitude of the night to explore that didn't involve running away from a bad dream. That was a novelty she couldn't resist. Pulling on her boots and slipping a warm flannel shirt on over her pajamas, Rohanna snuck out of her grandmother's house. Her steps were sure, the moonlight guiding her way as she followed the path out towards the barn.

Rohanna walked into the darkened interior of the old barn and inhaled deeply. The earthy smell of alfalfa, molasses, and oats belonged here, along with the soft sounds of the horses shuffling about in their straw padded stalls. A large figure appeared out of the dark in the main isle, a darker shape moving within the shadows where nothing should be. Rohanna startled. Her heart sped up, and she froze in place, her eyes straining to identify the intruder. She relaxed when the figure turned, profiling a familiar aquiline head. The barn had an escapee, a four-legged thief intent on stealing as much grain as they could from a bin that proved not to be horse proof.

The horse lazily munched on its stolen bounty, ignoring Rohanna's presence with a single-minded determination she had to admire.

"Sorry, buddy, no more snacking for you." Rohanna spoke in a soft, reassuring voice. The last thing she needed was a spooky horse freaking out and running around the inside of a dark barn. She grabbed a handy lead line from a nearby hook and headed for the hungry horse. The first order of business was getting them in hand. She would figure out what stall they belonged in after that.

She blessed the bright moonlight shining through the skylights. As she moved closer Ro was able to tell that the horse was a mare, and a very pregnant one at that. She needed to be doubly careful.

"Alright, missy, let's get you back to bed." Just as she reached out to click the lead on the mare's halter, she pulled her head away and trotted to the other side of the barn, spattering Ro with bits of grain as she zipped by.

"Dammit." Rohanna jogged after the errant mare, trying to catch her before she made it out the large bay door. The barn door had been left open to take advantage of the cool night breeze, but now it served as a handy escape route.

Rohanna would never admit to a single soul how the next few hours played out. The mare seemed pleased with herself, playing with Rohanna over and over again in what she had to admit must have been highly amusing to anyone watching their little comedy routine. The mare would placidly graze on the lush summer grass until Rohanna got close enough to touch her, then she would spin away and run off, digging up the turf as she went. Ro's irritation gave way to real concern when they reached the river. Headlights flashed ahead of her, travelling along the winding road that passed by the farm. If the mare crossed the river, she could end up on the road. She wasn't sure if there was fence up between the road and this section of the farm. There should be, but she wasn't going to assume anything, not when it came to keeping a horse safe.

When she was finally able to latch the lead line on the playful mare, she swore the darn horse was laughing at her, a horsy version of a Mona Lisa smile playing along her dark muzzle.

"You're quite the brat, aren't you?" She shook her head and looked around her, trying to get her bearings. "Now, where did our little wild goose chase take us?"

The house was nowhere to be seen, she'd lost sight of it several hillsides ago, along with the moon. It had been replaced by the faint pink glow of pre-dawn along the horizon. She had spent a good part of the night outside chasing the mischievous mare. A thin stream of smoke rose up over a hill to her left, and she headed in that direction, still peeved at her embarrassing ordeal. *Horses never, ever run away from me.*

She cast a disparaging glance at the mare and muttered under her breath, "Let's just keep this between the two of us, shall we?" The horse snorted and twitched its ears at her, then butted its head against her shoulder, unbalancing her enough to make her stumble. She fell flat on her face. A sudden, sharp pain in her knee gave birth to a string of colorful curses that echoed loudly in the early morning fog.

She pulled herself up, then looked for the offending stone that had found her knee. At least that could feel her wrath. She dug the stone out of the ground and shook it. "Let's see how you like living on the bottom of the river," she muttered, then kneeled back down when something else caught her attention.

"What the hell?" Rohanna brushed the dirt away from a yellow envelope the stone had been hiding. A sense of déjà vu traveled up her spine and left an itch in the back of her head. The envelope was old, stained and tattered from its time in the ground. It crumpled in her hands. She was left holding a small velveteen box, the kind jewelry came in.

Rohanna fell back on her heels, the mare forgotten as she stared at the contents of the box. Her hands shook, spilling a shiny silver chain out onto the ground. She plucked it up, then raised it into the early morning light, unwilling to believe her eyes. Dangling from the chain was a small pendant that spun lazily in front of her, defying her disbelief. It was a small stone cross, a Faerie stone much like the one she had lost years ago.

Rohanna scrambled to her feet. Her whole body trembled against the icy chill coursing through her veins. The cold sensation bore deeper, burrowing into her bones until she couldn't feel her legs, a feeling that had nothing to do with the early morning dew gathering on the grass and soaking through her pajamas. She swung her head around and stared at the river in front of her, the curve of the road above her, and finally...the grizzled and scarred oak standing a few feet away from her, its bark carved and deeply gashed as badly as an old warrior.

Ro ran her fingers across the scarred trunk, then gasped in pain. A thin trail of blood ran down her thumb and into her palm.

"Damn, that hurts," she said, pressing the pad against her mouth. The metallic taste of her own blood made her stomach twist. Golden sunlight crawled up the trunk like a sundial and flashed on something metallic. She moved in closer, then stumbled back against the mare's shoulder. Shards of sheet metal and mirror were imbedded in the gnarled oak. The mirror had cut her thumb, but the metal? The metal was rusted and bent, but there was no mistaking the dark green paint with just the slightest hint of gold trim.

"Oh, no. No, no, no," Rohanna cried out. A chorus of whinnies, thin and piercing, sounded over the hills. The mare called back, her nostrils flared and she pulled away from her, fighting the lead line. Rohanna followed her lead, trusting her ability to get them back home. "Find your friends."

***

Two figures stood in the shadows of the trees behind Rohanna, watching silently as she turned away from the place where her father had died so many years ago.

"The Fairie stone has returned to her at last."

"So it seems. It is what we have been waiting for."

"I don't understand. It was here all this time? We could have saved her so much pain if we had looked for it when John died, rather than wait for chance to step in. Look at how many years it took."

"Not chance, Shyann...prophecy, and you know as well as I do that prophecy doesn't work that way. It works in the shadows, twisting and turning around fate like the silver wire wrapped around that stone."

"Well, I don't like it."

"Nor do I, but it isn't up to us. We do not choose when or how, we can only observe and react. Anything I do to interfere could change things, perhaps for the worst. It is better to leave such things alone. We must let it play out as it is meant to be, not as we wish."

A low growl answered her admonishment, along with a flash of angry green eyes that carefully avoided Maeve's stern gaze.

"And this was fair to her? She was never told where her father died, or how it happened, just the lies Belinda has been feeding her all these years," Shyann said, sweeping her hand towards the damaged oak tree. The morning sun was emptying the meadow of its shadows, revealing more evidence. The unnatural furrow dug out of the roadside and leading to the river, rough stones that held a sharper edge than their field-mates, the violence done to the earth by John's pickup truck still marked the landscape. The pale gashes across the trunk of the ancient oak tree had aged over the years until they matched the grey-brown color of the bark around it, but there was no mistaking the damage left behind. Upside down and smoking, the truck had slammed into the tree with enough force to tilt the tree trunk so that it now grew twisted and bent, as if hunched around the old injury that still carried shrapnel beneath and within its skin.

"She knows he died in a car accident. She didn't need to know how it happened, not then. She was too young to understand everything. That knowledge wouldn't have changed anything, but it could have made things harder on her."

"I know, but..."

"No buts, Shyann." Maeve shook her head at her young protégé's anger. "Believe me, I love Rohanna just as much as you do and would do almost anything to save her pain, but in this, I cannot interfere. And, neither can you, not while you are acting on my behest," she added, noting how Shyann's frown deepened with every word. Shyann was young and full of all the bluster and heat that youth offered, which also meant the temptation to let her heart overrule her head was there. That could be disastrous, not only for Rohanna, but for all of them. Her words were sharp, spoken harshly then softened with an affectionate pat on the shoulder. She wanted Shyann to understand the importance of the situation, not encourage an act of rebellion.

"Now, let's get back home before Rohanna does. She shouldn't come back to an empty house. Goddess knows I could use the warmth of a good fire right now. It's been a long, cold night."

"That it has," Shyann agreed. She didn't feel the cold like Maeve did, or Rohanna...but she could eat.

Hunger existed in every creature, no matter what form they took. She took a few steps, following behind Maeve, then turned and looked back at the tree...her gaze slipping unbidden to the small patch of dirt that had hidden the Fairie stone from Rohanna for so long.

So unusual, that we would miss it that night, she thought, *or that it found its way under a flat stone the size of a plate. I won't ask, but if I'm right...Maeve is keeping her own secrets from me.*

"This is why I distrust prophecy," she muttered, not for the first time and she was sure, not for the last. You never knew what the hell you were supposed to do or not do. Inaction could be as deadly as action...and second-guessing everything you do was a hell of a way to do business.

CHAPTER FIFTEEN

Rohanna walked into her grandmother's kitchen after waking to the heavenly smell of breakfast wafting through the bedroom door. She had been half tempted to stay in bed rather than admit that the day had started, but her stomach growled like a wild animal, demanding her attention and overruling the yawn that almost convinced her to go back to sleep. From the amount of sunlight streaming through the windows, someone had already been in her room and pulled back all the curtains.

Rohanna whipped back the covers, giving in to the inevitable. More likely it had been Maeve wandering in and letting in the morning, but if she dallied any longer Shyann would be next, bouncing in and waking her up as creatively as possible. Cold feet and early morning pillow fights were never off limits, neither was yanking off every blanket on the bed and letting her freeze. The process usually included loud noises that Ro was not ready for in the mornings.

Wobbling down the hall like a drunk man in an alleyway, Ro bumbled into the kitchen, squinting through one eye at the other two women. The other eye refused to cooperate, it wanted to go back to sleep. Maeve stared at her and Shyann raised an eyebrow in her direction then snorted before pouring herself another cup of coffee.

"What?" Rohanna asked peevishly. Her head itched, and she felt like someone had tossed her down a hill, a very steep, very muddy hill full of brambles.

"Have you had a look at yourself?" Maeve gestured with the spatula she was holding. Rohanna looked down at herself and grimaced. She did look particularly disheveled, especially after last night. She was still in her pajamas, the same pair she had gone traipsing about the farm in for half the night. Dark patches along each knee were stiff with dirt, the same dirt dusted the cuffs of her pajamas. Shyann reached up and pulled a picker out of her hair. "Ouch!" she protested, pulling away from her cousin. Trying to smooth her hair down only made it worse, she found two more pickers in her hair and gave up trying to finger comb hair that she was sure looked more like a rat's nest.

"I can only imagine what the bed looks like."

"Adventurous night, eh, Ro?" Maeve and Shyann spoke at the same time, one playful and the other not so happy with her. *Great, now I get to add sleepwalking to all the rest of my problems.*

Ro's cheeks burned in embarrassment while she frantically searched for an excuse for her appearance. "I went for a walk, I wanted to check in on Galileo."

"Looks more like you went hunting for worms in the middle of the night." Shyann smirked.

"I couldn't sleep," Ro admitted.

"Could've fooled me, you were snoring loud enough to knock dust out of the rafters."

"That's enough, Shy," Maeve cut in. "And there isn't a single speck of dust in this house, other than what you two drag in."

That's when Rohanna finally noticed that, unlike her, they were both dressed and ready for the day. Shyann's boots were filthy, which probably explained her grandmother's ire. She didn't appreciate people tramping dirt into her house.

"It's almost nine, sleepyhead," Shyann quipped, catching Ro's quick glance.

"Sorry, Shy," Ro groaned, smacking her forehead lightly with her palm. She was supposed to help her cousin with morning feed.

"That's okay, cousin." Shyann grinned around a mouthful of potatoes.

Maeve put another plate of food down on the table, then sat down to finish her own meal. "Eat, Ro. Enjoy your morning. I'll worry about the sheets later."

"Thanks, Grandma." Ro tucked into her breakfast as if she was starving, then moaned around a mouthful of country potatoes. "This is so good."

Her grandmother just smiled and sipped her tea while Ro and Shyann chatted, a pleased expression on her face as she watched the two younger women eat. Sometimes Ro thought her grandmother would feed the world if she could, just to watch them eat.

"What's this?" Maeve asked, reaching out to touch Rohanna's necklace. Ro plucked the silver chain away from her neckline, dangling the small Faerie stone cross in the air between them.

"I found it."

"Hmmm, I haven't seen this since your father came and picked it up years ago. You say you found it? Where?"

"I, um...it was in a box on top of the dresser," Rohanna stuttered. That was where she found the necklace this morning, so why did it feel like she was telling a lie? "Wait, this is the same stone? The one I found all those years ago?"

"It sure looks like it. I wrapped the stone myself, and I remember this chain. Your dad gave it to for your birthday."

"How amazing," Ro murmured, gently running her thumb across the smooth surface.

Ro stared down at the cross. Oblivious to her audience, she didn't see the knowing look that passed between Shyann and Maeve, nor the slight shake of her grandmother's head when Shyann opened her mouth to say something.

"Shyann? Since you're done, why don't you clear these dishes?" The warning to wait was obvious.

Stiff backed and silent, Shyann did as Maeve asked, getting up from the table and taking her dirty plate to the sink.

Maeve shook her head. *Stubborn as a mule*, she thought, then cleared her throat. "I guess we should get the rest of our day started, if you want to get back home today."

"I guess we should," Rohanna responded dully. She really didn't want to go home, not yet. Taking Shyann's cue, Ro took her plate to the sink. She almost dropped the plate when she noticed her fingernails. Casting a quick glance over her shoulder, she turned on the faucet and washed her plate, surreptitiously scrubbing the dirt under her fingernails away at the same time. Her thumb stung. She rinsed away the soap and found a thin cut, not too deep but almost an inch long, right across the meat of her thumb. Dirty knees and clothes could be explained away if she was sleepwalking, she could have fallen down and not even realized it, but this? This was too close to her dream.

Not a dream, Ro thought. *It was all real.* She had knelt on the ground where her father had died and left her all alone. Her grandmother had to have known. All these years, and no one had told her where he had died, only that it had been an accident. A mad bubble of laughter threatened to escape from her. Why her grandmother had kept this a secret didn't matter right then. Because the only thing she could think of was that if last night's dream was real, how many of her other nightmares lived in reality and not just in her head?

Her ceramic plate clanged against Shyann's, loud enough to put her teeth on edge. She barely noticed. The impression of things shifting and moving beneath her reminded her of the time her school had sent the entire class to New York. The ferry ride out to see the Statue of Liberty had been rough on a lot of the girls. That up and down, side-to-side motion of water against the boat hull was unsettling until you learned how to use your legs. She felt that subtle movement now, the need to maintain balance despite unsure footing. Unlike some of the girls, who spent the trip bent over the side rails, she had quickly found her balance. Legs wide, braced against the wind and movement, she had spent the ride over grinning like an idiot at the bow while the salt air whipped around her like a maelstrom.

"I've changed my mind. I'm going to take Galileo home," Ro said. That announcement got everyone's attention. Maeve and Shyann both stopped in their tracks, leaving the room in a silent tableau for a full second before both women broke out into pleased grins.

"Are you sure?" Maeve asked. She wasn't doubting Rohanna. Her eyes shown with pride and she gave her a big hug before stepping back and wiping the corner of her eyes.

"Yes."

"Well, if that's the case, I'll head out and get the truck and trailer ready," Shyann said.

Rohanna turned towards Shyann, her eyes flashing with newfound confidence. "No, don't bother. I'll ride Galileo home."

"Are you sure?" Shyann asked, repeating Maeve's question.

"Don't task her, Shyann," Maeve cautioned her, then gave Ro a curious look. "What changed your mind?"

"I...I'm not sure. All I know is that the farm will be mine soon. I've spent all this time in college learning how to run it, and I've spent a good bit of time establishing myself as a competitive rider. I've spent all this time preparing. It would be stupid to go home and do nothing to improve the farm. The MacLeod family has always been on top, in the ring and with breeding. I can make sure we stay there. With Galileo, I can keep showing and winning, which means the farm's name stays on top." Rohanna stopped trying to explain something she was still trying to process herself.

Maeve hummed her approval. Her smile widened, deepening the subtle creases around her eyes. "I'm proud of you, Rohanna. It's a solid plan. It gets you out there, on the road and under the eyes of those who need to see you—who need to see who you are and what you can do." *And away from the one who doesn't need to be watching you every second of the day.*

Rohanna blushed at the accolades, then made a quick exit with the excuse of needing to get dressed for her ride home.

Once Rohanna was out of the room, Shyann leaned against the kitchen counter and crossed her arms in front of her, narrowing her eyes at Maeve suspiciously.

"And what was that all about, then? I thought we weren't allowed to interfere, nor give her a hint of what was to come?"

"Hmm. I didn't say anything but the truth, and she made the decision on her own, didn't she?"

"Did she? She sure seemed to grow a backbone all of a sudden. It wouldn't happen to have anything to do with that pendant, would it?"

Maeve's face remade itself into an expression of complete innocence before she answered. "I have no idea, Shyann. The stone was meant to protect her, but I had nothing to do with its gifting. That, as they like to say, is way above my pay grade."

Maeve turned and looked down the hallway, making sure it was empty before continuing. "You know as well as I that Bellaria has had too much influence on the child. Perhaps this is the Fates way of ensuring she has free will to decide for herself what is to happen next."

"I still think it has been ill done."

"True, but how else will she gain the strength to do what needs to be done? Bellaria has found nothing but frustration at every turn, failing at every attempt to make Ro do her bidding. Yet with every attempt, she is teaching Rohanna, whether she knows it or not. Her arrogance will be her undoing."

"You hope," Shyann added, doubtful of Maeve's confidence.

"I hope." Maeve left it at that.

"Do you think I should suggest taking her and Galileo home with the truck, rather than try the old trails? The last we checked, the way was blocked," Shyann asked.

"No, let her ride. It will give her time to think," Maeve answered. "Besides, I have a feeling the way will be clear for her now."

CHAPTER SIXTEEN

Rohanna was enjoying the quiet of the road. The wide grey strip of highway stretching out in front of her was comfortably familiar. She had travelled down it many times before on her way to various horse shows. The road's familiarity allowed her mind to wander. She could go on auto-drive, eating up the miles at a steady pace and putting distance between her and her stepmother's constant ability to find fault in her life.

Rohanna frowned.

The irritating woman kept straying into her thoughts, forcing her good mood to evaporate as quickly as the miles behind her. Their earlier conversation stubbornly replayed in her head despite her best intentions to leave it behind.

"Look Belinda, I really have to get on the road now. Is this really necessary?" Ro couldn't believe that she had let her stepmother get to her again. *Belinda's voice was creating a painful throb in her head, threatening a migraine that Ro couldn't afford on a show weekend.*

"I can't believe you are taking him again instead of one of the more important horses." Belinda's words emphasized *"him"* in an aggravated hiss, narrowing her eyes at Rohanna's favorite mount.

"It doesn't matter what horse I ride, it's still a horse from our farm and one that I have trained," Ro shot back, angrily tossing a couple of square bales onto the trailer.

"But why does it always have to be him?" Belinda asked, pointing at Galileo accusingly. *Her voice trailed off*

into a whine that still managed to sound dangerous, like the buzz of an irritated wasp. Belinda was trying to manipulate her, to make it seem like she was being the unreasonable one. That trick used to work when she was younger when Rohanna would cave in to her stepmother's wishes in order to keep the peace. It rarely worked anymore. Since Rohanna returned from college, the two women had clashed on a regular basis. It was only when Rohanna was on the road, showing Galileo or performing at the expos, that she had any peace at all.

A wicked grin split Rohanna's face. That Galileo was the only animal on the farm that Belinda had no claim to was a constant thorn in her side, especially since Rohanna continued to show on him almost exclusively. With each show, Belinda would rehash the same old argument— Rohanna's time would be better spent promoting their own stock and bloodlines, etcetera, etcetera—and it was that very argument that ensured Ro did exactly the opposite.

In Rohanna's talented hands, their horses would increase in value when they were shown and brought home ribbons. While impressive in themselves, you couldn't ride papers and good bloodlines didn't ensure the horse was going to be a winner, they needed to be well trained as well. Belinda's logic was solid. Rich buyers didn't want to buy prospects. They wanted proven show winners for their aspiring adolescent daughters and sons, something they would have to wait for until the MacLeod farm was back in Rohanna's hands.

Rohanna's stepmother grudgingly admitted that Ro had a talent for training and riding, but she would never admit that she needed her abilities to get their horses' sale ready. Rohanna used this knowledge to her advantage, pushing her own agenda as often as possible to keep

Belinda from over-extending their stock by overbreeding. Prospects were going to stay prospects until Ro said they were ready to show and sell. That kept the best stock right where they belonged, on the MacLeod farm—at least until it was signed over to her.

As far as Rohanna was concerned, she was not going to expend her efforts to line Belinda's pockets, not with her twenty-fifth birthday so close. Rohanna was sure she wouldn't see any of the money that did come in, so it made better sense to wait. Besides, anything her stepmother wanted that bad automatically became something Rohanna tried her damnedest to keep from happening.

"So close," Rohanna muttered to herself. She could practically taste her victory...because on the day the farm was signed over to her the first order of business was to show Belinda the front door. That vision was a favorite fantasy of hers, one that kept her going on days when it seemed like the hellish situation would never end.

Rohanna's heart skipped a beat when the dually shuddered violently, shaking Rohanna out of her reverie. She looked in the rear view mirror. The horse trailer was swaying back and forth as if being pushed by a heavy side wind.

"What the hell?" Something had to be wrong to make it sway like that. The trailer's weight was being thrown off balance, pulling dangerously against the truck's steering. Worried that something was wrong with Galileo, Rohanna slowed down and pulled over. Rohanna jumped out of the cab and walked back to the trailer. She stepped up onto the tire well to look through the escape door. Galileo was agitated, stomping around in the small area and rolling his eye at her until the whites showed. Ro was horrified to see one of his front shoes hanging loose. Shiny nails stuck out of the shoe, threatening to cut into the tender frog with each restless step and possibly laming him.

"Hush, Galileo, calm down, buddy."

She spoke soothingly, calming the agitated horse down a bit before running back to the trailer's tack room. Rohanna always kept a box in the small tack room where she kept a few emergency tools. It was a fact of life; horses would throw shoes, so it made sense to keep a shoe puller in the trailer...just in case. There was only one problem; the box was missing.

"I'm going to kill whoever raided my trailer," Ro cursed under her breath. Thanks to Belinda's little temper tantrum, she hadn't done a final check before leaving as she normally did. Now Ro had to find a farrier and get the shoe taken care of, rather than just pull the shoe herself. Ideally, she would have done that and waited until she arrived at the show to have a new one put on. There always seemed to be a farrier at every horse show, some young or not-so-young man hoping to establish themselves and drum up new business. Finding one out in the middle of nowhere and on short notice was an entirely different matter.

Ro huffed and kicked a rock into the roadside ditch before climbing back into the truck cab and digging out her cell phone.

Great, one small town and its way off the freeway. Her only option was to backtrack thirty miles and there still wasn't any guarantee of finding a damn thing. There wasn't a single online listing for a farrier, but that didn't mean there wasn't any, it just meant they hadn't bothered moving into this century. Not surprising. Most good farriers made a living by word of mouth. She was going to have to do it old school.

Rohanna started the engine and pulled out onto an empty highway. She was so not enjoying how her day was playing out.

About twenty minutes later, Rohanna slowed her rig down to the posted speed limit. As soon as she hit the little town, the country road she was driving along changed its name to Main Street and the speed limit dropped to 20.

Who still does that? She thought, half expecting to find old Studebakers and horse drawn carriages dotting the cobblestone edged street. Or maybe, a geeky little man in an oversized police uniform eagerly waiting for a stranger to wander into their midst's. She had been on the road long enough to know her rig was a ticket magnet...especially when she was out of state. She tapped the brakes, slowing down even farther. The diesel engine groaned, upset at having to crawl by at a piddly seventeen miles per hour, while she kept one eye peeled for a black and white cruiser and the other on her destination.

"No ticket for you today, Barney," Ro said, practicing her best "I belong here, just ignore me" slouch.

Main Street lived up to its name. An ancient strip of brick storefronts served as the center of an even smaller country town. If she had blinked, she would have missed the small sign proclaiming "largest selection of tack and feed in the county" tacked onto the side of an ancient two story brick building that had seen better days a few decades ago. Now it just looked decrepit and a little sad. Towns like these were rapidly dying, victims of shopping malls and big box stores that made it hard for country folk to keep small businesses running. Especially ones like this that were close enough to a freeway to bleed away jobs but too far away to be noticed by developers eager to find the next and best country getaway.

"Largest selection in the county?" Rohanna snorted. Put in perspective, they probably had the right to lay claim to that statement. She parked her truck and trailer and rushed across the street, praying that at least one farrier would have their card posted inside. She had yet to find a tack store that didn't keep some kind of community board up in the back, overflowing with ads for farriers, horses for sale, trainers drumming up some business, and various other leaflets for local shows, feed, and weekend revivals.

In her haste, Ro pushed open the door with more force than she meant, slamming the door against the sales counter. A raucous tinkling of bells above the door announced her presence, their frantic noise echoing Rohanna's own sense of urgency.

Ro stopped and looked around her. The tack store was considerably larger than it appeared from the outside and looked well stocked. Intent on her mission and distracted, Rohanna responded to the polite "hello" from the store clerk with an abrupt "Where can I find farrier ads posted?" The clerk frowned and pointed to the back of the store. A low "humph" behind her let her know the clerk thought she was being rude.

Ro blushed, but she didn't have time to worry about her. She scanned the paper-filled board, finding not one, but three farrier business cards tacked into the cork.

"Yes!" Elated, Ro pulled out her cell phone and dialed the number listed on the closest card. A few minutes later her victory turned into defeat.

Well, that was a waste of time, Rohanna thought. It had taken her less than five minutes to call every farrier on the board—five minutes to have each one tell her she wasn't going to get her horse shod today. After the last one called her "little lady," she was ready to scream in frustration. She turned away from the useless pegboard. She needed to get back to Galileo. Boots beating a rapid staccato on the wood floor, Rohanna was almost out the door when the clerk's voice interrupted her departure.

"Is there anything I can help you with?" the store clerk asked.

"Um, I was looking for a farrier, but no one seems to be able to see me on short notice."

"I see. I might be able to help you out."

"You know about another farrier?" Ro asked hopefully, flashing her best smile. "That would be wonderful."

"Let me make a call and I'll see what I can do." The clerk left Rohanna at the front counter while she disappeared into the back office. After a few minutes, the woman re-emerged with a business card in her hand.

"She'll see you. Here's her card and the directions," the woman said. She held onto the card when Rohanna reached out to take it.

"Now, I don't give this card out to just anyone, you hear? She's a friend, and I am doing this because I see you have a need." She looked Ro in the eyes and waited until Rohanna acknowledged the favor before letting go.

"She? Her?" she asked, "The farrier's a woman?"

"Is that a problem?"

"No, no. I don't have a problem with that at all," Ro said, back peddling quickly. "I'm just happy you found someone for me." Rohanna smiled at the woman and thanked her for her effort.

"That's fine. Just tell her that Dottie sent you, okay?"

"Yes, ma'am, and thank you again."

Ro rushed for the door, but just before she managed to escape, the clerk called out to her again.

"Dottie, don't forget my name now. Let her know Dottie sent you."

"Dottie, right." Ro felt she had to repeat the name, just to make the woman feel better. "Got it."

The door bells chimed behind her and she was back outside. It was getting hot, too hot to leave Galileo in a parked horse trailer.

What a strange woman, maybe she gets credit for referrals Ro thought, then discarded her interest for more important matters. *No matter, I've got what I needed.* Keeping a firm grip on the business card, she jogged back to her rig. She needed to get this done and get back on the road if she was going to make it to the fairgrounds tonight.

CHAPTER SEVENTEEN

Alex Strider pulled off her welding helmet and gloves before examining the unfinished metal sculpture in front of her. Wiping the sweat from her brow with her sleeve, she checked her last few welds and smiled. Pleased with the results, she ran her fingers across the still warm metal, caressing the curves and shapes she had pulled from the old steel plate through fire and effort. The seams were smooth. They wouldn't require much grinding to clean up the few rough edges left. Nodding her head appreciatively, she scrubbed her fingers together to work the residual tingling sensation out of her fingertips. Working with steel had its advantages and disadvantages, but she would never tire of the final product. Industry transformed into art. New and old mixing together and creating something infinitely more beautiful. A little discomfort was a small price to pay for her art.

Alex rolled her shoulders, feeling the tight muscles in her back and arms loosen up as she moved. She picked up her water bottle and finished it off, then leaned in the doorway. A piece this large was meant to be seen from afar, it was good to step away and see it as the buyer would, not as the artist. Most of her buyers would be attracted to the form, by the way it looked...and never feel brave enough to run their hands across the shapes. They should, but Alex had learned a long time ago that people tended to trust their eyes over any other sense. It seemed like such a limited way to live, but perhaps it was better that way.

"Not my concern, as long as they find beauty in the piece," Alex muttered. "And are willing to pay the price for it."

Alex ran practiced eyes along the lines of the sculpture lurking incomplete in her workshop. The area she had been working on had already turned cold and black, losing the organic feel of live steel. The glowing red of heated metal was almost hypnotic to watch, yet without the application of the torch, it would be impossible to make hardened steel bend and shape itself into the forms she saw in her head. She glanced at the tanks of gas strapped along the wall. Using the welder made the work easier, but she preferred the feel of a hammer in her hand and an old-fashioned forge fire. The solid ring of metal struck against the anvil was still preferable to the hiss and spark of a torch. It called to the past, and it didn't require anything more technical than her own two hands and a hot coal fire. That was why a lot of her work started in the forge room and moved here, where the parts of the whole could be joined together into large and complex sculptures that the customers seemed to demand.

The phone rang just as she pulled out a fresh bottle of water from the cooler tucked under the table. She tried ignoring it at first, then glared in the direction of the disruptive noise when it stopped then started up again. Whoever was calling was being persistent. The phone had rung at least ten times with no sign of quitting.

One of those old wall phones that still had a dialer, the yellowing plastic annoyance had come with the house and she had left it as a reluctant necessity. She never bothered upgrading it and probably never would. Alex despised the modern appliance and refused to have a cell phone anywhere near her.

"I really need to remember to take the damn thing off the hook when I'm working."

Another shrill ring brought a curse to her lips. Since both solitude and quiet had been lost to the incessant ringing, it was time to call it a day. She had already lost the feel for the form she had been working on and experience taught her it was better to step away rather than force it. The piece would have to wait for now, at least until the urge to create overwhelmed her and led her back into her workshop. Alex stepped inside the house and answered the phone with a resigned sigh.

"Dottie? Really, you know I'm too busy to take new clients," Alex said, tucking the phone under her chin so she could open her bottle of water. "Especially not a rush job." Alex concentrated more on drinking her water than paying attention to her long-time friend—at first. Then the conversation started to get interesting. She sat down at the kitchen table and listened. After a few minutes, she interrupted Dottie's sales pitch to ask a few questions of her own.

"Why would she interest me?" Alex asked, pulling another chair up to rest her feet on. For Dottie to insist that she should help this lady out was out of character, she usually respected Alex's privacy. She wouldn't normally risk offending Alex over a one-time client. Intrigued by what her friend meant by "it being worth her while," Alex finally agreed to the emergency visit.

"All right. I'll see her. Tell me what she looks like."

"She's your type, isn't that enough?" Dottie laughed. "I told her to tell you I was the one who sent her, just in case, but I don't think you'll have to guess."

Alex rolled her eyes and waited, holding both her tongue and her temper in check. She didn't like being laughed at, but she was willing to let it slip by this time, mostly because Dottie knew just what type of woman Alex was interested in.

"She's blonde—true blonde mind you, not bottle. She's about five foot three, slender but athletic. Just trust me, Alex. There's something about her," Dottie said.

Alex hung up then closed her eyes and took a deep calming breath. She could practically hear the smirking over the phone line and wondered what her friend wasn't telling her.

Alex stood up and stretched, then headed back into the workroom to take one last longing gaze at her almost finished masterpiece before heading for the forge room. She would have to stoke her forge up before the customer arrived. Alex tied a faded black bandana around her forehead to keep the sweat from rolling into her eyes then laced a thick leather cuff on her left wrist. Her hair was already pulled back safely. The thick braid running between her shoulder blades would keep it from getting too close to the hot coals. Humming a wordless tune as she worked, she pumped the billows until the coals glowed white-hot. Alex stared into the fire, enjoying the heat from the antique coal forge she refused to put aside. When she travelled she would occasionally use the small gas forge she kept in her pickup truck, but the smell of an old-fashioned coal fire brought back too many good memories to abandon so easily.

The familiar ritual allowed her mind to wander towards the mysterious woman whom she "just had to meet." *She did sound stimulating*, Alex thought, then grinned and shook her head. She hadn't even laid eyes on the woman yet and she was already letting her appetite rule her thoughts. As for Dottie? Dottie was clearly meddling in Alex's personal life, but since it had been a while since she had enjoyed the company of a good-looking woman, Alex really couldn't complain.

CHAPTER EIGHTEEN

Alex leaned against the forge room wall just inside the wide doorway overlooking the large courtyard behind the main house. The whole property was incredibly secluded, which was how she liked it. Both the house and meadows that stretched behind it were hidden by a dense stand of trees. The mix of tall pines and old oaks started along the roadway and was only broken by the winding gravel driveway she had put in with the least amount of cutting necessary. What she had to cut was now siding for part of the main barn. Waste not, want not.

The curve of the driveway prevented the casual visitor from accidentally showing up but also made it difficult to see any legitimate guests until they were almost on top of her. The crushed gravel balanced that out nicely. It made a nice loud crunching sound that echoed through the small forest. It was a great alarm system that never failed to warn her when company was coming, just like now. From the sound of it, the driver was moving slow and easy along the narrow passageway.

Even with the forge stoked up, the barn cast shadows deep enough to allow her to watch her new customer negotiate the courtyard unobserved. Alex could imagine their relief when they saw the large turnabout area she had left, especially after their quarter mile ride through the woods.

She smiled in amusement. The pickup truck and its matching fifth wheel trailer was ridiculously huge. The rig was worth well over a hundred grand and she was certain that the custom black and gold pin striping added a few dollars on top of that. Her eyes narrowed when the barn name plastered on the side of the rig came into view. MacLeod Farms was the biggest breeding and showing barn in the region.

Alex's anticipation dropped a few notches now that she knew who her customer was.

"Rohanna MacLeod—the darling of the show circuit," Alex muttered, trying to remember everything she had heard about the woman. Considering how popular she was, it was amazing they hadn't run into each other yet. But then, Alex didn't care to attend the horse shows so much as the fairs and expositions.

Alex pulled on her braid and frowned. She really didn't have time to deal with some horse diva or barn princess and she began contemplating doing something horrid to Dottie. Good friend or not, she should have known better than to send one of the snotty elite her way.

She could just make out a single silhouette inside the line of windows passing by her. Each window chugged past her like a row of train cars. Alex whistled. When you added the full living quarters in the front, the monstrosity was as long as a full size tractor-trailer.

"Amazing, and for only one horse," Alex murmured, disgusted with the sheer extravagance.

Her mood settled into the exact opposite of the bright summer sun, rapidly becoming dark and brooding. Dottie knew she couldn't stand dealing with rich folks, and Alex couldn't see how Dottie thought she would be interested in someone who drove such a ridiculous set-up. The sooner she took care of this "emergency call" the sooner she could get back to her art.

She was about to push off from her hiding place when the driver side door opened and a petite woman jumped out of the truck cab.

Her first view of Rohanna MacLeod was enough of a surprise to make her delay judgement. She relaxed back against the wall, deciding not to give up her shadowy vantage point just yet. A very casual looking flannel shirt, the sleeves rolled up to the elbows, and faded blue jeans just tight enough to show off her assets brightened Alex's mood considerably. That outfit told her that the woman might not be a complete snot. *From the way she fills out those jeans, I hope she isn't one, either.*

Alex wasn't prepared for her reaction when Rohanna turned around. Reddish blonde hair, cut short just above her shoulders, framed a smallish face that was both strong and delicate. Curiously, she looked directly towards her hiding place. Alex closed her eyes against the spine tingling spike of arousal that knifed through her, sharp and hot like the iron imbedded in the coal fire, then stepped deeper into the shadows. She didn't want the pale beauty standing in her driveway to see her jaw drop like some brain-addled fool who didn't have the sense to keep their mouth closed.

Goddess below, she's gorgeous, Alex thought, both forgiving Dottie and thanking her for sending this heavenly creature her way. A light breeze flitted across the courtyard and spun into the entranceway, tasting the dark before continuing along its way. Alex inhaled deeply, discarding the more familiar taste of iron and coal and flame to focus on the unfamiliar scents. She could smell her. Rohanna's scent reminded her of the glens and heathers of the old country, mixed with something heady and sensual. Alex's pulse quickened and muscles low in her belly tightened in response to thoughts more appropriate for the bedroom than the forge room, although she would be hard pressed to say which one would be hotter.

Unwilling to give away her presence just yet, Alex waited to see what Rohanna would do next.

"Hello?" Rohanna called out in a clear voice that carried easily across the courtyard. Delighted with the woman's independent nature, Alex watched Rohanna cross the courtyard with deliberate steps. Alex savored the visual feast striding towards her. The sway of her hips was almost hypnotic, the effect enjoyably exaggerated as the woman sought balance on the fine crushed stone beneath her boots.

"Hello?" Rohanna called out again, squinting against the bright sunlight while she scanned the courtyard for any sign of the farrier. The crushed stone crunched beneath her heeled boots, her normally bold stride held in check by the uneven surface. A small noise inside the larger barn caught her attention, and she headed for it. Ro stepped inside the dark interior and was instantly blinded. She blinked a few times, waiting for her eyes to adjust to the dimness. She had expected the shadowed interior to be cooler, but a dry heat assaulted her as soon as she walked a few feet into the room. A pale red light illuminated the various benches and tables around her. She was able to make out the outline of a large anvil and a tool shelf beyond the huge forge that dominated the center of the room. This was the source of the dim light, glowing lumps of coal sitting at the center of the forge. The floor was hard packed dirt, muffling her footfalls as she wandered farther into the silent room. The air smelled of heat, acrid with the scent of coal and steel that left a metallic taste in her throat.

Rohanna felt strangely jubilant. Her skull tingled pleasantly, much like it did when she drank too much, both numb and overly awake at the same time. Her vision wavered with the lines of heat rising from the red-hot coals, making her feel off balance. She turned around, trying to find the source of the strange sensation, then realized what it was. The forge room was completely devoid of any modern conveniences. There was nothing mechanical in the entire room, not even an overhead light. The farriers she knew used a modern gas forge, instead of the great coal forge and bellows that dominated the wood beamed room. Complete with pulleys and chains that hung like marionette strings from above, the room could have looked the same a hundred years ago as it did today. Ro felt like she had stepped far into the past. A sense of déjà vu passed through her, and she shuddered delicately despite the heat of the room. Disconcerted, Ro turned back towards the bright square of light behind her. The modern lines of her truck and trailer reassured her that she remained firmly in the 21st century.

Foolish woman, she admonished herself. Turning back towards the forge, she stared at the white tipped flames, caught up in their hypnotic dance. *Where is this farrier?* She asked herself. The strangeness of it all had started to get to her. Only her growing irritation at being left waiting kept her from screaming in surprise when a tall, slim figure materialized out of the darkness stubbornly clinging to the corners of the room.

"Hello." Alex had given the woman a few minutes to inspect the dim interior before stepping forward into the soft glow of the forge. She had no idea what possessed her to do that, other than working on pure instinct. Dottie was right; there was a strangeness about Rohanna that made her scalp tingle and the hairs on her arms stand on end. She needed a moment to compose herself, to shake the odd sense of déjà vu that sent her thoughts racing into the past. *Had they met before?* She had to say no. There was no way she would have forgotten this woman if they had locked eyes in the past, let alone spoke to each other.

Her dramatic entrance was not lost on her guest. Alex noted the suppressed gasp, the pursed lips holding back a startled scream. Rohanna's eyes widened, then changed to an expression of honest interest as she openly appraised Alex. A slow flush crept up from the woman's shirt collar, her breasts rising and falling enticingly with each rapid breath. Alex shifted her gaze. Rohanna's pulse quickened, bounding noticeably along her pale neckline.

"I'm sorry, I didn't mean to scare you," Alex said. She knew full well that the woman before her wasn't even close to being scared, startled, yes—but definitely not afraid. Alex nodded, impressed with her mettle.

"I'm Alexandria Strider. Call me Alex. And you must be—?" she asked. There was no reason to let Rohanna know she already knew who she was.

Alex looked down at the other woman and was captured by a pair of exquisitely colored eyes boldly assessing her. They were green yet not green at the same time. The reflection of early autumn leaves, they held flecks of blue-green and gold that couldn't be reduced to just one color. With her fine gold hair and pale skin, the petite woman looking up at her appeared frail, almost waiflike. If it wasn't for the eyes, today might have been the beginning and the end of their knowledge of each other. If not for those eyes, Alex wouldn't have pursued the woman any farther than a day's bit of work and perhaps a night's worth of pleasure. But, Rohanna's eyes smoldered with an otherworldly grace that was a rare find in this magic deprived world. Alex could feel the heat of that gaze like a second sun burning on the horizon.

That look told Alex all she needed to know and left her with more questions than she could find answers for. Desire, need, and hunger simmering in the liquid depths of those eyes, waiting to boil over if stoked by the right fire. They marked her, revealing an inner strength that attracted Alex and made her want to be that fire. The urge to lean down and thoroughly kiss this woman was almost overpowering.

"Fae," Alex murmured, the word escaping her like a sigh. *How extraordinary.*

A slow blink ended the moment and sent time back on its original course.

"Not Fay, Rohanna."

"Of course, my mistake." Alex nodded, amused at being corrected.

Rohanna's eyes changed in an instant, like a magician's illusion. Now Rohanna's eyes were hard, green malachite that gave nothing away beneath its surface. Alex watched as Rohanna forcefully swallowed her hunger, her passion, completely. She could practically hear the cold "snick" of armor plating encasing the woman before her piece by piece. As if the moment between them had never passed, Rohanna smiled at Alex. It was a smile that was impersonal at worst, professional at best, and never touched her eyes.

Alex wasn't fooled. She remembered watching a fire-eater once at the carnival. He would light sticks on fire then swallow the flame, then make a fine show of the doused stick as proof of his brave act. Alex had just watched Rohanna perform the very same trick. The difference was, Alex knew the flames the carnival man had swallowed weren't real. Rohanna may have "swallowed" her fire for now, but her flames were hot and they could burn. *Ice cannot stand up to fire for long, and if there is one thing I know, it is fire*, Alex thought.

"I'm Rohanna MacLeod. Dottie from the tack store sent me over."

"Well met, Rohanna." Alex took Rohanna's offered hand in her own firm grip. Electricity sparked between them where their palms met, much like a static charge but strong enough to create a tiny ball of electricity that vanished into the ether. Rohanna gasped and pulled her hand away, rubbing her palm vigorously. Alex coughed and pushed down the claxon bells going off inside her head, demanding she hear their warnings.

"Sorry about that, I was welding just before you came over." Alex made a quick excuse and then back-stepped a few feet towards the doorway. "Why don't we have a look at your horse, then? Dottie said something about a pulled shoe."

"Yes. Exactly," Rohanna said, still feeling a little out of it. *Maybe it's the forge smoke* she wondered, following the farrier out into the courtyard. She took a few deep breaths and shook her head to clear it. "I'll get him out for you."

With quick, practiced movements, Rohanna let the ramp down on the back of the trailer, then backed a very cranky and irritable gelding from the first slant stall.

"Come on, Galileo. Don't embarrass me now, not in front of this woman," Ro whispered.

After watching Rohanna fight with the energetic bay gelding for a few minutes, Alex pushed herself away from the tie out pole she had been leaning against. It was all getting a bit silly, and she was becoming bored watching the two of them fight with each other.

"Here, let me." Taking the lead line in hand, Alex tugged once, hard, and the gelding stopped dancing and pulling. The gelding turned to look at Alex, looking as silly as a 1400-pound warm blood could as he gave her a decidedly cross-eyed look down his long nose. Alex started to lead him towards the cross ties so she could see what kind of damage the loose shoe had caused, keeping an eye on how he moved.

"What are you doing?" Rohanna hissed.

Alex turned her attention back to her client. "My job. Is there a problem?"

CHAPTER NINETEEN

"You didn't have to do that, I was handling him just fine," Rohanna sputtered, barely able to speak past her anger and embarrassment. *How dare she just step in like that and take the lead line from me!* "He was just a little antsy from being cooped up for so long."

Alex murmured something to the gelding, just below Rohanna's hearing. He relaxed in Alex's hands, allowing her to guide him with a loose lead into the cross ties. After snapping his halter in, the now complacent animal dropped his head to be scratched, content to be in the company of the farrier. It was only then that Alex turned and looked at her.

"Horses are incredibly sensitive creatures. They can pick up your emotions better than you can, and react accordingly. I am sure you know this," Alex said, patting Galileo's shoulder. "Your horse was feeding off your emotions. Whatever conflict you are feeling is making him nervous."

"I'm not nervous."

"I didn't say you were nervous, I said you were feeling conflicted," Alex corrected her, then gave her a sharp look. "But since you brought it up, am I making you nervous?"

"Of course not," Rohanna scoffed, feeling the lie all the way down to her toes. The tall farrier did make her nervous.

"Hmm. That's good then, isn't it?"

Alex's voice slid across her mind like silk, caressing her skin and sending her thoughts skittering down dark paths lined with soft gasps and eager bodies slipping against each other.

What the hell?

Rohanna closed her eyes, swaying a little as she tried to banish the images in her mind. A firm hand clasped her shoulder, steadying her.

"Are you okay?" Alex asked.

Her voice was close, too close, it breathed against her like a hot wind spiced with the scent of cloves and apple groves. Rohanna felt drunk on it. She opened her eyes only to find the smooth tan skin she was fantasizing about a scant few inches away from her. *Christ, the woman was tall.*

She had to look up before she succumbed to the desire to look down, to follow the vee of her shirt where the slightest swell of flesh gave just a hint of what was hidden beneath the light denim shirt. Bright blue eyes gazed down at her from beneath the shadow of the black bandanna Alex wore across her forehead. The contrast was striking.

"Yes, I'm sorry. I must be overheated," Rohanna stuttered, backing away awkwardly.

"It can happen, the courtyard can get quite warm," Alex said, her lips twitching in a suggestive half smile. "You do look a little flushed. Is there anything I can do for you?"

"No, no...I'll be fine. I just need to cool off." Rohanna backed away some more until she ran into a solid wall.

"Okay. But if you change your mind, let me know." Alex's smile widened into a toothy grin. "I wouldn't want it to get out that I left a customer of mine unsatisfied," she added before she turned and walked back to Galileo.

Rohanna's jaw dropped. She tried to be outraged at the obvious proposition but she couldn't do it. *God help me, but I want what she's offering.*

Rohanna ran the back of her hand across her brow. She was perspiring, her palms were damp and she couldn't stop trembling. Worse yet, she couldn't stop herself from staring at the tall farrier. She ran her eyes over the long, lean form of the woman who seemed able to send her libido into overdrive just by her presence.

Unlike most of her male counterparts, Alex was trim and well groomed. As she worked, sleek muscles played across her shoulders and back. Alex was deceptively strong, muscular but not so heavy that she looked bulky or clunky. She looked more like a dancer, or a gymnast. The bulk of her muscle was in her upper body, accentuating a slim waist and hips that took nothing away from her more womanly attributes. A long, thick braid hung down past her waist, as black as a raven's wing. Rohanna had never seen hair that long or that lustrous. When she moved, strands glinted in the bright sunlight. Idly, she wondered how long Alex's hair was when it was unbraided and imagined what it would feel like sliding across her bare skin. Goosebumps rose on her arms and she felt the small hairs on the back of her neck rise in response. A chill ran down her spine that made her shiver in the heat, while other bits of her warmed considerably at the thought.

This is so not good, she thought.

"Here, it's cold." Alex's voice made Rohanna jump. Somehow, Alex had walked past her into the barn and returned without her noticing. She held out a cold bottle of water for her.

"Thank you." Ro took the bottle. Droplets of perspiration hit her wrist, and she flicked them off. As hot as she was, the ice cold water felt like fire against her skin.

"No problem." Alex took a swig from her bottle, then gestured towards Ro's horse. "I took a look at Galileo's hoof. Luckily, I was able to pull the shoe without causing any more damage. But I have to tell you, the work was pretty shoddy in the first place."

"What? We've used the same guy for years. That doesn't make sense."

"Well then, either you need a new farrier or he was in a hurry."

"What do you mean? Can't you just tack it back on?"

"No, in fact, the other shoes need to come off as well so that I can even out his toes. The back shoes had too much overhang, and the clinches were too big. That's why he was able to grab the front shoe and pull it off."

Alex wandered back to Galileo's side and started laying out her tools, leaving Rohanna alone to think about what she said. The poor quality farrier work didn't add up. She narrowed her eyes, immediately going to the one person she knew would and could arrange such a shoddy job. A bad shoeing could lame a horse. *If it was Galileo, all the better, right Belinda?*

"Fine, but can we hurry this up? I just need you to put my horse's shoe back on so I can get back on the road," Rohanna ground out between clenched teeth. Her attraction to the farrier was palpable, a physical force that made her uncomfortably aroused. Not knowing what else to do, Ro fell back into a more comfortable persona. "Bitchy woman" could fight the world, keep her safe from her stepmother's constant manipulations, and kept her from making any mistakes that might jeopardize her goals. She needed to step back and analyze what was happening. She couldn't afford to let her emotions ride her; she had to be the one with her hands on the reins.

Alex straightened up, and for the first time since Rohanna arrived she spoke coldly. "I don't rush, ever. If you want me to do the work, I will. But I will not be hurried."

Alex patted Galileo's back, running her hand along his rump in order to let him know she was crossing behind him. Alex then headed straight for her, her long legs breaching the distance between them in seconds. "You do want me to do this, right? It's your choice. I won't do anything you don't want me to."

Brilliant blue eyes scanned her face, flickering down to Rohanna's lips when she licked them nervously. Somehow, Rohanna got the distinct impression that Alex was asking her a very different question from the one she was hearing.

"Ah, um." Rohanna lost her voice again.

"I'll take that as a yes." Alex leaned in closer and continued in a more intimate tone. "We'll continue this conversation later," she promised, then disappeared into the shadows of the forge room.

Rohanna sagged against the wall behind her and breathed a sigh of relief. For a second there, she thought Alex was going to kiss her. She would have let it happen, too, and that realization scared the hell out of her. She should have shut her down immediately, told Alex she wasn't interested, but that would have been a lie. For the first time in her life she was more than interested, to the point of losing control of her emotions, and that wouldn't do. There was too much at stake in her life to add any distracting complications.

Ro turned and strode into the shade of the forge room, intent on finding Alex. The woman was obviously a player. She was way too smooth. The idea of being added to a long list of faceless conquests was repellent enough for her to resist the strange attraction she had for the farrier. She needed to let her know she wasn't interested now before things got out of hand.

She was brought up short when she collided into a very tall, very solid wall that slowly registered as Alex's abdomen and chest. Thrown off balance, Rohanna reached out blindly to keep herself from falling. It was Alex who kept her from falling on her ass, but before she could register that embarrassing fact, she realized she was firmly pressed against Alex's rock hard body.

Jesus, she feels like coiled steel, Rohanna thought.

Even in the dim red glow of the forge, Rohanna could see the hungry expression on Alex's face flickering in and out of the shadows in time with the dancing flames. A slow shudder rolled through her body in response to the intimate embrace.

"Umm. This is kind of awkward," Rohanna managed to say.

"Only if you want it to be." Alex drew her closer to the flames and away from the shadows. Fingertips grazed along her jawline, tilting her head up until their eyes met. "Do you want it to be?"

"I—I don't know what I want," Rohanna whispered, unable to look away. The dim light had eaten away the color in Alex's eyes, leaving only the thinnest corona of deep blue surrounding flame licked obsidian pupils. Rohanna swore she saw lightning possess the ink black wells, a miniature maelstrom furiously trying to escape its small world.

Alex leaned down much as she had done earlier, except this time, she didn't turn and walk away. This time she brushed her lips across Rohanna's. Rohanna sighed. As sweet as the kiss was, it awakened the fire inside her, the one she had so carefully kept tamped down for years. She struggled to free herself, fighting more with her desire than with the woman holding her tightly, then gave in. The next kiss wasn't as chaste as the first one, but it wasn't enough to quench the hunger burning like fire in the pit of her stomach. She reached for Alex, eager to even the playing field before losing herself completely.

The feel of packed dirt beneath her palms barely registered, all she could see was firelight and piercing blue eyes, a lopsided smile and the feel of impossibly hot hands burning her wherever they touched.

***

Ro groaned. Her body was stiff and aching from laying on the hard bench beneath her. She sat up too quickly, then brought her hands up to her temples when a sudden pain flashed through her skull.

"Ugh, what the hell?" She felt hung-over and not quite sure where she was. *Oh yeah...the farrier's. I must have fallen asleep.* Alex was nowhere in sight, but Ro could hear the soft tinking of a hammer out in the courtyard.

Rohanna stood up awkwardly, feeling oddly disconnected with her body. She had been dreaming about Galileo. Her head felt thick and full of cobwebs, refusing to give up details of the last hour of her life. Rubbing her temples seemed to help both her foggy head and her headache.

She remembered pulling her rig into the courtyard and introducing herself to the farrier and discussing Galileo. Alex offered her a cold drink and led her to the low bench just inside the forge room when she started to felt dizzy.

Galileo had been misbehaving badly, fighting her and being a total snot in front of an audience. *That can't be right.* The gelding was well trained. He never misbehaved that badly, especially not for her. That had to be part of the dream. She wasn't a stranger to odd and disturbing dreams. After years of unexplained nightmares and sleepless nights, she had learned to take them in stride. Rohanna scrubbed her face. It was unusual for her to have one during the day, especially one like this.

She had a sinking suspicion that this dream had more to do with Alex than anything else. The woman was handsome, cocky, and arrogant...not to mention incredibly attractive. She made Ro feel awkward and gawky, like a teenager experiencing her first crush. Wincing at how close that actually hit the mark, Rohanna ruefully examined her dream more carefully. Years of practice had taught her to remember her dreams, to recognize the ones that turned dark so that she could force herself awake before becoming trapped inside a nightmare.

Embarrassment flooded through her, making her cheeks burn. She might have kept herself from acting like a fool in front of the tall farrier, but her unconscious mind had made sure she understood just how attracted she was to Alex.

Nightmares were one thing, but having sex with a perfect stranger in a dream? Rohanna shook her head at how far she had fallen. Her body still hummed with leftover sensations. Her nipples were sensitive where they pressed against her bra. She felt slick and heavy; her pulse beat rhythmically between her thighs as if her orgasm had escaped the dream.

She needed to get Galileo and get the hell out of there. Rohanna's legs felt like rubber bands and she wobbled a little when she walked, but she was determined to leave before Alex started to ask questions. Straightening her shirttails and smoothing her hair, she summoned whatever few ounces of self-respect she still had and marched back out into the courtyard.

***

Oh, yeah, Alex thought as she watched the huge trailer disappear down the wooded driveway. *Dottie definitely called this one right.* Rohanna might try to pull off cool indifference now, but what they had shared earlier was neither cool nor indifferent. Of course, Alex would have preferred if things had happened differently. Alex hadn't expected to be drawn into the other woman's dream, but once there, she wasn't about to deny her the fantasy. She had to admit that Rohanna had quite the imagination, even as untried as she was in lovemaking. Alex pursed her lips, considering that bit of information. It was unusual for someone like Rohanna to be so inexperienced.

Rohanna didn't behave as any of the other Demi-Fae Alex had met. She didn't embrace her nature like others of her kind. She hid from it, denying herself pleasure when there was no reason to. *Or was there?*

Rohanna seemed ignorant of her heritage, which wasn't that unusual, but she also seemed determined to deny her true nature...and that was unusual.

Alex frowned. After generations of intermingling with humans, most Demi-Fae carried only a drop or two of faerie blood. That was the problem. With the veil closed for hundreds of years and most of the Fae choosing to stay on the other side, someone like Rohanna shouldn't be possible. As far as she knew, the only pure lesser Fae were the Mere folk, and that was because you were either born Mere or not. The lines never diluted.

Rohanna was different. Rohanna was an enigma, an impossibility in this mundane world. More importantly, she was strong enough to invite Alex into her dreams.

Alex rubbed her fingers together, reigniting the spark that had jumped between them when they touched. The current rolled between her thumb and forefinger like ball lightning, then dissipated when she spread her fingers wide. She stared at her palm, considering the strange occurrence. The sensation was very similar to what she felt when she touched bare iron, but instead of just pain, the promise of pleasure had sweetened the ache.

Alex was looking forward to running into Rohanna again and wondered how she should go about making that happen. The light breeze swirling through the courtyard picked up speed, birthing a small dust devil that delighted in tossing about the few bits of leaves dotting the stone landscape. It struggled with a larger bit of debris, a white sheet of paper that spun dizzily on the wind before landing at Alex's feet. She bent and picked it up, instantly recognizing the same Expo flyer she had tacked on her kitchen wall.

This is where she's headed this weekend? How convenient. Considering her booth there had been booked for over three months, it looked like the fates were playing on her side, handing her a winning hand before she even stacked the deck. She had planned to wait until this evening to head out for the fairgrounds, but now she was eager to get on the road. The coal fire would have to be put out first and her finished pieces loaded onto her trailer before she could even think of leaving, but that wouldn't take long.

Alex grinned. Her pulse jumped and her breath quickened in response to the thrill of the hunt. For now, anticipation would have to serve, but there was always plenty of down time at the Expo after the crowds left for the night. Alex was looking forward to spending that time with Rohanna.

CHAPTER TWENTY

"Oh my, will you look at that?" Shyann asked, tracing one suggestive finger along her lower lip.

Ro felt sorry for whoever had just piqued Shyann's short-lived interest. Her cousin was as well known for her wild ways as Rohanna was for being uptight. Despite living on the opposite sides of the sexual spectrum, the two of them had remained fast friends through the years. Ro often joked that she didn't need to have sex since she lived vicariously through Shyann's sexual escapades. In return, Ro often suffered from good-natured teasing for being the consummate "ice princess". It was an odd relationship, but it worked for them.

She looked down the row of tents and covered tables outside the exhibition hall to see who had captured Shyann's attention. Rohanna almost stumbled when she saw Alex standing in front of a small three-legged forge, working a piece of iron on a smaller version of the anvil she kept at her shop.

The heavy short-handled hammer made sparks fly with each solid blow. Alex handled the hammer with such ease that most people wouldn't realize it weighed almost five pounds. The same worn leather bracer she wore that last time they met supported her left wrist, and she wore a similarly worn leather apron to protect her from the heat and slag as she pounded the metal.

"Now, she is absolutely yummy looking," Shyann said. "And if my gaydar is right, which it always is—she definitely plays on our team."

"Keep your voice down, dammit," Rohanna hissed, looking around nervously. "What if someone heard you?"

"So what? Who cares?"

"I care, and there's no 'our team' so just stop."

Shyann rolled her eyes at Ro, grinning mischievously. "Yeah right, Ro. You can keep trying to fool yourself, but you and I both know the real deal. At least admit that she's hot, even if you aren't interested."

"Okay, okay. I'll give you that. Yes, she's hot." Rohanna threw up her hands. "Are you happy now?"

"More than you will ever know, dear cousin." Shyann wobbled left and bumped into Ro's shoulder.

"Hey, watch it!" Rohanna rubbed her shoulder, then gave her cousin the stink eye. "Tell me again why you came out today to support me?"

"Support you?" Shyann's eyebrow's climbed up her forehead. "I'm not here to support you. I'm here to make sure you have fun outside of that damn arena!"

"Hmm. Your kind of fun usually makes it hard for me to do well in the arena," Ro pursed her lips. "I seem to remember a particularly bad morning after a night of cheap whiskey."

Shyann's mouth fell open. "One, I never ever let cheap whiskey pass by these lips, and two, you didn't even drink that much. It's not my fault you're such a lightweight. That's embarrassing for a MacLeod, I'll have you know. Your ancestors must have turned in their graves."

"Hmm. Just because I can't drink like a fish like you do, doesn't mean I can't hold my liquor."

"I'll take that as a challenge, then, later tonight." Shyann turned her attention back to the other woman. "It's too bad, though. She looks like someone who knows how to take charge. Maybe she'd be good for you, Ro, if you'd just let go and relax for once."

"I'm just fine, Shyann. Even if I was interested, which I'm not, I don't have time for romance. I have the farm to think about. I can't afford to get distracted."

Ro hated lying to her cousin. Her attention was drawn back to the laboring blacksmith. Her gaze slid intimately along Alex's bare arms, the cut muscles rippling and flexing rhythmically with each hammer stroke. Her skin was damp with perspiration and flushed from the intense heat of the forge fire.

Alex turned away from the anvil and plunged the glowing metal into a bucket next to her, creating white steam that hissed and danced around her body. The steam carried the acrid smell of hot metal with it, reminding her of the last time she had seen Alex at her forge—and the dream that followed. Her body responded to the memory of the dream by tightening things low in her belly, sending a surge of adrenaline along a path that started between her thighs and raced up her spine, settling at the base of her skull and making it hard to think.

The sound of someone clearing their throat brought Ro back to reality. Shyann narrowed her eyes and stared at her suspiciously. Rohanna groaned.

"Uh-huh, so that's how it is." Shyann crossed her arms, tapping one finger expectantly.

A slow red flush started to creep across Ro's neck and cheeks, making her look feverish. Shyann had a feeling that her fever had nothing to do with the heat of the day, and everything to do with the look in her eyes. Ro was trying awfully hard not to stare at the tall woman at the end of the aisle.

"How what is?" Rohanna asked as innocently as possible. She was in for some merciless questioning if she couldn't satisfy Shyann's curiosity now.

"If I didn't know any better, Ro." Shyann started to tease her cousin, then stopped when Rohanna turned and refused to meet her eyes. "Oh, shit."

Shyann looked back at the blacksmith again and made the obvious connection. Although she was secretly thrilled at her cousin's audacity, she couldn't help feeling a bit disappointed. Her intended prey for the evening was now off-limits. *There's no way I'd ever poach someone Ro's interested in. Goddess knows, it's taken her long enough to find someone.* That it was a tall, dark, and handsome blacksmith was just too deliciously ironic.

"Come on, Rohanna, you've got to throw me a bone here," Shyann begged, trying to get her to admit to something, anything she could report back to Maeve.

"Her name's Alex. She's the farrier I told you about, the one that took care of Galileo yesterday."

"Alex, huh? Seems she's more than just a farrier," Shyann teased, tipping her head towards Alex's booth. "And from the look on your face, she took care of more than just Galileo yesterday."

"Now wait a minute," Rohanna said, turning on Shyann and making her step back. "Nothing happened." She paused, worrying her lower lip. "Well, nothing important, anyway."

"Oh, really?" Shyann drawled, "Then why are you so pissed at me? I tease you all the time. Why are being so sensitive now?"

"It's complicated, Shyann. I really don't want to talk about it. Not now."

Shyann allowed herself one last lingering gaze at the blacksmith's incredible body. There wasn't an ounce of softness in that impressive musculature, except where a slight curve and swell made it obvious that she was all woman. The blacksmith looked up from her work and looked directly at Shyann as she stood admiring her.

Shyann gasped. The blacksmith's dark hair and deep tan had made her assume she would have dark eyes as well, not the electric blue ones boldly assessing her now. Unable to look away, Shyann felt as if she was being appraised, her soul stripped and laid bare for inspection. The blacksmith's gaze slid away from her then, dismissing her with a slight frown before shifting her focus towards Rohanna. A slow, lazy smile slid across her face. *That is so not a nothing happened look,* Shyann thought. *Oh, Ro...what did you get yourself into?*

A woman leaned over the rope separating the blacksmith from the crowd and touched her arm. The smile disappeared in an instant, and while Alex was polite to the customer, she was definitely cool with her. The hammer was put away, and someone else took Alex's place at the front of the booth.

Ooh, so we don't like to be touched without permission, eh? Shyann watched the scene unfold with some amount of frustration. They were too far away to hear what was being said, and Shy was too damned curious for her own good. She headed down the aisle, dragging Ro along with her and blessing her good luck that the barns were in the same direction she wanted to go.

With a purposeful swagger, Alex turned and walked away from her forge, disappearing into a crowd that split before her, a stream of humanity changing course to avoid a stronger force of nature. Shyann's mouth dropped open. They didn't even realize what they were doing. They simply moved out of her way then closed ranks around her, continuing on their way as blithely and ignorant as a herd of cattle.

There was something wild and untamed about the woman that sent warning bells off in Shyann's head. There was no doubt in Shyann's mind that when Alex held out her hand, whomever she was calling would come to her, eager and wanting. Even Rohanna.

Shyann shook her head, trying to rein in her concern. Rohanna had lived her entire life with a single-minded purpose—the promise of finally inheriting the farm was the only passion she ever allowed herself.

Shyann had asked Maeve about this once, after Rohanna had found the Faerie stone. It seemed plausible that Belinda was behind Ro's disinterest in anything but the farm, since it was her talent that kept the place running. Even when she was sent away for school, she returned each summer, faithfully inspecting the new colts and assigning handpicked trainers for the ones they wanted to keep as prospects.

She had hoped that whatever influence Belinda had would weaken after Ro placed the Faerie stone around her neck, and it did, just not the way Shyann had expected. Whatever drove Rohanna now was of her own making. The Faerie stone had freed Rohanna's tongue and her mind, but it had also freed a simmering hatred for the woman who had married her father. Ro had no idea how dangerous this was, but Shyann had been told in no uncertain terms that she was not allowed to interfere, only to observe.

"Shy? Earth to Shyann. Shy? Hey, we've got to get going. I've got to get Galileo warmed up."

"What? Okay." Shyann stumbled over her words. "You gonna win today?" she jibed, poking at Rohanna's ribs to distract her from her lapse. She had let her thoughts wander where they shouldn't when she was around Ro.

"Of course!"

Shyann barked a quick laugh. "Only because I'm not competing," she boasted, following close on Rohanna's heels as she headed for the barns.

"You think so?" Rohanna fired back, as cocky as ever. "That reminds me, I need to see my young man. How does he look? Is he ready?" Rohanna fired off several quick questions at once, a sure sign of her excitement.

"He's fine, Ro. But if you want to see him, you have to go to the stallion barn. Which, by my watch, you don't have time to do right now," Shyann said. Galileo's younger brother was all grown up. The mare Rohanna chased the night she returned from college had thrown an elegant and well-conformed black colt later that summer. Now he was almost three and ready for the world to see. Both Rohanna and Shy had high hopes for the warmblood stallion. Even as young as he was, he was showing great promise as a future stud prospect. Belinda didn't know about him because Rohanna didn't want her to, which is also why he stayed with her grandmother. After the farm was hers, he would come home and be an amazing asset to her breeding program.

"Fine. Later tonight, then?"

"Of course. Then maybe we can go out and see what this town has to offer for a night life, hmm?" An exaggerated wink accompanied her less than innocent suggestion.

"You're never going to grow up, are you?"

"Not if I can help it. Perhaps someday I'll wake up old and grey, but until then...I'll live my life to the fullest." Shyann grinned broadly. The exchange was old and well worn, but it never failed to amuse her.

CHAPTER TWENTY-ONE

Rohanna scanned the field in front of her. Her eyes were only partially shielded from the bright summer sunlight by the hard brim of her riding helmet, but she refused to squint against the glare and ruin the perfectly smooth expression on her face. Her hands held Galileo's reins before her, perfectly still and at just the proper angle. The reins vibrated beneath her fingertips as the gelding fidgeted ever so slightly. Galileo tolerated the forced immobility because he was required to, but that didn't mean he liked it.

The merest hint of a smile touched the edge of her lips. She was sympathetic to the gelding's desire to enter the ring, to compete—and to win. These things were dear to her and Galileo was a kindred soul in that regard. Galileo's ears perked up when Ro's name was called, and horse and rider walked boldly into the arena. Galileo stepped out proudly, knowing that all eyes were on them as they approached the grandstand.

Once caught up in the familiar motion of their routine, Rohanna forgot about the people in the bleachers. The world shrank until she was only aware of the sand in front of her, the cadenced beat of Galileo's hooves, and the creak of well-oiled leather between her knees. Fierce joy swelled in Rohanna's breast as it always did when she rode. The thrill of competition fed her soul like nothing else in the world. Beneath her, Galileo outdid himself like normal. Arching his head gracefully, he placed each hoof carefully, elegantly, in a manner that was both art and design. Stopping in front of the judge, Rohanna sat quietly and awaited the judge's notice. A quick nod gave her permission to leave the arena.

She was called to the arena a second time, this time for the awards ceremony. For Rohanna there had never been any doubt. Her score lay well above the other competitors. She smiled broadly as Galileo was presented with the blue ribbon and leaned forward to pat the bay gelding's neck affectionately. As she passed by the other riders, she noted that among the well-wishers and cheers was the occasional surly nod, as well as one outright hostile stare. Rohanna's stomach knotted. The look was all too familiar, and difficult to ignore.

Rohanna disliked the power that hate had over her. Living under the untender tutelage of Belinda had attuned her to that particular emotion, in both herself and others.

Rohanna twisted around in her saddle to see if the rider was still glaring at her. She wasn't; now her ire was focused on her mount. Rohanna sighed. The other rider was the worst sort of competitor, a pouting rich brat that expected to win because her father could afford an expensive horse. From her expression, she obviously blamed the poor horse and not her inadequate riding skills for her failure. Ro's sympathy for the poor gelding ignited into outrage when the rider jerked her mount about by the reins.

A plow horse didn't deserve that kind of rough treatment. A nice looking animal like that didn't deserve to be owned by someone who couldn't appreciate what they had. As if hearing her thoughts, the big bay rolled one liquid brown eye back towards Rohanna. Rohanna sensed mischief a second before the bay acted on its impulse, tossing his head violently enough to yank the reins out of his unsuspecting rider's hands. The horse barreled past Rohanna and Galileo in a full on gallop and she swore the animal was smiling. The leather reins that were supposed to control 1100 pounds of hoof-powered muscle hung loosely from his bridle, eluding the desperate grasps of the rider as she tried to cling to his back.

Everyone in the arena froze. Not a single rider moved. Rohanna rolled her eyes and tapped Galileo with her heels. Galileo jumped at the chance to run, quickly overtaking the out-of-control horse. Leaning over, Rohanna reached out and grabbed one of the reins, then turned Galileo into the other horse, forcing him close to the fence. The other horse slowed down to a trot, then a walk. He was blowing hard, foamy sweat coating his chest and dripping down his legs.

"Are you okay?" Rohanna asked. The woman nodded, her head bobbed in quick short movements that mirrored her tense posture. The gelding danced beneath her and her eyes widened even more.

"Right. You need to relax. Your horse can tell you're nervous, and he won't calm down until you do." Rohanna dismounted, talking softly to the nervous horse while she moved around him.

"Here, take the reins," Ro said. "But for God's sake, be easy on them. He's got a soft mouth. You don't need to be so heavy handed."

Another nod, but this time the woman didn't jerk around like a marionette. "Good. Relax and he'll relax."

Ro walked the gelding out into the ring a bit while his rider got herself together. Galileo stayed put, content to watch until she returned to him.

"Ms. MacLeod?" A small voice called out behind her as she led Galileo away.

"Yes?"

"Thank you, and congratulations."

Well, how about that? Rohanna thought. Galileo snorted and tossed his head. Evidently, he agreed with her.

CHAPTER TWENTY-TWO

Alex stood next to the bleachers, carefully leaning against a wood wall that was covered more in peeling paint chips than paint. The layers of the years showed through curled edges, following the times like a wilted rose shedding stiff acrylic petals. Just the slightest breeze or finger-brushing would liberate thin leaves of old color that eagerly clung to any new surface it found...and so far they seemed attracted to every bit of black clothing Alex wore.

Eyes forward, she scanned the arena, looking for Rohanna. She stood up straight and paid attention when the judge called her name, eager to see how she would do in the competition. Rohanna was so intent on putting Galileo through his paces that she didn't even notice Alex despite passing a scant few feet away from her. Alex found her attention split between the rider and horse. Galileo was fine, his shoes had held and he wasn't tripping up at all after the corrective work she had done back at her place. "Very good."

Now that she knew Galileo was good, she could concentrate on the woman who had piqued her interest enough to search her out. Alex had to admit that Rohanna was impressive in the saddle. She had a gentle but firm way with her mount, never pushing him but always getting the most out of him. In return, Galileo stepped proudly, obviously responding to the crowd and enjoying every moment of their time in the limelight. Alex had learned a long time ago to pay attention to how people treated the animals around them. A human capable of cruelty to animals was rarely capable of compassion elsewhere in their life, and Alex would have nothing to do with them. Rohanna and Galileo were a team and that pleased her.

I wonder why Rohanna dreamed that he was misbehaving. Was it some secret fear or just nervousness on her part?

Alex stiffened and tipped her head slightly, catching the soft sound of footfalls on the grass right behind her. She glanced over her shoulder to confirm what she already knew. The woman Rohanna had been walking with earlier was coming up behind her.

"Well met, Shyann," Alex called out over her shoulder.

Shyann jumped at Alex's unexpected greetings but recovered quickly. "How did you know?"

"Is there something I can help you with?" Alex said, choosing to ask her own question rather than answer Shyann's.

"Well, I'm not quite sure. Maybe you could tell me what's going on between you two. Ro was quite tight lipped about it."

Alex laughed heartily. The woman was bold as hell. "I confess I'm confused. From the look of things earlier, you seemed to be working quite hard to beg Rohanna off me. In fact, I got the distinct impression that you had other ideas floating around in that devious little head of yours."

"No. Why would you think that?" Shyann sputtered.

Alex smirked at her. She was so damned obvious it was hysterical. Still, she couldn't help but tease the woman a bit before letting her off the hook.

"Perhaps it was the way you looked me up and down, or maybe it was how long you stared at this, hmmm? Alex asked, lowering her voice to a more intimate tone. She raised her left arm, displaying the wide leather bracer. The air shimmered around Alex like waves of heat coming off summer blacktop. Shyann swallowed nervously, stepping back from her and putting space between them. She shifted her gaze to the side, half expecting to see the poorly maintained wall behind them covered in melting paint.

"What are you?" she asked, almost whispering.

"Don't you know? I have to admit, I am curious at Rohanna's apparent lack of knowledge about her heritage. Here you are, reeking of Fae—all seduction and sexual tension, yet you are as ignorant of me as Rohanna is of herself. What gives?" Alex tried to rein in the aggression tramping through her heart.

Neither of these women were what she was used to finding, mostly human with a drop or two of Fae blood, enough to quicken her pulse and pique her interest. These two were altogether different. Rohanna barely tasted human and Shyann not at all. Both were fascinating in their own way, but it was Rohanna that set her blood boiling...despite her contrived and well-scripted indifference.

"That's not my place to say, I am honor bound not to interfere."

"Interfere with what?" Alex demanded.

"That's not my place either, Alex. I can't divulge our secrets."

"And yet you come to me, asking about Rohanna and me, and you wonder about this?" Alex frowned, rubbing the leather on her forearm. "You keep glancing at it. Why?"

"Because I care about Rohanna and don't want to see her get hurt."

"You think I have the power to hurt her?" Alex asked, contemplating the unexpected answer.

"I see that," Shyann reached out to tap the leather bracer, then snatched her hand away. "And I have to wonder, what is it hiding? If you aren't hiding anything, then it means something altogether different, now doesn't it?"

"So you are worried that what I want from Rohanna will hurt her," Alex said. She looked down at her arm. "Because of this." She looked up, searching Shyann's face and finding only concern and worry. "And what if it is both?"

"Both?"

"What if this hides something I do not wish to share, but it also conveniently states where my interests lie?" Alex asked.

"Then I am worried. Just like I am worried that you know who I am, and I know nothing about you."

Alex laughed. "This is quite a dance we are having, Shyann. I think I should end it now and give you what you want." She straightened up to her full height, drawing around her all the power and privilege of her rank. She wasn't worried about being seen. Alex had picked her vantage spot carefully; she knew there would be no witnesses to their little exchange.

"I know you Shyann, from seeing you inside Rohanna's dreams. I know you say you are her cousin, but you are not. Not technically. I see an old woman she calls Grandmother, whose soul and body do not match. I see many things, including what Rohanna holds dearest to her heart, and what she has kept buried deep in her soul all these years. This piece of leather hides the key to how I know these things, but the leather itself should tell you I

204

know how to break Rohanna free from her inhibitions." Alex's voice stayed low, but it carried force and authority behind it.

She had expected Shyann to cringe away from her, for fear to etch her brow with each piece of knowledge she laid out in the open. She didn't. Shyann held her ground, with only the least bit of fear touching the corners of her mouth.

"I disagree. Rohanna has had it rough. She won't respond well to a firm hand. She has known nothing about love and compassion for years but what little we, her grandmother and I, have been able to give her. What you think she needs could break her."

"Love is the law, Shyann. I have to follow that law as much as you do," Alex countered, arguing for Rohanna even while acknowledging that she was treading in unknown waters. What she felt for Rohanna was so unexpected and so overpowering, it frightened even her.

"Are you saying you love Rohanna? You just met. You barely know her."

"No. I am saying that I am drawn to her, and I must follow that imperative. She feels right to me. I cannot turn my back on the voice inside me that tells me not to turn away." She was angry now. Shyann was pushing her and she didn't like it. Her face must have given her away because Shyann backed off, making a peacekeeping sign with her hand.

"Look, I am sorry if I offended you. I just want what is best for Ro and you seem to affect her."

"Really, you think I affect her?" Alex drawled, narrowing her eyes at the other woman. "Well. Now *that* is interesting." Alex turned and walked away.

"Wait, you never answered my question," Shyann called after her.

"No, I didn't, did I?" Alex said. She had enough of her own questions. She wasn't in the mood for satisfying someone else's curiosity.

Shyann really had a problem with the leather bracer, or rather, what it meant. Sure, she would wear it around the forge on occasion, but she usually went for leather gloves unless she was working on something intricate and small. Alex wore the bracer when she had visitors, or like today, when she was working in public.

The intricate blue tattoo along her forearm was not for outsiders. It was forbidden to show it, just in case it was recognized and her people were discovered. The bracer had been a convenient way to hide the tattoo. It also made her natural inclinations a much easier thing to advertise when she went out at night. She discovered that many humans were just as adventurous in bed as the Fae were known to be. She had also discovered that the ones who were more likely to enjoy what she had to offer as a woman had Fae blood. It was fascinating, learning that those humans who identified as gay or bisexual had a drop or two of Fae in them. She had yet to meet someone who was not strictly heterosexual who didn't. It worked for her.

Alex found Fae blood subtly more aromatic, an aphrodisiac if you will, that identified others with a like mind. She had heard some humans call this Gaydar. The cute label was amusing, but it also revealed the differences between them.

Humans were so blind to their senses, ignoring what their noses and tongue told them. Smell and taste alone told her who was not locked into the strict duality that humans seemed so determined to adhere to. It amazed her how much animosity humans held against their own, especially if they thought another of their kind enjoyed pleasures with the same sex. Even sadder, they did it without knowledge of how they knew. They were so head blind it was ridiculous.

Alex shook her head then made a scoffing noise in her throat. She was an anomaly herself. She preferred only women, which was rarer than enjoying both sexes amongst her own people. This was one of the reasons she stayed away, but not the main reason. The main reason was more complex. There were no easy answers to that particular problem so she chose to live alone, without the comforts of the tribal community. It was a simpler way of living, not having to answer to others all the time, but that didn't mean it was easy.

Alex walked around the fairgrounds without paying much attention to where she was going. She didn't stop until she found herself at the entrance of one of the larger barns. *Huh, I wonder why my feet brought me here?*

The steady clop of metal shoes on concrete on the other side of the barn answered her question. The dim lighting didn't hide the identity of the horse or the person leading him—Rohanna was bringing Galileo back to his stall.

"Hello, Rohanna." Alex's salutation was met with a small squeak Alex thought was quite adorable. "How's Galileo's shoes holding up?"

Epona! What I really want to talk about, what I want to do. Asking about Galileo's shoes is the last thing on my mind. Alex realized she was tempering her conversation based on what Shyann had said. She was treating Rohanna more like a skittish colt than the woman who had let her into her dreams and shared her fantasies.

"Alex! You scared the crap out of me." Rohanna's heart was pounding so hard Alex could hear it from where she stood. The urge to reach out and touch her, to feel that bounding pulse beneath her fingertips, was almost overwhelming.

"My apologies, I swear that wasn't my intent," Alex said, offering Rohanna a lopsided grin. "I do seem to have a habit of doing that. Why don't you let me make it up to you?"

Rohanna stood frozen in place, the very image of indecision. Alex took a chance and reached for her hand. The same electrical jolt passed between them, making both women gasp. Alex didn't let go this time. Instead, she let the pleasant tingle travel up her arm and take up residence at the base of her skull. Rohanna closed her eyes and swayed in Alex's grip. When she opened them again, they smoldered with the same fire that had set all of this in motion.

"What is that?" Rohanna rasped, her eyebrows drawn together in confusion. Her voice sounded forced, hoarse, and low.

Alex stepped closer. "It's one of the things we need to talk about. Meet with me, tonight?"

"I promised Shyann I would go out with her, but in all honestly, going to a club doesn't appeal to me."

"Nor me, not tonight," Alex admitted, feeling the heat of Rohanna's gaze. They stood close together. The back of her hand rested along Rohanna's breastbone, the heavy drumming of her heart beating against Alex's knuckles. All she had to do was spread her hand, and she would touch softness. The thought was enough to ignite a blaze in her, burning her skin and heating her blood. The familiar warmth of arousal coiled deep in her belly, threatening her ability to think.

"Rohanna? I need to do something." She stroked the soft skin along Rohanna's cheek.

"What?" Rohanna trembled beneath her touch.

"Just this one thing," she murmured, running her thumb along Rohanna's lower lip. "So soft."

Rohanna's lips parted to accept the caress. It was enough for Alex. She dipped her head and tasted Rohanna's lips for the first time outside of the dream world. The two realities collided together madly, adding to the experience that was new and yet already realized.

She had no idea what might have happened next if they hadn't been interrupted. Alex wasn't above a wild romp in a haystack, and the way Rohanna was looking at her? She wouldn't have been able to resist. Unfortunately, another rider was making their way down the aisle, and whatever privacy they had was ruined. Alex growled in frustration. "Damn it all to Hell."

In an instant Rohanna was gone, out of her arms and back into her shell. The tired clop of a horse's hooves gave Rohanna enough time to pull away, both physically and mentally. She fiddled with her saddle, keeping her eyes on her work and away from Alex.

"Rohanna?" Alex asked.

Rohanna held up her hand, palm out, begging for silence.

"No, not here. We could have been caught. I can't have that," Rohanna spoke over her shoulder, her voice muted, low. "Tonight. We can meet tonight."

"Where?" Alex asked, letting her take the lead. Rohanna picked up her gear and turned towards her, holding her saddle in front of her like a shield.

"At your booth?"

"I'll be there," Alex readily agreed. For the chance of tasting those lips again, she would suffer the wait. Unfortunately, a good part of the day remained until nightfall, and she had a booth to attend to. Alex sighed. At least the busy work would keep her preoccupied.

CHAPTER TWENTY-THREE

"I hope you don't mind vegetarian?" Alex asked.

"Vegetarian? No, I don't mind," Ro looked around her. They had been walking for a while, leaving behind both the barn size halls crammed with vendors and the outside demonstration booths where she had met up with Alex. The fairgrounds were bigger than she had imagined, but then, she usually relegated herself to a strict triangle...riding arena, barn, and trailer. "Where are we going?"

"My place. I hope you don't mind," Alex said, making one last turn before leading Rohanna through the trees to her motorhome. The East Coast Equine Exposition was one of the largest shows of the year and it attracted a huge number of visitors, which meant the vendors were relegated to the farthest corner they could find to camp out in. Alex didn't mind; it was quiet and wooded and reminded her of the past. The hodgepodge group of individuals were about as close to a family of wanderers as she had seen in a very long while. Many of them had a gypsy heart, and she felt more comfortable around them than most humans.

"No, not at all."

Rohanna's eyes widened when she saw Alex's motorhome for the first time. She had set up the camp for comfort, with a large stone fire pit ready and waiting for an evening fire. There were other surprises as well, ones that Alex had prepared with Rohanna in mind. Alex grinned at Rohanna's expression. "Surprised?"

"A little," Rohanna admitted, sounding a bit awestruck. Rohanna looked around, then tilted her head back to look at the sky above them.

"Beautiful, aren't they?" Alex asked, following Rohanna's gaze. The moonless night made the stars appear all that much brighter for not having to compete with its bright glow. The Milky Way looked close enough to reach up and touch with her fingertips. Alex smiled. The wide belt blazing across the heavens seemed a worthy place to ride.

"Yes. I love nights like this."

"So do I," Alex said. "It would be a shame to go inside and miss such a grand display." Alex opted to start a wood fire in the stone fire pit and before long, she had a stunning array of vegetables grilling while they enjoyed a glass of wine.

While Alex worked, Rohanna sat on the makeshift log bench, silently contemplating the glass in her hand. She swirled the liquid around until it almost hit the rim of the glass as it circled, but had yet to raise the glass to her lips.

The fine crystal suits her, Alex thought, watching the subtle play of tendons along Rohanna's wrist. Her gaze moved to Rohanna's face and she rethought herself. The crystal was flawed and dull when compared to the woman. Cool and clear and finely wrought, something told Alex that with the right touch across that deceptively fragile lip a crystal note would sound, as true and pure as anything this world had to offer.

"Do you want something else?" Alex asked, pointing at Rohanna's full glass.

"No, no. It's okay. I'm just not used to drinking alcohol." *At least not with sexy female blacksmiths who make me lose my mind whenever they get too close to me.* She dropped her eyes, sure that Alex could read her thoughts and taste the lie. She felt awkward and obvious and altogether too transparent beneath that brilliant blue gaze.

Rohanna raised the glass to her lips and took a sip of the Pinot Noir Alex had bought on a whim. Her hand trembled slightly as she did so, giving away her nervousness. She smiled up at Alex, as delicately and sweetly as the wine wetting her lips, and it made Alex thirsty just looking at her. She raised her own glass and drank, just to have the same taste on her tongue, then frowned in disappointment. The wine was sweet but too cool, not what she wanted at all. She wanted warmth.

"It's very good." Rohanna looked up from her glass, bringing all the warmth and heat that Alex desired in one unguarded moment.

"Yes, it is, isn't it?" Alex agreed, lowering the timbre of her voice so it would slip across Rohanna's skin like a caress. Rohanna shivered in response, shifting her eyes back to the fire.

"You're cold," Alex said. She stood up and held her hand out to Rohanna. "The fire is dying down out here and we should let it. Why don't we go inside and finish our conversation there?"

Rohanna hesitated a moment before taking Alex's hand. Alex pulled her close. The stakes were about to get much higher and she had to know that Rohanna knew that, too.

"You don't have to come in, Rohanna. I can take you back to your trailer right now, if you want," Alex said. She didn't want to ask her permission, but she had to. Every fiber of her being had wanted to remain silent, to simply lead Rohanna through the door behind her and seek the intimacy they could find within those walls.

"No, I want to do this." Rohanna thrust her jaw out bravely, challenging Alex's attempt at chivalry.

"So brave," Alex murmured. "Is that what this is all about?"

She leaned down and brushed her lips across Rohanna's once and then again, ever so lightly, drawing from her what she needed to know. Being inside someone else's head made it hard at times. Especially when you knew that a brave front, was just that—a front. Alex had no doubt that Rohanna wanted to be here. Whatever power that was drawing them together had as tight of a hold on Rohanna as it did on her, making tonight as inevitable as the return of the new moon.

"No, I—I dreamt of this, you know, of you and me together." A deep red flush crept along Rohanna's cheeks, making her look even younger.

"And it made you curious?"

"No. Not curious so much as drawn. Yes, that's the right word," Rohanna said, her admission an uncanny reflection of Alex's thoughts. A cold chill ran up Alex's spine, defying the heat in her blood and setting off warning bells in her head.

Rohanna was trembling now.

"I have held myself apart from so much, for so long. I just can't seem to do that with you. Every fear I have, all the years I have felt nothing...and you just walk in and burn them all away."

"Not yet," Alex murmured, opening the door behind her and holding out her hand. This time there was no hesitation. She led and Rohanna followed, into the darkness and shadows where her bed lay.

I am actually here. This is really happening.

Rohanna stood in the dark, listening to Alex move around behind her. She jumped when Alex's hands slid across her shoulders, then melted against the taller woman when Alex kissed her, brushing warm lips against her neck.

"Lovely," Alex murmured.

Rohanna closed her eyes, removing the one sense she didn't need to fully savor the sensations Alex was drawing from her without effort.

Oh, God. She makes me feel so much. Her passion had sat inside her like a still pool for so long. Now it rippled and flowed like a spring, fresh and sweet and demanding. The emotion was so raw and powerful she should have felt afraid or overwhelmed, but she didn't. She felt exhilarated, her body taut with anticipation.

Alex continued to plant gentle kisses along Ro's neck, letting her fingers dance lightly up and down her arms, lighting small fires along their languorous path. Rohanna moaned. The light touches were torture. Her lips parted to beg for more, but Alex's voice silenced her, low and hoarse and sounding as desperate as she felt.

"I want you." Palms softer than Rohanna expected for someone who worked with hammer and steel all day slid along the back of her hands, then roughly pulled her shirt free from her jeans. Her stomach muscles twitched when Alex snaked her hands along her bare skin, circling the taut skin and skimming along the curve of her bra.

"Raise your arms," Alex whispered. She pulled Ro's t-shirt up and over her head in one quick movement. The bra came off next with practiced ease, and Rohanna's small breasts tumbled free from the last barrier between them. Rohanna arched her back, anticipating Alex's touch on her breasts. She bit back a groan of disappointment when Alex released her instead.

"Turn around," Alex commanded. She did. Deep blue eyes gleaming with dark desire gazed down at her. "Goddess, but you are beautiful."

She spoke with such reverence in her voice that it made Rohanna want to weep and cry out in joy at the same time. Alex planted a soft kiss on her brow, then captured her lips for a scorching kiss. Alex's fingertips mapped out her pulse line, tracing the line of her collarbone before laying a palm on her chest. Ro's captured heart pounded wildly beneath Alex's hand.

"So hot," Rohanna gasped. She felt like she was burning up, yet Alex's skin felt feverish compared to her.

"I do tend to run a bit warm." Alex grinned. "And the presence of a beautiful woman doesn't hurt."

Rohanna swayed in ecstasy when Alex found her breasts, first with nimble fingers then with her lips. Alex lowered her onto the bed, covering her body with her own before kissing her again. An insistent tongue sought entry and was given permission when her lips parted of their own accord. Alex's hand snaked down the flat planes of her stomach to finger the metal button of her jeans.

Alex continued her single-minded campaign. She slithered down Rohanna's body, peeling the offending jeans away as she moved, until Rohanna lay naked on the bed beneath her. Alex reared up, tossing the jeans on the floor before returning her attention back to Rohanna. Alex gazed down at her, eyes smoldering with pleasure as she watched Rohanna squirm beneath her. The movement seemed to excite her, so Rohanna did it again, writhing beneath the woman kneeling above her until Alex growled at her.

"Holy Hells, woman. Don't do that unless you mean it."

"Well? You do seem to have me at a disadvantage," Rohanna bluffed, smiling up at the still dressed woman as sweetly as she could. Her voice didn't waiver, despite her nervousness. Alex was right about one thing, she wanted this. Badly. *No*, she thought, *I want her, and there's the difference.*

"Do I now?" Alex asked, grinning down at her in a most delightful way. "Perhaps I should fix that?"

Alex pulled her shirt up and over her head in one quick movement. The shirt hit the floor, mingling with Rohanna's clothes. Rohanna openly admired Alex's sleek physique. Her breasts were small, the areolas dark and flushed. The golden tan of her skin held no lines or breaks. She either sunbathed nude or the coloring was naturally hers. The thought sent a flush of heat down her thighs, tightening muscles deep inside her. The world could have ended around them, and she wouldn't have cared. Alex slowly unbuckled her belt and then, with tormenting deliberateness, unbuttoned her jeans one slow pop at a time before returning to Rohanna's side.

Rohanna gasped then moaned deeply at the sensation of soft breasts pressing into hers, of a demanding mouth at her neck, and a wandering hand caressing down her stomach until fingertips found soft curls. Her hips jerked, trying to force Alex to continue along the path she had started. A low chuckle and a firm hand on her hip stopped her.

"So eager," Alex murmured.

"Yes." The word escaped her lips through clenched teeth as Alex slipped her fingers along sensitive lips to find the drenched folds hidden within. "Yessss."

The sheets twisted in her fists, her hips rocking against Alex's palm as she leisurely stroked her, carefully avoiding her swollen clit.

Rohanna gasped at the spike of pleasure that shot like lightning from her breast to her clit when Alex sucked her nipple, lashing the sensitive flesh with her tongue until her other breast ached for the same punishment. Emboldened, she threaded her fingers through Alex's thick hair, pulling her head back and guiding her lips to her other breast. Matching her boldness for boldness, Alex hummed her approval as she nipped and tugged on Ro's nipple, just shy of it being more pain than pleasure.

Cool air caressed her tortured breasts when Alex slid away from her to kneel on the floor. There was no place else for her to go, not for what she did next. She wrapped her arms around Rohanna's thighs and pulled her to the edge of the bed.

Rohanna had no time to respond. Anything she might have said was lost the second Alex's tongue found her center, the strong muscle so different from the simple stroke of a finger. Then she found Rohanna's clit, treating it to the same lavish attention she had given her breasts, and she lost the ability to speak.

Teasing along the hard bundle of nerves, Alex brought Rohanna close to the edge over and over again, only to back off at the last second. Rohanna groaned in frustration; the need to come was overpowering. Tossing her head back, she moved her hips frantically against Alex's mouth in a bid to find the release she desperately needed.

"Alex, please," Ro begged, her hips coming off the bed in response to one delicious swipe of Alex's tongue. Rohanna's hands convulsed around the bed sheets in rhythm with the sharp pulses of pleasure building inside her, before finding Alex's hands. When Alex flattened her tongue on her clit then drew it into her mouth, Rohanna screamed, grasping at the air.

Their fingers laced together in a crushing grip, Alex encouraged her to rise as she curled herself around her orgasm, her thighs wrapped tightly around Alex's head. Her whole body tensed, poised at the precipice for one long moment before tumbling over the sharp ledge of long held restraint. She fell back onto the bed, the deafening sound of her blood drumming in her ears in time to the sweetly aching pulse between her thighs. Alex continued her light teasing licks until she begged her to stop, but her begging didn't end her torment completely. Alex shifted lower, drinking deeply from the hot wetness she had created, curling the sweet essence along her tongue until Rohanna's thighs quivered uncontrollably and her begging was reduced to whimpers.

Alex crawled back onto the bed and kissed her. Ro could taste her own arousal still lingering on Alex's tongue and lips. A sudden, irrational, and completely overpowering desire to taste Alex made her shudder in anticipation. Ro wanted to run her tongue along those long thighs until she found the same sweet essence to savor, spiced by the sounds of Alex's moans and desperate pleas until she screamed out her pleasure. The aggressive nature of the fantasy almost derailed her in its intensity.

She had two choices: accept the depths of her fantasies and give herself the freedom to act on them, or back away now and crawl back into her fears and isolated life. Torn between the two paths, she took in a deep sobbing breath and lost herself in the scent of Alex's skin. Earthy and rich, it reminded her of sandlewood with just a touch of cinnamon, and beneath that was the heady scent of her arousal, sweet and aromatic. From lips to breast to the flat planes of her stomach, Rohanna traced the lines of Alex's body. When eager fingertips slipped along the damp curls between Alex's thighs, a soft gasp from the other woman made her look up.

"I want to taste you."

"I won't say no," Alex said. Her eyes glittered in the dim light, but there was no mistaking the heat in that heavy lidded gaze. The tableau froze between them. Rohanna knelt between Alex's thighs while she watched silently, waiting for her to bow her head and bring their night full circle. Alex reached down and stroked Rohanna's cheek with the back of her hand then ran the pad of her thumb across her bottom lip.

Her skin tingled beneath that gentle touch. The strange sensation rushed through her like a whirlwind, awakening and numbing the nerve endings circling her brow before racing down her spine. Rohanna felt something shift, both inside her and around them, as though some strange ritual was in action that required completion. She could feel the energy between them build. The tension wasn't just sexual. It held something else, something she couldn't quite put her finger on.

"What is happening between us?" Rohanna whispered.

"Nothing that shouldn't, and everything that should," Alex answered.

The cryptic answer made Rohanna frown. "I don't understand."

"That's okay." Alex brushed the hair away from Rohanna's brow before speaking again. "Rohanna, you don't need to fight this. Embrace who you are. There is only joy here, and the promise of release."

Rohanna bowed her head.

"My choice?" Mostly a question and just shy of a whisper, Rohanna tasted the power of those words before repeating them, stronger this time. "My choice."

A deep sigh drifted down to Rohanna's ears when she bent down and pressed her lips against the heated flesh waiting for her. She moaned in ecstasy at the first taste of Alex's arousal as she snaked her tongue out to explore the slick folds. The sound was almost primal, coming from deep in her throat, yet it was a pale echo to the sounds she drew from the woman arching into her as she urged her on. Rohanna's arousal reignited when she brought Alex screaming into the night, bringing a fresh flood of moisture. She felt slick and heavy, her clit swollen and hard from teasing Alex's orgasm from her.

Alex flipped her, pressing the length of her body against her as she moved between her thighs. This time she wasn't as gentle. Her hand slipped between them, seeking Rohanna's core, and slipped inside her without warning. Rohanna gasped at the sudden intrusion, her muscles clamping down on Alex's fingers as they slid as deep as they could go, only to withdraw again. Each time she did this, Rohanna felt a profound sense of loss. Having felt the fullness of Alex inside of her, she wasn't prepared for the emptiness left behind when she withdrew. She wrapped her arms around the woman towering over her, shamelessly grasping at the muscles flexing across Alex's back in time with her movements.

"Ahhh...Alex!" she called out, her hips pistoning frantically until the tension inside her unwound in one blinding flash of ecstasy. Her whole body shook, convulsing around Alex's fingers as she teased aftershock after aftershock of pleasure out of her.

The low, throaty sound of a pleased chuckle followed her into oblivion. Before she drifted off, she had a vague awareness of a blanket being thrown over her, Alex's warm body pressing into her from behind and a firm arm draped across her middle and pulling her close.

CHAPTER TWENTY-FOUR

"What the hell?" Rohanna sat up, pulling at tangled sheets as unfamiliar as the room around her.

What happened? What had woken her? Rohanna grasped her head, squeezing her temples almost painfully, willing the dream to make itself known. Frustration welled up inside her. She couldn't remember. She was sure it was another nightmare, but if she couldn't sort it out before falling back asleep, she would just return to the same bad dream.

"Dammit, why can't I remember?" Ro slammed her fist into the mattress next to her. She was getting so tired of the endless cycle of waking just to dread falling back asleep.

The bed shifted next to her, reminding her that she was sharing it with someone else. Rohanna was usually alone in the middle of the night with her nightmares, but not this night.

Alex. Oh, God...Alex. She had accepted Alex's invitation to dinner, but had ended up here, in her bed instead. Her stomach growled, reminding her that they had forgotten about dinner. Other hungers had demanded attention, awakening inside her with a ferocious need she couldn't ignore.

Alex's bedroom was almost pitch dark now, she was sure the fire had gone out long ago, burnt to ash and charcoal, their intended meal shriveled to nothing by the heat. She shivered. Only a scant few hours ago it had felt like summer inside the dark room, full of heat and humidity and blinding sunlight held at bay by closed eyelids. Old fears grew in the dark and quiet places; she didn't want to be alone with them.

"Alex?" Rohanna's voice trembled a little despite herself.

Alex's long black hair had come loose from its braid and now draped across her shoulders and back. Rohanna reached out and touched the thick tresses, fascinated by the heavy strands that spilled onto the bedsheets like a river of black ink. Her hair was so dark, it made the shadows look pale and grey in comparison.

"Alex, wake up, please?"

Alex made an odd noise in her throat, her body unfolding from where she lay.

"Ro?" Alex mumbled drowsily, turning to face her. Her hair fell away from her face, and Rohanna shrieked. Alex's confusion couldn't hide her eyes. Even with her eyebrows drawn tight and her face in shadow, they shone eerily in the dark around them.

"What's wrong?" Alex asked, instantly awake.

"Get away from me!" Rohanna managed to speak past the fear gripping her throat like a vice.

"Rohanna?"

"No." Rohanna shook her head violently. She had suffered through violent, even frightening nightmares before, but this one was exceptionally cruel. Her chest hurt, pierced with a blade of her own making. "This, you...nothing but another nightmare. I need to leave, to wake up from this."

"No, Rohanna! I'm not..." Alex couldn't say it, couldn't deny that she was a Nightmare. She swallowed her denial and tried again, skirting around the truth as tightly as she was allowed. "This isn't a dream, Rohanna. I'm real."

She reached out for Rohanna's hand, only to find empty air when Rohanna scrambled off the bed. She landed on the floor with a bone-jarring thud. Unable to tear her gaze away from Alex, she reached behind her for the clothes she had so eagerly discarded earlier.

"What are you?" Rohanna whispered, unable to contain her horror. She fled out the door, the sound of it slamming shut following her as she ran.

Alarmed and confused, Alex rolled out of the bed and strode to the door. Her words should have reassured Rohanna, not sent her skittering away like a frightened child.

She caught sight of Rohanna just before she disappeared behind a large stand of trees. She touched the handle, turning it a bit before remembering that she was naked. A string of colorful curses escaped through the door without her. Alex didn't care that she was skyclad. If she chose, she could arrive at Rohanna's destination before she did and clothes would just get in the way. She considered it, then discarded the idea. Rohanna would demand an explanation she couldn't give.

When she turned around to retrieve her clothes, she caught sight of herself in the small mirror behind her and gasped. A wave of nausea hit her. She felt the world shift beneath her feet, making her lose her balance. She slammed her palm onto the wall to steady herself, hard enough to make the trailer shake.

"Great Goddess, no wonder she ran," Alex said, trying to focus on the image in front of her. Flames danced in her eyes, the color of a gas jet—blue on white, without a hint of a pupil inside. Pain crashed into her, bringing her to her knees. She dug her fingers into her scalp, desperate to ease the razor's edge slicing through her brain. A hundred voices clamored for room all at once, all dreaming, all exposing their deepest desires as they slept. Their auras assaulted her senses. They pierced her mind, a hundred steel lances forcing their way in on singular points of pain until she could separate the clamoring hoard and push them to the edges of her consciousness.

Instinct guided her, along with the vague memories of old tales told around campfires. They were meant to instruct the earthborn children of Epona, to explain the reasons behind the sacrifices made in their name, but they had only angered Alex. The old stories had served to remind her of what her people had once been and how far they had fallen, now they guided her blood towards a long forgotten birthright.

Once she could sort them out, she cast about her more purposefully. Most of the auras felt crystalline and relatively free from corruption. She discarded them as harmless. One aura stood out from the rest. It was a sickly color, yellowish brown and black. It made her think of the filthy windows dotting the side of an abandoned factory. Filmed over and opaque from years of pollution and despair, it reeked of corruption, the edges eaten away from years of moral rot. Impressions turned into thoughts that turned Alex's stomach. She pulled herself upright, shuddering at the depravity of the man's desires. The need to protect what was hers reared up inside her when she discovered his sick fantasies included Rohanna.

Alex screamed, the sound becoming something altogether inhuman before ending abruptly. The silence that remained was deadlier in its absence of a warning.

The sound of thunder intruded on the middle-age man's dreams, bringing with it his first nightmare since childhood. His unconscious mind was just as corrupt and twisted as his waking mind. Dreams were a place to relive his sick fantasies over and over again, there was no guilt to seed nightmares meant to remind him of what was right and wrong...until tonight.

He had strategically placed his small trailer along the edge of the camp. As one who found excitement in watching others, he was paranoid of others observing him. Unfortunately, his purposeful isolation carried no protection from what was coming for him now. The second scream of the night was not one that could be heard by others. It happened in a place as alone and bereft of life as a storm tossed beach. Sharp white teeth and vengeful eyes followed his dreams and turned them into something else, a beast that ate itself from within. Not fair! Cries for mercy were ignored, much as he had denied the same to his victims, yet he felt he was deserving of them. "No mercy, no quarter. You have been found wanting, and this is the punishment for your crimes. Never again..." The voice was inhuman, cold and imperious, and it passed judgement on him without benefit of judge and jury. "Never will you hurt me or mine, or any other."

"Please?" He held out his hand, grasping at the air above him in one last, lonely attempt to save himself.

"No." White teeth and blue flames flashed into scorching pain. His screams lasted long after his voice gave out, but no one heard a sound in the waking world.

Leaving behind a shredded soul and a harmless mind, Alex ran into the night. She had to find Rohanna.

CHAPTER TWENTY-FIVE

Rohanna woke up in an altogether too familiar place, surrounded by the sweet smell of hay and horses

"Christ, how many barns am I going to wake up in?" She plucked a few pieces of dusty hay from her hair and then sneezed. Standing up a bit unsteadily, she brushed the worst of the dust off of her, then climbed down from the hayloft attached to the main barn. The aisle was brightly lit, but even that light couldn't bite far into the night. It pressed through the wide entranceway at the end of the barn, thick and oppressive and not the least bit inviting to venture out into.

"Can this night get any stranger?" Rohanna asked, her voice echoing hollowly in the cavernous building. A few nervous nickers answered her, their muted timber suited to the late hour. The horses were wiser than she. They knew better than to invite attention from things that hunted at night. She shivered against the feeling of déjà vu as remnants of her nightmare started to trickle through. The night had been strange enough as it was, why would she invite more strangeness into it?

Rohanna shook her head ruefully. This was the second time she had dreamed about Alex. She couldn't seem to shake her attraction to the tall blacksmith, not even in her sleep. "So real." Rohanna spoke aloud, brushing her hands down the front of her body. Her breasts felt full, her nipples sensitive and raw against the smooth fabric of her bra. She couldn't ignore what her body was telling her.

Had she really met with Alex for dinner last night? If she had, then what about the rest of the night?

The lines between dream and reality blurred for a moment, sending Rohanna to her knees.

"No, no, no," Rohanna cried out, refusing to accept her memories as true ones. Crouching in the dirt, she held her hands in her head and squeezed her eyes shut as tight as she could. Her mind stumbled and tripped through the jumble of images crowding her vision as she tried to make sense of things that made none and offered no logical explanation.

Something warm snuffled against her ear. Rohanna squeaked and fell back, awkwardly landing on her backside. She scrambled back, crablike, away from the shadow standing over her. Her heart climbed up into her throat, suffocating the startled scream that tried to escape. She looked up, then started laughing uncontrollably.

Ro recognized her laughter for what it was. It was that maniacal sort of laugh you do after something scares the crap out of you and then you realize that there wasn't anything to be afraid of in the first place. Ro scrambled to her feet, then took a few deeps breaths to calm down. A tall black horse stood in front of her, watching her compose herself. It took a little longer than she expected. She was jumpy as hell tonight, and her nerves felt as tattered and frayed as an old horse blanket. Only when she was sure she was done giggling like an idiot and jumping at every sound did she approach the strange horse. It was rule number one in her book. Never approach a horse with fear or anger in your heart.

"Now, what are you doing loose and running about, eh?" Rohanna asked, stepping sideways to get a better look at the mare. Pitch black and without a single white marking, the horse was impressively muscled and tall, almost a good seventeen hands. The elegant head and mane made her think of the Friesian breed, but she lacked the feathering and draft like thickness she associated with them. *Some kind of warm blood, then?* Ro thought, comfortably falling back into more familiar territory. She didn't know and she certainly would have noticed such an impressive animal out on the field yesterday. She made poor Galileo look absolutely plain in comparison.

Throughout Ro's examination, the black mare stood there, watching her without attempting to move away.

"As weird as tonight has been, I wonder?" Rohanna reached out to touch the black hide, stroking the velvet fur along her neck. The horse arched its neck and stomped one hoof softly, then went completely still. "I wonder who you belong to. You are beautiful."

Rohanna sighed. She would have loved to ride such an impressive creature.

As if on cue, the tall horse bent its knee and bowed its head, lowering the front half of its body in invitation. The soft brown eye rolled back and looked directly at her, as if waiting for her to mount. Rohanna's jaw dropped.

"Okay, that answers one question," she whispered. She must still be dreaming. A dream horse in a dream world had no owner—she was free to ride if she wanted to. Jumping onto the broad back, she had just enough time to tangle her hands into the thick mane before the mare surged upright.

The mare snorted once, her unshod hooves struck the ground, sparking like flint on steel before leaping into the night, taking Rohanna for a wild ride through the fairgrounds before taking an even bigger leap. With nothing but the sky and stars to guide them, she urged the black mare on. The wind whipped past them as they thundered along paths that blurred into so many pinpoint lights she couldn't say whether they were galloping along a marked path or The Milky Way arcing across the blue-black sky. She couldn't see much past the tears streaming across her cheeks, but she couldn't break the sensation that they were travelling at a great height. The air was too cold and crisp for a summer night, and she tucked closer to the mare to borrow some of her body heat.

Finally, Rohanna had enough.

"Enough!" she called out, and the horse slowed to a trot, then a walk. They stopped on a sandy hill by a small stream. Rohanna slid down off the mare and looked around. A full moon sat low on the horizon. In stark relief, large upright shapes loomed nearby, their height seeking the moon above them. As her eyes adjusted to the moonlight, her heart skipped a beat.

They were at the stone circle on her farm. But here and now, in her dream—the stones stood tall and proud and three times the size they were supposed to be.

"Well now, since it's my dream, they can look anyway I want them to, can't they?" she asked herself, bravely marching up to the stone circle. She fingered the Faerie stone around her neck. This was the place she had found it, and she had nothing to fear here. She caressed the stone, standing in the shadow of the gateway just as she had so many years ago. The stone grew hot beneath her touch. Like a living being, it thrummed with energy. Her palm started to tingle, and then burn. The moon dimmed and pulsed, fading into the background as the stones around her drew in the light until they glowed.

"Beautiful," Rohanna whispered in awe as electric blue-white light made its way around the circle until it found her. Her head snapped back with the power that raced up her arm and through her body. She snatched her hand away from the stone and the light vanished. Vigorously rubbing her arm, she backed away from the stone circle and ran into something solid. It was the black mare. The comforting presence of a horse, dream one or otherwise, calmed her. She pressed her forehead against the warm hide and took a deep breath in, expecting the familiar scent of horse and hay or perhaps, this being a dream...no scent at all. What she didn't expect was a newly familiar scent of sandlewood and cinnamon. Pushing away from the mare, Ro backed a step away and almost stumbled on the rough ground behind her.

"Alex?" she stuttered. The mare's head swung around and faced her, blue on blue eyes blazing at her, the same blue-white blaze that had stolen the light of the moon.

***

"Alex?" Rohanna struggled in Alex's arms.

It was early morning and the pale pre-dawn light was trying to find its way inside. Alex was curled up behind Ro, holding her in an intimate embrace. The tangled blankets had slipped from Alex's upper body, exposing her bare skin to the morning chill. She barely felt it; in fact, she was lending her warmth to Rohanna.

"Shhh," Alex whispered in her ear, stroking her arm to reassure her. "I didn't want to wake you, but you were calling out in your sleep."

"In my sleep? I was dreaming?" Rohanna twisted her upper body to look at Alex.

"I was just dreaming." Relief flashed in her eyes a second before she smiled. Alex's pulse quickened at the drowsy, half-lidded gaze of the woman smiling up at her. She almost chuckled. With all the strangeness of the night, and all that she had learned, all it took was a look and a smile to refocus her energies back on the physical. Even tousled and half asleep, Rohanna was a difficult woman to resist.

She dropped her gaze down to Rohanna's lips before looking back up, directly into Rohanna's eyes. She was willing to believe her, the look in her eyes said so...but it pained Alex to keep the lie going.

"But I'm not dreaming now?" Ro asked, running one tentative finger down Alex's cheek before tracing her lower lip. Alex captured the errant digit between her lips, sucking it gently before releasing it.

"No, you are definitely not dreaming now," Alex said. Her lips found the sensitive skin at Rohanna's neck and traced a hot line of kisses along her shoulder. Pressing her forehead against the bed, Rohanna moaned in the most delightful way, her body moving restlessly beneath Alex as she continued her campaign. Alex was intent on igniting Rohanna's passion. She continued to plant tantalizing kisses along Rohanna's back and didn't stop until she reached Rohanna's backside, licking along the soft curve of her spine and teasing the firm flesh of her buttocks with her teeth. Rohanna squirmed under her touch, then cried out when Alex reached between her thighs and found her already wet and ready for her. "Fuck," Alex growled, not expecting her to be so primed. She changed her mind and changed direction, even though her mouth watered at the thought of her tongue gliding through such sweet nectar. Curling up behind her, she wrapped her free arm around

Rohanna's waist before slipping her fingers inside. She loved this position, taking a willing woman from behind like this, feeling her move against her without being able to see their face. Her only guide was how they moved against her and the sounds they made. It made it more intimate and decidedly more exciting, learning to read a lover this way.

Her lips and teeth found Rohanna's flesh, tasting salt and desire. The added pain was a goad that sent Rohanna into a frenzy. The response was immediate. Rohanna whimpered, spreading her legs a bit wider to allow Alex more access.

"Oh God, Alex," she sobbed, her breath going ragged. "More."

She rolled her hips onto Alex's fingers with each deep thrust. Alex curled around her, trying to ignore what Rohanna was doing to her with each backward thrust. It didn't matter. When Rohanna threw her head back, crying out in ecstasy, Alex found herself thundering along the same wild path as the woman writhing against her.

A few minutes later, Rohanna stirred against her. Alex kissed sweat dampened hair and carefully withdrew her hand. "Are you okay?"

"Mm. More than okay. Starved, though."

Alex smirked. "I'm afraid dinner is done for." There was no saving the meal she had planned last night. All of her hard work had shriveled into barely recognizable blobs of charcoal after being left on the coals while other appetites had been explored. It was a fair trade, and one for which she would gladly miss any meal for.

Rohanna blushed when she saw Alex's face, then coughed. "Um, I..."

"You're cute when you blush like that," Alex teased her, then threw off the blankets and rolled out of bed. "I'll find us something to eat...and drink. I'm sure you're parched after last night."

Rohanna's blush managed to deepen to a lovely shade of pinkish red and she had to look away from Alex's backside before she disappeared into other parts of the trailer.

She was more than thirsty...and no wonder. She felt like every ounce of moisture in her body had been drawn out of her in a haze of passion. She shivered, not because she was cold, but because her body kept reminding her of how everything that happened last night-and this morning-felt.

"It's getting late. Don't you have to be at your booth soon?" Rohanna asked as soon as Alex returned from the small kitchen at the front of the trailer.

"No, I don't have a forging demonstration until later. And you? Are you showing Galileo this morning?" Alex handed Rohanna a cup of coffee then rejoined her in the bed. Rohanna had managed to salvage one of the blankets from the tangled mess on the floor, and was now sitting up in the bed with the woven fabric tucked around her.

"No, my practice hour in the arena isn't until noon. I do have to swing by the stallion showcase as some point, but that can be anytime this afternoon."

"And Shyann? Won't she be worried about you?"

"If anything, she'd probably be thrilled that I finally jumped into bed with someone."

"Oh?" Alex raised an inquiring eyebrow. *Just not me, I bet.*

Rohanna's pale cheeks flamed a lovely shade of pink almost instantly and she buried her face in her coffee.

"I've embarrassed you."

"No, not at all. I..." Rohanna started, then stopped to lick her lips. "I'm sorry. You're right. I have to admit, this isn't like me." Rohanna waved her hand between them, taking in the room, the disheveled sheets, everything.

"I don't understand. What isn't you?" Alex asked.

"I asked you what was happening between us, last night. I had a reason. I'm not usually so out of control, not with anyone, not *for* anyone. It isn't me." Rohanna licked her lips again before repeating the oft practiced excuses she had for everything, only this morning they didn't sit well on her tongue. "I have responsibilities. My farm. The horses. They come first. Before me or anyone else."

"Is this your way of telling me you had fun last night, but it's over now?" Alex asked.

"No! That's the problem. I don't want that at all," Rohanna admitted. "I barely know you, but I can't stop thinking about you, and that's scaring me to death. You make me consider doing things I've never considered doing, wanting things I never knew I wanted."

And don't forget doing...Oh, God...and that, too. Rohanna drew a ragged breath and waited. She had half expected Alex to call her a coward, instead she sat back and regarded Rohanna silently for a minute before leaning forward again.

"Look, Ro. There are things you don't know about me."

"I know you're into a pretty heavy scene," Rohanna said. "Shyann made sure I knew what this meant." She ran her fingertips across the wide leather bracer still laced on Alex's left wrist. "I think she was trying to scare me away from you."

"But, she didn't succeed?" Alex asked, her face carefully blank. She held her breath, waiting to see what

Rohanna would say next. The unexpected direction of their conversation held a level of promise in it she hadn't expected.

"After what we just did, you have to ask?" Rohanna laughed. "When we met, I thought you wore it to protect your arm from the forge."

"I do, but sometimes things don't always look like they appear, nor do they always mean what people think they do." Alex cringed at how cryptic that sounded. She had come as close as she could to the truth, and for the first time, she wished she didn't have to. She understood Shyann's position all too well; she was honor bound to keep certain secrets.

Rohanna nervously picked at the blanket wrapped around her.

"I have to admit, I don't know a lot about who you are." Suddenly shy, she dropped her gaze. "But, I would like to learn more…if you will let me."

The sharp rush of desire that those words released in her shocked Alex. They generated a deep hum that vibrated inside her skull like a well-plucked harp string. It coursed through her, finding its way along already primed paths and reigniting passions she had thought well satiated. The leather bracer felt like a firebrand against her skin. Somehow, the lie had become the truth. Or, perhaps it had always been there, waiting for the right person to awaken that particular desire. Tamped down, half realized…but always there. *Not the right person*, Alex thought, correcting herself. *Rohanna is Fae even though she doesn't know it…as Fae as I am and that means no holding back…no need to worry about going too far or letting my true nature come out and play.*

Running her index finger softly along Rohanna's cheek, Alex realized just how much she was caught within this mutual trap of attraction. Rohanna looked up. Her half-lidded gaze smoldered, capturing Alex with the promise of imagined pleasures.

"Perhaps later. But not now and not here." Alex regretfully declined the offer. Despite Ro's eager offer, Alex didn't think she was ready for what she was asking for.

Rohanna's hurt expression made Alex careless with her next words. "When you ask me again, we'll discuss it."

And by then, I will have spoken with GranMere. I need to be released from my vow. Rohanna deserves to know the truth.

CHAPTER TWENTY-SIX

Alex checked her rear view mirror to make sure the road was clear behind her before slowing down and turning right onto the small, unmarked dirt road no one ever noticed but had been there for more years than most of the locals could remember. Deceptively non-descript and more than a little dangerous looking, she was sure most people thought it was a dead end utility road and ignored it. She was deep in the boonies, in an area about as isolated as you could get in a world that was rapidly shrinking, on an equally non-descript road that was rarely travelled upon—but it never failed.

The minute she needed to slow down, some idiot would be right behind her, crawling so far up her rear it became a heart-stopping event. They would pull out and speed by, more concerned with applying their horn than the brakes in their misplaced anger. She didn't care about the middle finger flashed her way as much as being circumspect. She didn't need someone looking twice at the overgrown area surrounding the dirt road and taking note of it. GranMere would not be pleased if a group of hunters showed up unannounced one day, just because someone thought they had found a convenient back way into the woods that hid their trucks and campfire from the prying eyes of the local game warden. Worse yet, they might bring tales back to town of the small community of women living there, with all the speculation and sordid talk of mysterious communes tucked in their back yard. It had happened before, and in this county...curiosity like that was never a good thing.

Alex slowed to a crawl going past the switchback leading farther into the woods, keeping a close eye on the steep drop-off on the left and the sheer rock cliff rising up above her on the right. She tapped the steering wheel in time with the music on the radio, more out of nerves than actually listening to the tune. It had been a while since she had seen Kaleigh and she wasn't sure what to expect. Kaleigh was both her aunt and the GranMere of Alex's tribe, their leader. She doubly held Alex's heart and loyalty, but it had been a long time since they had seen eye to eye on anything of importance. The last time they met, Alex had left on her own accord, angry, frustrated and fuming at her aunt's demands. Kaleigh had told her then, she was always welcome back, but there was no mistaking it, she was an exile from her people. A self-imposed exile, that was true, but that didn't mean some of her people weren't happy to see her gone.

About a mile down the road, the heavy forest thinned, then cleared, spitting her truck out into a surprisingly large mountaintop meadow. Several dozen neatly spaced log homes and a few acres of well-tended gardens dotted the rolling landscape.

There weren't any power lines or sign of modern conveniences visible anywhere. If anyone accidentally wandered here, they would assume they had stumbled into one of those small Appalachian villages people liked to joke about and worried they would never escape. Alex smirked. One benefit of being out in the real world was exposure to human culture...including their odd sense of humor.

"Not a single banjo in the whole place." She chuckled, wondering how effective it would be to learn. Would an unwanted visitor flee in terror?

Alex found a dry patch of stony ground and parked the truck, then sat there for a few minutes, listening to the sound of the engine clicking while it cooled down. She was procrastinating, but couldn't help it. There was so much of her past here, in the sights, the sounds, the smells. She had grown up here, isolated from the rest of the world. Taught from childhood what it meant to be different and how important it was to stay hidden even in plain sight.

Alex tugged at her braid. A small part of her felt guilty for leaving every time she returned. Today was no different. The same things that drew her here were the same things that sent her away, reminding her why she had to leave each time she succumbed to memories that tried to edit themselves into the perfection of childish nostalgia.

Nothing had changed since her childhood, not the houses nor the farmland. There were a few goats and chickens running around, but other than that, there weren't any farm animals. Her people didn't eat meat as a rule; the goats and chickens were used for milk and eggs. The place was completely self-sufficient, if necessary, even though most of the women chose to work in order to enjoy the luxuries that the outside world offered. Unlike her, they returned here every night, and if they were forced to choose...they would return to the tribe.

She was the only one who chose to live apart from the others. She was a loner in a tribe that prided itself on being a community. Saying that her decision had caused some division in the tribe would be a huge understatement. There were some who used her voluntary isolation as proof that she didn't deserve to inherit her aunt's position as leader.

Some days she wondered if they were right.

Alex laid her forehead on the steering wheel, closing her eyes against the pain and grief of the past. It was a beautiful place. It smelled like home. The air tasted like home and made her want to weep, but she couldn't let loneliness sway her. She could never stay here, not as things were now. She couldn't bring herself to toe the line and be the woman that her aunt wanted her to be.

Taking in a deep fortifying breath to steel herself against the inevitable confrontation, Alex was reminded of the last time she was here. Memories of her last failed conversation with her aunt flooded in, shredding what little bit of calm and peace she had gathered about her. She threw her head back against the headrest, eyes screwed shut as the images played out behind her eyelids.

"GranMere, there is no reason that we can't mingle with them. You are denying us so much. Our human forms deserve to have the intimacy, even love, they can have with humans."

"Nonsense, child. We are Daughters of Epona. We have ever survived as myth and legend. Our safety is kept with secrecy. Would you have us go the way of other faerfolk who thought it better to share with humans, only to be mown down in their continuous wars?"

"Wars happen whether we want or not, and time and again we have been drawn into them. If we hadn't, the world would have been a worse place, for us and the humans who value freedom as well."

"True, but I remember how people feared us, and fear is a great motivator to destroy. We left our home to come here because we were tired of being servants, I'll not expose us to

those who would see us in chains. Do you think the Humans would be a more gracious taskmaster if they were given reign over us? They are cruel and capricious, more so because they have so little time between birth and death. I'll let them remember us as legend and myth, thank you. It is safer for us all, including you."

"The world is shrinking, GranMere. It is not so easy to stay apart from it," Alex argued, troubled at the way the world was moving. Without magic, humans had found science—and technology was advancing in leaps and bounds. Everything had to be counted, put on lists and downloaded. Data was everything to them, a bastardized curiosity that demanded knowledge of things that weren't important but were becoming increasingly troublesome to folk like them. Driver's licenses, Photo ID, taxes to the government that made sure nothing was ever owned and could be taken away at any time by the state. It wouldn't be long before some of her kin had to explain why their licenses seemed out of sync with their pictures or someone questioned why perfectly good land had somehow managed to escape the strip mining and insatiable demand for precious metals or stones.

"That may be, Niece, but for now, the old ways still serve us well. There is no need for us to change what has always been."

Alex opened her mouth, stubbornly prepared to continue her argument, but she knew it was useless. GranMere was as set in her ways as the humans were, and the violence and losses of the past was inarguable.

Kaleigh absently waved her away, turning her attention back to the text lying on the table before her.

Dismissed, Alex had no choice but to hold her tongue...until today.

Until Rohanna.

Her fists clenched ineffectively, missing the feel of the hammer in her hand. There was no outlet for her frustration here. She would have to suffer through this in order to find answers. She had no choice.

Anger wouldn't help her cause, but it rose up inside her anyway. As volatile and hot as her forge fire, it burned inside her like desire and tasted like conquest. Alex had grown up listening to the stories of the Great Hunt and how the Meres would ride out into the night to seek out their victims. The poor souls who had the misfortune of harboring ill thoughts and ill deeds could not hide from them. No matter how fast or how far they ran, they could not outrun a nightmare cloaked in darkness. This was before the veil closed, when magic ran rampant through the hills and flowed through the veins of every creature that claimed Fae blood.

Alex grinned, a grim baring of straight white teeth that clenched and ground against each other in response to the clarion call of the Horn she could feel sounding through her. It was real enough to make her look around, but there was nothing to disturb the peace around her. Her face flushed hot and then cold as she fought the surge of power that coursed through her veins and ignited the blue lines of her tattoo until they felt like a living thing moving restlessly beneath her skin. She shuddered, the delicate play of muscle and tendon reminding her how easy it was now to shed this form. The NightMere inside her was living far too close to the surface lately, and that was another reason she had to come.

It was Fae magic doing this to her.

What had been lost when the veil closed had somehow returned to her, and it had to do with Rohanna.

246

That she felt the call of the Wild Hunt would not be something Kaleigh would receive well. They had not always gone on the Hunt of their own will. The Greater Fae had delighted in making them go after chosen victims...forcing NightMeres to punish those who displeased them, rather than those who deserved such terror. That alone had been enough to send them here, where magic was weak and no one could call them by right or rank to do their bidding.

Alex finally climbed out her truck. Delaying would do nothing but keep her here past sun down, and she longed to return to her forge. There was only one thing left to do.

Alex leaned against the truck door and tore at the laces along her forearm until her bracer loosened enough to rip it off. She would not cover her arm here. To do so would be an insult, but more importantly, it was a reminder that she outranked anyone who would challenge her right to see the GranMere on short notice. She tossed the discarded leather onto the front seat and massaged her wrist, enjoying the feel of the cool breeze on her bare skin. The edges of the dark blue tattoo rose in response to the sensation as did the fine hairs along her arm. Sensitive fingertips traced the lines that looped and scrolled across her skin. The intricate knot work pattern was as familiar to her as her name. She mapped out the clean lines, remembering what they meant and why they were there.

Sighing in resignation, Alex turned her feet down the path that led to the main house. She would find her aunt and tell her everything she knew. She offered a quick prayer to Epona that her aunt would listen to her tale without prejudice.

Alex couldn't shake the feeling that there was so much more going on than she was aware of. She needed GranMere's knowledge, and if possible, her blessing.

CHAPTER TWENTY-SEVEN

Her instincts were proven right. The minute Alex walked into the old-fashioned parlor, replete with muted pinks and deep velvets straight out of the 1800's, someone cleared their throat behind her. Alex shook her head. As if the presence of the antique decorations weren't enough of a bad omen, turning to find her cousin standing in the doorway surely was. Even with a tea tray in hand, she tried to turn her nose up at Alex and pretend she wasn't acting as Kaleigh's personal assistant.

"Hello, Rosalind."

"Alexandria," Rosalind said, managing to make her name sound like something unpleasant. "To what do we owe the pleasure of your company?"

Alex had to give it to her for trying. Her cousin had minimized the spite in her voice quite well, but the quick glance at Alex's wrist gave her away. Alex hadn't imagined the flash of jealousy. She was all too familiar with it, having been victim of it for most of her childhood.

"That is between me and Kaleigh, Cousin," Alex responded coldly. It wasn't Rosalind's place to question her, and Rosalind knew it. Alex nodded her head towards the tray her cousin was carrying. "And since it seems to be tea time, I take it she is available to see me."

"Wait here. I'll see if her schedule permits an unexpected visitor." Rosalind sneered at her.

"Really Rosalind? We're going to play this game? What did you do this time to earn this penance? We both know GranMere requires no maid...and I'm pretty sure you aren't the volunteer type."

Her eyes flashed in contempt a moment before she opened her mouth to speak, but another's command cut off whatever she had to say. She remade her face into something a bit more contrite, at least for her, and mumbled under her breath. "It's my honor to serve, Alexandria."

Alex snorted. Rosalind acting meek was about as honest as a hornet pretending to be a butterfly. They would always sting, no matter how pretty they dressed themselves up.

"Let her in, Rosalind, and fetch another cup. Alexandria will be joining me for tea."

Alex grinned at her cousin. Rosalind turned on her heel and marched back into the kitchen, leaving Alex to find her own way into the back of the house.

"Alexandria! It has been too long." Kaleigh stood and embraced her.

"GranMere." Alex stooped down to embrace the older woman, then kissed her, once on each cheek as was her due. The GranMere was a small, non-descript woman, much like Rosalind and the rest. White streaked auburn hair flowed loose across her shoulders, framing a round face. High angular cheekbones, much like Alex's, accentuated chocolate brown eyes that were deceptively gentle. Alex's aunt carried an air of command that belied her diminutive stature, but it still saddened Alex. For a race that spawned legends of Amazon warrior and Valkyrie alike, the need to hide in plain sight had somehow lessened them over the centuries. Alex was a throwback, and her height and coloring had singled her out as a child. No one else in her tribe could claim her jet-black hair or bright-blue eyes.

When Alex attempted to kneel, Kaleigh stopped her with a touch on her shoulder.

"None of that, Alexandria. We needn't be so formal."

"As you wish, Aunt," Alex said.

"Sit down, please. Tell me what brings you back after all this time. Are you doing well?" Kaleigh sat down on the low couch nearest the fireplace and patted the cushion next to her.

Rosalind returned with the tray and set it on the coffee table in front of them. Alex noticed that she had added not one, but two additional cups. *How bold.*

"I'm doing well," Alex said, glancing up at Rosalind. Her expression turned grim. Whatever smile she had for her aunt melted away at the intrusive presence. There was no way she was going to speak in front of her cousin.

Kaleigh looked at her curiously, then leaned forward and picked up the third cup, handing it to Rosalind without taking her eyes off Alex.

"Rosalind, please take this back to the kitchen. Alex can serve me. I won't be needing you for the rest of the afternoon so you can go home." Alex winced. She knew what it felt like to be so summarily dismissed. If it was anyone other than her cousin, she might have been more sympathetic, but Rosalind had been behind too many miserable schemes over the years.

"Things are still bad between you two, I take it?" Kaleigh asked after taking a sip of her tea.

"She doesn't think I deserve this," Alex said, displaying the knot work circling her forearm. There was no hiding the animosity between the two cousins, not when it seemed to grow and fester with each year that passed. "Or the responsibility that comes with it."

"What do you expect? You live apart from us and rarely come home to honor the moon," Kaleigh said, her face the very picture of serenity.

Alex tensed up, threatening the fragile china in her hand. Carefully putting her cup down, Alex took a deep breath and tried to avoid the inevitable argument.

"GranMere, I am not here to re-hash old arguments. I am my mother's daughter. I cannot be anyone else but whom I am meant to be. Rosalind..." Alex stopped and took another deep breath. "Rosalind is a bully who wants what she cannot have. When I came here as a child, she made sure that I knew about my mother's shame—and she did it gleefully. You and I both know she thinks she should be the one sitting here with you, not me."

"She may, but we do not choose who wears the mark of Epona. For some reason, the Goddess chose you and that cannot be changed. Rosalind will learn to deal with it in time." Kaleigh gave Alex a sly look over the rim of her cup. "It would be easier, though, if you would come back."

"I cannot. There are things you ask of me that I cannot give. As for Rosalind, how much more time does she need?" Alex asked, then made an abrupt chopping motion with her hand. "But that is not what I am here for. I have met someone, Aunt...and I am not sure what to do."

"I am confused, I thought you said you couldn't..."

Alex interrupted Kaleigh. It was rude, but she didn't want her aunt's desire for an heir to become the focus of their conversation.

"A woman, Aunt—I met a woman. But unlike any woman, or human for that matter, that I have ever met. She changed me." Before Kaleigh could object to her announcement, Alex started to explain. As she spoke, the initial dismay in her aunt's eyes turned to concern. By the time Alex finished, her aunt looked troubled, her tea gone cold and long forgotten.

"Are you sure, Alexandria?" she asked, setting her cup down on the coffee table. Kaleigh's hands shook, making the porcelain cup skitter and scratch across the saucer. Alex looked away, giving her aunt time to recover from her momentary weakness.

"I am, GranMere," Alex said, reverting to the more formal address to cover her unease.

"We have been diminished since the veil closed, Alexandria. What you are telling me, I cannot even begin to fathom. You are describing abilities that have been lost to us since we chose to stay here." Kaleigh held up her hand. "May I?"

"Of course!" Alex said, surprised she asked permission.

Kaleigh leaned forward and grasped Alex's left wrist in an iron grip. The tattoo flared to life, making Alex's hand tingle painfully. A blue glow escaped from the gaps between her aunt's fingers, illuminating the older woman's veins across the back of her hand.

"Great Goddess," Kaleigh whispered, looking up at Alex in wonder.

The tingling sensation increased, then physically arched between them much like the arc of her welding tool. A sharp pain snapped across Alex's wrist. Kaleigh gasped and snatched her hand away a second before Alex did. Rubbing her hands together, Kaleigh stood and looked out the large picture window that showcased an immaculate wall garden.

"Who is this woman?"

"Her name is Rohanna MacLeod."

"MacLeod? As in THE MacLeod's?" Kaleigh asked sharply.

"Yes, why?"

"Nothing really. Just an old saying—If you dream of a horse you were sure to meet a MacLeod." Kaleigh turned back to face Alex. "I do find it ironic that the heart of one of the biggest names in the horse industry has been captured by a Mere. Does she know what you are?"

"If you are asking if I told her, no."

"But, I did not ask if you told her. I asked if she knows."

"To tell you the truth, GranMere, I do not know. Her mind, it refuses to see things as they are, as they should be. Her grasp on reality is questionable. Whatever she has trouble understanding, she ascribes it to a dream, or a nightmare," Alex said, furrowing her brow. "I told you about her cousin and her grandmother. How can she be so ignorant of her heritage when they are not? It is like she has blocked that part of herself away and refuses to acknowledge it."

"That is disturbing. I have to say that without knowing more about her, I am hesitant to expose ourselves to her. If she is as powerful as you say, how do I know she is not a threat to the life we have built here?"

Alex laughed, sounding loud and harsh in the otherwise quiet room. "GranMere. Aunt, I cannot leave this be. If we have any chance at all of being elevated back to who we used to be, what we should be, how can I ignore this?"

"Alexandria, the veil was closed for a reason, and we chose to stay here for the same reason. That this woman holds so much Fae magic?" Kaleigh paused and shook her head. "There shouldn't be that much magic in this world, Alexandria. What if she has the power to open the veil?"

The sobering thought turned into an unsettled silence. Even the air felt heavy inside the stillness. Alex hadn't been alive when the worlds were still one, but she had grown up hearing the stories. As one of the lesser Fae, the Mere tribes had not been treated kindly. The Greater Fae held most of the magic, and they used it without consequence or conscience. When given the choice, it had not been a hard decision for the Meres to choose to stay and deal with humanity, not when the alternative was servitude.

Alex bowed her head. "I understand. But I cannot just walk away from this, Aunt. As you so astutely noted, this is a matter of the heart. Not just hers, but mine as well."

"What? I can understand a human falling in love with you. It is a part of who we are, but you? Alexandria, you know how I feel about forming attachments to humans."

Alex felt her aunt's disapproval blow through her like a cold wind. As she had expected, the conversation had circled around to a place where she would not bend. Alex held up her hand to forestall the familiar lecture. "You and I will always disagree on this. I understand why you believe as you do, but I will not give up Rohanna for your rules. Dangerous or not, I did my duty to you by coming here. I only ask your leave to tell her about me. I will not mention that there are others, but she will find out what I am, sooner or later."

"It is cruel, Alexandria...to fall in love with a human, to watch them wither and die while you live on. You complain about my rules, but I have had centuries of experience dealing with this. We lost too many during the burning times. A wife who does not age was easily called a witch, and without the protection of places like this, a lone Mere was easy game."

"Then I must be cruel, Aunt, because I cannot see myself giving up Rohanna so easily."

"I can see that." Kaleigh's expression turned inward, processing everything she had heard before speaking again. "You say that her grasp on reality is weak?"

"Yes, her dreams and the real world have become tangled like a wild vine. I'm not sure how or why, only that she experiences her dreams to a depth I have never seen before."

"This is good, then." Kaleigh closed her eyes for a moment, then gazed down at Alex. This time, when she spoke, it was as her sworn leader. "As long as she believes what she saw was just another strange dream, she won't seek answers. See to it that this is how it stays until I can think upon this some more. She's awakened your abilities. It shouldn't be hard to manipulate her dreams, if it comes down to it."

"I won't hurt her GranMere. I won't bring terror down on her simply to hide myself."

Kaleigh shook her head and looked at her as if she was an errant child. "Tsk, Alex. You have a knack for bringing trouble with you. Let us hope this strange attraction you have for this woman is not the death of us all."

"That's not my intent, GranMere."

"I know, child." Kaleigh sighed. "I will think on this and let you know what I decide. That's all I can give you."

"It's enough for now." Alex kissed her aunt goodbye.

CHAPTER TWENTY-EIGHT

Alex awoke to the sound of the phone ringing. The high-pitched trill managed to abuse her ears all the way from the kitchen. Normally she would ignore such an early wake up call, but she forced herself up and out of the warm nest. Rohanna said she might call and check in this morning after she made it to this weekend's show.

Groaning in protest, she struggled to untangle her long legs from sheets that seemed intent on snatching her feet out from under her and rolled out of a comfortably warm bed that still carried Rohanna's scent.

"Let go!" Alex cursed, hopping awkwardly on one foot toward the practically antique wall phone after stubbing her toe. *I have really got to get a new phone,* she thought, even though she hated having the thing at all. Until she met Rohanna, its only job had been to connect her to her customers and buyers. If she had neither, the phone would have been gone long ago. If it weren't for Rohanna, she wouldn't be hobbling across the floor, eager to answer it.

Anticipating Rohanna on the other end, she answered the phone more enthusiastically than usual, despite having to massage her throbbing toe with one hand while balancing the phone with the other.

"Hello?"

"Yes, I am looking for Alex Strider," a haughty voice said. "The farrier?"

Damn, Alex thought, *a customer.* A delightfully colorful string of curses danced on the tip of her tongue. Only propriety held the well-justified words at bay, but they still begged for release. It was too damn early for customers to start calling. Even Alex understood that little bit of phone etiquette.

Now she had to deal with some rich old biddy who sounded like the world revolved around her and her own personal timetable. That was enough right there to turn Alex off. Already disinterested, she shoveled coffee grounds into the coffee maker, the phone tucked under her chin as she moved about the small kitchen.

"Yes, this is she," Alex said, automatically emphasizing the often-made correction. The long pause following her announcement wasn't entirely unexpected. It happened about half the time. She waited for the woman to make some excuse and hang-up, unwilling to believe a woman farrier could do the job. Alex really didn't care either way. She had enough farrier business to keep the place running. The funny thing was, she was stronger than most of the men out there doing the same work, if anyone ever paid enough attention to notice.

"I see," the woman said. "I have several dozen horses that need work. Can you do warmbloods?"

Her snide tone implied that it took some special skill to deal with the large animals, a skill she seemed to doubt Alex possessed. Still, a few dozen horses in one barn call was easy money, and the woman sounded like she had money.

Reassuring the woman that she could indeed handle her needs, she pulled out her schedule book and found an opening she could squeeze a new customer in.

"I can fit you in next Friday."

"That won't do. I need it done this weekend."

"I'm sorry, I don't work the weekends." Alex frowned at the phone. After making an exception, the woman was going to be difficult.

"I'll pay double your standard fee."

Holy Hells, that's a lot of money. Alex chewed on her pen cap and weighed her options. Deal with a woman she was already starting to dislike versus earning quick money. Doing this job would let her take more time off later in the month and buy some much needed supplies, besides, she could still finish her masterpiece on time even if she lost a day

"Fine. I'll rearrange my schedule. Can I get your name and address?" Alex asked, readying her pen to write the information down.

"Of course," the woman said. "I look forward to meeting you."

The standard polite response, spoken in a tone cold enough to frost the line between them, made the courtesy a lie. Reconsidering her decision, Alex was about to cancel the appointment when the woman spoke again.

"My name is Belinda MacLeod."

Alex clenched her teeth, now doubly sorry she had answered the phone.

Damn it, Ro's stepmother. I wonder what the hell she's up to. Rapidly scribbling down the address and directions on autopilot, she schooled her voice to absolute blandness. After hanging up the phone, Alex sat and drank her coffee while contemplating the possible motives behind Belinda's request.

Rohanna. Her thoughts immediately strayed back towards the enigmatic woman. The passion they had ignited their first night together had not lagged. In fact, it had become an almost addicting force that constantly distracted Alex, not enough to put her behind schedule on completing her sculptures, but enough to make her lose more sleep than she was used to.

Fortunately, there hadn't been a repeat of that first night's performance, not after speaking with her aunt and being given a few hints on how to keep her NightMere under control. The one time she had mentioned it, Rohanna acted as if she had already forgotten the strange experience, chalking it up to a weirdly vivid dream. Since Alex had not been given permission to speak freely in front of Rohanna, it was somewhat frustrating. It would be so much easier if Rohanna would just remember.

Since their first night together, Rohanna had found every excuse to slip away and be with Alex. They always met at Alex's place and she never stayed for long. The one time she had suggested dropping by Rohanna's farm, she had completely freaked out on her. It had almost spawned the one and only argument between them. It was only after she managed to calm Rohanna down that she had acquired even a minimal explanation. Rohanna told her that Belinda was something of a despot. She seemed scared to death that her stepmother would find out about the two of them and begged Alex not to call her on the farm's home line, and never to come visit her there.

And now this woman is calling me and asking me for farrier work, and on a day she knows Rohanna is gone and far away from home.

Alarms sounded a warning to beware of this supposedly coincidental call. She knew very little about Rohanna's stepmother.

Whatever hold Belinda had on Rohanna went deep into her psyche. Belinda was a complete blank in

Rohanna's dreams which, considering the obvious hatred she felt for the woman, shouldn't be possible. Usually, the object of such strong emotions made them sure visitors within the nightmare world. Not so with Rohanna's stepmother. Any images or conversations with Belinda were hidden from Alex's sight, existing only as unpassable walls inside Rohanna's mind that fractured her memories and forced her to skittle around corners and change direction to avoid them. Rohanna's mind was a maze, and everywhere Belinda existed inside it, there was a false hedge blocking her path.

Alex let her curiosity win out over her instincts. *Maybe Ro gave her my business card. There's no reason she should know about us, just that I was recommended as a farrier.* Alex snorted. There was no way Rohanna would have done that, not after making her promise never to visit unexpectedly. No, there was something odd about the request and the only way she'd find out what was afoot, was to go and see for herself.

The longer she thought about it, the more she wanted to meet this woman and find out if she was as horrible as Rohanna said she was. If the older MacLeod woman did have an ulterior motive for inviting her up to the farm, well then, Alex had a few surprises of her own.

Alex stretched her long limbs, enjoying the sensation of tight muscles straining against themselves, reveling in the strength of her bones as her back popped loudly. The adrenaline rush she felt coursing through her veins had nothing to do with the coffee she drank and barely tasted.

"Tomorrow is going to be an interesting day." Alex grinned, flashing white teeth at the empty room. "An interesting day, indeed."

CHAPTER TWENTY-NINE

Alex pulled her farrier rig up to the main barn at the MacLeod Farm. It hadn't been hard to miss; she had been able to spot the huge white building all the way from the main road. It sat proudly along the expanse of a flattened hilltop, dwarfing the older buildings hidden behind it that held the grace and solidity of age. If she had to choose between the chestnut beams and rough cut wood barns of the turn of the century buildings or the newer metal monstrosity, Alex would have gladly avoided the steel building. It had no soul.

The entire place was impressive. The grounds were extensive, dotted with well-bred horses grazing on green expanses that rolled along seemingly endless hills. In the distance, the forest was cut well back from the immaculate white fence that crisscrossed through the picture perfect pastures. The familiar smell of horse and thick green grass greeted Alex's sensitive nose like an old friend. The entire effect was pleasing to the eye and reminded her of her clan's own lands, except there was something wrong with the place she just couldn't put her finger on. She rubbed at her forearm through the leather bracer. It felt like her tattoo was shifting, the blue ink undulating like an angry serpent beneath her skin; a decidedly unpleasant itching sensation that made her want to rip off her bracer and scratch the hell out of her forearm.

It was a sunny day out, but Alex shivered despite the warmth. The closer she came to the main house, the more it felt like something was sucking the heat right out the native Earth. Alex was certain that without Rohanna's presence, even the sun would feel unwelcome here.

Scanning around for a tie out, Alex drove at a snail's pace until she found something or someone to tell her where she should set up. She didn't have long to wait. A lean older man emerged from the barn, waving at her to pull over near the large double doors she had just passed.

"Park'er here and get set up. I'll bring out the first horse when you're ready."

"Am I hot or cold-shoeing?"

"Neither. It's just the broodmares today. Trims only. You okay with that?" The man's gruff voice turned challenging, almost daring her to object.

Alex felt her temper flare, but pushed it down immediately. The amount of money she was going to make today was just cut in half. Arguing with him wouldn't help. He wasn't worth it and she had bigger things to worry about. She had yet to meet Rohanna's stepmother and find out if she was as fearsome as Rohanna made her out to be. Until she knew what was going on, she wouldn't ask, either. She needed to know how Mrs. MacLeod got her number and what she was up to.

"Fine. Just bring the first one out to me. I'll get set up while you're doing that."

For the next hour, Alex was busy doing her job, trimming several mares before she finally found the answers she was looking for.

The groom hadn't been any help. He remained rude and circumspect, content to deliver each mare in turn and disappear into the dark interior until she was ready for the next one. Her attempts to learn anything were met with a flat look and a well-timed sneer followed by a disgusting gob of tobacco hitting the worn dirt.

Alex turned to talking to the horses after the last time. He was getting way to accurate with that tobacco, and she didn't need to bring that smell home with her. *Disgusting habit.*

"Now this is an interesting turn of events."

Alex was working on a particularly fractious mare. The nervous horse kept wanting to dance away from her, and the small filly at her side was making the situation even worse. The mare would turn her head to check the filly's location, shifting her weight onto Alex whenever she got her into position to nip the last bit of overgrown heel.

With single-minded determination, she caught the bit of hoof between her nippers and squeezed, evening off what was left nicely. Grunting in appreciation, Alex stood up and untangled herself from the mare's leg, patting her rump affectionately before nodding to the groom to take her away. It was only then that she turned towards the voice.

"Excuse me?" Alex asked. A regal looking woman with flaming red hair stood several feet away, staring down her nose at Alex. For the first time in a very long while, Alex was confronted with a woman as tall as she was, a woman whose entire demeanor radiated superiority. It was pretty obvious that she thought she was better than Alex.

"Can I help you?" Alex asked casually, tossing her nippers and rasp into the back of her truck and grabbing a small towel to wipe her face and hands. If the expression on the other woman's face was any indication, she was done for the day. *This must be Rohanna's stepmother.*

"No, I don't think so, Alexandria Strider."

Alex bristled, not at the dismissive tone alone, but the fact the woman used her full name. She never told anybody her full first name, which meant someone had been doing some digging. Drawing herself up to her full height, she was oddly gratified by the fact that she was a fraction taller than the other woman.

"Your broodmares are done. If you will wait a moment, I'll get the bill ready for you." Alex turned away from Ro's stepmother. Whatever she was trying to accomplish, Alex wasn't about to rise to the bait. Then she spoke again and all of Alex's good intentions fell apart.

"I know who you are, Alexandria Strider." Belinda sniffed the air, then grimaced as if something foul had wafted by. "Merefolk. I didn't realize your people were here, but it does give me a great deal to think about."

"What are you talking about, Mrs. MacLeod?" Alex asked, carefully keeping her expression blank. *How does she know about my people?*

"Don't play coy with me, Alexandria. You and I both know that there is more to Rohanna than meets the eye." Belinda smiled evilly, her eyes narrowing to snake like slits. "And you, Alexandria? You surprise me. A Fae handling cold iron? How bold of you."

Belinda strolled a few steps closer to Alex. "Tell me, what drives you to handle the one thing that is anathema to your race?"

"What do you want, Belinda?" Alex asked coldly, purposely addressing her by her first name. Let her wonder how much Alex knew about her. "What does it matter to you that I work with iron?"

Belinda hadn't missed the subtle repositioning of her body, nor the tightening of Alex's fingers as if her muscle memory was seeking the comfort of a weapon in hand. For a Mere, she was an impressive specimen, one with a warrior's heart and instincts. She took another step just to watch Alex's reaction. The farrier shifted on the balls of her feet, angling her body to face Belinda while maintaining a defensive posture.

"Ahh, you mistake my question. I was not asking about your odd choice of vocations. I was asking about my stepdaughter."

"I don't understand." This time it was Alex who went on the offensive. Jaw clenched, hands balled into fists until the leather laces holding her bracer on creaked against the force behind them, she took one heated step towards the woman.

Belinda strode a few steps sideways, keeping Alex at a distance. *Like fighters circling each other in a ring, taking each other's measure.*

"Haven't you wondered about her? I know you aren't immune to her abilities. Do you think it was by accident that she was drawn to you? Or you to her? It is actually quite ironic, you know. I never considered she might be attracted to another woman. I wouldn't have wasted all that time and energy discouraging her from dating all these years."

"Explain yourself." Alex spoke gruffly. "I don't care for games." Her right hand convulsed, her fingers grasping at the air, not quite making a fist. That she wished for her heavy hammer right now was a warning she couldn't ignore. This woman was dangerous.

"Rohanna is a Gatekeeper. Do you know what that is?"

"No," Alex growled.

"She has the power to open the stone circles. To let the Magic of Faerie back into the world, along with every Greater Fae who ever laid claim to you."

"You're lying," Alex grated out. *How could this be?* Every fiber in her being was screaming at her, telling her that Belinda was not to be trusted.

"Am I? Are you willing to bet the safety of your tribe on it? I know why your people came here, Alexandria. I do not think that your tribe would appreciate you helping the one woman who could bring magic back into this world. I think you can guess what the consequences of that might be."

Is this what GranMere is afraid of? She would never allow her people to go back to the way it was. No Mere would be forced to participate in the Great Hunt against her will, nor would they allow themselves to be used as mounts, a mark of status by the Greater Fae to have such a steed under their control. The amount of tears her people had shed during those years was enough to fuel a raging river. If Rohanna had the power to bring Magic back, she would indeed be considered an enemy of her tribe.

"What do you want?"

"I want you to leave Rohanna alone. I am sure this dalliance of yours has been exciting, but it is dangerous."

"Dangerous? To you or to me, Belinda?"

"That's depends on you, my dear Mere, and on what you do after you leave here today."

"That sounds suspiciously like a threat, and I do not respond well to threats."

"Why are you making this so difficult?" Belinda sighed, shaking her head. "Fine, I will make it simple for you then. I know about you, and I know about your tribe. If you don't walk away from this, I can make sure that your tribe suffers for it. I will make sure that Rohanna suffers for it, and in turn, I will make sure that you suffer. Is that sufficient motivation?"

"You don't have the power to do that."

"Oh, don't I?" Belinda asked, her lips turning up just enough to show the sharp edges of her teeth. The feral grin made Alex step back a bit, not out of fear but to give her room to maneuver.

"From what Rohanna has told me, she inherits the farm in a few months. What can you do to her?"

"I can do plenty. She may get this farm, but she can do nothing if I sell all the stock before she inherits it. She will get this place, but it will be an empty shell. Think. Everything she has worked so hard for all these years, gone."

"Somehow, Belinda, I don't think that is the way you play," Alex gritted out between clenched teeth.

It was obvious Belinda was used to getting her own way and was amused at someone trying to say otherwise. She laughed in that throaty, over the top way someone did when entertaining the idea of doing something incredibly wicked before leveling those strange grey eyes at her, her mood shifting to something deadly and dark in an instant. Alex felt her tattoo flare in response to that look and struggled hard to keep that blue flame from travelling. She would not, could not, reveal herself that way.

"Now that, Alexandria, is the smartest thing you have said so far." Belinda's voice dripped with sarcasm. "No, that is not the way I play. The stakes here are so much bigger, and I do not need you interfering with my plans."

Electricity crackled in the air between them, generating a breeze that whipped through Belinda's red hair and tangled itself around Alex's heavy braid. The smell of ozone laced with sulfur tainted the air. Alex's nose wrinkled in distaste at the foul odor of dark magic.

"Witch woman," Alex growled, practically baring her teeth at Belinda. Not just any type of witch, but the worst type, one who had embraced the darkest forms of magic.

"What do you want with Rohanna?" Alex demanded, concern for her new lover skyrocketing after Belinda's display of power. The small hairs on her forearms stood at attention from the residual static. The air still smelled charged with electricity, hot and dry like the rare summer storm that refused to bring the rain with it.

"Oh, I won't make it that easy on you. All you need to know is that I will not tolerate any interference from you. Rohanna will perform the task I have groomed her for all these years," Belinda said, waving her hand dismissively. "I think it's time for you to leave now. Peter here will pay you what you are due. I suggest you think on what I have said. Good bye."

The groom appeared out of nowhere to stand just behind and to the side of Belinda. There was no hint of the surly man Alex had been dealing with all morning. He stank with fear and old tobacco, the sour odor permeated the air around her. Belinda turned on her heel and strolled away, leaving her alone with the obviously terrified man.

"How much do we owe you?"

Pulling out her receipt book, Alex quickly tallied up the bill. More pressing matters occupied her mind. The witch woman was an obvious threat to her people. What was going on between her and Rohanna was one thing, Belinda was another matter altogether.

Tossing her hoof stand into the back of the truck, she stuffed the money Peter held out to her into her jeans pocket without bothering to count it and jumped in her truck to leave. The stakes had been raised, along with a number of new questions. What was a Gatekeeper and why did Belinda need her? More importantly, what had she been doing to her all these years?

The trip down the blacktop driveway seemed to take longer on the way out, adding to her agitation. Her back tires squealed and tossed gravel behind her when she turned onto the state road and could finally hit the gas pedal as hard as she wanted.

Alex couldn't get home fast enough. She needed to get in touch with her aunt and tell her about Belinda. Kaleigh had been afraid of the magic Rohanna carried. Even untrained and ignorant of her talents, she had considered Rohanna dangerous. What would she do once she knew someone had been grooming those talents?

CHAPTER THIRTY

Rohanna was in a terrible mood.

A brief, sudden summer storm had come in earlier, catching her and Galileo out in a torrential downpour. The rain had soaked both of them through and through, making for a miserable ride that ended in disappointment. The arena had quickly gone to mud, becoming too slick and dangerous to ride past a sedate walk, and the judges had called it a day and cancelled the rest of the show. "A long drive and all that preparation and not a single ribbon to bring home, what a waste of a day," she grumbled, untacking Galileo and hitting the road early.

Rohanna crawled into the truck cab and waited for the windshield wipers to clear the dust borne mud smeared across the windshield before pulling out. Her hands shook and her stomach did a nauseating flip-flop when the trailer slipped in the mud behind her. The tires finally found gravel to dig into and soon after that, she was back on the blacktop.

The road was solid, but it didn't make her feel any better. She hated driving in bad weather, especially with a horse and trailer, but if it was going to rain while she drove, she'd rather do it during the day. Rain and nighttime driving brought back too many painful memories.

She finally made it home, happy to have made it in one piece, only to discover that she didn't want to be there.

"Oh, you have got to be kidding." Rohanna squinted up at the sky. The minute she led Galileo towards the barn the rain stopped and the sun broke through the clouds. She shook her head. The show should have kept her away from the farm all weekend. She really wasn't ready to deal with Belinda, and while she could always find a place somewhere and sleep in the horse trailer, another option came to mind. A better option. Ro grinned at the bay gelding. "What do you think, Galileo? Should I go see Alex?"

"Alex?" A youngish looking woman interrupted her aggravated muttering. "The farrier?"

"What? Yes, why?" Rohanna asked sharply, taken aback by the question. She hadn't seen the girl before today. *Probably one of the locals picking up a few hours.* She had a pitchfork in hand and a wheelbarrow full of manure so she'd gotten stuck with the crap job—literally.

"She was here earlier, trimming the broodmares."

"Was my stepmother around?" Rohanna asked, biting her lower lip nervously. What was Alex doing here with Belinda?

"Mrs. MacLeod? Yes. They were talking and then it looked like they had a bit of an argument and then she left without finishing all the broodmares. Mrs. MacLeod looked pleased with herself, which don't make much sense. She did pay her for her work though."

The young woman was trying to be honest, but Ro could tell she was nervous. One of the senior grooms frowned at her and she went silent.

"Thank you, uh..." Ro held out her hand. She didn't know the girls name.

"Darla, Miss Rohanna...I live right down the way on Sycamore Lane."

Rohanna nodded. She knew exactly where that was. A patch of antique single-wide's set on a hillside off of a dirt road, there was only one way in and it was a dead end place to live in more than one way. The families there were dirt poor, and this job was probably a Godsend.

"Thank you, Darla, I appreciate the help."

Galileo got the quickest wash down and squeegeeing of his life. The poor thing looked slightly shell-shocked after the rough rub down that removed the majority of wet off his dark hide. Between the rain and the wash rack she was still soaked. She locked her gear up and parked the rig. There was no reason to go through all the hassle of disconnecting the diesel when she had her baby back.

Ro headed for the old wooden barn. Deemed unsafe for live animals, it worked just dandy as a trouble free parking garage. Her dad's old beat up green and gold truck resided there. It had been given a facelift after college, thanks to all those show winnings she kept squirreling away. It was now a shiny new classic truck, replete with fresh shocks, new seats, and a glossy new paint job.

She couldn't risk going up to the house and changing, not if Belinda was there. Shivering against the cold and wet, Rohanna grabbed an old flannel shirt from the back seat and did a quick change before digging the keys out of their hidey-hole. The engine roared to life, and she turned up the radio the minute she hit the driveway…loud enough to give her an excuse if anyone tried to call out to her.

At least the top half of me is warm and dry, she thought, turning the heat up full blast. Her jeans felt gross, clinging to her legs like wet leaves and cold as hell— hopefully they would dry out soon.

The green truck ate up the miles between her and Alex. The road was wet and there was a lot of water in the ditches, but not too much on the street itself. That was the good. The bad was the glare from the sun setting ahead of her, coupled with a dense fog rolling in from the surrounding hills.

Rohanna's pulse jumped erratically when a small group of deer suddenly materialized out of nowhere.

I have to slow down, she thought, gripping the steering wheel tight enough to turn her knuckles white. The deer had practically leapt over the hood of her truck, unseen and unheard until they showed up in her headlights. Even as slow as she was going, she almost missed the turn off to Alex's house. The fog had thickened with each mile until she could barely make out the telephone poles lining the side of the road. Trees loomed out of the grey mist for brief seconds before disappearing, wet green and browns fading to mere shadows of themselves before being replaced by the next set of silent sentinels.

She was so intent on finding the turn off she didn't notice Alex's truck barreling towards her.

The sound of gravel flying accentuated the squelch of pained brakes as she brought her truck to an abrupt stop just shy of the driveway. Alex jumped out of her truck and motioned for Rohanna to pull off the road, then walked up to her window and leaned in.

"Ro, what are you doing here?"

Alex sounded angry. It was not the greeting Rohanna had expected.

"I heard you were at the farm. I wanted to see you, make sure everything was okay," she mumbled, now wondering if she had made a mistake. "Geez, that made me sound like a stalker, didn't it?"

"No, not at all." Alex gazed at her and then turned her face away, watching the road behind Rohanna's truck. Even softened by the fog, Alex's face was all angles, her cheekbones casting shadows that made her face look drawn. The muscles along her jawline tensed and jumped, making the shadows dance. Her tongue snaked out and wet her upper lip a second before troubling the tender flesh with her teeth. Alex looked distracted, her eyebrows drawing together for a second before nodding her head. Whatever silent conversation she was having with herself must have concluded. She closed her eyes and took a deep breath before turning back to Rohanna. Her expression remained guarded but at least she wasn't looking at Rohanna as if she was miles away.

"Ro, I have something I need to do. I can't explain right now, but I'll be back later. I...we need to talk. Will you wait for me here? The forge room isn't locked. You can go through my workshop to get into the house."

Alex's request both disturbed and reassured Rohanna. We need to talk rarely meant something good. She felt her heart drop to the floor. *What happened today?*

"Does this have anything to do with meeting Belinda today? I heard you two argued."

Alex's face darkened, but she didn't answer her question. She reached in and took Rohanna's hand, lowering her head to press a quick kiss across her palm. Ro's pulse jumped, quickening at the brush of lips so near her wrist.

"Wait for me, Ro. You have my heart, do not worry about that." Alex's words were so unexpected and spoken so earnestly that it sent Rohanna's mind reeling. She knew she had fallen for Alex weeks ago. Since their first night together she could barely think of anything else, but until this moment, she hadn't been as sure of Alex's feelings.

"Okay," Rohanna rasped. Her lungs burned from holding her breath for too long.

"Good. I won't be long. I promise." Rohanna watched Alex climb back into her truck and pull away, leaving her alone with a growing sense of frustration as her sole companion. She had so many unanswered questions, and now she was supposed to wait.

The idea was maddening.

She could still see Alex's running lights as they receded into the distance. The pale red glow was the only color in an otherwise grey world. In a few seconds they would be gone, swallowed whole by a world gone eerily silent except for the rumbling growl of her truck's engine. The normally passive grumble spoke to her, daring her to rev the motor into a deeper roar and enter the chase.

"Screw it," Rohanna said. Throwing the truck into drive, she took off after Alex.

The feeling of being left in the dark too many times drove her to follow her lover. She wasn't willing to just sit and wait while things happened around her anymore. Determination found its way into her heart. She could no longer be a passive observer in her own life. Alex had woken something inside her, a hunger for life and passion that had been kept chained and bound for far too long. Straightening up in her seat, Rohanna focused resolute eyes on the road ahead of her. Belinda would not interfere with what she had with Alex—not now or ever. The vow sunk in, unspoken, but still incredibly powerful.

Rohanna trembled, feeling something that had been coiled and silent inside of her begin to unravel and stretch towards some invisible light. Why it felt like she had done something forbidden, like opening a metaphorical Pandora's Box, she had no idea. All she knew was that she was chasing the future in a pair of bright blue eyes and it felt wonderful.

CHAPTER THIRTY-ONE

Night had fallen rapidly. By the time Alex pulled her truck off the main road and onto a poorly marked side road, a full moon had replaced the setting sun with its own haloed glow and Rohanna was starting to rethink her plan. Or, more accurately, her lack of one. How was she supposed to explain to Alex what she was doing, following her like this?

Her internal war didn't stop her feet from moving forward. Like many people doing something foolish and emotional, Ro didn't let indecision keep her from doing something even she had to admit was stupid. Her stalker joke didn't seem as funny now, not when she was creeping about in the dark out in the middle of nowhere, following Alex's trail by the thin light of the moon.

Alex hadn't noticed Rohanna following behind her. She was busy watching the moonlit path in front of her, stepping carefully across the uneven ground as she mounted a rounded hillside. Still, the woman was moving faster than Ro thought possible. Most of the time she was travelling blindly, trusting the path Alex had gone to not trip her up.

She almost missed when Alex's silhouette crested a small hill ahead of her and disappeared. Ro scrambled after her, descending into dark shadows that fought with the fog that had continued to thicken and was now earnestly seeking out the dips and hollows around her.

Ro's heart pounded in her ears and her lungs burned from the effort of climbing.

After watching Alex ascend, she made sure she stayed low once she reached the ridge. Crouching down on all fours, she peeked over the edge and gasped aloud. The slight noise seemed to travel on the fog and she clapped her hand over her mouth before someone heard her, then stared wide eyed, at the strange scene below her.

A large open glen where there shouldn't be one stretched out as far as she could see. There were old-fashioned torches placed at regular intervals where the forest butted against the glen, and a pavilion perched next to a stream that bubbled along the bottom of the crescent-shaped field. The well-manicured, almost park-like setting was a surprise, considering how far out into the countryside they had driven.

Rohanna looked up at the sky, frustrated that she couldn't see more. The full moon would have made it easier to see if the sky was clear, but the heavy grey fog rolling in softened and blurred everything around her, making her vision seem cloudy and unfocused. Eyes straining to see, she slipped over the ridge and kept moving forward. Staying on the trail had its own dangers. The dirt was loose and rocky and she risked giving herself away with every step, but she couldn't help herself. If she could just get close enough, she could discover what Alex was up to.

She almost jumped out of her skin when she heard voices, then realized that Alex was talking to someone else. She whipped her head around, expecting to find Alex right on top of her, then sagged in relief. A trick of the fog made it sound as though they were standing right next to her. Then a twig snapped near her and she did jump. Resisting the urge to run like hell, she ducked behind a large half-fallen tree, praying that the pounding of her heart only sounded that loud inside her head.

A woman stepped out of the fog and greeted Alex with the familiarity of an old friend. When she spoke, Ro relaxed perceptibly. This was the other voice she had heard moments ago. She risked moving just enough to get a better view, finding a thin spot in the branches to peek through unobserved.

"Alexandria. It is so good to see you. It has been too long since you have joined us!" Grasping the woman's outstretched hands, Alex leaned in and kissed first one cheek then the other.

"Thank you, it is good to see you as well," Alex said. "Is GranMere here?"

"She is. But Alexandria, what brings you here on this night?"

"It's a long story, Elphie, and not one I am allowed to speak freely about," Alex said.

"I've heard rumors," Elphie lowered her voice.

"What rumors?" Alex's voice sharpened enough Ro expected to see the fog between them sliced clean through.

"That you went to see the GranMere."

"Aye, that much is true."

"Might I ask why? After all this time?"

"I've met someone important to me."

Rohanna wanted to growl in frustration. She felt like a child, hiding in the woods and listening to conversation she desperately wanted to hear, and now she was completely lost. *GranMere? What and who were they talking about?*

Rohanna felt like she was listening to a conversation from a different time and place. Even Alex's voice sounded odd; her cadence and demeanor completely different from the teasing, playful manner Ro was familiar with. Even Alex's accent had changed. Rohanna shook her head, trying to remember. Had Alex ever told her where she was from? Now that she thought about it, Alex didn't sound like a local.

"No, she isn't." Alex spoke again and Rohanna cursed under her breath. She hadn't heard the question.

"A woman?" Elphie asked. "I take it Kaleigh was not pleased."

Alex nodded. "You know how she is, Elphie. She should know by now that I won't bow to her demands."

"She must be something, then, for you to come back." The woman's curiosity was patently obvious, even from where Ro was hidden.

"Ah, you are too smart for your own good." Alex shook her head, a ghost of a smile touching her lips before disappearing. "And yes, she is something else, that is for sure."

Ro felt the small hairs on her arms raise in response to Alex's comment. *What did she mean?* There was something odd about how she responded, a secret code that Ro wasn't privy too. *Christ, why did I follow her? This is getting stranger by the minute.*

"And you cannot tell me a thing, can you?"

"No. Not until I speak to GranMere again."

After staring at each other for a long moment, Elphie shrugged her shoulders and took a deep breath. Alex hadn't budged on giving up more information, and it was doubtful she would. Without warning, Elphie lunged forward and squeezed Alex unabashedly, then stepped back. She gripped Alex's upper arms and looked up at her. "Alexandria, I will always love you. No matter what, we are sisters. Do you understand?"

"I love you too, little sister." Alex returned the embrace, then turned her attention towards the canvas pavilion. "Where is she?"

"She has already honored the moon. You will find her in the glen with the other Meres." Elphie turned and started up the path. "I'll come with you as far as I can, but my job tonight is to stand watch."

"You don't have to, Elphie. I know the way."

"This is true, but still, I will attend you as far as the tents." Elphie paused. "You need to shed your human trappings before approaching her. Tonight she feels the need to honor the old ways."

"Where are they?" Rohanna whispered, trying to control her growing frustration. She could no longer see Alex or the woman she was talking to. Desperately scanning ahead of her, she sighed in relief when a thin spot in the fog left a clear window for her to see through. She caught a brief impression of movement that coalesced into a human body. A triumphant surge of adrenaline pumped through Ro's veins; she had found her. The fog swirled around Alex, then slithered away like an undulating mass of smoky grey satin. Its movement reminded Ro of the flourish at the end of a magic trick, and like the magician's dramatic reveal, it ended in a surprised gasp.

Alex was completely nude, her body bathed in pale moonlight.

Ro's breath caught in her throat, and with good reason. Alex was breathtaking to watch. Freed from the usual braid, her hair hung loose in a long flowing mane that swayed across her back in time with her strides, accentuating her slim waist and ending just below her firm buttocks. Unable to look away, Rohanna watched in awe as Alex's long legs took the steep slope in great strides, the muscles in her thighs and calves contracting rhythmically beneath flawless skin. Then the fog closed in around her again, releasing Rohanna from the hypnotic scene. Rohanna sagged against the fallen tree, trying to make sense of it all.

Was this her secret?

Rohanna had stumbled on something she had no understanding of. The other women obviously knew her, and Alex had called her "sister" so she must be a part of Alex's family. But who was this GranMere, and why was Alex naked? She had to know and to do that, Rohanna had to find a way up the hillside without being discovered.

Rohanna finally managed to make it to the top of the hill, but not without suffering for it. She had bruises and scratches on her arms from picking her way along the dirt path, and she had fallen, twice. She found a good hiding place and caught sight of Alex, standing alone and proud in the middle of a large, almost flat, field. Surprisingly, the fog hadn't found its way there. The full moon was high above the horizon now, casting a cold white light across the entire field. Alex's shadow stretched out behind her, inky black and as sharp as the gnomon on a sundial. Other than the sound of the creek below them running across its rocky path, the normal sounds of the night were eerily absent. There should have been frogs speaking to each other along the creek bed, the rustle of night creatures hunting for a meal. Even the soft hoot of a lone owl would have been welcome, yet there was nothing...except for Alex.

Alex stood in the middle of all that silence, unmoving and silent. Rohanna found herself holding her breath. They were both waiting, but Ro had no idea what it was for, only that the night felt pregnant with strange energy. Hypersensitive to every sound and smell, she swore she could feel the damp air moving across her skin, plucking at the hairs at the nape of her neck in a silent rhythm she felt she should recognize.

Several minutes passed by and still Alex stood there as solid and straight as a lodge pole. Ro wasn't faring as well. Damp and cold and already on sensory overload, she had to pee badly but couldn't leave her hiding place without revealing herself.

"Screw this," Ro finally muttered, rising up on her knees. She had screwed up, following Alex like this...and it was time to fess up and take the hit. *Hopefully Alex will forgive me for this stupid stunt,* she thought. Before she was able to scramble to her feet, an impressively massive horse thundered out of the woods across from Alex. Its steel grey coat gleamed with silver highlights as it tore great chunks of grass out of the earth with every hoof strike. Rohanna's heart reeled. The horse was charging straight for Alex!

Rohanna lurched forward, her hand stretched out in front of her as if she could physically pluck her lover out of the path of danger.

Before she could shout a warning, the horse slid to a stop in front of Alex. Blowing hard, it pawed at the ground and tossed its head. Rohanna watched as incredibly, unbelievably, Alex knelt before the horse. It was all so surreal. Rohanna rubbed at her eyes, unable to reconcile what she was seeing with her concept of reality. When she looked again, the scene only got stranger.

Alex appeared to be addressing the grey horse, speaking too low for Rohanna to hear. With every minute that ticked by, the horse became increasingly agitated, stomping and snorting frequently.

"What are you doing, Alex?" Rohanna whispered, worriedly gnawing her lower lip. Alex was kneeling so close to those dancing hooves, there was no way she could move quick enough to avoid injury if the horse reared up or struck out at her. As the strange meeting progressed, Rohanna became hyperaware of more minute details. Alex's body language didn't register fear. Rohanna shook her head. Fear made sense. That close to danger anyone would be afraid. *They would also be trying to get the hell out of the way.* Rohanna grimaced, then narrowed her eyes when another explanation surfaced. Alex's behavior made zero sense to her. *Nightmare? Is this all a dream, and I'm really back at Alex's, asleep on the couch while I wait for her to return from her errand?*

She pinched her arm, hoping the pain would waken her, and earned nothing but a bruise for her troubles. "Stupid me, it never works, yet I try it every time," she muttered, returning her attention to the strange scenario in front of her. If she couldn't wake up, she could at least pay attention and try to decipher the meaning behind the dream.

Despite her kneeling position, Alex's tall, sleekly muscled body refused to remake itself into passive submission, every line screamed defiance. Secretly relieved, Rohanna realized that some strange battle of wills was taking place. She had only seen Alex in control, strong and assured of herself. To see Alex bow to another was disturbing enough. To witness her acknowledging their superiority? That would have been devastating.

An inhuman scream broke the silence and echoed through Rohanna's skull. She had heard this sound before, in another dream. Rubbing her forehead, she tried to pull the memory of when out of her head without success.

All of a sudden, the horse wheeled around on its hind legs and took off, running full out for the edge of the forest and rapidly disappearing. Alex stood, then bent over to brush off her knees. She didn't see the other horses emerging from the nearby woods, not until dozens surrounded her, every one of them with hides as black as night. They galloped around her, circling closer until Rohanna was sure one of them would run her over...and not a single one made a sound.

One mare broke away from the band and headed straight for her. It reared up, teeth bared and ears pinned back, and lunged out at Alex aggressively. Alex didn't even flinch. The mare spun and kicked out, her rear hoof making contact with Alex's body. Instead of scrambling to get up, Alex fell to all fours, her own scream of pain ending abruptly.

Rohanna watched in horror, sure that the woman she loved was being trampled beneath the milling bodies. Several of the horses struck out at each other, white teeth flashing savagely in their attempt to bloody the other. Rohanna clenched her fists, her body vibrating with the need to do something. There was no way she could make it through to Alex without being trampled herself, but she couldn't just sit there and watch, either.

"Hey! Hey, whoa there!" she yelled as loudly as she could, jumping up from her hiding place and running straight for the small band of horses. Legs pumping, she waved her arms, trying to get their attention. It was incredibly stupid and dangerous, but it was the only thing she could think to do.

As soon as it began, the violent attack ended. As if responding to an unspoken call, the entire herd took off for the hills. The ground shook violently beneath their hooves as they thundered past Rohanna. Her heart in her throat, she watched them pass by at breakneck speed until they disappeared down the steep hillside.

Turning back to the now empty field, afraid to her core of what she would find, she ran as fast as she could to the last place she had seen Alex. Terrified, her fear pushed her onward as she scuttled crablike towards the still form lying on the ground ahead of her.

She expected to find Alex's battered and bruised body. Instead, another black mare lay there. She was breathing heavily and various cuts and bites marred her coat. Bright red blood glistened in the pale moonlight as it ran down her hide in muddy rivulets. Then, the mare opened her eyes and looked at her. Blue on blue and glowing softly, with no pupil set inside that strange light, Rohanna found herself looking back at the same mare she had dreamed about weeks ago.

"A horse that wasn't a horse. She took me to the stone circle riding a road made of stars, and then...and then, she was something else."

Rohanna's mind rebelled and then blanked completely. Her body went numb as shock set in, forcing her to sit down before she fell down.

Attempting to sooth the injured mare, she cradled its head and ran her hands across the silky fur of its neck. She scanned the meadow around her but couldn't find Alex anywhere. The ground around her was torn up, masking any signs of her escape. The woods were a mass of darkness. If Alex had run for the safety of the trees, she would never find her.

"Alex?" Rohanna called out. "Alex? Please, answer me if you can." Rohanna didn't know what to do next. She could feel her panic growing, threatening to escalate out of control.

"Alex, where are you?" Rohanna asked tearfully. Her voice cracked, reducing her plea to a whisper. The black mare nickered weakly, moving fitfully beneath her hand until Rohanna looked down.

"Alex," Rohanna whispered. Inside the bright blue light of impossibility, Rohanna reached out into the night and for the first time in her life, purposefully tore down the cobwebs guarding the hidden corners of her mind. A million points of pain pierced her skull, sending waves of agony across her temples and blinding her momentarily.

"A horse that wasn't a horse," she murmured, *and was also, somehow, Alex.*

Ro cradled her head and rocked back and forth, refusing to lose the knowledge...refusing to let it slip away like it had so many times before. She felt lightheaded. Her vision went fuzzy, then blackness rushed up to greet her as she collapsed to the ground next to the injured horse.

✳✳✳

Rohanna. Rohanna, wake up.

Rohanna groaned. Someone was calling her name. She pulled herself up on her elbows, every muscle and bone protesting the movement. Her body was stiff from lying on the cold, damp ground. She couldn't move her legs and she panicked before she realized that there was something lying across her hips. Blinking rapidly, she brought her eyes back into focus and directly onto Alex's pale face.

"Rohanna," Alex croaked, then licked her lips before trying again. "Ro, baby, what are you doing here?"

Rohanna swallowed nervously.

291

"I followed you. I couldn't help it, I'm sorry I...and then I thought this was all a dream, and now I know it isn't, and I'm so confused about everything."

"Shhh." Alex reached up and touched Rohanna's lips. "It's okay. We'll work this out together, but not now. Now, we need to get out of here. You shouldn't be here, it's not safe."

Alex tried to sit up, failing miserably to hide her pain and weakness. She finally gave up and fell back to the ground. The attempt made Alex's face go beyond pale.

"Here, let me." Rohanna scooted free then kneeled above Alex, noting the multiple bruises and cuts. A large cut above Alex's eye had bled profusely, leaving dark streaks running down her cheek and neck. Now it was closed shut by the mud caking most of Alex's body. A particularly nasty bruise ran across most of Alex's flank and ribs on her left side. Rohanna delicately explored the area with just her fingertips, eliciting a muffled groan.

"Um, Alex? I think you're really hurt. We need to get you to a hospital."

"No, no hospital." Alex wrapped her arm against her ribs for support and rolled to the side so she could get her legs beneath her. Every breath she took was a sharp knife slipping between her ribs and every attempt to move brought fresh tears to her eyes. Breathing fast and shallow and grinding her teeth hard enough to make her jaw crack, she made one huge effort to gain her feet. The muddy ground made it hard to balance and if wasn't for Rohanna's steadying hand, she would have fallen before taking a dozen steps.

"But, Alex, what if you're bleeding inside? I don't know what to do."

Alex closed her eyes. Silently, she had to agree with Rohanna. She was hurt badly. There was no doubt she had more than one broken rib. Her head throbbed and her entire body ached fiercely. She could feel the damp earth seeping into her joints, and she was staving off shivering like a lost puppy by will alone. She wanted nothing more than the heat of her forge to warm her and a soft bed to lie in while she healed.

Opening her eyes, she captured Rohanna's concerned gaze.

"No hospital, Rohanna. Please, just get me home."

CHAPTER THIRTY-TWO

Rohanna awkwardly dropped the phone back down on the table and resigned herself to the wait. She was too exhausted to do anything else. It would take her grandmother a little over an hour to get there.

She looked up without even bothering to try and raise her head. Rohanna just wanted to close her eyes and sleep but she could barely stand to blink, not when the inside of her eyelids felt like sandpaper. Trying to focus on the view from the picture window made her eyes hurt. The normally peaceful scene was a blur of colors and shapes, but that didn't matter, she couldn't look at her hands any longer. Her fingernails were filthy, a stomach churning combination of dried blood and dirt that stubbornly clung to her despite scrubbing them twice in the kitchen sink. Alex's blood.

Rohanna knew she was approaching total exhaustion. Her whole body trembled with a bone deep level of fatigue that made even the thought of moving from her chair a daunting idea.

Before she called her grandmother, she had managed to start a fresh pot of coffee. Now it called to her, enticing her to drag herself up from the kitchen table and over to the counter where the steaming pot awaited her.

After almost losing the entire carafe to barely working fingers, she managed to pour a cup, then stood at the counter and started ruining the coffee so she could drink it. A few healthy spoonsful of sugar, followed by too much creamer. She didn't stop until the coffee became unrecognizable, a creamy light toffee color that didn't just mask the bitter taste, it overwhelmed it into complete submission. Even complete exhaustion wasn't enough of an incentive to drink her coffee black. She inhaled deeply before drinking, then almost gagged when the scent of old blood and peat overwhelmed her.

The cup almost broke when she dropped it back down on the counter.

"Dammit." Ro squeezed her eyes shut and clung to the countertop while the world tilted and whirled around her. "Keep it together, Ro. You've got to hold on to yourself."

The pep talk echoed hollowly in the tile-lined kitchen, mocking her weakness. For the third time today, Rohanna ran the water as hot as she could stand it and hung her hands under the faucet. Steam billowed up towards the ceiling but Ro barely felt the heat, not even when her skin started taking on a bright pink hue. She scrubbed at her hands, desperate to remove the reddish brown lines etched into the creases of her palms. Tears came and she couldn't stop them from flowing down her cheeks. Washing her hands wouldn't take away the scent of fear burned into her nostrils, or remove the taste of iron sitting at the back of her throat.

Ro gave up and returned to her coffee. Her hands shook horribly, bad enough to form circular waves across the surface. It took both hands to steady her cup enough to make it to her lips.

"Fuck." Rohanna scowled. The coffee was too hot. It burned going down, but she gulped it eagerly, even though she could tell she was scalding her tongue. The coffee didn't do anything for her, but at least the foul taste was gone.

Ro left the mug on the counter and found her way back to Alex's bedroom, thankful that the narrow hallway was pretty much devoid of any obstacles. More than once she reached out a hand to steady herself before she stumbled over her own feet.

Alex was far too still. Rohanna rushed to her side, her heart skipping a beat before she caught the subtle rise and fall of her chest beneath the blankets. She had never been so attuned to the simple sound of someone breathing as she had over the last twenty-four hours.

It had been a hellish night. After dragging the taller and heavier woman up and down the treacherous trail back to her vehicle, she had driven back to Alex's, white knuckling it the entire way. Alex was slouched over, barely conscious in the passenger seat, and each time Ro hit a bump she would moan and start mumbling something. None of it made any sense to Rohanna, hell, she wasn't even sure if it was all in English. By the time she got Alex into the house and bundled in to bed she was exhausted and Alex felt like she was burning up.

She collapsed onto the bed and hadn't moved since then. Ro had spent the entire night awake, watching and waiting, too afraid to leave her alone. She had managed to clean most of Alex's wounds last night but it was her ribs that worried her most. Swollen and tender, the entire flank was a mottled palette of red, purple, and black bruises. When morning came, Ro was able to wake Alex long enough to get a couple sips of water into her. That had made her brave enough to leave Alex's side and call her grandmother.

If anyone knew what to do, it would be her.

Rohanna made sure that Alex was comfortable, fussing with the blanket and checking her bandages, before heading down the hall to the bathroom.

A quick check in the mirror showed Ro what she already knew. She looked horrible. Her clothes were grass stained and filthy, moving stiffly against her skin as she walked. It was a decidedly unpleasant sensation that made her long for a hot shower. Rohanna plucked at her shirt, grimacing in disgust. Her grandmother would be there soon and Ro didn't want to answer the door looking like a survivor of a major disaster.

No one would begrudge her a quick shower.

***

"Well, hello again, sleepy head."

Alex woke instantly, thrusting out her hand and grabbing Shyann by the front of her shirt before she could move out of the way.

"Shit, Alex, let go!"

"Shyann? What are you doing here?" Alex asked, then winced when the slight movement made it feel like her brain was beating itself against the inside of her skull. "Dammit. That hurts."

"Yeah. I wouldn't move too much, Alex. You've got some broken ribs and a nasty cut on your forehead. Probably a concussion too," Shyann told her a second before she tried to sit up.

"I'm fine," Alex made a second tentative attempt to sit up, then started coughing. Wracking pain circled her chest and clamped down on her lungs like a vice, making her eyes water.

"Hurts to breathe, does it?" Shyann asked, gently prying Alex's fingers from the front of her shirt. Alex took the hint and released her. "Here, drink this. It will help the pain."

Alex narrowed her eyes at Shyann, then gave the drink an equally distrusting glare.

Shyann shook her head. "It's just juice with a little something to ease your pain, Alex. I'm not trying to poison you."

Alex let Shyann place a straw between her lips, sipping gingerly before deciding it was safe to drink. The drink hit her stomach cold, but soon sent a warm flush through her body that chased away the worst of the aching. Her vision was still fuzzy, but it was clear enough to recognize the figure watching her from the doorway.

"You must be Maeve," Alex spoke by way of greeting. Her voice was rough, and it hurt like hell, but the juice had soothed her throat enough to speak.

"This is Rohanna's grandmother, Alex," Shyann corrected her softly.

"Is she now?" Alex asked, keeping her eye on the other woman.

"Yes, Alex. For all intents and purposes, that is who I am," Maeve answered. She sat on the edge of the bed, looking down at Alex with eyes as ancient as time. "But that is a conversation for another time. Right now, we have other problems. Alexandria, where is Rohanna?"

"What do you mean? She's here. I mean, she brought me here last night." Alex tried to sit up. Sharp pain lanced through her middle, pulling the oxygen from her lungs. Breathless, she fought to remain conscious.

Shyann responded to some unseen sign from Maeve. She nodded at both of them and left the bedroom. Alex could hear her moving about the house. Alex shot a questioning look towards Maeve, only to be shushed in a most grandmotherly way. Maeve smiled sweetly at her and patted her hand.

"Patience, my dear. Let's see what Shyann can find. She is good at such things."

"I don't think so, not where Rohanna is concerned," Alex practically growled. "Why isn't she here? She would have told me if she had to leave."

"I think I have the answer." Shyann walked into the room and held up a familiar silver chain. "I found this in a pile of dirty clothes on the bathroom floor. It was tangled up in her shirt. The clasp had fallen open."

"Rohanna's pendant? I don't understand."

"You will, Alexandria. But for now, you need to rest and get your strength back." Maeve took the silver chain from Shyann's hand, cupping it gently in her palm before closing her fist around it. "Sleep now, we will talk when you wake up."

***

Alex woke up alone in a darkened room with a dry mouth and no concept of how much time had passed. *What the hell did she give me? I don't even remember falling asleep.*

Tossing the blankets away from her, she swung her legs over the side of the bed, ignoring the sharp twinge of pain across her ribs. She took an experimental breath, then a deeper one, expanding her lungs fully. It hurt, but not bad enough to keep her in bed. She heard Shyann and Maeve talking in the kitchen so she turned her feet in that direction.

"Have you found Rohanna?" Alex asked, leaning heavily on the doorframe. Two pairs of eyes turned towards hers, one shocked at seeing her upright while the other mildly observed her over the lip of her coffee cup.

"You shouldn't be up," Maeve said. Her chair scraped across the floor as she stood up. "Sit. Let me make you something to drink."

"And you shouldn't be keeping me from finding Rohanna," Alex said, waving the other woman away from the coffee pot. "I'll make my own, thank you. I don't need another nap."

Maeve's eyelids fluttered just the tiniest bit, acknowledging Alex's shrewd assessment. Her eyes glittered in amusement before lowering herself back onto her seat.

"Tell me, Alexandria. Did you dream about Rohanna today?" Maeve's unexpected question almost made Alex drop her cup.

"What?"

"Let's not dissemble, Alexandria. We know you are Merefolk. Rohanna told me what happened last night."

"Really? I don't think you know as much as you think you do," Alex said, looking away.

She didn't want to talk about the Merefolk with these people. She had gone to her aunt asking for help and had been turned away, in the worst way possible. She was no longer a part of the tribe. Just like her mother before her, she was now an outcast, regardless of Epona's blessing.

True to form, Kaleigh had chosen safety and isolation over risk of exposure. She didn't want to expose the tribe to Belinda or help her protect Rohanna. That was made very clear to her last night. The cuts and bruises she bore didn't hurt nearly as much as her heart did right now. There was only one thing keeping grief and sorrow from overwhelming her, and that was Rohanna. She had lost everything else; she couldn't afford to lose her, too.

"Okay, fine. So you know about me. The answer to your question is no, I did not dream about Rohanna today." Alex pulled out a chair and sat down. She was sore and tired, and these two were holding something back from her. "Now it's my turn. I want to know why you keep dodging my question. I want to know why Rohanna isn't here. You said she called you and told you about me, and now you are here, in my house. Tell me, Maeve, how is it the two of you are in my house and Rohanna is not?"

The two women, young and old alike, gave her a look so akin to the other it made Alex want to beat cold iron. Gritting her teeth in frustration, she tried very hard to keep her temper in check. Laying her palms out on the table very carefully, she closed her eyes and just breathed for a minute, concentrating on the simple task of taking air into her lungs and exhaling.

"Tell me. Did she leave because of last night, because of me?" Alex finally asked the question she had been avoiding.

"I wish it was that simple, but it isn't," Maeve answered. She dropped Rohanna's necklace on the table between them. "Do you recognize this?"

"That's a stupid question. You know I do. It's Rohanna's necklace." Being drugged into oblivion was making her a very cranky woman.

Shyann scowled at Alex. "That's not..."

Maeve held up her hand and Shyann fell silent. "Peace, Shyann. She doesn't know what I was asking. It's not her fault. I have a feeling a great deal of knowledge has been lost over the years, whether by design or negligence, I cannot say."

"My apologies, Maeve." Alex bowed her head. "I am not usually so rude."

"Tsk. It's nothing, Alexandria. This is more than just a necklace," Maeve said, pushing the plain stone cross across the table toward Alex. "This is a Faerie stone. It was given to Rohanna many years ago, the first time she managed to activate a circle on her own. It was meant to protect her from harm, a gift from the Fae."

"Protect her from what?" Alex was beginning to dislike the direction their conversation was going.

"Actually, it was from who more than what," Maeve corrected her.

"Belinda! You're talking about her stepmother."

"Partly, yes. Really it is to protect her from any who would wish her harm."

"What kind of harm?" Alex asked.

"Magic, Alex. You know this."

"There isn't supposed to be that much magic here," Alex growled, finally understanding why her Aunt feared it so much.

"And yet you've met two in as many months with more magic than you thought possible."

"So without this?" Alex pointed at the Faerie stone.

"She is without protection."

"And?"

"More than likely, Belinda has called her back," Maeve said.

Alex launched from her chair so quickly it bounced across the floor behind her. "Ro's stepmother is dangerous. How can you be so calm about this? You know what she is, you have to know."

"Yes, Alex, we know, probably better than you. But think, you can't do anything right now. Despite the fact that you are actually vertical, you are still badly injured. You can't just bull your way past Belinda and take Rohanna, not in your weakened state."

Maeve's words barely registered with Alex. She had been preparing to do just that until a gentle hand touched her shoulder.

When did she leave the table?

"We need to get you well and then we need to work together. Belinda won't do anything to Rohanna. Not yet anyway. We have a little time."

"How do you know?" Alex demanded, pulling her shoulder away from the older woman.

"I just do. Alex, please. Just sit and listen to me. Then you can decide for yourself what you think is best."

CHAPTER THIRTY-THREE

Alex had tried, she really had. It was only after Maeve's story revealed just how bad it was for Rohanna that she retreated to her bedroom. It was either that or throw the two women out of her home; she was that angry.

She needed time to process what Maeve had told her. She couldn't do that though with Shyann slouching against her door frame, arms crossed and doing her best to look inconspicuous.

"Following me in here might not be the best thing to do right now," Alex warned her. She wasn't ready to continue discussing Rohanna, prophecies—or Belinda for that matter with Shyann.

Shyann raised one cinnamon-colored eyebrow at her and shook her head before returning her attention back towards a particularly interesting knot in the floor. "You shouldn't be that hard on her, you know."

"Why not?" Alex asked, picking up the argument right where it had left off. "She knew Rohanna was in danger all these years and did nothing. Absolutely nothing. Do you have any idea what it's like inside Rohanna's head? What Belinda has done to her? Not only is she completely unaware of who she is, you can't even tell her that she's Fae. Her mind runs and hides every time something happens around her that she can't explain." Alex threw her arms up in the air, not in frustration, but because she needed to do something physical. Even if that something was an ineffective gesture, it was still action.

"Maeve told you why, Alex. It's not that she didn't want to help. She was not allowed to help, only observe," Shyann said. "She wasn't aware of who Belinda was for a very long time. It was only after Ro's father died that we figured out that she was actually Bellaria. By that time, Bellaria had shipped her off to boarding school, and was using every human law there was to keep us from her. As soon as we were able to find her, Maeve sent me to her, to protect her as best as I could. Can you imagine? Me stuck at a prep school? Do you have any idea how much glamour it took to make me look like a teenager?"

Shyann shuddered. "It was emotional roller coaster hell. I have no idea how humans ever survive adolescence."

While Alex appreciated the humor involved in Shyann's admission, it only left her with more questions. "So, who are you really?"

"For all intents and purposes, I am Ro's cousin. Maybe a few more times removed than most, but still, we do share common blood."

"You're like Bellaria, aren't you? You aren't from this side of the veil."

"I am nothing like Bellaria, she was human once and still holds on to all the worst characteristics of a human. Greedy, power hungry and shouting unfair at every twist and turn in her life. She is jealous of our nature and wants to be like us, not fade away into the dust like most of her kind."

"You are right about one thing though. I'm not from here, not originally," Shyann continued, grinning mischievously. She still had her secrets and seemed intent on keeping them. "In a way, neither is Maeve, but that is her tale to tell. I wouldn't suggest pushing it though. Even I am not privy to all of her secrets. She is a good person, despite her stubborn ways. We've learned to agree to disagree on how some matters should be handled."

Alex swung her head around to face Shyann. Something about the way Shyann defended Maeve made Alex wonder if she didn't quite share her sentiments. Was she offering to help? If she was, it was certainly worth exploring further.

"Why are you here, Shyann?" Alex asked gruffly. "Did she send you in to try and change my mind?"

"No, Alex, I think getting you to change your mind is about as easy as convincing the sun to rise in the west."

"Hmmpff." Alex launched herself away from window to stand in front of the dresser mirror. She scowled at her reflection. It was fitting; she was just as mad at herself as everyone else right now. The laceration above her eyebrow had been cleaned and dressed and was already starting to scab over and itch. The bruising around it had already faded to a pale purple color tinged with green. She pulled up her shirt, knowing she would find the same—angry bruises that were fading as quickly as her body healed.

It still hurt a bit to take in a deep breath. Bones took longer to knit together, but at least the pain didn't steal her breath away anymore. If she turned too quickly, she could feel the bone crackle and shift beneath her skin. As long as it did that, she was forced to wait. Broken ribs were one thing; a punctured lung would delay her recovery.

"You're healing fast," Shyann observed, raising an inquisitive eyebrow in Alex's direction. "Faster than even I do. How are you managing that?"

Alex shifted her scowl towards Shyann's reflection, hoping she would get the hint and leave. It didn't work. Shyann just leaned in the doorway and crossed her arms over her chest.

"Stubborn ass Faerie," Alex grumbled. Trying to get rid of Shyann was as hard as picking burrs out of a horse's mane without poking yourself. Impossible.

"You betcha."

"I was attacked in my human form. I changed. It helped me survive my wounds," Alex admitted, then shrugged her shoulders. It really didn't matter anymore. Alex clenched her teeth together until her jaw popped. What she could not and would not tell Ro's cousin was that if she hadn't managed to change into her Mere form, she probably wouldn't have survived the night. The sharp blade of betrayal carved deep into her heart, and unlike her physical injuries, she doubted it would ever fully heal.

"Uh, huh. Sooooo...do you have a plan for getting her back? I mean, other than rushing in and just stealing her away?" Shyann asked casually. When Alex shot her a sharp look, Shyann simply smiled, all innocence and guile, then proceeded to inspect her fingernails. Alex bit her lip to keep from laughing aloud. Rushing in and stealing Rohanna away was exactly what she had been thinking of doing.

"No, not yet. But Shyann, I can't just sit here and wait. Without that stone around her neck, Belinda-Bellaria, whatever the hell her name is, could be holding her against her will and we'll never know!" Her voice rose a few octaves, falling just short of outright yelling. Alex angrily tugged at her thick braid, a sure sign of just how close she was to exploding. She was beyond angry and had nothing to lash out at.

"Rohanna is gone and I can't do a damn thing to get her back. Maeve's reassurance that Rohanna is safe doesn't mean a damn thing to me. I need to see for myself."

"I understand, Alex—I really do. But Maeve is right. You have to heal first. Bellaria is extremely powerful. To go against her now would be careless."

"And alone, let's not forget that," Alex muttered miserably, tugging at her braid again. As much as she hated to admit it, Shyann was right. If she tried something now she risked both her and Rohanna's lives.

"What?" Shyann risked touching Alex, turning her around so they faced each other. "What are you talking about?"

"Last night..." Alex began, then looked down at her hands to hide the fact that she was about to choke on her words.

They were strong hands, with tendons and sinew hardened from years of hefting a hammer and shaping hard metal. Not now. Now they trembled uncontrollably and all she could do was glare at them for their failure to remain strong. Even raising her arm was an effort, but the leather bracer had to come off. She wasn't sure why Rohanna had left it on, but she did and now Alex had to unlace the dirty leather cords with equally stiff fingers. Stubbornly, she continued to pluck at the laces until the thick leather bracer fell to the carpet and Shyann could see the delicate blue lines decorating her wrist.

"This tattoo marks my rank and position in the tribe. Until last night it was a living thing, the blessing of Epona given to me when I was tested for leadership. Now it's nothing more than plain ink, dull and lifeless. It's a mockery of everything I used to be, of what I was meant to do." Alex curled her lip in disgust. "Last night I went to the leader of my tribe, to beg assistance from the herd about Rohanna and to tell them about Belinda. Rather than stand behind me, they denied my request. My own people attacked me, Shyann! I am no longer part of them."

Alex choked on her grief, then swallowed the pain so she could continue. Living apart from her people was a vastly different thing than being banished. She felt hollowed out inside, like an old oak tree whose heart had been eaten away by time.

"When I go against Bellaria I will be going alone. I have lost everything else. I will not lose Rohanna. She is my only family now."

"No, you are not alone, Alex." Shyann's playful grin fell from her face like a party mask. What Shyann revealed in its place was something harsher, more prone to violence and keen on battle than Alex had thought possible from the good-natured Fae.

Obviously, there was more to Shyann than she had let Alex see. It didn't take much imagination to visualize this Shyann with a sword in hand and a shield on her arm. She strode across the room until the two women were almost chest-to-chest. Grasping Alex's forearm, she spoke quietly but with a force behind her words that made what she said next more of a vow than a simple promise.

"Alex, you do not have to do this alone. If there is any way I can help you get her back, I will."

Alex searched Shyann's face carefully, looking for any signs of subterfuge. All of her life Alex had been taught to distrust the Greater Fae, yet here was one willing to stand with her when her own family would not. After a moment, she nodded. Alex grasped Shyann's forearm in turn and clapped her shoulder soundly. It was a warrior's greeting, a bond of its own given freely by two Fae, acknowledging their solidarity and willingness to fight together.

"Thank you, Shyann," Alex said. "But, won't Maeve be upset about this, with all her talk about prophecy?"

"Who am I to decide what prophecy requires in order for it to come to pass? Act or don't act, what if it's all the same? I am sure that if a prophecy requires a certain ending, it will figure out how to get there on its own. I am not bound to being an observer like Maeve. I am in my own time and my own life." Shyann paused then, her focus travelling to some inner place before speaking again. "I think she is held to a different set of rules than the rest of us. At least for now."

Alex shivered against the sudden cold. Whatever force spoke through Shyann bled power into the room around them, a power that disappeared when Shyann came back to herself.

"Are you okay?" Alex asked, searching for something alien behind Shyann's eyes, then exhaled in relief. There was nothing hidden there that would suggest Shyann wasn't herself.

"I'm fine, why?"

Alex wasn't sure how to answer that, so she chose not to say anything at all. The strange message was obviously meant for her ears alone. Whether it was a warning or not, only time would tell.

"Nothing at all. Look, I have an idea that should work, if you are game?" Alex smiled, purposefully mimicking Shyann's mischievous grin. "How good are you at sneaking into places you don't belong?"

"Well now, that would be one of my specialties, and isn't that convenient for you?"

CHAPTER THIRTY-FOUR

Bellaria walked along the stone path with all the grace and airs of a Queen inspecting her personal guard. The sky had grown dark with the promise of a suitably violent storm. Ominous clouds churned above her, carrying restless air currents that funneled down to the earth to grasp at tree branches, encouraging them to sway ecstatically. The movement was hypnotic—row after row of ancient oaks all caught up in the same sacred dance.

Bellaria was immune to nature's charm, her only concern was the energy it brought with it. She was focused on the coming ritual. Much like the mounting storm, it churned and blew through her like a cold wind, caressing her veins with its icy power.

It was the first night of the full moon and everything was ready. Her lips curled up at the corners, an invitation to a smile that harbored nothing but evil intent. Whatever emotion that passed for joy in Bellaria's twisted soul made her heart race in anticipation.

Bellaria didn't know what had possessed Rohanna to remove her Faerie stone, but she was perfectly happy to take advantage of the unexpected boon. The cursed thing had kept her from completely controlling Rohanna since she came back from college and she hadn't been able to separate her from it no matter what tricks she had tried. Bellaria had assumed it was destroyed years ago, when she took care of Rohanna's father.

How it reappeared out of the blue to hang around Rohanna's neck was a mystery she had yet to solve, but she had her suspicions. Maeve, Rohanna's grandmother, was a constant thorn in her side...and John's truck had crashed on her property. The stone was never recovered from his body or the vehicle. She often wondered if the old woman had found it and returned it to Rohanna.

"Troublesome woman," Bellaria muttered, wondering why she hadn't put the old hag out of her misery long ago. "No matter, I have what I want now, I can take care of her at my leisure once this is done."

Bellaria turned onto the hidden path that led to her goal. Just ahead of her lay a clearing devoid of any vegetation. Stark and sterile, the circle's true boundaries were invisible to most, but even so, no animal or bird would voluntarily cross the woven strands holding the circle together. Thirteen forms stood waiting for her, thirteen hooded forms that turned towards her in unison when she arrived. *Twelve plus another to replace Siandra, there had been no repeat of that one's insolence since my demonstration. There was always another one eager to join, eager to lap at the leftover's I toss to them. Pitiful.*

She ignored their obeisance, the cowled heads dipping in acknowledgement of her presence. The still figure standing in the center of the circle was the only one who mattered.

A swift slicing motion opened the circle and then closed it behind her. Now that she was near enough to sense the delicate threads, she was gratified to find Rohanna bound quite nicely by her spell. Rohanna's eyes rolled back in her head until just the whites showed as the power within her tried to free itself, her body writhed within the restraints as something greater than herself beat against the frail vessel. Bellaria had no sympathy for the pain she knew the young woman was suffering. She had laid claim to Rohanna's magic a long time ago, considering it her own as much as the land and people around her by virtue of all the time and energy she had spent developing Rohanna's skills. It was time for Rohanna to pay her back in full for her investment.

"It is time," Bellaria announced.

Thirteen hoods were thrown back, revealing thirteen women who were alike in only one aspect. They were the strongest witches she could find on this side of the veil that craved power as much as she did. Other than that, they had nothing in common. Young or old, pale or olive skinned, tall or short— it didn't matter to her. They were vessels that could hold what she craved most—power.

She felt their eyes on her, anticipating the rewards she had promised for all their years of loyalty. Bellaria sneered in derision. All of them were fools, down to the last one. Their greed had blinded them, much to Bellaria's amusement. She was not the type to share. *If they haven't figured that out on their own by now, well, more's the pity for them.*

"Let us begin."

***

Alex was forced to wait another night before she could go after Rohanna. Her wounds itched like hell, making sleep almost impossible, but they could only heal so fast. She tossed and turned and tried not to scratch most of the night. In the morning, she took a quick shower.

The healed scabs fell away from fresh pink skin to circle the drain and disappear. Any residual dirt and dried blood likewise found its way down the drain. She turned the water on as hot as she could stand and just stood there, head down, and let the water beat down on her shoulders until steam rolled off her skin. It felt good to be clean again.

After drying off, she stopped in front of the mirror and dropped her towel, wiping the steam from the long glass in order to inspect her torso. Grunting in satisfaction, Alex ran her fingers along ribs that were still sensitive, but no longer creaked whenever she took a deep breath.

"Soon, Ro..." Alex promised, re-wrapping her ribs with the compression bandage Shyann had scared up before throwing on a robe.

It was time to see what the day held.

Alex walked back to her bedroom and listened to the common noises the old farmhouse made, seeking comfort in their familiarity. Instead, the cadenced hum of strange voices rose and fell in the familiar rhythm of casual conversation. Maeve and Shyann were waiting for her in the kitchen, but she had no desire to join them. The forced inactivity of the last forty-eight hours was taking its toll on her temper. She was acting downright bitchy, which made her guests decision to stay while she recuperated a surprising choice.

Her people had stayed on this side of the veil to get away from all the politics and power plays that the Greater Fae seemed to rejoice in, yet somehow she had landed square in the middle of something she had very little understanding of. Belinda, or Bellaria—it didn't matter what her name was—was a dangerous person who held no qualms about hurting Rohanna. That made Maeve and Shyann her allies, for now. That didn't change her feelings. A lifelong distrust towards the Greater Fae could not be overcome in a couple of days. They were incidental allies; it would take time to see if they were as true as they claimed to be.

She had learned a hard lesson this week. Friends could become enemies in the blink of an eye. Just because they were on the same side now didn't mean that Alex's goals and their goals would remain the same. It was a shame because Alex really did like Shyann.

Alex grimaced at the painful reminder. *Friends is one thing, but family? When family turns on you, there is no hiding from that pain.*

She was running blind into the future. Maeve believed that her fate had already been settled by some ancient prophecy and that she couldn't just walk away. Belinda had made it very clear that her presence was not welcome—suggesting that she should just walk away.

Belinda's warning was obvious; there was no subtlety there. Maeve was an unknown, her reasons were her own and even Shyann questioned some of her decisions. While Belinda's option seemed the safer one for her and the Mere tribe, she found she simply couldn't do it. Something had been set in motion the minute she met Rohanna, and it was still running its course. Alex felt like she had been cast into the water by something more powerful than she was and told to swim against the rushing current the best she could. That there were rocks hidden beneath the rolling surface was never mentioned, yet that was the most dangerous part...what was unseen and hidden until it crashed into you and left you bleeding.

The urge to scream in frustration rose up in her throat, as bitter as the lingering taste of betrayal. The forge room called to her. It offered her some sanctuary from her guests and the sound of unwelcome voices. Hammer and hot steel would relieve her of some of her frustration and allow her to test her muscles. If she could tolerate a few hours at the anvil, she should be strong enough to go after Rohanna.

Slipping out through the back hall, Alex headed for the forge. The familiar actions of stoking the fire and pumping the bellows gave her the first sense of peace she had felt since meeting Rohanna's stepmother. The smell of hot metal and burning coals radiated warmth that heated the small room enough to send small rivulets of sweat running down her brow. She picked the tools she needed and plucked out a small length of flat steel and thrust it into the coals.

The calming effect was almost instantaneous.

Alex was most at home with herself when she stood next to the heat of the coal forge, felt the heft of the heavy hammer in her hand, the sound of metal ringing in her ears. She loved the sense of creation it gave her when she worked steel, the dull grey of the cold metal changing to crimson and gold, made soft and pliable by the glowing coals.

With her thoughts attuned to heat and softness, an image of Rohanna surfaced in her mind. Rohanna had come to her cold and hard, her life dull and listless. Alex had taught her the joys of standing within the flame, feeling the heat, and craving it, forging Rohanna's passion much like she forged steel. Even with total ignorance of her heritage, Rohanna had embraced the unrestrained desires that her Fae blood craved. In turn, Rohanna's wantonness had inflamed Alex to seek even more creative heights.

Captured by her own creation, Alex had discovered too late that the flames of their passion had forged an unbreakable bond between them. She was in love with

Rohanna, and it was this knowledge that had kept her firmly planted in that cold field, preparing to confront the one person that could still claim rule over her. Kaleigh was lead Mere. Her rule was absolute, yet Alex had gone against thousands of years of tradition to defy her and for Rohanna, she would do it all over again. Love would always be the ultimate law above and beyond any other bond or vow.

Enough time had passed. Alex plucked out the slim piece of metal from the hot coals and brought it up to eye level. It glowed dimly, dull orange against the muted background of amber light illuminating the forge room. The flames had burned low, leaving only the red-hot coals to cast their primitive light across the room. Irreverent shadows danced gaily in the far corners, while tendrils of darkness licked back at the tongues of light invading their night borne life. Larger shapes lurked inside those happier shadows, layers upon layers of dark and light trying to share a common ground. Goaded by her dark mood, those shadows didn't dance in the firelight. They twisted slowly, seeking a way to escape the light and seek darker things in the night.

A quick twist of the wrist brought the blower beneath the forge back to life, sending sparks shooting across the top of the coals. Alex made a sound deep in her throat. Dissatisfied with the color, she thrust the glowing metal back into the forge, burying it far into the pile of red-hot coals.

Alex stared moodily into the white-hot heart of the stoked forge. Sweat poured down her forehead, burning her eyes, but rubbing away the moisture would only leave more soot streaks on her face. While she waited for the iron to turn, she took a quick drink of water from her ever-present water bottle. The action was more automatic than anything else. Her body demanded repletion of lost fluid, there was no enjoyment there, only practical necessity.

While she worked, she let her mind wander freely, hoping it would stumble on a feasible plan to rescue Rohanna. And, much like it always did when she was at the forge, time slipped away from her. The world was reduced to the rhythm of hammer on anvil and the hiss of hot coals whispering to each other in the background.

CHAPTER THIRTY-FIVE

"I think the steel is hot enough, don't you?" a rough voice asked.

A quick shallow breath was all Alex allowed herself. She had been distracted enough that someone had invaded her sanctuary without her knowledge. Her fingers tightened around the smooth maple handle of her heavy hammer, not so much that she couldn't switch her grip, but enough to put a bit of strength behind her next blow without shocking her wrist. She rarely considered her blacksmithing tools as weapons. They were better suited to creating than destroying, but her heavy hammer would do.

Twisting away from the light of the forge, Alex blinked twice, quickly, trying to clear her vision. She scanned the darkness for the source of the voice, but all she could see was unrelieved black coming in through the doorway. She stepped away from the anvil, balancing lightly on the balls of her feet and giving herself room to maneuver. A second step might give her intruder the idea that she was retreating in fear. They would be wrong.

A low chuckle followed her movement.

"Your mother's daughter to the last, Alexandria." A low, masculine voice spoke out from the shadows. The lightly mocking voice carried with it a soft brogue that marked him as coming from the Old Country. "You can put the hammer down. You have no cause to fear me, nor would I ever harm you. Besides, a blacksmith's forge is sacred."

As he spoke, he emerged from the shadows. A tall man, he was wide in the shoulder and broad across the chest in the way that only blacksmiths could be. His plain white shirt and leather pants were worn but clean. The shirt could have been in fashion a hundred years ago or yesterday, but appeared homespun. He stepped closer to the forge and details of his face emerged. He had dark hair that would have fallen across his forehead in loose waves if it wasn't pulled back along his skull by a long braid, framing a face that seemed too young for his build. He was beardless but his jawline was too smooth to ever have seen a razor. A heavy brow shadowed his eyes, his cheekbones were high and accented by shadow as well. His looks gave him away, as much as his words did. *One of the Old Ones*, Alex decided, *the Tuatha De Danann*. Alex became even more wary of her guest. If he was strong enough to cross through the veil on his own volition, he was also strong enough to be a serious threat.

Despite his reassurance, she didn't relax her stance.

"What do you know of my mother?" Alex demanded. The man's calm assurance of superiority set her teeth on edge. He might have stated his intentions were peaceful, but he still hadn't told her why he was here. Until then, Alex would treat him as what he was, an intruder.

The strange man looked up then, revealing bright blue eyes that glowed like the purest sapphires. The air crackled around them, charged with all the power of a storm that threatened to bring the lightning just so the thunder could make its voice heard. Light seemed to gather about him, making the shadows cringe and retreat into the darkest corners.

"I know much, Alexandria. Things you should know. Things you need to know." The man's voice was gentle, although his tone was urgent. "Things aren't always what they seem. Truths and lies can become twisted until no one knows which is which. What I do know and what you should have been told years ago, is that your mother loved you very much. After she died, I didn't know what else to do. I still regret leaving you with your aunt, even though I knew it was for the best."

"I don't understand. My mother is dead?" Alex shook her head. After so many years without knowing, a part of her wanted to clap her hands over her ears and take back what she had heard. She found she was afraid of what this stranger would say to her next. Taking a jagged breath, Alex gave into the long suppressed rage she had nursed for so many years it had become a part of her. Her hammer came up, pointing directly at the stranger's chest like a judge's gavel.

"No. You lie! My mother left me when I was a child. She left me with the tribe while she stayed with her human lover. She abandoned her family, her position as the leader of my people, and left me to fend for myself."

"So much anger, Alexandria. Yet, here you are, living apart from your people...choosing a human over your tribe. How can you deny your mother what you have sought for yourself all these years?"

"That's unfair! I wasn't responsible for a child. She left me to fend for myself, the daughter of a traitor. I was an outcast long before I ever left that place."

The stranger stepped closer until he was face to face with Alex above the iron anvil that separated them. Two sets of bright blue eyes blazed defiantly, each refusing to break eye contact first. Two equally strong jaw lines clenched stubbornly.

Alex was of a height with the stranger and found herself staring directly into eyes that looked overly familiar, eyes that looked exactly like the ones that stared back at her in the mirror every morning.

"Alexandria, your mother made me promise to send you to Kaleigh. On her death bed, she did this. I could not deny her at the time. Do you not think it pained me as much as it does you, losing the only thing left of her that I loved?"

Alex's hands went numb. She heard the dull thump of her hammer hitting the packed dirt beneath her feet. Her knees threatened to fail her as well, trying to follow gravity's path. Grasping blindly, nerveless fingers found and then clung desperately to the solidness of the heavy anvil while her world spun around her. Pain streaked through her, travelling up her arm, and lighting her body on fire. Strong emotions warred within her, simultaneously demanding attention, all wanting answers, all crippling her with the need to know.

"It hurts you still, the touch of cold iron?"

Of course it does, Alex thought, her teeth clenched against the discomfort. But it was real, it was solid, and it was something she understood very well. It grounded her.

"My poor child, have you never wondered why you are drawn to the forge? Why you can tolerate the touch of iron while your kinswomen cannot?"

Realization struck Alex as his words sunk in. All those years of being teased, all those years of whispers that stopped whenever she walked by certain cabins. They were the same ones that grumbled and fussed when Kaleigh announced that Alexandria was chosen to succeed her rather than her own daughter.

She was always too tall, too different, too noticeable for a tribe that prided itself on its survival by being perfectly unremarkable. No one noticed them because they were beneath notice and that made them feel safe. It was a pitiful tribute to a race that used to make men tremble and fear their own dreams.

Blue eyes, black hair. None of her people had her height or her coloring...but this man did.

My father. Suddenly the ground beneath her didn't feel quite so solid. Her knees betrayed her, and she sunk to the packed dirt beneath her feet.

This stranger, her father, gathered her gently in his arms and lifted her up.

"I know you have many questions, Alexandria, but this is neither the time nor the place. Rohanna will be coming soon, and you have important work to do. Know this, whatever happens, Bellaria must not be allowed to return to the Shadow Lands. That she sought out Rohanna as a child is no accident. With Rohanna under her control, she can devastate both worlds, and that cannot happen. Each of you has a part to play in this, and you are strongest together. Kaleigh has crippled you with ignorance by keeping me a secret. In doing so, she denied you your birthright. It is time to correct that mistake, and not in a way of my choosing, but out of necessity."

"Ro? Coming here. How?" Alex said, her voice hoarse. There was too much information coming at her at one time, too many questions and too many answers being given that in turn, lent themselves to more questions.

Alex's father grasped his daughter's hands within his own, calloused and rough from hours at the forge. They comforted her in their familiarity.

"Even now, you ask of Rohanna first, despite the questions welling up in your mind. The heart demands its answers, and so her name is first upon your lips. It is well, Daughter, that you have found such a love. Perhaps it will let you open your heart more generously when you reexamine your mother's choices."

"That still doesn't explain why you didn't come to me before this." A slow tremor travelled through Alex's body, which was suddenly cold despite the heat of the forge room. Alex started to shiver, her teeth chattering in response to the chill.

"I know, and I am sorry. Time is limited, and there is no other way to do this, Daughter. Know that I do this out of love," he said, grasping Alex's left arm firmly within his large hands. "Your mother was ever so much wiser than me. I thought this was something you should have never been denied, I see now that it was better this way. You have forged your own strength without my gifts and you are stronger for it. I am so very proud of you."

Her father's touch made her fingers tingle, as if a low electrical current was passing through her skin. Alex felt the small hairs on the back of her arm raise in protest, then the sensation spread, travelling to the base of her skull. The sound of his voice echoed around her as if coming from a long distance yet it filled Alex's ears louder than any drum.

"I am Gofannon, the forge is my domain. No daughter of mine should feel pain at the touch of cold steel. Your strength has always been that of black iron torn from the earth. Through my blood, your heart carries the fire of falling stars. I give to you your birthright. I fear it is no gentle gift." Regret and love colored the deep voice. The words circled around them, gathering power as they rang out into the night.

Without warning, the tingle in her arm became sharp pain. Alex's vision bled bright red with the intensity. The pain was pure agony, unforgiving and relentless. The sting of a thousand fire ant bites escalated into the burning of the purest fire pouring across her skin like liquid sun. Alex threw her head back, her spine arching as she howled her pain into the sky. She felt the shock of her knees slamming into the hard soil as her body betrayed her, folding onto itself before she lost consciousness. Red bled to black, her mind racing into oblivion to escape the pain. Before absolute darkness descended on her, she felt strong arms catch her.

"When day and night meet at the forge of souls, the midnight sun will bring mixed blessings. The one who is two, shall lose and gain a crown. One will be given their hearts desire, while another shall be torn asunder." Gofannon repeated Maeve's prophecy with a heavy heart. Prophecy always required sacrifice.

Very carefully, he lowered Alexandria's unconscious body to the ground. A small towel became a pillow to cradle her head. It was the only physical comfort he could offer her, and she would need her strength in the coming hours. A single caress along the cheek of a daughter he had not seen in four hundred years was all he allowed himself before stepping aside. He was here for a purpose and there was one last thing he needed to do before he could leave.

He picked up Alex's hammer and hefted it in his hand, impressed with its weight. Looking down on Alex's still form, he murmured softly, "You've met your sun, Alexandria, and lost your crown. Another waits for you when you are ready to take it."

Hefting the hammer in his hand, he raised his arm up three times, striking the anvil in slow succession. The anvil pealed loudly under the force of each swing, ringing heavily across the silence. Cocking his head to the side, he waited a moment, listening intently. A rumble of deep thunder answered the lightning that danced upon the cold surface of the iron anvil. Satisfied, he laid the hammer upon the now silent anvil and walked into the waiting storm.

CHAPTER THIRTY-SIX

"Noooooooooo!" Rohanna screamed, pulling away from Bellaria's grasp. Lightning danced in the clouds above them, adding an ozone smell to the sharp taste of magic coiling around Bellaria's circle like a deadly serpent. The sudden illumination revealed the thirteen women standing around Rohanna. They managed to stand steady against the sudden onslaught of wind and rain. Not even the frozen drops falling like icy spear points disturbed their chanting.

Then a sudden boom sounded close to them and stole their words. Thunder shook the ground with such violence that some of them stumbled and fell.

The chanting stopped, and with it, their control of the wild power they had been gathering. Tossed into the maelstrom without a guiding hand to shape it, the wind gathered up the loose strands and sent the torn roots scurrying for the safety of the wet earth. The circle shredded into nothingness.

"This isn't working, Bellaria!" One hooded figure screeched, pressing her hands over her ears against the sudden change in pressure. She crawled to the nearest woman and rolled her over. Blood leaked from her eyes and nose and she stared blindly into the storm. The rain pelted her and still she did not blink. Her throat gurgled like a fountain from the rain running down her and into her mouth. The storm was slowly drowning her, and she did nothing to resist it. Horrified, the woman managed to make it to her knees and crawl towards Bellaria. "We need to stop, now."

"I will not!" Bellaria bellowed, desperately reaching out to gather up the fractured threads. "I will not lose what I have gained!"

She grabbed for Rohanna, digging her nails deep into Rohanna's arms until she drew blood, trying to realign the threads of control and stop whatever was happening. Rohanna spun in her grasp, flinging her arm wildly and almost knocking Bellaria over.

Bellaria's rage ignited into something red hot. It scorched the air around her and even set the rain on fire. The witches scattered, scampering across the wet ground like spiders seeking dry ground.

"Foolish women, I am not done with you, yet," Bellaria snarled. She reached out once again, this time snatching at the life threads of her coven and reeling them back in.

Crawling in the mud like the grotesque creatures they were, not a single one of them deserved her mercy, not even the one clutching at her robe and begging her to stop. She kicked out viciously. The woman whimpered and rolled away, already half forgotten.

"You will not defy me!" she bellowed, shaking Rohanna like a ragdoll. Bellaria continued to draw down the raw energy around her until it felt like her skin was on fire. Ignoring the pain, Bellaria screamed her defiance into the storm. "I will not be denied my revenge."

Without warning, the world exploded into blinding white light.

Bellaria found herself lying on her back in a puddle at the edge of the circle. She scrambled back to her feet only to wobble like a newborn colt struggling to find its balance.

Bellaria turned in a circle, blinking away the spots dancing across her vision as she sought out her prize. She found Rohanna standing in the center of the circle, her head thrown back and her arms raised to the sky. Lightning danced with and around her, filling the circle with enough energy to make Bellaria's skin crawl.

Bellaria hesitated. Fear crept into her heart for the first time since her exile so many years ago.

"Rohanna. You cannot control this. You need my help before you get hurt," Bellaria yelled. It was a desperate lie, but she had to try something—anything to keep Rohanna in her control.

"No! I will not listen to your lies anymore, Stepmother. I am the Gatekeeper. I know this now. I claim this circle as mine. I will take what is mine and everything that you have stolen from me." Rohanna did not yell, yet her voice carried easily across the distance between them.

"Please, Rohanna." Bellaria feigned weakness. She held her hand out, beseeching her to help an old woman.

"Never again. Do you hear me? Never again," Rohanna roared, then cocked her head as if she was listening to something in the wind.

Thunder boomed across the sky once, twice, then a third time, rumbling across the sky as clear as a drum beating out the rhythm of creation. Bellaria heard nothing but the howl of the storm around her, but Rohanna smiled and nodded before taking a single threatening step towards Bellaria.

"I know your true name, Bellaria. I know who you are and I will never be your pawn again!" And with that, she was gone.

A pale afterimage flickered in the dark, a play of light and dark in the shadows that faded with the spent storm. Bellaria gathered her rage into one last surge of energy. Drawing heavily from the witches scattered around her, she hurled one last curse like a javelin towards that flickering image before it faded completely.

Frustrated beyond belief, Bellaria turned, seeking some outlet for her anger and finding none. She called for her witches to attend her, but they failed to move, nor did they speak to her. "What is this?" she whispered, reaching out to touch the nearest woman. Her fingertips found nothing but stone, hard and cold and beyond her ability to reclaim.

"What is this?" she asked again, but there was no one left to answer her. Thirteen stones stood motionless in a circle around her, as tall and twisted as if they had been teased from the earth beneath them. Bellaria's frustration turned into black horror.

The newly formed standing stones stood cold and still, but their shadows still danced behind them. Thirteen black souls stood caught beneath the weight of their stone bodies. Unable to flee their punishment, they screamed silently into the night.

***

Alex woke to the sound of rumbling thunder crashing down around her and cold rain blowing in sideways through the forge room door. She had no idea how long she had been out but she knew it hadn't been long. The coals still burned in the forge, and the room still glowed a dim ruby red, but the storm made it difficult to say if it was day or night. Inside the forge room, it was eerily silent, except for the occasional sizzling hiss from the raindrops that found their way to the fire.

"Ugh, my head." Alex pulled herself up from the floor, her body protesting every movement. The dirt floor made a terrible bed. While she stretched her stiff muscles, she took a quick inventory of the rest of her body. Her ribs and forehead still hurt but not as bad as before. The headache was fading rapidly, but now an annoying ringing in her ears was taking its place. She scrubbed at her wrist, then rotated her shoulder until she heard it pop. Her left arm ached terribly but everything seemed to be working okay.

Water was her next thought. She desperately needed something to drink, which struck her as funny since she was half soaked by the rain.

Stumbling into the main house, Alex grabbed a bottle of water and drank until the bottle was empty. Lightning flashed wildly, illuminating the house with odd black and white images of the room around her. The next crash of thunder shook the rafters above her so hard she fought the instinct to duck.

"That one was close." Shyann's disembodied voice spilled out of the darkness. Alex almost jumped out of her skin. After what happened in the forge room, her reactions were primed and stripped bare of any restraint.

"Shyann! Don't do that. I almost took your head off."

"That might be harder than you think," Shyann said. She actually sounded amused until she turned on the light. "Are you okay?"

"I think so."

"Really?" Shyann pointed at Alex's arm. "Then perhaps you wouldn't mind explaining that?"

Alex looked down at her forearm. Her eyes widened.

The ornate tattoo along her left wrist now travelled halfway up her forearm. More importantly, the tattoo was no longer dull and lifeless. It blazed, a living thing that moved restlessly beneath her skin, like a serpent swimming slowly across a smooth lake. In addition to the deep blue, shades of magenta and gold accentuated the complex knot work.

"Great Goddess, what is this?" Alex whispered. An echo of a voice answered her question. *"I give to you your birthright. I fear it is no gentle gift."* Lightning crashed above the house again, and the tattoo flared even brighter. The two women stared at each other, then spun in unison towards the front door. The frame shook with the force of something slamming hard against it.

Shyann raised a warning finger to her lips then padded silently to the door. She looked back and Alex nodded, expecting the worst. Shyann opened the door. Alex was ready for anything except what they found waiting for them on the other side of that door.

"Rohanna!"

Soaked to the bone and shaking like a leaf, Rohanna stood in the pouring rain. Both arms wrapped tightly around her middle, she could barely hold her head up, let alone stand. She swayed dangerously, then. She held a hand out towards Alex and before collapsing. Alex managed to catch her before she hit the floor. Shyann was a close second behind her.

"She's freezing cold. We need to get her warmed up and out of these wet clothes," Alex said. She easily picked the smaller woman up and carried her to the living room sofa.

"How the hell did she get here?" Shyann asked.

"That's not important right now. Just get the fire stoked and grab some dry clothes from my room," Alex said, unable to tear her gaze away from Ro's face. Her lips were blue, and she was incredibly pale.

When Shyann didn't move right away, Alex grabbed her shoulder and shook her. "Now, Shyann. Move."

Alex pulled a blanket around Ro's shoulders, then wrapped her arms around her, hoping to share some of her body heat. "Rohanna? Ro, baby? Talk to me, sweetie."

"Alex," Rohanna moaned.

Her teeth chattered violently and she could barely speak but she managed to make herself heard. "I heard you, in the thunder, calling to me. It showed me what I needed to do. I told it to take me to you."

"Told who what, Ro?" Alex asked, rubbing the color back into Rohanna's hands. She sounded delirious.

"The circle. I told the circle to take me to you." Rohanna opened her eyes and smiled at Alex in a way that made her heart want to break. "I love you, Alex."

Rohanna's words faded to the barest of a whisper. It faded like her smile as she lost consciousness, but that moment would be engraved in Alex's memory forever. Those words and that smile were hers, and she would do everything in her power to see them over and over again.

Alex ran the back of her hand over Rohanna's forehead, then snatched it away. She had gone from freezing to boiling hot in a flash.

"Shyann! Maeve! Get in here now," Alex roared. She felt her skin shift, her Mere restless in its need to seek vengeance for hurting the one she loved. *Not now*, she muttered, gritting her teeth against the urge to course through the night in search of the one who did this. Ro needed her here.

"What's wrong?" Maeve ran into the room with Shyann close on her heels. She took one look at Alex and stopped in her tracks. "Great Mother of All, Alexandria."

Shyann was not as eloquent, borrowing a common human expletive. "Holy fuck, Alex."

"She's sick, Maeve. A fever, I think," Alex said, her attention on Rohanna's face. "Something's not right. She's Fae...she shouldn't have a fever."

When neither woman moved to help, she looked up to find both of them staring at her.

"What is wrong with you two?" Alex demanded to know.

"Your eyes, Alex...they've bled out," Shyann said, shifting nervously from one foot to the other.

"I know. I can feel it," Alex growled. "You know what I am, why does this surprise you?"

Maeve stepped forward.

"I've seen NightMeres before, Alex...on the Great Hunt." She shivered at the memory. "Gleaming black hides that make the darkest night seem pale in comparison and eyes that glowed like the hottest coals."

"So?" Alex frowned. "Are you afraid of me?"

"No." Maeve and Shyann exchanged glances while Alex fussed over Rohanna.

"Then help me," Alex pleaded with them, sure that they had no idea how hard that was for her to do. She closed her eyes and willfully shoved down the power coiling inside of her. When she opened her eyes again, her skin felt like her own and she could no longer sense the dream world that existed within and under the world around them. She cast a contemptuous glance at her visitors. "Better?"

Maeve could claim lack of fear all she wanted, but it took that show of self-discipline to get the woman moving, and she did...she took over immediately, much to Alex's relief. Ro looked so very human lying there, so frail and weak and fragile. It scared her more than she would like to admit.

Maeve kneeled at Rohanna's side and practically pushed Alex away. After a moment she sent Shyann scurrying into the kitchen for supplies. "You too, Alex. Hovering over her won't help but she'll need the tea Shyann is making. Help Shyann. I'll stay with Rohanna."

CHAPTER THIRTY-SEVEN

Ro's body healed quickly in the days following her escape, but her mind remained lost in the fog and pain of her ordeal. Alex's heart ached to the point of breaking. The fiery woman she had fallen in love with sat listlessly before her, dull eyed and uninterested in the food she tried to tempt her with. Rohanna had lost weight; her hair felt brittle and appeared washed out, no longer the color of spun gold that seemed to shine like the sun itself. Now that sun lay behind dark clouds, leaving only a shadow of Ro's former self.

Alex gave up trying to get food into her and led Ro over to the overstuffed sofa. Ro took wooden, automatic steps, going where she was directed but no farther. Once on the sofa, Ro curled up in a small ball and hugged herself with too thin arms. Alex gently brushed the hair out of her eyes, then kissed her forehead.

"So cold," Rohanna chattered, shivering despite the heat. This lingering chill troubled Alex. Ro's fever had responded well to Maeve's treatment, there was no reason she was still so cold. Alex laid a thick woolen blanket over Ro's body and threw another log on the already blazing fire. Rohanna closed her eyes, passively accepting Alex's gentle ministrations before drifting back to sleep

Alex collapsed on the floor beneath the crushing weight of what felt like an overwhelming hopelessness. The bruised circles beneath Ro's eyes grew darker every day.

Overly pale cheekbones stood out in stark relief, leaving her face etched in deep shadows that only served to illustrate the obvious. Rohanna was not getting better.

Alex took Rohanna's hands in hers and closed her eyes, following the path of sleep until she reached Rohanna's dreams. A cold, hard lump of despair settled deep inside Alex's belly. Her throat burned with the sour taste of failure.

Rohanna's soul felt thin. Her dreams were one-dimensional. Like images on a movie screen, they slid through memories of the past, not the future. Swallowing hard against a sudden wave of nausea, Alex realized that Rohanna, the one woman she loved more than her own life, was slowly dying. Too much of who Ro was had been damaged by Bellaria. Her body was strong, but the injuries sustained by her soul were proving to be insurmountable.

Covering her face in her hands, Alex pushed back the tears that threatened to come. She pressed the heel of her hands firmly against eyes reddened by too many sleepless nights. The cool, firm edge of her leather bracer pressed hard against her cheek.

She had taken to wearing it again since that night at the forge, slipping it on while the confusion around Rohanna's unexpected arrival kept everyone occupied. Maeve hadn't noticed the marking when she took over Rohanna's care, and Alex had acted purely on instinct. No other reason guided her action and she couldn't even be sure that Shyann hadn't told her. Something told her she hadn't.

"I should just take the damn thing off, there's no one here to see anything they shouldn't." Both Shyann and Maeve were gone now. She had sent them away in a burst of overwhelming rage. They were the nearest targets, and she cared nothing for their own pain, only that their weak excuses and half-answers had infuriated her. Her actions only added to the guilt she was feeling now.

A flash of lightning and the subsequent roll of thunder heralded the beginning of another summer storm. They had been frequent and violent over the last week and were a constant reminder of finding Rohanna shivering and wet in her doorway. Ro moaned in her sleep, shifting restlessly beneath the blankets. Alex was at her side in an instant, comforting her the best she could. She sandwiched Rohanna's hand between her own, then searched her face for any sign that she felt her touch.

"Fool woman, you couldn't even give me the chance to rescue you, could you? You had to go and do it yourself," Alex whispered. Like something alive and full of teeth actively chewing on her insides, her guilt fed on her self-doubt and assailed her with a dozen what if questions.

What if she had gone to her that night? What if she had ignored Maeve's warning and done as she had wanted, attacking Bellaria head on? Would Rohanna be like this now? Those questions sliced apart her self-confidence. If they had a physical presence, her skin would be bleeding from a hundred wounds.

Another lightning strike crashed around them. Blinding in its intensity, it was followed by another furious roll of thunder that shook the timbers of the house. Momentarily stunned by the bright flash, Alex blinked against the after images burned into her retinas, flashing balls of light dancing across her field of vision. The logs in the fireplace sputtered and hissed, then died a moment before the lights flickered and the power went out completely, plunging the house into complete darkness.

Unable to see, Alex's other senses took over. She could hear the heavy patter of rain striking the metal roof above her. It had started raining again. Underneath the smell of rain and damp smoke, she caught the acrid scent of magic, a sulphur like smell that made her nose twitch in irritation. She moved rapidly, standing in front of Ro to protect her from the unseen presence. Another flash of lightning momentarily silhouetted a still figure in the doorway. Hidden in shadow, it made no move towards them.

"Who's there, show yourself." Alex's challenge was answered by a voice as deep as the rumbling thunder. It rolled through Alex's consciousness, speaking a word of power that echoed through the room. The knot work hidden beneath her bracer blazed to life, its heat trapped beneath the thick leather.

"Holy hells," Alex roared, grabbing at her wrist. It felt like her entire forearm had caught fire. She yanked at the laces, managing to loosen it enough to pull it off despite the pain. The scorched leather fell to the floor, a lone tendril of smoke let her know how close the tough hide had come to igniting.

Alex held her hand up in front of her, expecting to see charred flesh. She gasped and stumbled back, almost falling over the couch and onto Rohanna.

Shining like a beacon, electric blue lines pulsed and danced across her skin, flaring with each lightning strike. The fine hairs on her arms stood on end, sensitized to the subtle currents of air and power that surrounded her.

"Father," Alex nodded at her visitor. She recognized that voice now.

"Hush, child. There isn't much time. You can still save her but it won't be easy."

"I'm listening," Alex said.

As much as she hated being ignorant of her own past and of her mother's life, she had to put aside her anger and bitterness. She had to, if Rohanna was to survive long enough to see another sunrise. She bowed her head and listened, not because she forgave him for years of absence, but because his presence here tonight had nothing to do with the two of them.

Tonight he came as a God offering the chance at accomplishing the impossible, and when the Gods chose to be so generous, it was wise to pay attention.

***

"Alex? What's happening?" Ro asked weakly, "It's so dark in here."

"What?" Alex shook her head, trying to clear it. She stood in the middle of the living room with no memory of how long she had been there and only a vague sense of how much time had passed. Had she been called into a dream? She didn't think so. As surreal as the experience had been, it did not bear the hallmarks of the dream world.

"Alex?" Ro called out again. Her voice trembled and faded at the end, but it was more than she had said in a week. Alex rushed to her side.

"I'm here, Love. The storm knocked out the power."

"Oh," Rohanna sighed. Red rimmed eyes squinted up at her then closed again. "I thought someone was here."

"No, Sweetheart, it was just the lightning."

Rohanna's breathing slowed until it was so shallow Alex had to strain to see her chest rise and fall. She was about to move away when Rohanna took a deep breath and fidgeted beneath the blanket.

"I'm so cold, Alex."

Alex's heart nearly broke. "I'll warm you, Love. Here, let me hold you."

Alex settled on the couch and pulled Rohanna up on her lap. Ro curled up against her, then promptly fell asleep with her head tucked under Alex's chin. With nothing left to do, Alex stared blindly at the low flames eating at the logs in the fireplace. She didn't need the light to see; her mind was elsewhere. Light and sound would only distract her.

All her life, she had known she was different from the rest of her tribe. A throwback to the time when it was more common for Mere and Greater Fae to intermingle. It had been enough to mark her as different, subject to the constant taunts of her childhood peers. Wearing the face of their oppressor did not make her popular, not when they had sacrificed so much to be free of them, neither did her Fae nature. Cruel and capricious, the Greater Fae never apologized for their appetites...and she had many of the same desires. Desires she spent many years tempering with her own moral code.

I thought choosing to live apart from the tribe and working the forge was an act of rebellion. Now, I am not so sure.

All her life, Alex had clung to that bit of humanity her father's blood gave her as if it was a shield against her Fae nature. That shield was now shattered, and within those shards lay a lifetime of lies. She had spent so much energy trying to convince her tribe that there was no shame in love...that they didn't have to follow the old ways. Now she felt like a fool. Her father was not human. She had been fighting the wrong fight. No wonder Kaleigh had fought her so vehemently...*and no wonder that she took advantage of the first valid excuse to kick me out of the tribe. It's pretty clear to me now that she would have never let me ascend to her position. Epona blessed or not.*

She gazed down at her arm and shuddered.

Goddess help me. I know what I need to do, but can I bring myself to do it? Alex looked down at Ro and her heart started to pound again. *Will Rohanna let me do what is necessary?*

Alex wrapped her arms around her beloved and whispered a soft question. It was time to find out how far trust and love could go. Dull green eyes slid open, a small gleam of light gathering deep in them as she answered.

"Yes."

It was such a simple answer, but it held worlds of possibility. Alex felt hope leap and dance inside her. The sharp teeth of fear gnawed relentlessly at the edge of that hope, but Alex willed it back into its dark cave where it belonged. She could not doubt herself. She could not doubt Rohanna.

Alex brushed her lips across Rohanna's forehead. "Sleep, Sweetheart. Save your strength."

***

Alex's words gathered power as she moved about the room, lighting candles in a large circle. Her movements were slow and elegant. With each candle lit, the shadows danced eerily across the darkened room, growing paler until the gathered light finally chased them away. Alex spoke not only for Ro's benefit, but for her own, finding calm within the ritual movements and forms.

345

"Few people understand the controlled violence of striking steel on steel. Forging is not simply a matter of pummeling hot metal with a large hammer. Yes, the mallet is heavy. But if there is no control, no exact knowledge of the force behind the swing, no measure of accuracy in the strike, there will be no finished project. The difference between a work of art and a lump of misshapen metal lay in the ability to discern when rough metal glows hotly enough to be malleable to the blacksmith's art. Cold metal is often too brittle, and brittle steel shatters easily under the blows of even the most talented blacksmith."

Finally, the last candle was lit, and Alex ended her circle where she had begun. The first and last candle stood together, one white and one black. Their flames danced close to each other, rightfully attracted to the other's light. The circle complete, she turned to face the center.

Rohanna stood silent, listening to the cadenced tone of Alex's words. Their eyes locked. The smell of burning wax combined with the scents of fear and excitement filled the air with electricity.

"Tonight we will be forging our souls, Rohanna. This is old magic, and like all magicks, it has its risks. Are you sure you want to go through with this?"

"I trust you Alex. I want to do this. I need to do this."

"If it becomes too much, just tell me and I will stop," Alex said.

If I stop she will die, but I cannot do this against her will.

CHAPTER THIRTY-EIGHT

Alex towered gracefully above Rohanna. Rohanna kneeled before her, her body held upright by the restraints buckled to each wrist. Alex's arm, sleekly muscled and solid from hours working at the anvil, barely felt the weight of the leather flogger in her hand.

A soft pink glow was growing slowly across Rohanna's smooth back and firm bottom, evidence of Alex's art with the soft leather. Able to caress with kisses as soft as a butterfly's wing, it could also lash out like a scorpion's sting to lay long, angry welts along willing flesh. She wanted Rohanna to sink into the pleasure of the stinging pain she rained down upon her, to soften into the caresses of the leather flogger. Too much would break her, but if Alex failed to go as far as was needed, Rohanna would be lost forever. Alex wanted the softly moaning woman to lay pliable before her, every inch of Rohanna's skin needed to feel alive, to remind her that her body and spirit belonged together. Only then would Alex be able to identify the intruding spells that bound Rohanna and disrupted the energy paths that fed her soul.

Alex took a deep breath to center herself. She was breathing hard, not from exertion, but from excitement. Her father's blood sang inside her; newly awakened, it was all the more powerful, even stronger than her Mere blood. Her father had not lied when he told her his gift was no gentle thing.

347

Fae blood held an edge to it that craved the darker things, including levels of passions few humans would find enjoyable let alone survive, and it was too easy to succumb to the love of pain.

Her hand tightened around the whip until her knuckles cracked and she felt the leather give. *I will heal Rohanna,* she vowed. The trick was not losing herself in the process.

Restraint. Alex raised her arm. She would not tempt her darker side with harsher play of the lash, especially with Rohanna's life on the line. Black leather cut into her wrist just below her tattoos, twisted until it was almost too tight. One by one she forced tense fingers to release their hold on the floggers handle, then let the strap slip loose. Alex dropped the flogger on the floor and gazed down at Rohanna's back.

Rohanna's skin glowed brightly, much like the steel Alex forged. She admired her work, knowing that like that glowing metal, Rohanna was now able to be shaped by the power of the fire within her, without fear.

Rohanna was soaked with perspiration. It dripped from her brow, her body covered in a light sheen that glowed with the muted candle light. Head thrown back, eyes closed and lips parted slightly, the long line of Rohanna's throat begged to be kissed. Alex's gaze took in Rohanna's firm breasts thrust proudly before her. Her nipples were hard and swollen, begging to be suckled and roughly fondled.

Alex became aware of her own ragged breathing. *Not for me, this is all for her.* Alex reminded herself, swallowing around a suddenly dry throat. *Goddess, this is harder than I thought it would be.*

It wasn't a matter of curbing her arousal, the sexual tension was a part of the magic between them. The goal was not to remain unaroused. The goal was to bear her arousal, gathering it inside her until her veins burned with power. Only then could Alex set it free in one glorious push, pouring her power into Rohanna, joining them together, and setting Rohanna free from Bellaria's influence. If she succumbed to greed and demanded her own satisfaction, the magic would unravel and everything she had accomplished so far would unravel.

Alex kneeled behind the restrained woman. Alex passed her hands over Rohanna's glistening skin, never actually touching her but still tasting the heat of her aura that poured off her in waves. The pale yellow-orange of Ro's aura sparked and shone within Alex's vision; it turned a bright gold as delicate fingers of color melded with Alex's own red tinged aura.

Awed by the deep connection they had made, Alex reverently gathered Rohanna's body within her arms. She had refrained from touching her since they had both entered the circle and not since she had stripped naked. When their naked bodies connected, she gasped aloud. Their auras flashed, dancing across her vision with the same ethereal light that created the Northern Lights. Their individual colors bled together, binding them more firmly then any rope or chain ever could. The exquisitely intimate moment threatened to overwhelm Alex's fragile control.

Alex lowered her lips to meet the soft flesh along the muscled curve of Rohanna's neck, tasting only salt and sweat with no trace of the metallic edge that would have indicated fear. If Rohanna succumbed to fear now it would only increase the risk for failure and Alex could not allow that.

Rohanna moaned and tipped her head to the side, offering her neck to Alex's sharp white teeth and talented lips.

Alex's hearing was attuned to even the slightest sounds. She could hear Rohanna's heart galloping alongside hers, accompanied by the restless whisper of leather and hiss of flame on candle-wax, but it was Rohanna who sang to her with every catching breath, every low moan ending in a sudden gasp. She sought out that music like someone starved for beauty and the woman restrained and kneeling before her was her instrument.

Calloused and work roughened fingers sought out and captured Rohanna's nipples. She rubbed her palms across them roughly, then teased them mercilessly with her fingertips, knowing what brought Rohanna the most pleasure. Abandoning the soft flesh of Rohanna's breasts, Alex leisurely slid one hand down, circling taut abdominal muscles that flexed and fluttered as if anticipating her destination, the soft curls already damp with arousal. Cupping Rohanna firmly within the palm of her hand, Alex paused, feeling the incredible heat and wetness emanating from between those trembling thighs. Biding her time, Alex forced herself to stillness, patiently waiting.

Moments passed in silence, with only the sound of their breathing marking the time for them in the otherwise quiet room. Rohanna's pulse bounded beneath her lips, its frantic rhythm echoing against her palm pressed solidly over Rohanna's throbbing clit. All too aware of her own arousal, Alex felt the same hot wetness gathering between her thighs. It took all of her self-control not to thrust her hips forward against Ro's tight ass. Alex's swollen clit begged for the release that Ro's touch would offer.

Ro moved first, rocking her pelvis into Alex's cupped hand with a desperate whimper. The tantalizing motion brought the firm globes of her ass in contact with Alex's hypersensitive clit. Moaning softly into the golden halo of Rohanna's hair, she slid two fingers between Ro's glistening lips, capturing her engorged clitoris between them. With her fingers held still along either side of Rohanna's hardness, Alex limited Ro's stimulation to her own movements. Knowing that the indirect stimulation was maddening to her lover, she allowed one quick flick of her thumb over the sensitized clit. Rewarded with a sharp gasp and frantic movement intended to extend the pressure, Alex changed tactics. Circling down, she rested firm fingertips just outside of Rohanna's wet center, pressing the remaining length of her fingers against her slick folds. With the utmost control, Alex prevented Rohanna's rapid hip thrusting from enveloping her fingers, teasing her unmercifully.

Bringing her lips close to Rohanna's ear, she whispered tenderly, "Tell me what you need, Ro. Come back to me. Feel me here, with you." From the moment Alex had buckled the wrist restraints on Rohanna, the proud woman had refrained from uttering a word. Now, given leave to ask, Ro found herself begging. Her need was so great, and she had held her voice for so long, that her words came out as a choking sob.

"Please, Alex, please...I want..."

Another whispered command caressed Ro's burning skin. "Tell me, tell me what you want!"

Urgent, demanding, the voice was reinforced by two slick fingers gliding shallowly into Ro's depths and then withdrawing. The empty ache that filled Ro's heart and mind for so long now seemed centered between her thighs.

Ro wanted so much to be filled, to feel the ache of fullness that Alex's fingers promised.

"I don't want to feel empty any longer. Please, Alex, help me."

Reality shrunk around Ro's fevered mind, until it contained only her and the woman pressed against her. Nothing else mattered accept heat, and wet, and need. Her universe shifted, revolving dizzily around the core of her being. Her body was on fire. Her veins pulsed in time with her heartbeat, which in turn followed the frantic throbbing between her thighs. She could no longer tell what led what, only that her body demanded to be claimed by the one woman who truly understood her. She felt the heat along her back from Alex's whip, a mere shadow of the warmth radiating from her thighs. Alex's fingers felt like two flames licking at her core. She wanted to take Alex's fiery passion within her and make it her own.

"Then find me, Rohanna. Take what you need and find yourself." Alex urged her on.

As the maelstrom whipped and burnt around and through her, Ro experienced a moment of absolute clarity, her passion free and unencumbered by convention and rules; she felt power enter her chained body. Finally, totally, and without reserve, she gave herself over to Alex, accepting the gift she was offering.

"Please, Alex, please…I need to feel you inside me." Her words were spoken clearly, demanding and full of power, heralding her transformation.

Alex's power responded in kind. Her eyes bled blue and the familiar realm between dream and reality surrounded them. Rohanna strained against her restraints, then threw her head back violently and howled her desire.

Awestruck at the sheer wildness of her lover, she could only watch mutely while Rohanna cast off the mundane bits of herself, exposing the fierce spirit underneath that transcended every false belief and human frailty she had cloaked herself in.

Feeling Rohanna open to her in both body and spirit, Alex slid first one finger, then another, deep into Rohanna's wetness, allowing her to take as much as she could within her. Ro's slick walls contracted against her soaked fingers, capturing her in their muscular grip. Alex began to move slowly, savoring the tightness of velvet muscles clenching around each thrust of her invading fingers. Plunging deeper with every stroke, Rohanna's hips rocked forward to meet each thrust, demanding more. Bringing the calloused pad of her thumb into play, she pressed gently against Ro's clit. The answering buck was violent, setting off a wave of frantic thrusts against her captured hand. Ro was straining against her restraints to gain more leverage, throwing her head back against Alex's shoulder. Ro's pulse bounded noticeably beneath skin flushed red from arousal and exertion.

"Oh God, Alex," Rohanna sobbed. Her vision bled to red, fiery images of molten lava dancing before her as their passion brought forth the first stirrings of orgasm. Crying out, she thrust fiercely against Alex's hand, her hips bucking wildly. "I'm going to come, please let me come!"

"Not yet, Love, not yet," Alex whispered. Alex slid a third finger into Rohanna's tight depths, driving her over the edge. As Rohanna tumbled into orgasm, Alex held on tightly, feeling the rhythmic clenching of Rohanna's muscles as she came, wetness flowing copiously over her captured fingers.

Alex remained still, her fingers buried deep inside Rohanna's silken walls, feeling the contractions slowly diminish in force. Gradually, Alex began to move inside her, flexing her fingers slightly, the shallow strokes bringing Rohanna back to the brink of orgasm. She abandoned her earlier subtle movements, just shy of hard enough to bring Rohanna again, and stroked her in earnest. She did this without mercy, ignoring the begging sobs coming from the racked woman arching into her.

When Rohanna came again, it was to the sound of blood pounding through her skull and power rushing through her veins as Alex finally released the power she had held so carefully inside her, letting it flow between them until Rohanna's spirit snatched it up greedily, feeding the faded flame of her soul. Rohanna threw her head back and howled again, a primordial sound that reverberated through her soul and ripped away the shackles of her past. Spent, Rohanna dangled bonelessly from the leather restraints at each wrist. Even kneeling, her trembling legs felt too weak to support her. She had no doubt that the restraints were the only thing keeping her upright at all. Rohanna's voice felt raw from screaming her climax, her throat dry from lack of moisture. As the endorphin rush fled her exhausted body, a stinging pain was making itself known along her back and buttocks. Salt burned into her reddened skin from the trails of perspiration that marked her journey to this point.

Alex stood slowly, exhausted and shaky from the intense magic she had wrought between them. Reaching up, she gently removed the soft leather cuffs restraining Rohanna's limp hands. Lowering her gently to the ground, Alex brushed damp hair away from Ro's face. She slept now, exhausted by her ordeal, but she would recover and be well again, given a bit of time.

Raising her hand in front of her face, Alex watched the play of pale blue flames casting their hue across her splayed fingers. The same aura glowed softly along Rohanna's skin, shimmering through her aura. Wherever they touched, the faint blue hue flashed to the purest white, tendrils of light reaching out between them as if drawn to each other. Alex felt the small hairs on her arms rise in response to the faint electrical charge between them. She lightly stroked Ro's arm, then snatched her fingers away when the same sensation slid across her own skin.

"What have I done?" she whispered. The obvious answer did not placate her as it should. The foul taste of Bellaria's magic was gone; Rohanna was free of the tangled skein of spell after spell designed to control her. Alex had fumbled her way through the most dangerous of magicks, and they had both survived, but there was no room for pride in her accomplishment. Alex had almost pulled Rohanna's soul apart in order to separate her from the spells that Bellaria had woven through her.

"No one told me. I didn't know." Alex rocked back on her heels. Terror and madness bubbled up inside her, followed by a healthy dose of anger at her father. He had given her the power to heal Rohanna yet failed to tell her what the consequences might be.

"You never told me. You should have warned me." Shaking with rage, she roared her displeasure into the night before returning her attention back to Rohanna. She still slept. She didn't know. Relief flooded through her, followed by a different sort of terror.

"Goddess forgive me," Alex whispered. The magic had worked and Ro was safe, but at a cost.

She had taken Rohanna and worked her flesh much as she did the raw metal at her forge, hammering out the impurities in order to find the shining core that could survive the heat and flames. But in doing so, Alex had also burned away the brittleness of humanity. Without meaning to, she had taken away the part of Rohanna that made her human. Demi-Fae were not immortal. They may live extended lives, but they aged and died just like everyone in this world did.

What will she do when she finds out? Alex tried to placate herself with the fact that Rohanna never asked what side effects the ritual might hold, but knew she was fooling herself. Rohanna trusted her. She wouldn't have thought to ask.

She could only hope that Rohanna would understand and accept what had been done to her when the time came to tell her.

CHAPTER THIRTY-NINE

Making that one phone call was the most difficult thing Alex had ever done in her life. Listening to Bellaria's triumphant crow made her want to strike the wall in front of her until her knuckles were bloodied. She balled her fist tight enough to make her arm shake. Alex used the pain of sharp nails digging into her palm as a substitute for following through. She had to keep her eye on the goal, and could not risk steering away from the course she had laid out for them.

Alex hung up the phone, dropping the fear and indecision in her voice as easily as an actress shed her character once off stage. She turned towards her remaining audience, her lip curled up in a distasteful sneer. Just telling Bellaria that she needed her help, that she was too weak to help Rohanna, left a bad taste in her mouth. Not as foul as the witch herself, but it still made her stomach turn.

"It's done. Bellaria is expecting us tonight." Alex tugged at her braid. "Goddess below, but that was hard."

"I'm sure it was." Shyann jumped up on the kitchen counter and took a huge bite out of a stolen apple. Her legs swung back and forth, making her look deceptively young and vulnerable. *Fae camouflage meant to distract and deceive, nothing more*, Alex thought. She was pretty sure that out of all of them, Shyann was the deadliest of all.

Shyann tipped her head, narrowing her eyes at Alex for a moment before grinning at her.

"Don't underestimate yourself, Alexandria," Shyann said. "Bellaria's arrogance is her greatest weakness. She thinks she's won, let her believe that. She won't see you as a threat if she thinks you're weak. We need to use that to our advantage."

"But I'm not weak, not anymore," Alex answered bleakly. "My father's 'gift' took care of that."

"Careful, Alexandria, or I might think you're buying into Maeve's insistence that we are doing nothing more than fulfilling a longstanding prophecy."

"I could say the same thing about you, Shyann," Alex grumbled, reflexively rubbing at the leather bracer, a part of her mind always aware of the markings hidden there. "You come and go at her request, how do I know I can truly trust you. She might have told you to befriend me."

Anger flashed in Shyann's eyes like a flash fire. Her mouth dropped open, the apple forgotten in her hand. "Alex! I've already betrayed Maeve just by coming here today, how can you say that?"

"I'm sorry. Ever since I was a child we were fed horror stories about the Greater Fae. I see you, and I hear my aunt telling me how they were made to do terrible things, many times on a whim or simply because they wanted to remind us that we were less than they. It's hard to reconcile what I know of you with those stories."

"I can see that. Trust is hard to find and even harder to keep. I hate Bellaria with every fiber of my being. She is the worst of the worst, but I cannot condemn all witches because of one. There are many women who follow a gentler craft and abhor what she's become. She is sick and twisted and as addicted to power as some of the Fae, I will give you that. We are not all innocent, and it is good to remain wary. I'll not tell you a lie and say your aunt exaggerated."

Shyann suddenly became quite intrigued with counting the number of seeds she could pull out of her apple core. "But, um, Alex? You have to realize something."

"What?"

"You really haven't made the connection yet, have you?" Shyann's gaze slipped across Alex's leather bracer before meeting her eyes. "If your father is who you say he is, you aren't Lesser Fae, you never were."

"Oh, hell." Alex blindly reached behind her for a chair and sat down before her legs gave way. "I...I don't understand any of this. My father. Why did he show up now after being absent all these years? Would he have even bothered if it wasn't for Bellaria and Rohanna?"

"I don't have those answers, Alexandria." Shyann felt horrible for her new friend. She had every right to be angry at her father, and she doubted he would ever give his daughter the answers she needed. It was just the way it was with the most powerful of their kind. "I'm sorry it had to be me, but someone had to tell you. Bellaria might figure it out and if she does, she will try to use that knowledge to derail you. News such as this in the heat of battle can be the difference between victory and death. Truth can wound a warrior as easily as a blade, and knowledge can make you bleed. You need to be alright with this before you go against her."

"I need to be alright with it," Alex muttered. "So much easier said than done."

She jumped up from her seat. It was always easier to deal with things when she was on the move. Hand's clasped behind her back, she stopped at the picture window and gazed out at the green grass and blue sky above. How she wished she could leave all this behind and just run. It would be so easy...shed this life for another and exist for the night. Goddess knew there were plenty of souls that deserved more than one visit from a true NightMere. She would have purpose...but she wouldn't have Rohanna.

"Accept an unpleasant truth or lose the girl. How very Fae, hmm? I thought I was the master of the forge, but I feel like I'm the one being tossed into the fire and tempered beneath a ruthless hammer."

Shyann shrugged. "I won't argue with you. The question is, Alexandria Strider, will you be alright with this or am I wasting my time here?"

Alex spun back around. Shyann was still on her countertop perch. She looked like a child sitting like that, ankles crossed and swinging a good foot off of the floor, but there was nothing childlike in the challenge she issued. Alex cast a troubled look towards the back bedroom where Rohanna slept, unaware of their meeting, then met Shyann's gaze.

"I freed Rohanna of Bellaria's spell, but she's still a threat. No matter what, if we do nothing, Rohanna will be in danger."

"Yes. I believe so. Once Bellaria has her eyes on a prize, she will never go away, she will never stop trying to claim her, and if she ever becomes useless to her, she will kill to keep anyone else from having her."

"I can't allow that," Alex growled. There really was no choice, not unless she was willing to cede the win to Bellaria and lose Rohanna in the bargain. "If your offer still stands, I will gladly accept your help."

Shyann's face lit up, eager and cruel and altogether too excited about the coming battle. Alex half expected to see her rub her hands together gleefully, but she simply grinned and jumped off the kitchen counter. As light on her feet as a cat, she headed for the front door.

"Okay, then, I guess that's my cue. I'll see you at sunrise." Shyann stopped at the threshold and looked back at her. "One last thing, Alexandria. Maeve and all her talk about prophecy can be annoying, but look at everything that has happened to get us to this point. So many coincidences, so many unexpected and unexplained endeavors. There has to be a pattern, and if you see prophecy as an attempt to explain those patterns...to make them easier to recognize, it might help you trust Maeve a bit more."

"Good hunting," Shyann added, and then she was gone, leaving Alex alone with her thoughts.

The afternoon sun streamed through the window at a harsh angle. It flooded the room around her with a red-gold glow that cast the world into a mockery of hellfire. Soon, very soon...she would have to do something she abhorred doing.

"Trust Maeve," she muttered. *I'll trust the woman as far as I can throw her, and even then that would be stretching my trust farther than I like.* Maeve knew more than she was telling, and that smug, superior smile masquerading as complacent acceptance did nothing but infuriate Alex. She didn't believe in the infallibility of fate nor the immutable quality of prophecy. Anything could be made malleable with the right leverage.

Maeve was too pleased that Rohanna had found her power in time to escape from Bellaria, and all too certain that Alex had the knowledge to heal her. It was as if their hard won victories proved that she—Maeve—had been right all along, trusting her ancient prophecies. Alex trembled in remembered anger. She had wanted to strike out at Maeve that night but sent her on her way instead.

All she cared about was Rohanna, not some ridiculous prophecy or pre-ordained battle with Bellaria, and yet here she was, ready to do just that.

Bellaria. From what Alex had gleaned from Rohanna's confused memories, she wanted to control the Shadow Lands, to return to Faerie and continue her war there.

Bellaria wants to go home. Well then, far be it from me to keep her from her goal.

CHAPTER FORTY

"Remove the bracer, Alexandria. Now!" Bellaria demanded.

The witch gripped Rohanna tightly from behind, a sharp knife held against the flesh at her throat. A thin trickle of blood ran down the smooth skin. A light breeze carried the sharp metallic scent towards Alex, making her wary. This wasn't exactly how she had expected the night to play out. *I'm going to have to improvise.*

"Truly, you need proof?" Alex asked. "You know who I am and what I am."

"Yes, I would see for myself. You are useless to me without the markings, and there are rumors..." Bellaria licked her lips, her tongue slipping out between wolfish teeth before her jaw snapped shut. Only a fool would think it a sign of nervousness, and Alex was no fool. Bellaria knew something. Something she shouldn't know and had almost revealed.

"As you wish, then, but you're just wasting time." Alex's gaze never left the other woman's face while she unlaced the wide leather cuff encircling her left forearm. It felt strange removing it in front of Bellaria, and on her command.

The heavy leather was solid black, surprisingly free of scuffs and scratches you would expect from someone who worked long hours at a forge. Even the leather laces were shiny and new, sliding easily through the holes punched evenly along the underside of the bracer.

Careful, don't give anything away.

Unceremoniously dropping the bracer onto the ground in front of her, Alex slowly raised her left arm across her chest. Every muscle in her body felt strung tight as a bow, practically quivering with the desire to act. She was careful to keep her fear for Ro buried deep, just in case the witch could smell it.

The full moon had reached its highest point above them. Alex's raised arm caught the delicate beams, illuminating the details of the intricate blue tattoo that wove across her wrist and forearm.

"Is this sufficient proof?" Alex asked, ignoring the shocked gasp that escaped from Ro as the ancient markings came alive under the light of the moon. "This is what you wanted to see. What you needed to see?"

She lowered her arm. Two sets of eyes followed the designs that danced against her skin, seeming to be both a part of her while somehow alive.

"Is it, witch?" She shook her fist at the shadow-clad woman. "You know what this means, and what I can do. Only certain Meres are marked in such a way, these markings are a testament of my rank."

Alex avoided looking at Ro directly; she could not risk giving away how deep their connection went. *Let her think I want the human, nothing more. Bellaria understands greed and power. Rohanna is safest if she thinks I am acting on baser desires.* "You don't need to threaten her anymore. She's still too weak to be of use to you, but I can take you back to Faerie on my own."

"You will take me back to Faerie?" Bellaria jumped on Alex's offer all too eagerly. "Of your own free will?"

"I will take you to Faerie," Alex agreed.

"That's not good enough." Bellaria backed away from the stones, the sharp blade still pressed to Rohanna's neck. "I want to know why you offer yourself in place of Rohanna."

Alex thrust out her hand towards the two of them before she could stop herself. "Think, Bellaria...all these years you have tried to get Rohanna to do your bidding, and after all these years, has she ever managed to open the Gateway? Spill her blood tonight and you may find your way home, but what if it doesn't work? You will fail, and there will be no second chances. I, on the other hand, can give you want you want."

"And in return?" Bellaria narrowed her eyes at Alex.

Alex chuckled. "I enjoy her presence, Bellaria. She is, how do I say, compatible with my needs. Look at her back. See how I've marked her. How many humans do you think I could find that enjoy such play, let alone survive?"

The tableau froze between them. Alex trying so hard to be someone she wasn't and Bellaria sensing that something was wrong.

Rohanna clung to Bellaria's knife arm, barely able to swallow let alone speak, that's how close the knife sat against her veins. One wrong move and she would bleed. It would only take one moment of carelessness on Bellaria's part...or Rohanna losing her nerve and trying to run.

"Alex?" Rohanna's lips moved, but no sound came out. She beseeched Alex to end this before Bellaria's paranoia got the best of them with a look. Alex stepped forward, hiding the subtle movement of her head in the motion...the quickest of warnings that Bellaria missed but Ro did not. She closed her eyes, her eyelids fluttering in protest. Self-preservation demanded she remain watchful, and it took a huge effort to fight her natural instincts.

"Bellaria," Alex leveled a lethal stare at the witch woman. "I will take you to Faerie—of my own free will."

"Prove it," Bellaria gestured wildly with the knife. The silver blade flashed, casting a crimson arc between them. Drops of Rohanna's blood spattered across the stone arch, waking the ancient circle. Rohanna clasped her palm across the wound and whimpered, her eyes never left Alex's face.

"It's just a small cut," Bellaria sneered. "Now show me what you can do."

Alex glowered at the witch-woman but held her tongue. Losing her temper would do neither of them any good, no matter how much she wanted to tear Bellaria apart with her bare hands. She turned her back on the witch to gaze on the stones standing sentry behind her. The sacrifice stone hummed in anticipation of offered blood. Rohanna's blood. Alex ran her left hand across the stone, quieting its muted song.

Alex wheeled around at the sound of Bellaria's triumphant cackle. Rohanna lay crumpled at her feet, unmoving, and barely breathing. Fearing the worst, she was at Rohanna's side in less than a second, peering into her pale face. A low moan escaped from Rohanna's lips.

"Why?" Alex demanded.

"Why?" Bellaria spat, mocking Alex's question. "Because you are a fool."

Bellaria had discarded the subtle disguise she had kept while pretending to be Ro's stepmother, revealing her true nature. She was tall and unnaturally lean, with feral eyes that held the silver glow of a predator. Those eyes were fixed on Alex now, urging her to fear her like the prey she thought Alex was.

No, she thought, *this is but one, not a pack.* She visualized the witch as a lone wolf, left to skulk in the shadows and survive alone. This close, she could smell Bellaria's desperation. Her desire for power was so intense it had overcome all other needs, including any joy she might have been able to find on Earth. *She is consumed by this dark and twisted quest,* Alex thought. *There is nothing else left for her.*

"I know how much this woman means to you," Bellaria said, waving her arm in Ro's direction. "You thought you could control this game, hide your connection with Rohanna. You cannot hide *anything* from me!"

Alex listened in silence to the woman's ranting, her heart beating madly in her chest. The desire to do something, to act, was so strong that it hurt.

"I can smell you on her, in her. Her aura is so tainted with yours. I wonder if she knows what you have done to her," Bellaria continued, enjoying Alex's growing discomfort.

"Do not speak of what you do not understand, witch!" Alex growled, risking a quick glance at Rohanna. She was still unconscious, unaware of this last scene being played out above her.

"Tell me, does she know? Should I wake her? Tell her what has happened?" The witch pressed on, her voice arrogant. She looked delighted at the prospect of tormenting Alex with her knowledge.

"No," Alex spoke barely over a whisper. "I love her. If you do that, she may never trust me again." Her voice broke with emotion. The words had been spoken aloud. The three of them were inside the sacred circle—the stones now knew her secret.

Alex lowered her eyes and bowed her head before the cowled woman.

She could not risk Bellaria learning anything more about her. Dropping her shoulders, Alex feigned defeat.

Let her think she has broken me.

"Ah. At last, the truth." Bellaria laughed. "You have allowed yourself to become weakened by love, Alex...a weakness no Mere is supposed to succumb to. How deliciously ironic considering how much effort I took to make sure Rohanna found no man to her liking. It never crossed my mind that she would take an interest in the fairer sex, although I have to say you are a magnificent specimen, regardless of your gender."

Bellaria reached beneath her cloak and tossed something heavy on the ground in front of her.

"Pick them up and put them on. I can't have you getting away from me."

Alex looked down at the familiar shape of iron shackles. Placed on a Mere, the iron would make her weak, easy to control. Alex gasped and backed away from the evil things. Bellaria meant to make her a slave. "This wasn't our agreement. I told you I would take you home, isn't that enough?" Alex didn't want to put the shackles on, but the die had already been cast. She had to continue this to the end.

"You have made a fatal error tonight, offering yourself up to me. A captive Mere has its advantages, especially the heir to the GranMere. You have given me your word, and you cannot be foresworn. So honorable, the Merefolk."

Bellaria pulled herself up to her full height and gazed down at Alex.

"I am not content with your offer. I am a Queen and I deserve a mount worthy of my station. You, Alexandria, will be that mount...and when your GranMere dies—and mark my words she will be the first to die—you will take over leadership of your tribe and I will have all of you. No army can stand against me, not when they are shitting and pissing themselves while they run like rabbits from the Wild Hunt. I will teach your people to enjoy blood again!"

"And Rohanna?" Alex rasped.

"Rohanna is a Gatekeeper, the first one born in a very long time. She and only she can open the gates between the Shadow Lands and Earth. Can you imagine how much power the one who controls the gates between magic and technology can gain?"

Alex's face went blank as shock took root. Bellaria's desire for power was even greater than she had thought. *She's mad, thinking she can rule both worlds.*

Bellaria's voice cut through the air, sharp and insistent. "Put the shackles on. You will do exactly what I want when I want...or you will both suffer for it."

Alex bent over and picked up the heavy shackles. The thick links clinked against each other as she hefted its weight in her hand.

"It is true, Bellaria, that I will not be forsworn. But it is you who have made the fatal mistake." Alex held the heavy circlets of iron out in front of her, taking care to let Bellaria see her lock each circlet around her wrists. "You have dwelt so hard on who and what I am, on who my mother was, that you forgot to ask about my father."

"What does that matter? He was probably some poor dirt farmer. I know your kind's penchant for human lovers, taking what you need and discarding your male offspring."

"Ah, but my father was not some dirt farmer, as you put it—and I am not just a Mere."

It was Bellaria's turn to look confused. She stepped back a pace.

"Cold iron will not hold me." Alex grinned at Bellaria, her lips stretched across teeth that shone white and straight against the night. She raised her arms; light erupted from the fine lines drawn into her wrist and crawled across her skin. The metal shifted, warping of its own accord as it slid away from her wrists and landed with a muffled thunk at her feet.

Alex could taste Bellaria's fear; she could see it grow in her eyes as she watched the cold iron fall to the ground.

"That's impossible. You shouldn't be able to do that, not even the Greater Fae are immune to cold iron," Bellaria said. "I saw you. Even working with the horses, you wore gloves to protect you from the steel."

"Did you now? Are you sure that is what you saw?"

Bellaria stepped back again, almost tripping over Rohanna. She drew her dagger, pointing it wildly in Alex's direction.

"I can still get to Rohanna before you can reach me. I will kill her!"

Alex ignored her desperate threats. She needed to finish this. She chuckled, knowing that humor would distract and enrage her enemy.

"You know us as the steeds for the Wild Hunt, but here we are our own rulers. Haven't you ever wondered why we chose to live here, instead of staying in Faerie? Humans have such lovely dreams, and such vivid nightmares. How could we ignore that feast, that bounty of fear?"

Alex stepped sideways, watching the movement of Bellaria's dagger weave towards her like a snake threatening to strike. Her movement kept Bellaria's attention on her, and that was exactly what she wanted.

"But I digress—or perhaps, not? Weren't you human once, Bellaria? Or near enough to one, even after all your attempts to learn Fae magicks? You dream, do you not? I am sure even you have your nightmares."

Bellaria's face blanked then paled as she started to make the connection Alex was so cruelly hinting at. "Ah, I see you have at last realized your mistake. You see, Rohanna can do so much more than open gateways, she can unlock old magick and give back what was lost so long ago. A dream can exist within a dream, Bellaria...and what you desire most can create an incredibly powerful lie."

A flash of lightning struck, close enough that Alex's skin crawled with its power. A boom sounded, once, twice, and then a third time. Alex tipped her head, listening to the hidden message within the coming storm. She laughed then, a mad laugh that held notes of the Wild Hunt within it. A laugh that any human would respond to with irrational terror, their ancestors having learned to run from it long ago.

Bellaria retreated even farther until the sacrifice stone behind her blocked her path. The stone hummed, sensing the wild magic.

Alex's eyes bled to the purest blue, not the bright blue of a human's eye, nor the deep blue of her Mere form, but the wild blue of lightning as it crossed the night sky. No pupil showed in that pure hue as Alex gazed down at Bellaria, capturing her with all the power she had always coveted and would never own.

"The thunder has sounded, and the lightning has struck, Bellaria. I am here to do as you asked. It is time for us to ride the storm and pierce the veil. You will have what you demanded of me, even if it is not in the way you desired. I promised to take you to Faerie, and I will. It is unfortunate for you though, that your physical body remains apart from this place—still asleep in your bed."

Alex felt no remorse as she gathered the woman's soul in her arms. Bellaria screamed when the first lick of blue fire touched her. Caught in a nightmare woven of her own dark desires, she was powerless to prevent Alex from taking her.

CHAPTER FORTY-ONE

The maid hovered in front of Miss Belinda's bedroom door, wondering if she should knock on the door. The staff weren't allowed to knock on her door; they were expected to be in front of the door at a certain time and Miss Belinda would call for them.

She nervously tucked a stray lock of hair under the crisp white cap of her maid's uniform and tried not to fidget. The traditional uniform was dreary and uncomfortable, but worst of all, it itched like crazy the minute you started sweating. As nervous as she was at the moment, the wool was starting to feel like a swarm of mosquitos had taken up residence under her dress.

The maid stared at the door, then down at the breakfast tray in her hands, contemplating how bad it would be to just turn around and go about the rest of her day. "Oh, it would be so bad," she whispered, knowing in her heart of hearts that if she left, she might as well just go home. Belinda would fire her for sure, and probably dock her last paycheck just for spite.

Miss Belinda was a stickler for form and function and she made sure that every member of the staff understood their place. They were the servants, she was the head of the house and that was that.

Her family didn't understand why she would work for someone like Miss Belinda, but she needed the job so she kept her mouth shut and put up with her employer's outdated ways. Besides, no matter how bad it was here, it was better than being a drone at the local factory, which was about all there was available for someone like her.

The silver tray was getting heavy. She wasn't willing to earn the woman's wrath because she didn't get her breakfast on time, but now she was worrying about serving Miss Belinda a cold breakfast.

That won't do, either. She had to make a decision. Miss Belinda had been very specific in her orders about not entering her private rooms unless invited, but she was also just as punctual in her daily schedule as she expected her employee's to be. The door should have opened by now.

Chewing her lip, the maid shifted her weight from one foot to the other, unable to decide what to do. Setting the tray down, the maid tread softly towards the door, pressing her ear tightly to the door. Unable to hear anything through the heavy wood, she sighed in resignation. Smoothing her apron down, she gathered up her tray and entered the room, praying she wasn't making a mistake.

"Miss Belinda? I'm sorry to come in like this, but your breakfast is getting cold and I know how hot you like your tea." The maid was so nervous she practically tiptoed into the room with her eyes firmly planted on the carpeting at her feet. A wind gust blew the curtain in on her as she passed the window and she squeaked like a frightened mouse. The rug was drenched and a stream of water ran along the baseboards. "Miss Belinda? Did you leave the window open all night with the storm? There's water everywhere!"

She set the tray down and rubbed the goosebumps popping up on her arms. "It's freezing in here. Let me close the window for you."

She'd done everything she could to avoid meeting her employer's face, but she couldn't procrastinate any longer.

She took a deep, fortifying breath, hoping to find a little courage before picking the tray back up, then turned to face the grand four poster bed.

"Oh, God, no!" she screamed. The tray fell from nerveless fingers to clatter across the floor, the hot tea spilling across the already damp rug.

The sound of silver crashing brought the rest of the house staff running. Their footsteps faltered when they reached the maid. She stood shaking in the doorway, eyes wild with terror, her clenched fist pressed to her open mouth. Blood ran down her wrist where she had bitten her own knuckle. Queries were met with the strangled cry of someone screaming in their sleep. All she could do was shake her head and point towards the bedroom door. A piteous wailing ghosted out of the room, gaining volume until she was forced to clamp her hands over her ears.

"Oh, make it stop, please!" she begged.

The other staff pushed past her. Someone grabbed her firmly by the arms and moved her out of the way while the cook and one of the grooms bravely surged forward. Their forward momentum wavered, then fell apart completely, stumbling over each other in a competition to see who could retreat the quickest.

Peter, the head groom, stomped up the stairs in his boots and pushed past the two men. "Fools, what are you doing in Miss Belinda's room?" An older man with greying hair and a slim beard cut tight around his jawline, he took one look inside the room and started demanding answers. "What has happened here?" he asked, then made a curt motion with his hand. He turned on the other men and shoved them towards Belinda. "Never mind. You two, get ahold of her before she hurts herself."

Miss Belinda was curled up in the corner of the room, the expensive silk threaded wallpaper above her shredded and hanging in tendrils as if she had tried to dig through the wall with her fingernails. Her nightgown lay loosely about her thin shoulders, bright red splotches of color dotting the otherwise pristine white where she had scratched bloody nail marks across the fabric.

"Go!" he bellowed again. Everyone in the room jumped. The two men couldn't have moved faster if Peter had taken a whip to their backs. They rushed forward to help the ailing woman. When they touched her arms, she shrieked and violently lashed out at them with hands warped and twisted into claw-like appendages. Both men backed away when she lifted her head. Blind eyes sought them out, then settled on their faces.

"Holy Mary, Mother of God," the cook cried out, crossing himself even as he skittered away from the jagged fingernails slashing in his direction. "Look at her face. What's wrong with her?"

The slate-grey eyes that could stop a person in their tracks with a single imperious look were now a pale milky white. Her red hair stood out crazily about her head, a wide streak of white running across her temple like a banner. Dried blood filled the lines around her mouth, oozing from dried and cracked lips whose only moisture came from the spittle running down her chin.

"A good question," Peter said, turning on the maid. "Was anyone up here before you?"

"I don't know!" she cried. "We sent up her evening tea like we always do, and she sent us home. She does that sometimes, lets us go early. No one else was here last night that I know of."

Belinda shrieked, a high pitched howl that devolved into piteous wailing. The ghostly sound grew louder until it was almost unbearable to listen to. It was the sound of a trapped animal grieving its own death because it hadn't the sense to know it was still alive. The noise finally, mercifully, descended into mad laughter so ragged it might have been described as cries of grief if it had been anyone else. Of all the emotions they had thought the cruel woman was capable of, fear and sorrow rarely came to mind.

"We can't just leave her like this, we need to call someone." The men looked at each other. They seemed unsure what to do as if each of them was waiting for the other to act first.

"Miss Belinda?" Peter finally asked, kneeling in front of his employer. He reached out to try to calm the crazed woman. He snatched his hand back when she growled at him, her teeth snapping towards his open hand. Bloody spittle oozed from her gaping mouth, flying about her when she began hysterically laughing again.

"Leave her be."

Peter looked behind him. A young maid stood there, staring down at Miss Belinda with a look of pity on her face. "Can't you see that you're scaring her, crowding so close? I'll keep an eye on her. Someone should probably call an ambulance."

"And who are you to be telling me what to do?" Peter asked, bristling at the young woman's cheekiness.

"Why, I'm no one at all, Peter. It's just obvious that it needs to be done and don't you think the one in charge should do something so important?"

She turned her attention to her audience and addressed them as well.

"I think Miss Belinda's maid could use a cup of tea to calm her nerves. Do you think you could do that for me?"

The room cleared out as quickly as it had filled.

As soon as she was left alone with Belinda, Shyann squatted down close to the insane woman.

"Ah, Bellaria. It would be so easy to be cruel to you now after all the things you've done to Rohanna...all the things you've put her through." Shyann reached out to caress Bellaria's face. She screeched and pulled away, twisting her body at an unnatural angle to avoid Shyann's touch, but the old woman was no match for her speed.

Shyann smirked. Bellaria's soul no longer occupied this body; what was left was just a hollow shell...a repository for a lifetime of bad dreams that swam in the murky waters of what was left of her mind. Not a single spark remained that could be recovered and made whole again and that made her very, very happy.

Satisfied with what she found, Shyann walked away, leaving the woman to drown in her own personal nightmare.

No one saw her leave, just as no one had really noticed her arrival. Red lights flashed through the windows, letting her know that the ambulance had arrived to take Bellaria away. On her way out the kitchen door, Shyann murmured a quick suggestion that perhaps someone should let Rohanna know what had happened. The stunned maid just nodded, staring down at the teacup in her hand. She hadn't even bothered to look up at her. Shyann was pleased. No one would remember the extra maid that had been so helpful last night, offering to prepare Miss Belinda's evening tea and bring it up to her. The one originally assigned had been too happy to be relieved of the onerous duty and too thrilled to hear that she could leave early.

She headed for the nearest trail and didn't stop until she was well within the tree line.

"Time to go home," Shyann murmured, smiling up at the heavily crowned forest rising above her. She tore the maid's uniform from her body and crumpled it into a small ball, grimacing at the uncomfortable and demeaning outfit before finding a fitting rock to cram it under. If she had her knife, she would have cut it into ribbons so that some animal or another could use it to line their nest.

Alex is so going to owe me for the indignity of wearing such an ugly garment, she thought, *even if it does give me an excuse to run sky-clad through the forest.*

***

The ambulance pulled away from the house, its heavy springs creaking as it drove down the driveway. The paramedics were polite young men who efficiently packed up Miss Belinda, promising the staff waiting outside that they would take good care of her as they securely buckled the struggling woman into the stretcher. The staff simply nodded and waited until the red and white box van rolled away before returning to the house.

"What do you suppose happened to her?" one of the staff asked. "Do you think it was a stroke? My aunt had a stroke, but she didn't act like that."

"I don't know. Maybe things finally just caught up with her. It's probably best not to ask questions we don't want the answers to," another answered before heading back into the house.

CHAPTER FORTY-TWO

Alex slipped back under the blankets and curled up next to Rohanna as if she had never left her side. She didn't bother with pajamas. She enjoyed the feel of Ro's bare skin against hers too much, and after last night, she didn't want any barriers between them.

Alex could never explain how comforting the sound of Ro's steady breathing was, or how Ro's heartbeat seemed to meter out the time they shared together, beating in time with hers. All she knew was that she would never tire of holding Ro in her arms and listen to her dreaming. Alex made a silent oath to Rohanna then, brushing her lips through the silken-blonde hair and inhaling her scent. Rohanna would never feel the terror of another nightmare, not as long as Alex was there to keep them away. That was one promise Alex could be sure of—that and her love.

Alex yawned, feeling exhaustion setting in. Despite her abilities, she still required rest, real rest that didn't involve invading others dreams, and while the night sky had not yet given way to the morning sun, pale streaks of pre-dawn blues and greys were already combing greedy fingers through the fading stars. Venus still hung low in the sky, its brighter light winking at her through the bedroom window and reminding her to sleep while she could.

Several hours later, Rohanna opened her eyes and groaned. Her body resisted doing her bidding. Her joints popped stiffly when she tried to move, every muscle protesting by sending sharp pains travelling down her back.

One particularly nasty knot settled solidly between her shoulder blades, making it hard to turn her head.

She groaned a second time, this time in blissful submission when a pair of warm hands found her tight and aching muscles and began to knead out the small balls of pain running the length of her back. Small noises escaped from her that told her lover how wonderful it felt while begging her not to stop.

Despite her hedonistic desire to continue enjoying Alex's massage, Ro had too many questions about last night. She turned onto her back to look up at Alex. While effectively ending the massage, her movement left other parts of her body open to Alex's touch. An insistent mouth descended on her own, soft lips teased a chaste kiss from her that took a decidedly more intimate turn when Alex's tongue slipped between her lips, seeking out Rohanna's. Before the kiss could build irreversible momentum, Rohanna pulled away. She did it reluctantly, her breathing already ragged from the first wave of desire Alex's kiss awakened in her.

"Stop, wait," she gasped, trying to gather her thoughts about her. Every time she thought she had them, they danced away from her. Like a child trying to catch fireflies with a jar, every time she opened the jar to catch one, another would escape her.

"Am I distracting you?"

"Yes, you know you are." Biting her lip, Rohanna tried to make sense of the confusing images in her mind, wondering if it was all a dream. "Last night...?"

"Yes and no," Alex answered Rohanna's unspoken question, then smiled and kissed her again. She didn't want to discuss last night. She wanted nothing more than to continue kissing her beloved and pretend that their day did not have to start just yet.

Her desire had been kindled by the touch of their lips, her passion driven by the need to reclaim the woman she almost lost forever. A sudden stab of fear shot through her at the unbidden thought of what she could have lost had things gone differently, making Alex gasp. Her emotions gathered one upon the other, like storm clouds gathering head on into an opposing wind, almost painful in their intensity. Hot tears gathered in the corner of her eyes, blurring her vision. Blindly seeking out her lover's hands, Alex laced her own strong fingers through Rohanna's smaller ones. With one sudden powerful movement, Alex straddled Rohanna, capturing Rohanna's hands high above her head.

Despite being held, unable to escape or move, Alex could sense that Rohanna wasn't frightened. The wild look in Rohanna's eyes mirrored her own. They held the same passion and desire roiling through their depths that Alex felt. Rohanna bucked beneath her, fighting against Alex's hold on her, a mock battle they both enjoyed. A low sound, almost a growl, escaped from her lips, ending in a deep moan of need.

The next kiss was fierce. There was no tentative meeting of lips on lips, no gentle buildup of passion as fires were lit along the lines of their bodies. A collision of desire, demanding and urgent, kindled and consumed what restraint they may have held in reserve. Releasing Rohanna's hands, Alex ran her nails lightly along Rohanna's taut abdomen, then teased aroused nipples until they stood proud and hard between her fingertips. When Rohanna moaned and arched into the touch, her breath coming in short, ecstatic gasps, she gave up her cruel teasing and soothed the hot flesh with light flicks of her tongue.

Alex tapped impatient fingers along Rohanna's thighs, then slipped her fingertips between the hot, slick folds that Rohanna eagerly opened to her exploration. Abandoning Rohanna's breasts, Alex slid down her body until her tongue found Rohanna's clit. She bucked beneath Alex, grasping at Alex's head and urging her on. Wrapping one arm around Rohanna's thigh, Alex slipped her fingers along one trembling thigh, pausing for just a moment before slipping inside her. Rohanna cried out, her heels digging deep into the mattress to force her hips up off of the bed, thrusting eagerly against the sudden intrusion.

Alex let her ride out her orgasm, nipping gently along her inner thigh until she felt the rhythmic contractions weaken, then gently removed her fingers before shifting position. Her lips weren't content to nibble and tease, she wanted to taste Rohanna's passion. Eagerly lapping at the sweet nectar, she gathered it onto her tongue, savoring the taste of pure ambrosia while her lover squirmed beneath her.

"Ah, Alex...please, stop. I can't take anymore." Ro begged. Alex grinned and crawled back up the bed to join Rohanna there.

Intense blue eyes gazed into hers.

"You taste like forever."

Alex drifted back asleep a few minutes later, leaving Rohanna alone with her thoughts. For a while she was content to lay against her lover's shoulder and listen to the sound of her heartbeat slow down as she fell into a deep sleep. Rohanna slowly ran her fingertips up and down Alex's forearm, enjoying the feel of firm muscles beneath the smooth skin.

Travelling farther down her arm, Rohanna massaged across the hard gathering of tendons at Alex's wrist, their strength a testimony of hours pounding metal at the forge. At the edge of sleep herself, Rohanna didn't realize at first what her brain was trying to tell her—she was stroking Alex's wrist, *her left wrist.*

Alex wasn't wearing her leather bracer. Images tumbled through her head, images that Alex had managed to distract her from with their lovemaking. Rohanna sat up in bed, rudely dislodging her sleeping companion. Alex grumbled and opened one disgruntled eye at her before rolling over on her side. Rohanna grabbed Alex's wrist and examined it. Except for being a little paler than the flesh around it, her arm was completely bare. There was no tattoo; absolutely nothing marked her skin

Rohanna raised a questioning eyebrow. "Um, Alex?"

Alex just looked at her. She didn't say a word for a very long time. Rohanna matched her stare for stare.

Alex finally sighed and swung her long legs out of bed and headed for the kitchen.

"I'll get us some coffee," she said. Alex stepped gracefully across the wooden floors, her long black hair flowed freely, framing her shoulders and accentuating her muscular buttocks nicely. Her annoyance at the delaying tactic didn't keep Rohanna from admiring the lithe body.

And I've never seen the woman take a brush to that mane of hair. Not once since I met her, how unfair is that? Ro's own hair suffered from a bad case of bed head that she suddenly felt the need to finger comb, half expecting to find burrs caught up in the tangled mess.

Rohanna gathered a blanket around her before following her lover to the kitchen. The floorboards were cold but the long bench by the picture window was perfect.

She could watch Alex from there and tuck her half-frozen feet beneath her, shamelessly attempting to warm them while Alex walked around appearing perfectly comfortable despite the chill in the air.

"I don't know how you manage it. Not feeling the cold like that," Rohanna said, gratefully accepting the steaming hot mug of coffee Alex brought her.

"My blood runs a bit hotter than most," Alex said, joining Rohanna on the bench. "But that isn't what you wanted to ask me, is it?"

"No, it isn't," Rohanna admitted, lifting up the edge of the blanket so she could join her. Alex wasn't lying about being warm; she was already getting toasty beneath their shared blanket.

"Mm, you really are better than an electric blanket," Ro admitted.

"All the better to entice you into bed, my dear," Alex teased, her lips twitching into a satisfied smile. "But, seriously, if you're cold, I can start a fire."

"No, I'm good right here." Rohanna cuddled in closer, pulling Alex's arm around her.

They stayed like that for a few minutes, enjoying their coffee and gazing out at a small herd of deer that had snuck into the courtyard behind the house so they could nibble at the lush grass there.

"You know, it's still there," Alex said, finally breaking the silence between them. She was still gazing out the window, her eyes level above her cup of coffee as she took another sip.

"What is?" Ro asked. Between the view and the warmth, she had started drifting off.

"The mark, the one you saw last night," Alex said. Her mild voice was completely at odds with the mischievous smile playing across her lips.

"When I thought you were passed out," she added, raising her eyebrows at Rohanna's suddenly innocent expression.

"Well, it seemed like a good idea at the time to lay low," Ro joked, trying to quell the uneasy feeling deep within her stomach. "But seriously, Alex, what happened? Was it real or just a dream?"

"Or both?"

"Alex, seriously, I'm not joking. How much of this, of us, is real and how much has been a dream?" For a late summer morning, it was unusually chilly outside. She reached out and touched the window pane, the fogged glass felt ice cold to her and very real.

"Everything between us is real, Rohanna. Whether it is here or in your dreams," Alex said, pressing her palm against the glass. The fog raced away from her imprint, leaving only clear glass behind.

"I thought I was going crazy, imagining all sorts of things that couldn't possibly be happening. Last night. That was Belinda, wasn't it? You called her Bellaria." Rohanna pressed her fingers into her temples, trying to wrap her head around it all.

"Yes."

"But, I was there, too. Not just you and her. It was real. I felt her knife at my throat, the pain when she struck me and I fell." Her hand went to her throat. A small bandage was taped to her neck. How had she not noticed it before?

"I taped it up this morning. It's not deep enough to need stitches, but I'd avoid getting it wet for a while." Alex looked away before Rohanna saw the guilt in her face.

She had been so sure that Bellaria wouldn't risk hurting Rohanna. That was a serious misstep on her part, one that almost ended in tragedy. She wouldn't make that mistake again.

"Everything in my dreams is real, just as real as this place. I exist in both places. Like rooms in a house, it is simply a matter of walking from one place to the other. My only concern had been to eliminate Bellaria. In trying to eliminate a threat to you, I put you in danger. I should have known better, I'm sorry."

Rohanna shook her head. The more Alex explained the more confusing everything became. "Stop, wait a minute, I'm confused. If you could take Belinda, uh, Bellaria like you said, why did you need me?"

"I couldn't take her. Not on my own. I lied."

"Then how?"

With impeccable timing, Rohanna's cell phone rang, giving Alex the perfect excuse to avoid answering the question.

"I think you should answer your phone first, then we'll talk some more." She plucked the cell phone off the kitchen table and handed it to Rohanna. "Meanwhile, I'm going to go get dressed. It's going to be a busy day."

Rohanna didn't get a chance to call Alex on her strange behavior. Her caller ID flashed. It was the farm calling. Not the house itself, but the barn phone, and that was unusual.

She swiped the button and said hello, then listened quietly while the rest of the puzzle fell into place, minus a few pieces.

CHAPTER FORTY-THREE

Returning to the MacLeod farm was hardly anticlimactic. It wasn't because of the staff or the daily running of the farm—that seemed to keep operating as efficiently as it always had without much interference by them. What made the return to the MacLeod farm beyond disturbing was what they found left behind. On the second day, they found the witches circle, the one that Rohanna had broken free of when she found her way back to Alex.

"Get Maeve, Shyann."

A few hours later, the three Fae stood at the edge of the clearing. Alex closed her eyes and rifled through her memories. "This isn't the same circle Bellaria brought me to. It's..."

"Foul." Maeve visibly shuddered.

"So what do we do?" Shyann asked.

"Nothing," Maeve said, turning her back on the clearing and heading back towards the house.

"What do you mean, nothing? We need to show her," Alex insisted, catching up with Maeve and blocking her path.

"No, we don't. Not yet, at least. Let her get settled in here first, she needs to know this place is hers. Traumatize her now and she might leave."

"So? She has that right." Alex crossed her arms and stared Maeve down. The old woman didn't budge from her position, and Shyann proved to be no help. She looked at both of them, shoved her hands in her pockets and walked away.

"You would like that, eh? She'd come home to you and all would be well." Maeve stamped her walking stick into the ground. "This land must stay in MacLeod hands. She can't leave and that abomination cannot remain on MacLeod lands."

Shyann started whistling. The irritating noise whined in her ears like an angry hornet, strafing her already abused nerves. The place made her skin crawl.

"Fine, I'll play it your way, Maeve. But only because it is best for Rohanna, not for you." Alex threw up her hands and stalked away, but not before taking her ire out on Shyann. "Gentle Epona, Shy! I thought all Fae could at least hold a tune, stop whistling before my ears bleed."

Several days passed by without another word about speaking to Rohanna. More mundane worries kept Alex occupied, things that needed to be done in order for Rohanna to take over the farm. What could have been a long and expensive process was made ten times easier when she produced her father's will. With Bellaria incapacitated, the farm went to her immediately. That was the one and only convenient thing about the entire process.

The bloated staff was another matter.

"I don't need a maid, Alex...or a cook. That was all Bellaria's doing."

"That's completely up to you, Ro. I can't make that decision for you."

"I'll not fire a single one of them, not while they need work," Rohanna announced to everyone's relief. "Except for one."

"That, I will do gladly," Alex readily agreed. "I know exactly who you are talking about."

Alex jumped up and was gone in a flash, leaving Rohanna alone with a decade's worth of legal documents sitting on her desk. She ignored it all. Peter had been a thorn in her side for years. Always up Bellaria's ass, he was the biggest snitch of them all...all to curry whatever favor he thought it would bring him. He was supposed to be the head groom but instead he acted like he was the barn manager, and he sucked at both jobs.

"Peter's gone," Alex announced, returning to Rohanna's study empty handed. "Probably right after he realized Bellaria wasn't coming back."

"That's probably just as well."

Bellaria's trip to the Emergency Room and her subsequent hospital stay found nothing wrong with her, other than an acute case of Dementia that didn't seem to respond to any treatment. The best the doctors could suggest was medicate her so that she wouldn't harm herself or the nursing staff and suggest a facility that could deal with her violent outbursts. Alex had gone with Rohanna to sign the necessary paperwork. Neither of them worried about the questioning looks from the doctors, nor did they care that the staff seemed to think that a familiar face might be helpful in her treatment. Ro refused to enter her room or promise to visit. Let them think she didn't care. They knew the truth, and that truth was not something they cared to share. The facility she sent Bellaria to wasn't a place to heal, it was a prison, pure and simple.

Alex cleared her throat. "Stop dwelling on her, Ro. She can't hurt you anymore."

"I'm sorry," Rohanna apologized. "I just. I don't know. I just can't shake the feeling there's something else."

Alex pulled Rohanna out of her chair and kissed her soundly.

"Are you trying to distract me again?"

"Maybe?" Alex grinned. She tapped her fingers on the desk, noting the huge pile of folders neatly divided into four smaller piles. "Do you have anyone in mind to replace Peter?"

"I do," Rohanna said, shuffling through a stack of papers to find the one she was looking for. "Darla Simpson. I've got her application right here. Seems Bellaria thought it was a fitting joke to hire a woman with a degree from the best equestrian school in the country and put her in the barn to muck out horseshit."

Rohanna narrowed her eyes, remembering that last day in the barn. Despite the risk, Darla had been the only one brave enough to go against Bellaria's wishes. "I'll fix that mistake on Monday."

"That sounds good to me," Alex agreed. It was time for one last thing. She had been putting it off, but Maeve insisted it had to be done. "If we're done here, there's something else I need to show you. But first, I have something for you."

Alex pulled the Fairie Stone necklace out of her pocket. The silver chain flashed when she uncoupled the clasp and held it in front of her.

"My necklace!" Rohanna gasped. "I thought I'd lost it."

"You did, but Maeve found it and gave it to me. I repaired the clasp so it won't fall off again."

Rohanna pulled her hair out of the way and turned around so Alex could put it on. Alex checked twice to make sure it was secure before taking advantage and pressing her lips along Ro's neckline. "There, now it's safely where it belongs."

Alex closed her eyes and took a deep breath. *I hope you're happy, Maeve.* She opened them to find Rohanna gazing up at her. "Where are we going?"

"Not far, just a short walk."

At first, Alex led the way, then she stopped where the hidden path lay and waited for Rohanna. She pulled aside a low-lying branch and waited to see what Rohanna would do when they made the clearing.

"I know this place," Rohanna said, her voice trembling with emotion. "I don't remember it, but I know it."

Thirteen pale stones stood in a circle, warped and twisted in a study of pain that made Alex's stomach turn. Rohanna approached the circle, running her fingertips along the granite like surface, only to turn deathly pale as she sought out Alex's protective embrace.

"What's wrong, Ro?" Alex asked.

Rohanna turned her head to stare at the stones. Her fingertips sought out the Faerie stone around her neck, seeking its comforting presence. Alex wasn't even sure if she realized she did that, but it seemed to reassure her.

"The stones, Alex…I can't, it's so horrible."

Alex reached out and touched the stones. The surface crumbled into a fine powder. She brought her fingers closer to her nose and sniffed. "It's not stone, it's salt."

"No, Alex…not just salt. Bellaria used these witches; she must have burned them out, trying to keep me. That, or I did this." Rohanna's words held such horror in them. "Look closer, Alex, they are all turned to stone. The salt is their tears."

"Ro, you can't feel guilty for this. They were evil women. What happened to them is not your fault. This is their punishment for aligning themselves with Bellaria in the first place and for trying to hurt you."

"No, you don't understand. Look at their shadows." Rohanna pointed at the ground.

"So? They have shadows, I don't understand, Ro. Everything casts a shadow." Alex was confused now. *Why did this bother her so much?*

"Look at the sun, Alex. It's almost noon."

Alex squinted at the cloudless sky, then back at the ground. A chill that had nothing to do with the temperature crawled down her spine and she instinctively stepped back, away from the nearest shadow. It danced and twisted against the burnt grass, stretching toward them like a living thing. Alex pulled Rohanna farther away from the unnatural circle. There was no way she wanted any of those shadows falling across their feet. Alex looked around her; not a single tree or rock cast a shadow against the noonday sun, yet each misshapen stone held one.

"What is this, Rohanna? Why do they have shadows?"

"They're trapped, Alex. Their souls haven't been set free, and they are in pain. How they suffer! I cannot bear it. I can hear them screaming, inside here," Rohanna said, tapping her temple.

"What can we do? They were witches, Ro. Perhaps this is their punishment?"

"No, I will not have them here, poisoning this place. Alex. They were evil, yes, but they were also tainted by Bellaria's touch. They deserve another chance. If not in this life, then in another. Please?" Rohanna had tears in her eyes. Alex brushed them away, awed that Ro could shed tears even for those who had tried to hurt her.

"You are an incredible woman, you know that?" Alex asked, lifting Ro's chin up so she could look into her eyes. "Do you truly want to free them?"

"Yes!"

"Then we'll do it," Alex said. "You can free them, Rohanna."

"How can you be so sure?"

"Because you are the Gatekeeper, Rohanna. There is no one else like you in this world and there hasn't been in many, many years. You control the stone circles. I told you that morning. I lied to Bellaria about being able to take her to the Shadow Lands, yet she believed me. Why?"

"Because the stones responded to you. I heard them singing," Rohanna said.

"Exactly. You heard them, Rohanna. You made them sing, not me. I was able to take Bellaria because you knew I needed the Gate opened. You opened it, for me."

"How? Bellaria tried to teach me. I failed every time."

"You didn't fail, Ro, you won. Every year, against everything she ever did to you. You fought against her and refused to give her what she wanted. You didn't fail because you couldn't open a Gate for her, you won the long battle. The power has always been yours, to use or not. If she did anything, it was to make you strong, resilient...stubborn. These aren't bad things to be, but you shouldn't have been subject to such abuse to gain these skills." Alex caressed Rohanna's cheek, wiping away a single tear before it could fall.

"That night you thought I saved you—but it was you all along. You saved us both." Alex turned towards the circle. "You've done this before. There is no one here forcing you. Save them, Ro...give them peace."

Rohanna nodded and put on a brave face, then marched towards the stone circle. Alex struggled to remain behind and let her do this alone. *Maeve, I swear. If this hurts her, I will hunt you down myself.* Controlling a stone circle was one thing, Rohanna intended to destroy this one. There was no other way to free the souls trapped there.

Rohanna reached out and tentatively touched one of the stones. Alex growled when the thing shimmered and reshaped itself. Stone does not move. Rohanna reached out with her other hand and touched the next stone. A drumming sound, loud and dissonant, echoed throughout the clearing. Power flared around her and the scent of dry lightning filled the air. Alex felt her eyes bleed through, blue on blue, and her skin crawled with the need to shift. Here were thirteen women that deserved the type of justice she was made for, what she had been born to do. She knew without a doubt that if she let her NightMere loose, she would shred those souls for the crimes they committed.

Alex dropped to her knees. Thirteen heartbeats hammered against their granite prisons, each begging to be let free. Stone hearts couldn't bleed, but she could hear them weeping, assaulting her ears with the cries of damned souls.

"Rohanna! I shouldn't be here; I can't be here. Not while you do this." She dug her hands into the barren soil until she felt the bite of sharp gravel digging into her palms.

Suddenly, Shyann was at her side, pulling her up out of the dirt. "Alex! Listen to me, you are more than this. Not just Mere...not just Fae."

Shyann grabbed her arm. "Look at your wrist. Your father's gift to you, remember? Alexandria, remember who you are."

Her tattoo flared to life, coiling beneath her skin to remake itself into a new pattern. The sacred horse of Epona still rode within the flowing lines, but now another design made its way to the surface. "It's all I know," Alex rasped. "I don't know who I am anymore."

"You do know, just like Rohanna knows." Shyann's voice changed. "You two have such a journey ahead of you. I promise you that all your questions will be answered in time, but right now you have to help Rohanna."

"How?"

"She can destroy the circle, but if she does..."

"The souls will shatter with the stone," Alex finished Shyann's sentence. *That can't happen,* Alex thought. In a moment of clarity, she realized why the fates had brought them together.

"Free them, Alex. Don't let their deaths weigh on Rohanna's soul."

Alex pounded the earth with both fists. "I am more than this."

She took a deep breath, and exhaled inside the world of dreams, surrounded by thirteen women's nightmares. The shifting views moved around her like a mad kaleidoscope in an unsettling view that made her stumble like a drunken sailor. Here, the witches were not stone, yet they could not leave their place inside the circle. They writhed in agony, hot tears ran down their faces as they howled out their grief. Alex bared her teeth. White and strong and meant for rending, they now gathered the witch's souls as delicately as a child plucked flowers from a field except these flowers tasted as greasy as frog carcasses and smelled just as bad.

Now what? She hesitated, unsure what to do next.

A dark figure beckoned to her from the edge of the clearing, urging her to leave the circle. "Hurry, there is danger."

The stones song changed, vibrating with a crystalline hum that inched towards the edges of human hearing. She broke into a wild gallop a second before the world went black, then felt herself falling.

"Holy Hells, but that hurts," Alex groaned, pulling herself up on her elbows and looking around. The ground around her was a lunar landscape of small rocks and large craters. "Rohanna!"

The sight of Rohanna's prostate body lying close to the edge of the clearing was enough to make Alex forget about her own hurts. She ran to her side and rolled her over, then breathed a sigh of relief. She wasn't broken or bleeding, and that counted for something.

"Ro, sweetie, wake up."

"Huh...did we do it, Alex? Did we save them?" Rohanna struggled to stand up.

"Easy now, you're still wobbly." Alex helped her to her knees, then braced herself when Ro leaned on her to stay upright.

Rohanna finally got her feet under her and managed to get a good look at the clearing. The place looked like a war-zone. "Holy crap, did we do that?"

"I'm afraid so."

"How are we going to explain this?"

"I don't know. Maybe we can claim a gas leak. There's tons of old natural gas wells all over this area."

"Ugh, I hurt like hell." Rohanna made a face. "And I feel like I've eaten half a pound of West Virginia dirt."

"Maybe not, but you look like you're wearing at least that much." Alex grinned at her.

Rohanna looked down at herself and laughed.

"I think you're right. Come on, let's get out of here, I feel the need for a drink or two and maybe a bath...or four."

Rohanna tried, but Alex was still the stronger of the two. After several brave hobbling steps on an obviously sprained ankle, Alex swept Rohanna up into her arms. Her weight didn't even slow her down, she strode away from the destroyed circle with long, ground eating strides that would get them home in no time.

"I still have so many questions. I feel like I have been living in the dark for so long. I know nothing about your people, let alone my own."

"I know, and I will do my best to help you. But Ro, you have to understand. You are asking me to go over thousands of years of history. History that has been passed on in legend and myth, so distorted that even I have trouble determining what really happened. Too often, those who were left to tell the tale were the ones deciding what was truth and what was myth."

"It's okay, Alex. I don't need to know everything this instant. We have a lifetime to spend together, and right now, I want to explore us. That is more important than any ancient history, right?"

"Right." Alex leaned down and kissed Rohanna the way she deserved to be kissed. "I love you, Rohanna, now and forever."

"And I love you," Rohanna said, a bit breathless after the soul searing kiss. "I want to go home, Alex. This isn't home yet, not until I purge Bellaria completely from this farm. Take me back to your place."

She didn't notice the troubled look in Alex's eyes, the fleeting look of guilt that Alex blinked away before Rohanna caught a glimpse of it.

Alex had no doubt that Rohanna meant exactly what she said, but would she still mean it when she found out that a lifetime really meant forever?

"Home it is, then," Alex said, turning her feet away from the house. The truck was farther away than the house, but she didn't care. If she had to, she'd walk the whole way home...unless Rohanna wanted to ride. Then there was no limit to where they could go.

EPILOGUE

The overly perky nurse's aide was all too happy to lead Miss Belinda's niece to her room. The moment she arrived, Rosalind was informed that the poor old thing hadn't had a visitor in months.

"It's almost Christmas, you know. Even busy families try to come up on the holidays and I try to make the place as festive as possible. We even keep a tree in the lobby although we ask family members to leave presents at the desk."

As she escorted Rosalind through the facility, she kept a running dialogue going, enthusiastic in telling her how well her aunt had been doing. Rosalind wasn't fooled. She saw through the candy-coated descriptions of Belinda's "improvements." The glowing reports were easy to decipher. They were making sure Miss Belinda was heavily medicated and kept their interaction with her to a minimum. She had to resist laughing at the woman's attempt to reach Belinda.

"She's in there, somewhere. If she only had a familiar voice to help her back from wherever she's wandered off to inside her head, she might come back to us," the aide said.

Rosalind wanted nothing more than to tell the irritating woman to shut the hell up, but instead, she simply nodded and agreed with her.

She knew that Belinda wasn't wandering around inside that empty head. Her soul was elsewhere, compliments of her cousin, Alexandria. She had to thank her cousin, though, for not being as dangerous as she could be. She may have shredded Belinda's psyche, tearing her soul from her body without a second thought. But, she didn't have the killer instinct to finish the job, even going so far as to ensure that Belinda's body remained intact and cared for.

Rosalind was led into an overly pink room decked out in Christmas red and green. She sniffed delicately, offended at the musty smell of old woman and dirty diapers. Still, she had a part to play so she pretended to smile and be happy to see her aunt, lavishing a kiss on the wrinkled brow and holding her hand affectionately. Belinda stared blankly at the TV in front of her. It might have been a wall, for all it mattered. Straightening up, Rosalind turned towards the helpful aide and thanked her for all her help. The woman smiled, and Rosalind knew she would help her in any way she could. Simple kindness and courtesy was the coin and currency of a place like this.

"Can you please ask the clerk to get the paperwork together? I want to take my aunt home. It's only right that she should be around family, among those who love and want to care for her," she said, sending the aide on her way with another pleasant smile. Rosalind checked the hallway, making sure there was no one within hearing range of her before turning back to the old woman cackling away at nothing in particular.

"Well now, Bellaria. Let's get you out of here and see if we can piece you back together. You made a promise to me, one you have yet to keep. Alexandria still bears the marks of leadership you promised me. They should have been mine, and you are going to make sure that Alexandria pays for stealing my birthright."

Another cackling fit followed her statement, sending threads of spittle flying from the old woman's gaping maw. Rosalind grimaced and wiped her sleeve carefully. *How disgusting*, she thought, *but very motivating*. A clerk knocked on the doorway, a clipboard in hand along with a sheaf of release papers as well as an outline of Miss Belinda's medication schedule.

"Miss Strider? All of the paperwork is done. All I need for you to do is sign this release form."

"Certainly." Rosalind cheerily scrawled her signature where the clerk pointed at and handed the clipboard back to her.

The clerk looked through the paperwork one last time, then neatly tucked the forms away. "You're a good woman, taking her home for the holidays like this. She'll be so much happier with loved ones."

"Thank you, I'm sure she'll be much better once she's back on familiar ground."

"Oh, one more thing, Miss Strider."

Rosalind had just turned to leave. She froze and stiffly turned back around, a plastic smile plastered on her face. "Yes, is there a problem?"

"Oh, no ma'am. I was just wondering if Miss Belinda needs transportation. We can get an ambulance van to take her home."

Rosalind relaxed perceptively.

"Oh, please, call me Alexandria, dear. But no, I have a van waiting outside, if someone could bring us a wheelchair?"

~ ~ ~ ~ ~ ~ ~ ~ ~ ~ ~ ~

If you enjoyed this novel, please check out more offerings by Rhavensfyre.

Follow on Facebook @ Characters of Rhavensfyre

www.rhavensfyre.com

twitter@rhavensfyre

Works by Rhavensfyre

LIFE IS NOT A COUNTRY SONG

This romantic novella is book one of Chase and Rowan's adventures.
Rowan St. John is on her way back home with an empty horse trailer and down a driver.
Chase Meadows had it all, until she came home one day to find her lover in bed with another woman. Now she's left with nothing but her truck, her horse and a definite need to find a new start. California was about as far away from North Carolina and the past as she could go. All she had to do was get there with her pregnant mare, Smoothy—the only thing she had left in her name that she would never give up.
When Rowan St. John responds to her ad for a last minute horse transport, she thought she had finally gotten a break. A deal is struck that benefits both women, more than they ever expected.

LOVE IS NOT A ROMANCE NOVEL

This romantic novella is book two of Chase and Rowan's adventures and the sequel to Life is Not a Country Song.
Chase and Rowan are given some time to learn more about each other when the last leg of their trip is delayed.
Rowan sees it as a way to show Chase everything the Southwest has to offer, including her, while Chase is more worried about earning her keep and making sure one special little colt is strong enough to travel. Trust and understanding are tested, and some internal demons are laid to rest against the backdrop of sun-kissed mesas and tall pines.
Both spiritual and sensual, the ladies discover that some journeys aren't

measured by how many miles you travel, but by how far you are willing to take your heart.

LIFE, LOVE, AND LOYALTY

This lesbian romance is the third in the popular Chase and Rowan Series. After a few detours along the way, Chase and Rowan have finally made it to California and are settling into their lives at the Flying S ranch. An urgent call sends them back on the road again when wildfires get close enough to threaten an old college friend's farm. Without a second thought, Rowan agrees to help evacuate her friend's horses, and from there on nothing goes as planned. Rowan and Chase find themselves in a volatile situation that places them both in danger.

A CHRISTMAS PROPOSAL: A CHASE AND ROWAN NOVELETTE

Chase and Rowan have been through a lot together but this Christmas will be their first. Plans change and Chase is still learning a lot about family, but when it comes to Rowan, she has a steep learning curve. This romantic novelette is exactly what it says, all you have to do is read till the end to find out if it's a yes or no. Of course, getting there is the best part of the story.

TIE DYE AND FLANNEL

Dr.Stacie Phillips' comfortable, pragmatic life is about to be turned upside down. Dr. Phillips is a young Veterinarian caught up in her carefully constructed life, trying to protect her family, her new career, and most of all-her heart. Her best friend, Josie, only wants what is best for her, and if that means meddling in affairs of the heart she will do it. Josie has her own reasons for wanting Stacie to be happy, and the last thing she wants is Stacie putting off her life to help Josie deal with hers. Stacie meets Maria, a free-spirited herbalist from Arizona, when her goddaughter Rowan literally runs into her at a farmer's market. Unfortunately, Rowan's mother, Josie finds out about the chance encounter and things start to spiral out of Stacie's control.

SWITCHING GEARS

There is a saying among the old ones, "If you dream of a mare, a MacLeod is sure to be near." Rohanna MacLeod grew up listening to her grandmother's stories of her family and the old country, the myths and legends of the Fae becoming dearer to her with each loss in her young life. True to her family name, Rohanna carries the MacLeod gift with horses. With single minded determination, she denies herself everything else that life offers in order to keep what is hers, to keep and preserve the family farm from an abusive stepmother she abhors.

Everything changes when she runs into trouble on the way to a horse show. A chance offer and a plain business card sends her to the Ladysmith, a farrier and blacksmith with a mysterious past.

Alexandria Strider is drawn into Rohanna's world. Caught between new bonds and old oaths, Alex holds the key to Rohanna's past and an unrealized destiny, if she can find the strength to do what is necessary.

SABRE

During the Civil War, hundreds of women cut their hair and donned the uniform of the common soldier on both sides. History tells us they did it to follow their husbands and brothers to war, rather than stay behind to uncertain destiny. A few, though, found their freedom beneath the heavy wool uniform and shorn hair.

These are the few that are not spoken of, the ones who desired no husband and found liberation behind the blue or the gray. Meet JC. Resigned to a solitary life, an unexpected gift changes everything for this Union soldier.

This short story is a historical lesbian erotic romance.

STEPPING OUT

Enter Micah and Olivia's world from Switching Gears and enjoy a tale of a night out on the town that was so deliciously naughty it was too hot to keep hidden away. Join Micah as she takes a walk through her past, leathers and all, for a night she soon won't forget. What can we say? Some fantasies can't be put to sleep until they are put to bed.

THE POTTER'S WHEEL

Would you dare love a Goddess?
The Potter's Wheel is a lesbian erotic romance. A short tale of epic love, both lost and found, and the undeniable passion between two unique and otherworldly women.

THE MISADVENTURES OF TWO RELUCTANT ZOMBIE HUNTERS: ZOMBIES AT THE CON

No one expects the zombie apocalypse…not even those who make a living pretending it exists. When a troupe of Zombie Hunters find themselves in the midst of a real zombie apocalypse they have to find a way to escape. After all, there aren't any real weapons allowed at the Con…and only wits and ingenuity will keep them alive long enough to make it home.

REST AND RELAXATION

Prescribed some R & R, overworked executive Allyse DeLeon heads for the country, where she meets quirky loner and farm owner, Dani Saxon. Dani. Allyse finds herself attracted to this unique and solitary woman, and soon finds out her heart is in more danger there than it ever was back home.

www.ingramcontent.com/pod-product-compliance
Lightning Source LLC
Chambersburg PA
CBHW071220250626
47163CB00001B/55